FROM THE CASE FILES OF
STEVE ROCKFISH - 2

SEE YOU NEXT Tuesday

KEN HARRIS

Black Rose Writing | Texas

ISBN: 978-1-68433-989-1
PUBLISHED BY BLACK ROSE WRITING
www.blackrosewriting.com

Printed in the United States of America
Suggested Retail Price (SRP) $20.95

See You Next Tuesday is printed in Baskerville

*As a planet-friendly publisher, Black Rose Writing does its best to eliminate unnecessary waste to reduce paper usage and energy costs, while never compromising the reading experience. As a result, the final word count vs. page count may not meet common expectations.

Praise for
See You Next Tuesday

"Harris has created his own sub-genre with this series, which is a beautiful and unique thing to see. Beloved characters must brave the most dangerous, harrowing journey yet. The suspense woven through this tale is done with a finesse rarely seen, and ensures we stay glued to the page."
–Ben Eads, author of *Cracked Sky* and *Hollow Heart*

"The second in the Rockfish and Jawnie detective series begins with separate cases involving a cheating husband, a corrupt religious cult, a stockpile of poison gas, and a currency scam. The cases come together in a wild ride worthy of a chase scene in a movie, as the detectives pursue the cult leader in a rip-roaring page turner of an ending."
–Carolyn Geduld, author of *Take Me Out The Back* and *Who Shall Live*

"Harris takes you on two journeys you hope will never happen to family members but fear it could. The emotional roller coaster you will ride, keeps you reading and hoping the end comes with a taste of sweet revenge. Harris finds a way to weave a story that keeps you turning the pages and wanting more Rockfish."
–Stephen W. Briggs, author of *Family of Killers-Memoirs of an Assassin*

For Bill – Thanks for the fuel you've given my fire

For Brent – Thanks for talking me off the ledge

For all the Killer Termites and Squirrels for without your support this sequel might never have happened

SEE YOU NEXT Tuesday

PROLOGUE - RECONNECTING

Elon Musk Crushes the Competition with NikolaTV's First Blockbuster Series

The Pine Barrens Stratagem - Second Only to Disney's The Mandalorian in Pandemic Streaming Sessions.

By Timmy Gallagher
TV Reporter | October 11, 2021 @TGReporter - Twitter/IG

In what one could call the strongest streaming launch for both a new service and its premiere show, NikolaTV and *The Pine Barrens Stratagem* have captivated housebound Americans as COVID-19's third wave spreads. As of September, forty-five million Americans have signed up and binge-watched.

The True Crime docuseries follows a private eye, as he tries to uncover the truths behind murder and child trafficking in rural Southern New Jersey during the 1940s. Through the investigation, he meets the great granddaughter of a policeman who went missing investigating the original crimes. Together, they map out a criminal organization that stretched from the local police to the Mafia and over to the Catholic Church. This alliance spanned seventy-five years and regrouped during the pandemic to upgrade their illicit activities to include defrauding the Federal Government's Paycheck Protection Program.

Like all of his previous endeavors, Musk's announcement last year that he would launch his own streaming service to compete with Netflix, Hulu and Disney+ was met with skepticism, but much like Tesla, Starlink, and SpaceX, it's Elon having the last laugh.

"The minute Angel Davenport laid out this storyline to me, I was instantly sold and knew that most of America would be, too," Musk said. "This type of True Crime, innovative storytelling, is exactly how I wanted to launch NikolaTV. I owe it all to Angel. I only provided him the stage to showcase his creation." The creative mind behind *The Pine Barrens Stratagem*, Angel Davenport, previously worked as a podcast producer for the All Things True Crime Podcast Network, before a chance meeting with Elon Musk sent his career on a SpaceX-type of trajectory.

"Elon got it, right from the start, and that was something I hadn't run into trying to promote and sell this series to the other streaming networks. His hands-off approach and full faith in myself and the team gave us the independent, creative space needed to bring this true story to life. I'd also like to thank Steve Rockfish and Jawnie McGee, because without their investigative tenacity, these crimes would never have come to light and justice not served."

Rockfish and McGee are dealing with their new-found celebrity and fame the best they can as they continue to operate their joint private investigative endeavor in Linthicum Heights, Maryland.

When asked during a press junket in support of the season finale, Rockfish had this to say on how their day-to-day operations have changed:

"I have to tell you. Things couldn't be better. The success of the show has brought new business opportunities and our phone rings off the hook. Each caller wants a 'famous' private detective to help them with their unique problem, but the influx of income from the network and new clients allows us to be more selective. Potential clients now pitch us on why we should take their case.

"The merchandise side is something we're getting used to. A Hot Wheels version of Lana and a Junior Jawnie Detective Kit for your inquisitive middle schooler, or under-achieving sophomore, are a few clicks away on our website."

Touching on his partner's impact on how he now conducts business...

"Jawnie's absolutely great. She's currently studying for her private investigator's final exam, and I've felt her impact on day-to-day operations since she came onboard. She's brought me into the 21st century with a small business network, new computers and the long-term goal of digitizing all my old case files. No more colored pencils and 3x5 index cards for me!"

As 2021 draws to a close, life for the private investigators is good. Business even better.

CHAPTER ONE

This is Steve Rockfish. At the tone, leave your name and message. I'll get back to you. [Beep]

"Stevie, you probably want to update this outgoing message since you've taken on a partner and..."

Rockfish recognized his father's voice and cringed.

"Yeah, why haven't we changed the outgoing message yet?" Jawnie said. "Even your dad noticed it's less than partner'y."

Steve Rockfish and Jawnie McGee sat in the open area that each preferred to their own small private offices. The partners had soon recognized that the space led to better collaboration. A large sofa, two recliners and a small conference table facing a retractable screen for presentations filled the space. The sofa was a sleeper for those late nights when a case or one too many Jamesons kept Rockfish overnight. A partially stocked bar lined the wall behind the recliners with a small refrigerator for cold drinks and DoorDash leftovers.

Rockfish sat in one recliner with his after-hours, decompression Irish whiskey in hand. Jawnie took up her normal spot on the couch, her ever-present laptop open. The meeting had become a reoccurring routine on Thursday evenings after one of them locked the door and flipped the sign to closed. This time was best used for strategizing on pending cases and brainstorming to confirm neither had overlooked any minor detail. Last, they would discuss potential clients and any administrative housekeeping issues.

The first item on this evening's agenda was slightly different. The State Board notified Jawnie two weeks prior she had passed her final exam and was now Rockfish's peer. At least on paper. It would take some more convincing and a ton of field work to make him admit it aloud. Tonight was the first time either of them had the time to stop, take a breath, and celebrate. Business had been that good.

He walked out from behind the bar with two rocks glasses and a bottle of Freixenet Brut Cordon Negro.

"Don't give me any shit. I like it and Costco sells it for something like fifteen and change for a two-pack," he said. "Although I dropped the ball. The engraved flutes I ordered from Things Remembered, over at the mall, to mark the occasion, are still in transit." Rockfish shrugged his shoulders and handed Jawnie a glass. He poured like the pro he was, and the bubbles stopped at the rim.

"Let me guess, you're going to blame our yet to be hired receptionist?" Jawnie said and grinned.

They laughed and clinked glasses. Rockfish didn't have a way with words, unless he was trying to sweet talk some information out of someone or avoid a solid punch to the nose. He kept his words short for this occasion and drained his glass before speaking.

"Welcome to the team, officially, I mean. It's not like you've been sitting around here with your nose in a textbook studying for the exam. Your ideas, technology, and thinking outside the box have really helped us out around here and, as important, how I look at things. I'm not sure what that whole outside the box thing is all about, but Mack said it would be a good thing to say."

Jawnie smiled and lifted her glass again. "Here's to things staying as smooth sailing as they are now."

"Amen. Now, let me top off your drink before we start. This shit goes straight to my head." Rockfish refilled Jawnie's glass, placed the bottle on the coffee table in front of the sofa and picked his whiskey back up.

"Wait, and sipping whiskey doesn't?" Jawnie said with a shake of her head.

"Look, I don't tell you how to vegan, and you don't tell me how to unwind. I thought we had an agreement," Rockfish said with a coy smile. "Okay, back to the grind. I've only got one case I need an update on. Donnelly. We know he went missing the evening of the 14th. Have you figured where he went after he left work?"

"I talked to a few co-workers and got bupkis," Jawnie said.

"What?"

"Nothing," she said, and took a sip of champagne before continuing. "I followed a few of them last Friday to a bar, three blocks over from their office. Then I laid on my womanly charms, batted a few eyelashes. You know, the usual."

Rockfish rolled his eyes. *Ha. Anne Arundel County's first black hipster, lesbian P.I. was a lot of things, but she wasn't a flirt. If the planets had aligned that night and she wasn't working, I bet she would have walked out of that place with a broad under each arm, if only to piss off the regulars.*

"Finally, one opened up. A guy named Tommy James sidled up to the chair next to mine. We had some small talk. I gave him a fake number and yada, yada, he told me Donnelly and a bunch of his co-workers went to Moe's Tavern later that evening. The last any of them saw of Donnelly was at last call when he was leaving with some redhead with giant boobs. She was holding him up as they left."

"A regular hook up of his?" Rockfish wondered aloud.

"Doesn't seem to be, at least according to Tommy," Jawnie said. "I went down to Moe's and talked to the bartender. He remembers them, but swears it was the first night he'd seen her in the place and she hasn't been back since. There's a camera out front and he said he'd have someone see if there are a few decent frames of them leaving or even her walking in that evening. I told him there's $200 in it if he can pull some decent footage."

"I can call my buddy Decker over at Baltimore PD and see if her description matches any other cases they have of Johns being rolled. We might get lucky if this is her usual M.O. Or maybe Donnelly's sitting on a beach somewhere with the new love of his life, forgot to call his kids and let them know of the change of plans. Speaking of which..."

Rockfish stood up and placed his glass on the table. He reached over and grabbed the small tactical binoculars from the bar before walking towards the front door.

"Checking on our friend?" Jawnie said.

"Yup," Rockfish said, and shook the binoculars in his hand. "Best four hundred dollars you ever made me spend." He stopped at the large floor to ceiling windows that ran the length of the storefront. Rockfish parted two of the slats in the blinds and looked through the binoculars past the parking lot and into the strip mall across the street. The yellow Nissan Xterra sat in its normal parking spot. The rusted front bumper guard was a dead giveaway. As was the very attractive young woman behind the wheel.

"She's back?" Jawnie said.

"Yeah, sitting in the same spot, staring at her phone. It's amateur hour out there. She's not even trying to be discreet."

Rockfish turned and walked back to his recliner, but stood behind it, his forearms resting on the back. He dropped the binoculars onto the padded seat and contemplated their next move.

If I was back working out of the trailer, I would have already grabbed a bat and put the fear of God into whoever she was. But now, I've got a partner to consider, and the last thing I want to do is something stupid and scare away future business. Not to mention there ain't a damn thing illegal about sitting in a parking spot, no matter how many consecutive days.

"Three out of four work days this week," Jawnie said.

Rockfish snapped his head around. They were partners for less than a year, not an old married couple. But somehow, she continued to finish his thoughts.

"And not like with these blinds she can see shit," Jawnie added. "You sure she's not a disgruntled old client, or girlfriend?"

"Please. You sure she ain't one of yours?" Rockfish said. Jawnie wrinkled her nose and shook her head. *She still couldn't take as well as she gave.* Rockfish laughed aloud. "She isn't breaking any laws, but I'm damn tired of this game. Maybe Decker can get a uniform patrol to drive past and see what she's up to."

"Works for me," Jawnie replied.

"But in the meantime, I'd suggest not biking in until we find out who and what this is all about. I can pick you up and drop you off."

"Hmm, if you paid attention to half the things I say, you'd know I've got a car. Bought it a month ago. Parked at the condo."

"Lord, it's not one of those boxy Scions again, is it?" Rockfish said.

"No, I went the safer route this time. Subaru Outback."

"Color me surprised. Still, I'll drop you off tonight."

4

"Aye, aye, Captain. Do you have another bottle of that fancy schmancy champagne? One or three more for the road won't hurt, as I'm not operating any heavy machinery. Plus, we still have to—"

The opening notes of Rob Zombie's *Thunder Kiss '65* filled the space and Rockfish reached for his cell.

"Uh huh, yeah. I'll be there in 20," he said into the phone and cut the call short.

"Who's pooping on our party?" Jawnie said, refilling her glass.

"Mack's at Saint Luke's. Iggy thinks Dad had a heart attack."

****

Rockfish pulled into Saint Luke's emergency room parking lot at the eighteen minute and forty-five second mark and found a parking space beneath a light pole. He had made good time with Lana's Hemi, rocketing him through a couple of intersections with questionable yellow lights.

Christ, I hope the county hadn't gotten around to installing those red-light cameras. Rockfish cut the engine and grabbed his mask before climbing out of the car. The DMV fines didn't worry him anymore; it was the points on his license. He shook his head. *I've got bigger things to worry about.* He glanced back over his shoulder at the lamppost. The small square sign read A13. He pulled out his cell and opened the Notes app.

"Parked under the light in A13," he said and gave a silent thanks to Jawnie for that nugget of tech insight. He jogged along the lighted pathway towards the giant neon sign that flashed *Emergency Room.*

Rockfish spotted Iggy before he entered the ER. The old man paced back and forth inside the sliding glass doors while nervously rubbing his temples. Iggy wore a pair of overalls a size too big for his thin frame and a John Deere trucker cap that had seen better days. Rockfish was familiar with Iggy's retirement uniform of choice. A blue disposable mask rested just under the old man's nose. *Why am I not shocked Iggy's a believer in the great hoax?*

Iggy Towski had worked overnights at the Mobil Oil Refinery coker plant alongside Mack for as long as Rockfish could remember. The friends retired a year apart and were inseparable, as their standing daily lunch date showed. They fished during the day and at night watched the Orioles or John Wayne movies in the offseason. Iggy had been part of the family and was the uncle Rockfish never had.

"Stevie, Stevie," Iggy called out as Rockfish entered the waiting room. "You made it."

Rockfish walked over and grabbed Iggy by the elbow before the old man continued to wear a path in the carpet. They embraced and Rockfish noticed that up-close, Iggy looked like death warmed over. The bags under his eyes had doubled in size since the last time they spoke. Rockfish took his hand off the elbow and laid his arm around Iggy's waist. He fully expected Iggy's legs to go out from underneath him in the next couple of seconds.

"Let's get you in a seat before you have a freakin' heart attack, too," Rockfish said. He guided Iggy towards two unoccupied chairs on the far side of the room away from the blaring television. He didn't want to constantly shout over a Flex Seal infomercial.

Rockfish helped lower Iggy into the chair and sat beside him.

He looks a goddamn mess. How the hell am I supposed to get anything out of him? Rockfish glanced over and saw that the admissions desk was vacant. *Okay, Iggy, you're my best shot at the moment.*

"Look, Iggy, I need you to take a deep breath, pull that mask up over your nose and tell me what happened," Rockfish said, and he placed his hand on Iggy's shoulder. "You need a glass of water?"

"No, no, I'm fine, Stevie," Iggy replied and pulled the mask to cover his nose. "They moved Mack up to a room on the fourth floor. They're done running tests, and the nurse said she would come get me when he's settled and can have a visitor. And they haven't told me yet what any of the tests showed."

"I'm his goddamn son and not a visitor, so I need you to tell me how the hell this happened and then I'm going to find a nurse to take me up there, stat."

Iggy didn't say a word, but his chin dropped to his chest. Rockfish ran his left hand through his hair. *What the fuck is this guy hiding?*

"Iggy, Mack's going to be okay. He's strong as a bull, but the two of you aren't spring chickens. Were you moving that damn washing machine out of the house like I told you not to?"

Iggy glanced up and shook his head. "Mack's been under a lot of pressure lately. We all have. I know he's been meaning to talk to you about it, but you know—"

"Steve!"

Rockfish swiveled his head, first to the still empty admissions desk and then one hundred and eighty degrees to the entrance. Jawnie moved across the floor towards him with an obvious takeout container in hand. He stood up and met her halfway.

"What are you doing here? I told you to go home. I got this," Rockfish said. She hadn't changed clothes, and he assumed she came straight from the office. *A full partner for a couple of weeks and already blowing off my orders.*

"How's Mack doing?" Jawnie said. "Here, I grabbed dinner for you on the way over." She pressed the Styrofoam box to his chest and Rockfish reluctantly took it.

"I haven't seen him yet. No one is around to tell me anything. Iggy said they were taking him up to a room and we have to wait. This old guy doesn't look too good, but I'm trying to pull out of him what the hell happened, but he's stammering and not saying much. Maybe he's traumatized too, I don't know. Did I mention there hasn't been a goddamn person at the admission desk since I got here?"

"Is that Iggy?" Jawnie said. She pointed across her chest at a pair of coveralls slipping past the sliding glass doors before they closed.

"Iggy!" Rockfish said and took a step towards the exit.

Jawnie grabbed Rockfish by the arm. "Let him go. You said he was acting strange. Everyone handles this stuff differently. Plus, you're here for Mack. If there's a story to be told, let your dad tell it." Her grip loosened. "I can only imagine you going up to your dad's room all accusatory and shit. For his sake, stop and take a breath. You need to be in receive mode, at least until you learn what's going on."

Rockfish knew it was the right course of action. But too many years of operating solo and flying off the handle at every cock-eyed situation was a hard habit to break. He moved back to his chair and Jawnie sat in Iggy's vacated spot.

"You said no one's helped you yet. Do you want me to put on my best Karen face and find a manager? Because I can do that."

"Thanks, but, Jawnie, you didn't need to come; risk driving over here." Rockfish said.

"I took an Uber, Grandpa. We're a team, remember?"

"I do," Rockfish said. "But that team runs a company. Look, I don't know what's up with Mack or how long he'll be in this place. But I'm not planning on leaving his side until he's home. And I've got, ah, I should say, you now have a ten o'clock with Claudia Coyne tomorrow."

"I didn't see it on the office calendar."

"I might have forgotten to put it on the computer." Rockfish watched Jawnie raise her eyebrows and purse her lips over his answer. To her credit, she didn't lecture him, and he was thankful.

"Okay, what do I have to know?" Jawnie said.

"Claudia Coyne's married to some rich son of a bitch that's stepping out on her. Simple pre-divorce case. Follow the guy, get some pictures, bing, bang, boom, get paid."

"That's it?"

"That's it. You got this," Rockfish said. "You don't need me sitting at the conference table with you. I know you are more than ready. Shit, you were ready months ago. Hit me up on my cell if anything goes sideways and I'll let you know what's happening here when I finally figure it out."

They made small talk for another few minutes before Rockfish could convince Jawnie that he'd be okay, and she needed to head home with the takeout he forced back on her.

A nurse emerged ten minutes later and called out for a Mr. Towski...

* * * * * * * * * *

An orderly led Rockfish up to the fourth floor and they followed the winding red line on the ground through half-a-dozen hallways before stopping in front of Room 4127. The hallway lights were dim, but Rockfish chalked that up to the night shift. *What night shift?* The nurses' station was as vacant as admissions. *This place has the most patient-attentive employees in the world, or I'm walking straight onto the set of Halloween II.* He took a deep breath and pushed the heavy door.

"Hey, occupied." Someone said on the other side.

Rockfish leaned forward and peeked around the door. A nurse met his gaze. She stood next to a wall-mounted automatic hand sanitizer dispenser dressed in maroon scrubs and a pair of small reading glasses perched on the end of her nose.

"Evening, ma'am. Sorry about that."

"Not your fault. There wasn't a lot of thought placing these things when the 'rona hit last year. Previously, there was one unit outside each room, but the board of directors went with the more is better approach. And now I have left arm bruises from all the doors."

"Can I come in?" Rockfish said, still peaking around the door. "Mack's my father. I'm Steve Rockfish."

"Nurse Packer. Nice to meet you. If you don't mind, we can step back into the hallway and I can catch you up. He's finally asleep, and I'd rather not disturb him. He needs his rest."

How bad...oh God...how bad? Rockfish followed Nurse Packer down the hall to a small alcove where there was some privacy.

"Mr. Rockfish, is this okay with you?" Nurse Packer said. "Or would you like to go somewhere you can sit?"

"I've been on my butt for the past hour downstairs. I'm good standing."

Nurse Packer recounted the events that led to Mack's admittance and how a barrage of tests since then had led to a diagnosis. Rockfish hung on each word she spoke. He listened, unlike client meetings where he'd drift off and quickly find himself on the back of a buddy's boat, catching an imaginary twenty-five pound-Blue fish.

"Non-cardiac chest pain," Rockfish said. "You're sure of that?" His fingers went straight to his temple, and he shook his head.

"Your father's heart is healthy, as it can be for his age. His problem is with his blood pressure and some severe gastroesophageal reflux disease. Has he suffered the loss of a close family member recently?"

"No, unless he's got a secret one he never told me about. Can you give him some Tums and I can take him home?"

"It's more complicated than that, although I expect they'll keep him here tomorrow for observation. You need to understand there is something eating at your father," Nurse Packer said. "Stress, anxiety, and depression. He's got all the symptoms. At his age, this could be as detrimental as a heart attack. Tums won't solve his issue, but in the words of my granddaughter, he needs to take a chill pill."

"Obviously."

"Look, ah, Mr. Rockfish. Someone will be around in the morning to talk to you regarding counseling and other options, but until then, he needs rest. What I gave him will keep him down for four to six hours. And looking at you, I recommend you go home and get some rest. Come back in the morning. These types of things are hereditary."

Rockfish looked at Nurse Packer. He wasn't sure if she was bullshitting him to get him out of the way for the rest of her shift, or as a health professional, she was truly concerned. *Goddamn it, Dad. I need this like I need a hole in the head. First male pattern baldness and now this.*

"All the same to you, ma'am, I'm going to pull up a chair and contemplate my life's choices until he wakes up."

"Your choice, Mr. Rockfish. You'll need to keep the mask on at all times in this ward, even if you are vaccinated. If you need anything, please ring the call bell and I'll get down to the room as soon as I can. Or else I'll be back in at three to check his vitals. Oh, and coffee is behind the nurses' station. Starbucks in the main lobby doesn't open 'til 8am."

"I will, I am, and thank you a ton for taking good care of him," Rockfish said. "I'll follow you back to grab a cup before I hunker down."

A few minutes later, Rockfish pulled the small recliner closer to the hospital bed and balanced the Styrofoam cup on the arm. Mack looked peaceful, despite the *weight of the world on his shoulders* speech Nurse Packer relayed.

Christ, Dad, what the hell is going on here? Life ain't been better for us. What could you be hiding? He dropped his head into his hands. *Come on, Rockfish! Think. What could it be? What did you miss?*

More than likely, the answer was nothing. Like father, like son. Mack had never been a touchy, feely, emotional type, and after Betty's death, he had raised his son the same way. Bury your feelings deep inside and don't let anyone in. Ever. Unless you've got a dog. And it had been quite a few years since Mack had a four-legged buddy.

I'm a licensed professional investigator, for Christ's sake. I should be able to put this together and come up with an answer. But tonight, Rockfish had nothing to work with. Not one clue, and the only witness had fled the ER when the first opportunity presented itself. Rockfish stopped and realized he was rubbing his temples again. *Must be some sort of world record.* His dad worried him. *This wasn't like Mack. At all.*

The hours and cups of garbage coffee ticked away, and Rockfish was never within reach of an answer. He found the recliner comfortable enough that he dozed off a few times, only to awake at the last instant before knocking the coffee cup to the floor. The caffeine and the small wall light behind Mack's bed were no help. A few minutes later, he finally succumbed, and the empty cup skidded across the floor.

A little past 2am, Rockfish snapped to attention.

"Stevie, is that you?" Mack's voice was weak, but it pierced Rockfish's subconscious and brought him back to the land of the living.

"Yeah, Dad, it's me. Take it easy, don't sit up. We're all good here," Rockfish said. He shook his head to clear the cobwebs.

"Can you get me some of that ice water out of the pitcher? The cups are right next to it on that wheely table over there."

Rockfish stood up and walked across the room. He poured a small cup of water and pulled the table over the bed so Mack had somewhere to rest his cup. Rockfish sat back down and glanced at his phone. *2:45am. Nurse Ratched will be in to ruin the reunion episode shortly.*

"I told Iggy not to call you," Mack said, his voice sounding a little stronger. The water had lubricated his vocal cords, to some extent.

There was fight left in the old man, but it was the wrong time for the great 'I told Iggy' debate.

"Dad, you went to the hospital under the guise of a heart attack. Do you really think he would listen? Look, this is not the place for this. The nurse will be here in a few to check your vitals. You want to go home at some point, right?"

"Yes," Mack replied.

"Well then, we need to show her you're calm, cool, and collected. I'll explain later."

They made small talk, dominated by the Orioles spring training success, and each differed on if the momentum would carry over into the regular season, until the nurse finished with the blood pressure cuff. She walked over to Rockfish's chair and leaned over.

"Please don't keep him up any longer, he really needs his rest."

"Scout's honor," Rockfish said. "I'm only going to sit here until he drifts back off."

The door hadn't closed completely when Mack spoke up. "Son, I gotta come clean with you."

"Dad, whatever it is can wait. You heard the lady. If you don't go back to sleep, she's going to give you something to force the issue. Let's try to stay focused on you following the rules to get discharged in a timely manner. As comfortable as this chair is, I've got a business to run."

"Fuck 'em. I should have told you this a month ago. Gimme ten minutes, so your old man can unburden himself. Do that for me?"

"Nurse said they would set you up with a counselor for that. We could always check with Father McMurphy, if you don't like the counselor."

"Shut up and listen, Son. This is between us. Keeping it in, hiding it away from you is the problem. I done fucked up. Iggy met this really nice gal. Pretty young thing, and she had some investment deals going on. He said he made a huge return with her and, well, if he trusted her, I thought it was okay. I wanted to earn my keep around the house."

"Pretty little thing, huh?" Rockfish said, noticing the volume and strength returning to Mack's voice with each word.

"Yes, reminded me of your mom, the way she wore her hair."

"How much did you lose, Dad? Be honest."

"Seventeen thousand, give or take. If I ever run across any of them, I'll shoot every one of the bastards. Mark my words."

"Dad, you were in the Navy. They don't teach you to shoot on a boat. Don't make me take that rifle away from you. Let's calm down and think reasonably here."

Rockfish ground his back teeth and made sure Mack couldn't read an ounce of emotion on his face. His fingers dug into the arms of the chair. *He wants to hunt them down and shoot them, for Christ's sake.* After a couple of seconds, Rockfish stood up and moved closer to the bed. He reached out and touched Mack's arm.

"It's going to be okay. I'm going to get it back for you. You have my word. Now, gimme a second, will you? I gotta use the head and get a refill on this coffee. I'll be back in a sec. Close your eyes and practice. Think happy thoughts."

"I ain't going nowhere."

Rockfish forced a smile and walked out the door into the hallway. He kept going past the nurses' station and took the elevator down to the first floor. He exited out the only doors open at that hour, and after looking around to make sure he was alone, he punched a brick wall until his hand bled.

* * * * * * * * * *

The sun crept over the horizon as Jawnie crossed the parking lot and unlocked the office door. Her hands shook, and it took a second for the key to slide in. She stepped into the office space, glanced around, and waited for the automatic lights to activate. The last step in opening was to disarm the security system. Opening was old hat to Jawnie. On most days, she was the first in the office, with Rockfish bringing up the rear after stopping at the McDonald's drive-thru for breakfast. But today was different.

It's all me today. Jawnie took a quick run around the 'client area' and straightened up. She looked in all directions and admired her handy work, as her hand subconsciously moved to her abdomen. She dressed to kill for her first solo client meeting. Her mind told her she was ready to ace this test, but like her hands a few minutes ago, her gut told a different story. Jawnie had skipped breakfast at her condo, as she wasn't a hundred percent sure it would stay down. She knew it was nerves, knew that she would overcome the anxiety, sign the client and Rockfish would give her an attaboy. But someone needed to convince the pit in her stomach.

Jawnie's plan was to ignore it, knowing it would dissipate as the meeting went on. By lunch, she would laugh about it. Now, though, she needed to stay busy. In her office, she turned on the computer. She owed it to herself to read the background information in order to prepare for the meeting with Mrs. Coyne, but first she needed to check in with Rockfish. She picked up the office phone but changed her mind to a less intrusive text message. *I don't want to bother him if he's at home catching up on sleep or still with Mack. A quick note to let him know I'm thinking of them.*

Jawnie hit send and turned her attention to the Coyne file. She had two hours before the meeting. Her mouse moved across the screen and checked for any folder Rockfish could have saved the information to, since it didn't appear to be in the Potential Client directory.

"Shit!" she said, but it didn't surprise her. Her brow furrowed as she reviewed the files created over the past week to see if he had screwed up the naming convention. She came up empty.

Those borderline Boomers/Gen X'ers are the worst. I created this system for him; I went over this system with him and still it's like pulling teeth to get his buy-in.

Jawnie got up from her desk and walked across the hall to Rockfish's office. He had closed the door, and she respected his privacy, but his screw-up now constituted an emergency on her part. She tried the knob, and the door swung open. She stepped in and the overhead light illuminated the small space.

The office was bare bones and the desk immaculate. A large calendar blotter took up most of the surface area, with the only other items being #4 pencils and a computer monitor. Before searching the desk, she looked at the floor and located the remote to turn off the television on the wall. Jawnie shook her head and, in the back of her mind, wondered if she was a partner or transitioning to a caretaker.

She sat down and looked at the blotter. *Seems like a logical starting point. If he couldn't be bothered to enter the appointment in the shared office calendar. It has to be around here. Somewhere.* Her eyes went immediately to Friday, March 18, and the pencil scribblings gave her an answer and cranked up her anxiety at the same time. She wouldn't need the allotted two hours to prepare.

Claudia Coyne, 10:30am, husband banging unsub

With time to kill, Jawnie looked down at her phone. The text to Rockfish was still marked *delivered*.

Ten-thirty, 11am and 11:30am came and went without Claudia Coyne gracing *Rockfish & McGee – Investigative Specialists* with her presence. Jawnie reminded herself the wealthy ran on their own time and as the clock inched closer to noon, she felt as if she could keep some food down. She had closed her desk drawer when the phone in her pocket vibrated. The alert signaled that someone had walked through the front door. Jawnie put down the small bag of vegan sweet potato puffs and walked around the corner to the front.

A woman stood a few feet inside the doorway. Jawnie's first reaction was to wonder if Cruella de Vil and Divine had a baby and that child grew up to marry into the wealthy Coyne family. The woman looked as if the DNA from each fictional parent fought for dominance daily.

"Mrs. Coyne, hello, I'm—"

"Yes, my dear, can you please get me a Pellegrino mineral water and watch Pookie for me?" Mrs. Coyne handed over the teacup Maltese and walked towards the rear of the client area. She stopped and looked back over her shoulder at Jawnie. "And let Mr. Rockfish know I've arrived and am ready to meet with him."

Jawnie took a deep breath and enjoyed Pookie's kisses for a minute before putting on her partner hat.

"By the way, I'm Jawnie McGee, *the* McGee in Rockfish & McGee. Mr. Rockfish is unavailable for this meeting because of a family emergency. I'll be handling your case and if you have issues with me or my perceived lack of what you think a hard-nosed P.I. looks like, you are free to go elsewhere. And if you're going to have a dog this small, you might as well have purchased a cat." Jawnie returned Pookie to Mrs. Coyne, and the woman looked back, aghast.

She's on the ropes. Jawnie continued. "If you think enough of Steve Rockfish to give him your business, don't assume he would half-assed the selection of his only partner." *TKO. Rockfish would be proud.*

"Shall we?" Jawnie said. She then led a stunned Mrs. Coyne over to the conference table. Once seated, Jawnie broke the ice with small talk until she felt Mrs. Coyne appeared to relax and had moved past her earlier faux pas. Jawnie then opened her laptop to take notes.

"You think Mr. Coyne—"

"Roan. His name is Roan and I'm Claudia. I think we're past the point of formalities. Also, before we dive into specifics, I want to make you aware that Mr. Rockfish has already discussed his—"

Jawnie cleared her throat and smiled.

"—the firm's daily rate and expenses with me. I have no objections and concur with your billing cycle and upfront retainer."

"Excellent. Our meeting is because you presume—"

"I *know*."

"Understandable," Jawnie said, after another deep breath. "You know Roan is cheating. And you've come to this conclusion from..."

"A change in the pattern of his behavior," Claudia said. "For the past six weeks, on Tuesdays and Thursdays, he has not come home until well after ten o'clock. The other three days of the week, he's through the front door no later than six-thirty. His excuses are paper thin, although I have not punched holes in them because of a rather fragile male ego."

Jawnie met Claudia's eyes and nodded. She didn't know about the male ego from experience, but a few of her girlfriends liked to vent occasionally.

"My forensic accountant discovered a connection between these tired excuses and cash withdraws from a previously unknown savings account," Claudia said.

"How much are these withdraws for?"

"I'd rather not say."

"If I could get the contact information for your forensic accountant," Jawnie said, "a brief conversation with him could benefit my investigation." Jawnie bit her lower lip. She knew the answer before Claudia spoke.

"My Dear, you do not need to know anything about my finances, other than I can and will compensate you for a job well done. Follow him and you'll find the slut. That is all I ask of you and your firm." Claudia tapped the table with her index finger with each word spoken. "Be at his office this coming Tuesday night and follow at a safe distance. Provide me the harlot's name and address the following morning and I'll pay the rest of your fee."

"Okay," Jawnie said. She was a proponent of having as much information as possible, but from this meeting, she knew she'd be working with the bare minimum. *Bing, bang, boom, get paid. My ass.* "Can you share with me the company and address for Roan's employment, not to mention the make and model of his car?"

"He's the Executive Vice President over Acquisitions and Mergers at *Wilhelm, Gicobe and Stottlemyer.* They've got a building downtown, off South Gay Street. His car? It's a blue something or other. I don't know cars. I have a driver."

Jawnie knew with that answer Claudia had reached the end of cooperation time. *Best get her moving so I can get started.*

"Well, Claudia, I apologize for taking up too much of your time this afternoon. This predicament sounds rather cut and dry. This coming Tuesday I'll follow him and report back to you on what I find."

"*Who*, you find. I want the tart's name and address, remember?"

With that, Claudia stood up, stuffed Pookie under her arm and headed for the door. Not a goodbye, good luck, or good riddance, and Jawnie was okay with it. She closed the laptop and unlocked her cell. The notification for her earlier text had changed from delivered to read.

Progress.

CHAPTER TWO

Jawnie pulled into the office parking lot a few minutes after nine on Saturday morning. There were no days off in the world of private eyeing, and she loved that about the job. Each day came with challenges, some more exciting than others.

This early morning challenge came through John Nicholson, a former Columbia City Fire Department employee. Mr. Nicholson had been away from the job for the past six months on disability because of a back injury sustained in the line of duty. The Columbia City Council had hired *Rockfish & McGee* to look into reports that Mr. Nicholson was faking his injury and bilking the city out of much needed funds.

Jawnie's third stake out of the Nicholson residence paid off. After talking to some neighbors, she learned he liked to do his yard work in the early morning hours. *Away from prying eyes.* This morning, the Nikon D3500 DSLR with a giant telephoto lens captured Mr. Nicholson carrying large logs from one side of his property to the other before using a splitting axe to make fireplace-sized pieces. *Not every case is worthy of a TV movie of the week, but these incriminating photos should pay the bills.*

Jawnie had driven back to the office for two reasons. She needed to return the camera and lens to the office for safekeeping, as she did not believe in holding company property at home. There were always going to be times where she couldn't avoid keeping equipment overnight, but over a weekend went against everything Rockfish had taught her.

Nothing we buy anymore is off the shelf from Walmart, he said. *If any equipment goes missing from the office, insurance will cover it. If some junkie breaks into your place, Mutual of Omaha could tell us to go pound sand.*

Second, with details fresh in her mind, Jawnie could write and complete her report for submission to the Columbia City Council first thing Monday morning.

Jawnie walked across the parking lot. The camera strap swung over her shoulder and stepped onto the sidewalk. Something caught her eye, and she stopped in front of their door. The lights were on, but she didn't expect anyone in the office. *Strange.*

Jawnie reached out and pushed the door. It didn't budge. She grabbed her keys and unlocked it. *Were the lights on the fritz? Not like it was the first time the newfangled motion detectors went haywire and how did I forget to set the alarm last night?*

Her eyes scanned the front area and then to the bullpen. The couch and recliners weren't out of place. Matter of fact, nothing seemed out of the ordinary, or at least that she could tell. A solitary light shone from the hallway leading to their offices. Erring on the side of caution, she pulled the phone from her back pocket and pressed 9-1, her finger hovering over the second 1.

"Hey Rockfish, is that you? I must have missed Lana out front."

A second later he came around the corner, and Jawnie canceled the pending call.

"Steve, you look like shit," Jawnie said. "But, important stuff first. How's Mack doing?" Jawnie gave him the once over and didn't like what she saw. Rockfish wore a yellow hoodie and plaid pajama pants. Large dark circles hung under each eye. While the clothes gave her pause, the bandages and wrapping around his left hand worried her. *That has to be a sore spot with him. Better tread lightly around it and not mention the ignored texts from yesterday.*

Jawnie tilted her head towards the couch and Rockfish sat down.

"I'll go put on a pot," Jawnie said. She put the camera down and stepped over to the coffee machine.

"I only stopped by for a minute," Rockfish said. "Needed to look up some information but came up empty. I'm going to head back here shortly to be with him."

"How is Mack?" Jawnie sighed deeply, hoped he realized its meaning and that he ignored her the first time.

"Mack's doing better. He didn't suffer a heart attack but more a mix of crippling anxiety, high blood pressure and some gastrointestinal issues." Rockfish glanced at the coffee machine, then over to Jawnie and finally back to his lap. "I'm hoping they'll release him sometime later today, but the nurse told me it could be tomorrow. It all depends on his blood pressure. The doc wants to see it below a certain point before they'll discharge him."

"Well, that's awesome," Jawnie exclaimed. "He'll make a quick recovery and be back at the house, annoying you. Glad to hear the good news."

"When you hear heart attack, I guess anything below that on the severity scale is good news." Rockfish's eyes moved to the coffee again. He stood up and walked over to the machine before continuing the conversation.

Was he trying to will the machine to brew faster? How are his own anxiety issues?

Rockfish poured two cups and returned to the couch where he recounted the story of lovelorn Iggy Towski and the great internet scam of 2022.

"... surprising no one, after meeting her at a cafe and handing over the cash, the woman disappeared. Mack was afraid to tell me. Afraid or embarrassed. Pick one. The old man thought I'd stick him in a home or kick him out." He sighed. "So... how was Coyne yesterday? She sounded like a real piece of work over the phone." Rockfish raised his eyebrows and sipped his coffee.

Jawnie noticed how quickly he moved on. She contemplated circling back, but he had been a little forthcoming, and she didn't want him shutting down. *Men do that. Or so I've been told.*

"She was worse in person, if you can believe that," Jawnie said. "The woman walked in and began barking orders. Speaking of barking, she literally handed me her dog, confused me for your secretary."

"Still need to hire one of those."

"Preaching to the choir," Jawnie said. "But other than that, the meeting went well. All she wants is the name and address of the other woman. Her husband, Roan, stays after work to see the woman on Tuesdays and Thursdays. Allegedly. Claudia also mentioned some bank withdraws on those days. Some new account, a numbers guy she hired uncovered. I asked if I could talk to the guy, but she shut it down. Said her finances were none of my business and only offered it up to corroborate the husband is lavishing this whore with money. Her words, not mine." Jawnie shook her head and shrugged her shoulders.

"It sounds easy enough," Rockfish said. "Follow him, then follow her home. Cash that check and move on to the next one."

"Dude, since I've met you, I can count on one hand the number of times things were simple and went according to plan, and once was this morning."

"First time for everything," Rockfish said. They shared a laugh and Jawnie could tell he was calmer, looser than when he first emerged from the office and stared down the coffee maker.

"I'll believe it when I see it. Anyway, I'll stakeout downtown Tuesday night. Oh, I meant to tell you, I nailed Nicholson this morning playing Paul Bunyan in his backyard. The client will be extremely happy."

"Excellent," Rockfish said with a grin and a nod.

They sipped coffee in silence until Rockfish stood up. Jawnie wondered if he had finished talking and watched as he moved over and refilled his cup before returning to the couch. She saw her opening and addressed the elephant in the room.

"Steve, I have to ask. What the hell happened to your hand? Please tell me you didn't get into a fight with one of Mack's doctors."

Rockfish took a deep breath, and then slowly grinned. Jawnie let out a sigh of her own. *Okay. Still on his good side.*

"Took you long enough. I had to let off some steam, and there was a brick wall between me and sanity. I lost a split-decision thanks to the judge from Estonia scoring it 10-8 in the wall's favor."

"Tough break," Jawnie said.

"Yeah, the conversation with my dad didn't thrill me. Left a nasty taste in my hand." Rockfish ran his unbandaged hand through his hair and all the way to the base of his neck.

He's stressed, no matter how calm he tries to sound. Rehashing how this woman ripped off Mack is a sore point.

"I mean, I moved him into the house so I can keep an eye on him," Rockfish said.

"You're not his parent. You can't watch his every move or be there for every decision," Jawnie said.

"I know. I'm beating myself up over this. But I came in this morning to see if I could remember how to use those social media tools you installed on the computer. I need to find this chick. She's my only clue, and to my surprise I kept your instruction cheat sheet."

"Blind dog finds a bone every once in a while."

"Wiseass. But speaking of a dog, I was thinking about getting one for the old man. We haven't had one in years. Maybe it's the companion he needs when I'm not around."

"Now that sounds like a plan. I've got a contact at the county shelter, if you're looking to adopt."

"Yeah, text it to me. But back to the broad. No luck on my end. She's scrubbed everything from Facebook. That's where she first contacted Iggy from, and they only communicated through the site. My single lead is this cafe where Iggy took Mack and physically handed over the cash."

"That isn't much, but I've seen you do more with less," Jawnie said. She wanted to stay positive, based on how focused he seemed to be on the matter.

"I'm going to be honest with you. I'm going to work the fuck out of this and get his money back. Iggy's too, if the cards fall right. Don't think I'll be a shitty partner and ignore my case load here. I won't be around much unless I need something. Any free time I have is going to be devoted to finding this broad and putting her head in a vice 'till she tells me where the money is."

Would he be willing to travel to Nigeria and punch a prince sitting in an Internet cafe to get the money back? Or could it be Romania where traffickers turned the cash into meth and shipped across the Baltics? She didn't have high hopes for the recovery effort, despite her belief in her partner's abilities. But by the sounds of it, Rockfish believed the cash remained local.

"... Hopefully, but I'm not too confident. It probably ended up in her arm or up her nose. But I've got to get going. Too much time wasted this morning as it is. Headed back to the hospital. I'll swing by the health spa and talk to the manager regarding the slip and fall case Bridgeport Insurance hired us for. If I have time, I'll check out the pound. I'll be on my phone if you need anything."

Yeah, right. On it, but will you respond? "Gotcha, boss. Give Mack a hug for me."

****

"Stevie, you look like your housemate defrosted the freezer with a claw hammer."

Rockfish looked up from his morning paper, this chilly and overcast Monday morning. It wasn't the weekend, but he enjoyed that ritual of coffee and headlines on the deck. *Sometimes you need to stretch that weekend one more day. At least that damn television money got me out of that trailer. Always better to have an actual view of the water than claim to.*

Rockfish's long-time friend and steadfast con artist, Raphael "Raffi" Pérez, walked up the deck steps after letting himself in through the side gate. His Hispanic afro caught Rockfish's eyes before the rest of his body became visible. For a Monday morning, Raffi wore his usual three-piece, pinstriped suit with a large turquoise pinky ring. *Give him credit. The man plays the part twenty-four seven.*

"The last three days have been a kick in the pants," Rockfish said. "Mack's hardly gotten out of bed since they discharged him yesterday afternoon. Swung by the pound too. Got him a dog for companionship when I'm out."

"Nice. Old people love having someone to talk to," Raffi said.

"Yeah, a five-year-old silver Labrador. Named Zippy. House trained and everything. He's up on Mac's bed as I speak. After one day, they're thick as thieves. And now I have two to take care of."

Raffi laughed and smacked his friend on the shoulder.

Rockfish and Raffi grew up together as best friends and ran scams from John Carroll LeGrand Elementary through high school graduation. Pomp and Circumstance led the friends down the forked road to adulthood as Rockfish joined Mack at the refinery and Raffi graduated to richer marks and more elaborate schemes. Raffi always amazed Rockfish by remaining one step ahead of the law after all these years, and Rockfish knew his old friend was the perfect wingman for this mission.

"Well, Stevie, you know I'm not one for family drama, but I'm glad to see Mack hasn't changed," Raffi said. "Still ordering you around. And now with his little buddy by his side. But your message said there's an angle for us to work. Like old times. What's my cut?"

"Two c-notes a day," Rockfish said. "Only an hour or two per afternoon 'till we find this broad."

"Two-fifty and I'm intrigued. Go on."

"Take it easy on me, huh, Raffi? I've got a rash of incoming medical bills that I'm betting insurance won't cover. Not to mention a shitload of vet bills to get this mutt checked out."

"Stevie, you're like family. I can't charge you mark-rates. Tell you what, you got me for ninety minutes, then I've got to get over to Shady Dell Rest Home and—"

"Raffi, the less I know, the better. Plausible deniability is my best friend whenever I run into you." Rockfish shook his head and poured another cup of coffee. Raffi declined, pulled up a patio chair, and Rockfish outlined his conversation with Iggy from the previous day.

"We hadn't been home for over twenty minutes when the house phone rang, and Iggy wanted to know if he could come over and see Mack. I figure it's good the old man sees his friend. He's angry one minute, happy the next. Iggy coming over can only help. Then the guy shows up at the house and I can immediately tell he's gun shy after our talk in the ER. Probably also because he knows Mack told me everything. But I'll give the old guy credit, he's got balls walking into my house." Rockfish paused and sipped his coffee. "I sat Iggy's ass down and wouldn't let him up the stairs until he told me everything. Then Zippy gave him the once over before prancing back up the steps." Rockfish stopped and took another sip. He saw Raffi leaning in and wanted to make sure the story had his friend's full attention. "I wanted to compare stories."

"At some point, you're going to get to why you need me, right?" Raffi said. "I got people, I mean things to get done."

"Three hundred if I have your full attention. You'll need the backstory for what I want to accomplish."

"For three bills you can have the password to my mamacita's OnlyFans." Raffi scooted his chair closer. "And I'll take a cup of that coffee now."

Rockfish did not know what that meant, but filed it away to ask Jawnie. He walked back inside and grabbed a cup for Raffi before continuing.

"A month back, this hot young thing on Facebook messages Iggy. Basic conversation at first, but soon the topless shots flooded his inbox. It's been centuries since anyone's given this old fuck any kind of attention, let alone sent nudes. He's in heaven and with all the blood not rushing to his brain, dumb fuck couldn't see straight." Rockfish raised his eyebrows and nodded. Raffi nodded back. *He knows where this is going.*

"Long story short, she sells him on this investment strategy for a new cryptocurrency a friend developed. She sends him pictures of a fancy car, claiming it's hers and other shit. Asks him if he wants in and his pea brain tells him, if you say no, the boobies will end abruptly. Iggy gives her a grand and three days later she hands him back fifteen-hundred. This broad's no dummy. She lets that percolate for a week and asks for five grand. He doesn't hesitate and in return gets back seventy-five hundred. That's when she puts the bug in his ear about if you know anyone who needs some quick turnaround cash, we have a big event coming up..."

"And Iggy runs right to your dad, titty pics in hand," Raffi said.

"He actually printed them out and kept a couple in his wallet."

Raffi did a spit take and Rockfish couldn't stop laughing, despite being sprayed. Rockfish regained his composure after a few seconds and continued.

"They went to the bank together and, against the advice of the teller and bank manager, took out twenty-five thousand and seventeen thousand, respectively. They met up with her at a coffee shop. Iggy assumed she worked there and turned over the money."

"I mean, I've seen how this movie ends, but now you're a world-famous P.I. What do you need old Raffi for?"

"All I got is a name, Shae La Guardia, and a profile picture from Facebook. The account no longer exists. But those clowns met her at a place called Jamocha Jubblies. Mack thinks she worked there."

"Never heard of it," Raffi said.

"It's new and on the Gen Z side of town, so understandable," Rockfish said. "Think of a mashup of Starbucks, where people go for coffee and do work on their laptops, but all the servers have giant racks like Hooters." Raffi's eyebrows rose to attention and Rockfish grinned. "Iggy said he staked the place out on his own but never saw her again. He claimed to have gone in with the picture, but no one would listen to him. I'm sure he's not making anything up, but I think this broad is, could be, window dressing for something or someone bigger."

"Right, she's a roper. Steers the mark to the inside man. But in this case, these two marks hear about him, all the great things he can accomplish with a little capital, but never meet or lay eyes on him."

"Correct. I need you to dress like you do and hit Jamocha Jubblies every day for a couple of hours and pretend to work. Talk big time mergers or deals on your phone. Hopefully, the sight of a fresh fish will draw her out of the woodwork. If that happens, call me. I'll be there as fast as I can. Oh, make sure you take a mask. I can't afford any hospital bills while you're working for me."

"No problema. I'm one shot down, one to go. I'm gonna say three hundred plus expenses," Raffi said. "Think of it as a Covid surcharge and also guessing those Jubblies don't come cheap."

"They never do, but pay for your own damn coffee, Raffi, and it's a deal." They laughed again. *I have no idea why we don't get together more often. Oh yeah, that's right, he's always one step away from Decker slapping cuffs on him and I'm a potential accessory after the fact.*

"If I find this broad, you gonna lay the verbal smack down on her right in the store, or should I put on the charm and lure her outside?"

"Keep it in your pants, Romeo," Rockfish said, holding up his hands. "At that point, I'll release you on your own recognizance. My job will be to hang around and follow her home after her shift ends. I'll confront her when she gets out of the car. She can get me the money, take me to who has it, or I'll call the cops on the spot. That oughta do it."

"What's the plan if a couple of days go by with no nibbles?"

"If this Shae isn't around, I'm hoping another will bite and try to run the scam on you. A scam like this doesn't operate with only one roper. You know better than anyone. Once burned, you fill the spot with another to keep the money coming in. Unless it gets too hot, then—"

"They shut the whole shebang down," Raffi said. "For your dad's sake, let's hope the temperature is still somewhere around medium. It ain't much to go on, brother, but I'm in. Nothing beats putting the band back together." Raffi smiled and rubbed his hands together. "Now introduce me to Zippy."

* * * * * * * * * *

The rain had come down harder since Jawnie pulled up across the street from the Wilhelm, Gicobe and Stottlemyer building. It had started as soon as she left the office, yet the weather report for Tuesday evening didn't call for rain. She sat in her Subaru, dripping wet from having to pick up quarters off the sidewalk she had dropped when attempting to feed the meter. The dashboard clock glowed 5:47pm and the intermittent wipers hummed every five seconds.

Claudia had provided only one significant piece of information concerning her husband. Roan would leave the office each evening, exactly at six. He would not exit out the front doors, but from a second-floor glass enclosed walkway. It ran from the office building, over the street, and into a parking garage designated for employees. From this angle, Jawnie could not make out the faces of anyone as they crossed above, and the weather wouldn't allow her to exploit the powerful, tactical binoculars which lay on the passenger seat.

Jawnie had circled the block twice before finding a parking spot. She killed time by texting Ned Hasty, a friend from New Jersey she had made prior to moving to Maryland. Hasty was the current chief of the Elk Township Police Department and had played a supporting role in the events that brought Jawnie and Rockfish together. Hasty shunned the Hollywood spotlight and instead concentrated on the job the people of Elk Township elected him to.

Jawnie texted a short thank you. *Thanks for the info on the Aston Martin. I'm sitting on it in the rain.*

No worries, Hasty replied.

She texted back and continued to vent. *I didn't want to bother Rockfish with all the stuff he's handling now.*

Well, you mentioned yesterday, he's not replying to you anyway, Hasty texted.

She couldn't disagree with his logic. *True, but in my last conversation with him I got a strong Taken vibe.*

Huh? Hasty texted.

Jawnie laughed and did a quick IMDB search to get the spelling and words correct. *From the movie with Liam Neeson — "What I do have are a very particular set of skills; skills I have acquired over a very long career; skills that make me a nightmare for people like you."*

You think he's gone rogue and out for blood? Hasty replied.

Hasty implied exactly what Jawnie was afraid of. *Yup, think so.*

He'll be fine. Give it time. He'll come around, hat in hand, Hasty replied.

Jawnie was grateful for her text buddy, understanding what she was going through. *Thanks Ned!*

Be careful out there, Hasty replied.

It rapidly approached 6pm, and Jawnie dropped her phone into the cup holder. *No distractions. Now to figure out which of these people is him.*

At six on the button, three men walked out of the WGS building and out onto the walkway. All three white male executives looked the same to her, even as they passed almost directly above. Ten minutes later, no other men had exited when a blue Aston Martin Vanquish pulled out of the parking garage and Jawnie shifted into drive.

The rain made her first solo night surveillance more difficult than snapping a few pictures of lumberjack Nicholson at the crack of dawn. She hung two cars back and leaned out over the steering wheel to keep a visual. Roan headed southwest, and after hitting every stoplight on the way, he pulled into a McDonald's drive-thru across the street from Oriole Park at Camden Yards. Jawnie followed him into the parking lot and swung around the back of the building. There she waited in a space across from the pickup window.

Google had informed Jawnie that Roan's car cost a little under three hundred thousand dollars. *I would have expected him to eat better, if certainly not more expensive. How do you think he got so rich?* Jawnie looked over at Roan and realized that he had spent longer than a normal customer would at the pay window, before finally inching forward. The woman at the second window leaned out and pointed towards a vacant parking spot, outlined in red paint.

"Jesus Christ!" Jawnie exclaimed and sunk down in her seat. The spot was directly next to her. She reached behind the seat and nervously fished for the hat she placed there for such an occasion. Her hand found the large, brimmed beach hat, and she pulled it down over her ears.

The Aston Martin slid into the spot and Jawnie stared straight ahead. *Keep your eyes forward. Don't give him any reason to look over.* Her right leg bounced faster on the ball of her foot, and she tried to take a deep breath. *Please don't look over at me.* She crossed her fingers on each hand.

After fifteen minutes, three employees carried out armfuls of bags to the car, and Roan stepped out. He opened the driver's side rear door and Jawnie saw her opportunity as he interacted with the employees. She turned and looked. Roan was a rather heavy man, dressed in a dark color suit with what looked like coke-bottle glasses and an out-of-place porkpie hat. After the employees loaded the bags into the backseat, Roan pulled out his wallet and handed bills to each of them.

What the fuck? A binge and purge eating disorder? Some weird sexual fetish he shared with whoever Claudia thinks he's cheating with? Roan's actions confused Jawnie, but she loved this part of the job. *Where would this Big Mac trail lead?*

Roan pulled out and Jawnie again let a couple of cars get between Roan and the Subaru as the rain finally subsided. She hung further back than before as her night vision improved and she switched off the wipers.

He drove north on South Martin Luther King Jr Boulevard. He didn't deviate from the street until fifteen minutes later when he pulled into a well-lit, abandoned lot. *Was this home to his deviant fast-food activities? A little scary if you ask me.* Jawnie drove a little further down the street before hanging a U-turn and parking on the opposite side of MLK Jr Blvd. Roan had come to a stop directly under a lamppost and stepped out. Jawnie reached for the Nikon and waited.

She watched him through the lens. Roan leaned against the left rear quarter panel and seemed to not have a care in the world. Jawnie scanned the lot and spotted a group of walkers headed towards the car. She blinked and shook her head. They were homeless, not extras from The Walking Dead, and she blamed too much time with Rockfish for allowing her mind to go there. She watched in awe as Roan handed bag after bag to each person, and when the back seat was empty, he reached for his wallet and handed out cash to those remaining.

Screw you, Rockfish and double to you, Claudia. This guy is a freakin' saint. Out here doing the Lord's work and you think he's gallivanting with another woman? For a second, Jawnie hoped Claudia would get her divorce, in order for a man like this to start over and not have to worry about the wicked witch of Federal Hill.

In a matter of minutes, Roan finished and was back on the road. By 7:30pm the two-car caravan arrived in West Baltimore. At one point, they passed a storefront for a business called Jamocha Jubblies, and the name made her laugh harder than she had in weeks. *People are damn crazy.* At one point she feared losing Roan because of the tears welling in her eyes. But her worries were for not as he soon made a right turn into a back parking lot and pulled into a space against a brick building. The sign read Allison's Adult Superstore and the laughing fit started all over again. *How much weirder can this night get?*

Jawnie continued past the turn and quickly circled the block, hoping she didn't lose him. She spotted him sitting in the Aston Martin as she pulled into the lot's back row and slouched down. He remained in the car until 8pm, when he exited and headed down an alleyway between two buildings. Jawnie slipped out of her car and tried to shut the door as quietly as she could before following. The alley was dark, filled with trash dumpsters and dirty brick-lined the walls. It smelled of rotten food, urine, and some other bodily fluids she'd rather not think about.

Halfway, she looked forward and then behind her. He had vanished. *Did he skip out the far end and go left or right?* Jawnie picked up her pace and came out of the alley in front of Allison's. There was no sign of Roan, left, right or across the street, and Jawnie's heart sank. She had lost him. The only thing she could think to do was retrace her steps and hope she got lucky. *Oh my God, all this way and I lose him on foot. You idiot!*

Back at the alley's halfway point, Jawnie stopped and saw it. A small stone staircase went down and appeared to lead beneath Allison's. There was no light, so she couldn't actually see where it led. She swallowed hard and descended the stairs. At the bottom, she stopped short of running face first into a steel door. Four glass panels comprised its top half. She used the darkness to her advantage and looked in. The room was well lit. Someone had spaced out folding chairs in two circles, one inside the other, with a dozen people milling around. Roan was holding a red solo cup and Jawnie had a pretty good idea of what was going on. *It may not be Alcoholics Anonymous, but it definitely is some sort of addiction meeting.*

Jawnie went back up the stairs and headed for her car. Three steps down the alley, she tripped in the dark, but caught her balance before taking a header. She stopped and looked behind her. She noticed a pair of legs sticking out from against the wall.

"Sorry about that, ma'am," a female voice said.

"It's my fault," Jawnie said. "I should have been watching where I was going. Are you okay?"

"Overall? It's debatable. But right now, I'm not too bad. No one bothers me back here."

Jawnie's mind raced back to Roan's actions earlier, and she reached for the ten in her front pocket. She handed the bill to the woman and repeated Hasty's words from earlier.

"Be safe out here."

Back in her car, Jawnie attempted to make sense of all that had occurred since she had started the surveillance. The one thing she knew was she needed to wrap her head around it before she spoke with Claudia in the morning.

She waited in the dark for Roan. At one point, she reached out to Rockfish via text and when a reply didn't come; she dialed the number and left a message.

"Hey, it's Jawnie. I'm sitting here outside an adult bookstore. Wait till you hear about my night. Anyway, I'm going to go, stay safe. Give Mack & Zippy my best. Yeah, Joanne told me you picked out a winner."

Roan emerged from the alley a few minutes after 10pm and started his car. Jawnie followed suit and uneventfully tailed him back to his house before calling it a night.

* * * * * * * * * *

Rockfish brought Lana to a stop and parked on the street a block and a half away from his destination. He grabbed his cell phone from the dash mount, hit the lock button, and hustled down the sidewalk. *It's a beautiful afternoon to get some payback.*

Raffi had called thirty minutes ago and repeated the phrase that pays, Pioneer Aviation.

The words came from an old episode of M*A*S*H that had cracked them up as kids and forty-some years later still served as a code word hinting Raffi had come across something. A nugget worthy of Rockfish dragging his ass down to the cafe to check out.

Wednesday afternoon was Raffi's second day working on site at Jamocha Jubblies. The previous day had been a complete wash. All Raffi uncovered that day was that after four Sloppy Top dark roasts, his acid reflux came at him like he owed it money. He ended up calling Rockfish shortly after leaving and insisted Rockfish reimburse him for the bottle of antacids purchased at a gas station on the way back to his apartment.

"Come on, Stevie, how was I supposed to know each one of those delicious drinks had over 300mg of caffeine?" He'd said. "They go down so smooth. If you won't reimburse me for the coffee, at least Venmo me a couple of bucks to help with the antidote."

Rockfish had reminded Raffi that the caffeine count for the drinks was most likely printed on the menu, and he would have known that if he had taken his eyes off the jubblies.

"Wednesday, go decaf or go home," Rockfish had said. "Mack and I need you there tomorrow." He had hung up, hoping that throwing in Mack's name would play on Raffi's emotions.

Rockfish slowed his walk as he approached Jamocha Jubblies from the left and passed the small, attached parking lot. Something caught his attention, and he came to an immediate stop.

Can't be. But it is. A yellow Nissan Xterra sat in the parking lot. *But is it THE yellow Nissan Xterra? Only one way to find out.* He stepped off the sidewalk, crossed the narrow berm and up onto the asphalt. There it was. The rusted front bumper guard.

Rockfish's mood shifted from kick ass and take names to straight up caution. He had always been a firm believer in coincidence and things happened for a reason, but this one had him second and even third guessing. *Maybe the stalker likes coffee or has a part-time job to fund her stalking hobby. No, this is too fluky.* Normal SOP in a situation like this called for a step back and to reevaluate the way forward. But this Wednesday afternoon found him standing in an open area, in full view of half the cafe patrons, if they bothered to take their eyes off the jubblies and glance outside.

He went against his better judgement and continued on towards the front door. From the outside it looked like any chain restaurant, but when he stepped inside, it oozed of sex appeal. *Gotta love the outfits. More places need the less is more look.*

"Stevie!" Raffi shouted from a booth along the far wall. Rockfish passed the 'seat yourself' sign, maneuvered his way between the floor tables, and slid into the empty side of the booth.

Raffi played the part like Rockfish knew he would. And then some. Raffi had dressed to the nines. There was a laptop open on the table and two cell phones lay between it and the edge of the table. Raphael Pérez, high-powered financier, was on the scene.

"When do I get my six hundred, Stevie?"

"Keep it down. We'll hit an ATM at some point. Don't you worry," Rockfish said, his voice at a much lower pitch than his partner's.

Raffi looked around and leaned in. "Okay, I trust you, Stevie." He carried on how his server, coincidently the same one from yesterday, had begun with small talk, before quickly moving to questions about his job and investment strategies. "I bullshitted the best I could and called you right away. She's mighty curious about investing in Pioneer Aviation now. Maybe we can get some cash out of her today?"

"Which one?" Rockfish said, ignoring his partner's question.

"I think she went into the back. I'll point her out when she's on the floor. You want anything? I got a tab going. Reimburse me later, since we're stopping at the ATM."

The two men made idle talk and tried to blend in until the server emerged from the kitchen area. Raffi pointed her out. Rockfish let out an audible sigh. She wasn't the same woman who had spied on the business from across the street in the yellow Xterra. *But damn, if young and blonde was a trait, she could be a close relative.* The server walked by the table and held up a finger to let them know she'd be right with them. She wore a white, maybe a size too small, Jamocha Jubblies t-shirt with a plunging neckline and tied an inch above her navel. Black leggings and pink high-top Nikes completed the outfit.

Rockfish's eyes followed her as she checked on a handful of tables before working her way back towards the booth. *This could be the break I'm hoping for, but what about that damn car outside?* Rockfish ran a hand through his hair and sighed. *Was this more than a one scammer or roper operation?* Either way, he felt his own little plan was headed in the right direction.

When the server made her way over to the booth, Rockfish ordered a coffee, black. As she walked away, Raffi went into further detail having to do with their interactions prior to Rockfish's arrival.

"She wanted to know about my job, how successful I was, and mentioned she had dabbled in foreign exchange currency trading." Rockfish leaned back in the booth to avoid getting hit by Raffi's hands. They moved in tandem with his words. "She knew of some friends that had opened an investment company and if I was ever interested, she'd introduce me. We were getting along great. Apparently, there's a great up-and-coming cryptocurrency opportunity I need to jump on. Or so she keeps saying."

Rockfish grinned and imitated reeling in a heavy fish with his hands. *Oh, we've got one on the line here. Time reel her in.*

"No, Stevie, I think she really likes me. I mean, we had a connection."

Rockfish rolled his eyes. "Yeah, the dancers at the Red Daisy all fall for you too," Rockfish said, and laughed out loud.

"Look, man, she gave me this." Raffi pulled a piece of paper from his jacket's inside pocket.

Sunshine West, Facebook.com/SunnyWest69

"Believe what you want, but she told me her DMs are open. You know what that means..."

"Actually, I don't," Rockfish said. "And you're here to play her, not vice versa. But I'll give her points for the profile name."

"Tsk... tsk... always with the negative waves, Stevie. Her parents might have been flower children of the 1960s."

Rockfish noticed the server walking back towards the booth with his coffee and kicked Raffi in the shins.

"OMG," Sunny said as she set Rockfish's drink in front of him. "You're Steve Rockfish, that famous private detective from television. Can I get an autograph?"

Rockfish smiled, and at that moment, he realized he no longer needed Raffi to play the mark. He was perfectly capable of the job. *Might even save me some time and money in the long run. Ah shit, though. Now she knows who I am: a damn good, famous and handsome P.I. I hope that doesn't ruin this.* Rockfish pulled out a business card and signed the back.

"O-M-G, thank you very much," Sunny said before turning towards Raffi. "Hey do you have that slip of paper I gave you earlier?"

"Sure do, darlin'," Raffi said and smiled.

"Good," Sunny said as she plucked it out from between Raffi's fingers and handed it to Rockfish before walking away.

"Well, easy come easy go," Raffi said. "How 'bout my money now?"

"Come on, Raffi, put those sad puppy dog eyes away," Rockfish said. "You weren't born last night."

"I could have got her," Raffi said, and leaned across the table. "You haven't seen the ladies that I'm pulling in on the regular. I got pictures. You want to see?" Raffi held up his phone but cautioned Rockfish from swiping left. "Go right, you don't want to see those others."

"Put your phone away," Rockfish said. "Did you drive here?"

"No, I took an Uber."

"Good, scoop up your shit and take my keys," Rockfish said. "Lana's parked on the street, a block and a half up. Wait there, I'll be out shortly."

"But—"

"No, forget her and I'll toss in another twenty," Rockfish said.

"*Who*? Get my tab for me, will you?" Raffi said and was out the front door.

Rockfish finished his coffee and raised a finger for another. Sunny nodded and grabbed a carafe off the front counter.

"Where did your friend go?" Sunny asked as she filled his cup and, as Rockfish expected, slid into Raffi's side of the booth.

Seat wasn't even cold.

"Raffi's late for a meeting with his parole officer," Rockfish said. He chuckled to himself at the confused expression on Sunny's face. *I'm going to enjoy fucking with these clowns at every opportunity until I get Dad's money. Buckle up, honey.*

"I'm a huge fan of your show," Sunny said. "I signed up for whatever that channel is because of all the hype surrounding it."

Rockfish wanted to give her points for at least attempting her homework. *A channel does not equal a streaming service launched by one of the richest men on earth.* Instead, he smiled and said thanks.

"I loved how you single-handedly took on the establishment and came out on top. You're like Captain America, or something," Sunny said, as she leaned over and pressed her elbows against her chest.

Rockfish admired the view, but the hypnosis trick didn't work on him as Sunny expected. *Not my first rodeo, honey. But if I'm going to have to play the part of the dimwitted guy with disposable income, I'll give them a good stare. All for the client.*

Sunny blathered on about her interpretation of *The Pine Barrens Stratagem*, when Rockfish realized he needed to fall back and assess the situation, especially without the distractions. *While this bimbo isn't the same one that scammed Dad, I'll hold off applying pressure until I've got a better link between the two. I've accomplished what I needed here. Any more time and I bet she'll try to pull me into the men's room and brush her charms across my face.*

"I appreciate it, really do. Love my fans, but I've got to get going myself. Tell you what I'm going to do. I'm going to go home and make me up one of those Facebook profile page things and send you a request. We can be buddies," Rockfish said. He finger-gunned her as he stood up to emphasize his point.

"Oh, come on. You off to go play Hollywood detective and help Kim with her divorce from Kayne or something?"

"I'd have to know who they are first. But yeah, duty calls," Rockfish said.

"Promise you'll send me a message when you get online? Cross your heart and hope to die? I really want to talk more, you know, about Hollywood. I can tell we have a lot in common." Her elbows tightened, and Rockfish paused for a second to admire the view.

In common? Other than my dad and his partially depleted retirement fund? Get the fuck outta here.

"Can't wait. Goodbye, Sunny," Rockfish said. "This oughta cover the tab and leave a little something for your troubles." He tossed a few bills on the table and when she didn't react negatively to the amount, he turned and walked towards the door.

Rockfish let the door close behind him, then waited until he was a half block up the street before he pumped his fist. *Oh, how I've missed this feeling. Dad, I'm gonna give 'em hell. And then some.*

CHAPTER THREE

Thursday night found Jawnie back in the parking lot behind Allison's Adult Superstore. The night sky was clear, and the moonlight gave her an unobstructed view of the alley's entrance. Ten minutes ago, she had shifted the Subaru into park and watched as Roan exited his car. She contemplated following him and taking a gander through the door to make sure the chair circle was actually his destination. She could hear Claudia now, if Roan had walked straight through the alley and gotten into a waiting car. *That would go as well as our talk yesterday.*

The previous morning, Jawnie had called Claudia to report back on the very uneventful aspects of Tuesday night's surveillance. Jawnie had hoped the woman would accept the truth, offer to drop off a check later, and then Jawnie could focus on the Andrist investigation or the next client through the door. But it didn't go as planned. *Never does with this lady...*

Claudia didn't want to hear any of it. She, in no certain terms, let Jawnie know her husband had played her. That everything he did that evening was a distraction to keep her from finding out the truth.

"He obviously felt something was off," Claudia said. "Or he identified you in the McDonald's parking lot. Did you forget to remove the magnetic advertising sign off the side of your car before you started following him?"

Jawnie muted her end of the call and let out a lengthy *Fuuuuck Yoouuu* and dropped her head into her hands. The conversation was quickly deteriorating into the worst-case scenario; having to continue working the case and deal with this Karen of a client. *There's no way Rockfish would let me drop it. Well, maybe he would, but definitely not in his current frame of mind. I can't get a text returned, let alone expect him to sit down for a conversation on cutting ties with this woman.* No matter how bad Jawnie thought Claudia would be, no matter how much she had hoped and prayed the woman would be civilized and understanding, she was going to have to deal with it and push forward. Jawnie unmuted her phone and dove in.

"Claudia, that wouldn't explain why he ordered all that food before pulling into the parking space next to me."

"Don't you patronize me, little girl. You work for me and I expect customer service worthy of the price I'm paying. I also insist your boss call me back to detail your firm's plan for this Thursday night."

"As I stated to you last Friday, Mr. Rockfish is handling other matters at the moment," Jawnie said. "I am and will continue to be your point-of-contact for this case until you no longer require our services. If that is your decision at the end of this call, we will expect payment for services rendered to be received at this office by the end of the week, per the agreement you signed last Friday, the eighteenth."

"I will do no such thing..." Claudia said, and Jawnie's shoulders dropped. *There's no getting out of this one, kid.* She could hear Rockfish in the back of her mind.

"... he played you and I will not stand for any slander. My husband is not an alcoholic, drug or sex addict of any kind. He obviously uses that low-class meeting location as a cover for his dalliances. I expect, at a minimum, this Friday you will have identified this floozy. Good day." Claudia ended the call.

Still on the case some two hours ago, Jawnie trailed the Aston Martin, but much to her surprise, there was no Costco-sized run at a fast-food restaurant. She hoped Claudia was right, no matter how painful it would be, and tonight's travels would lead to a fancy hotel. There she could enjoy a nice dinner and wait for the extra-curricular activities to finish up.

But nothing went as she hoped. Roan had driven out Fifteenth Street and came to a stop at the Graceland Park Soup Kitchen. He pulled his car around back and Jawnie frantically looked for street parking. She found a space one block over and jogged back to the soup kitchen, wondering if she would have to roll around in the dirt and pretend to scratch at meth bugs to blend in and locate Roan. *What would Rockfish do in a case like this?* And then it hit her. She knew exactly what he would do. She hurriedly scanned the line and went with her gut.

"Hey buddy, you wanna make a quick twenty," Jawnie said, and held up the bill. The young man wore a bright green Puma sweatsuit and the scars on his face gave off a meth-vibe. Yet, he looked the least homeless and most trustworthy. "Can you tell me what this guy is doing inside?" She handed him a picture of Roan.

"I mean, I can," the man said and took the bill from her hand. "But then again, you can walk over to those windows and look in yourself." He pointed towards the side of the building. "Ain't no one gonna stop you."

Goddamnit!

The man smiled and turned away. "Thanks for the handle of vodka," he said.

"The what?" Jawnie watched as he shuffled forward in line. It hit her a second later. Embarrassed, humiliated and thrilled no one she knew was around to witness that, Jawnie walked over to the windows on the side of the building. She had to wipe the dirt from the pane, but there was Roan. He had substituted his suit coat for an apron and was ladling soup into empty bowels for each man that stopped before him.

Oh, I hate you so fucking much now, Claudia! Did I say the man was a saint before? This confirms it. Jawnie pulled out her phone and snapped a couple of pictures through the window. *He is the world's sweetest man or feels the need to atone for something he's done. I need to figure out exactly what's going on in the chair circle and then put Claudia in her place. Why? She'd reply that all this was a front for something more devious. I need to wash my hands of this couple and dig up some free time to help Rockfish get Mack's money back or wrap up the Andrist case. There was always work to be done on Andrist.*

Jawnie had stuck around the outside of the soup kitchen until she saw Pope Roan the First take off his apron. She glanced at the time and knew where he was headed. She ran back to her car, played a hunch, and planned to be waiting when he pulled in.

Back at Allison's parking lot, Jawnie finally got out of the car and walked down the alley. She still wasn't sure what she was going to do when she reached the bottom of the steps. Walking through the door was the only way to solve this riddle, but she risked running into someone she knew. *That would be my luck.*

This time she paid more attention to the ground as she entered the alley and wasn't too surprised to come across the same set of denim covered legs sticking out from behind a dumpster. Jawnie looked over at where the woman sat, her back to the brick wall.

She doesn't look homeless. The woman's orange knit hat hid her hair and her UMBC hoodie and jeans looked relatively clean. *I wonder if my failed soup kitchen routine would work better this time?*

Jawnie took a chance and introduced herself to the girl. "You might remember me. I was the one who tripped over you and gave you a ten a couple of days ago. I've got a proposition for you, if you're interested."

The woman stood up and stepped towards Jawnie. *Her face seems not dirty enough for an alley urchin, not to mention the Doc Martens on her feet.*

"I remember you, but I won't lie and say I used the cash for above-board purposes. I'm Gwendolyn Hurricane-Tesla."

"Can I call you Gwen?" Jawnie said. *Christ, I thought growing up as Jawnie was a bitch.*

"Lynn will work."

"Not a problem. Can I pay you to help me out over the next hour or two? We can negotiate if that will help you decide."

"I don't swing that way," Lynn said with a wrinkled-up nose.

Could we get off on the wrong foot more if we tried? Jawnie's brow furrowed. "That's neither here nor there. What's important is the meeting going on, down those steps and through a door."

"Yeah, I've seen the people going in for the past month. Figured it was some sort of sex offender convention because of the jerk shop above."

That makes absolutely no sense. But Jawnie wouldn't let it detract her from getting Lynn through the door. "Twenty bucks and all I need you to do is go in, grab a seat. Take it all in and come back out and let me know what in the world is going on in there. And look for this guy." Jawnie handed a picture of Roan to Lynn and shone her phone's flashlight on it. "Let me know if your womanly intuitions give you any kind of vibe that he's banging any of the other participants."

"That's all I gotta do?" Lynn gave Jawnie a look as if she didn't believe a word.

"Scout's honor. By the looks of the last meeting, there should be snacks and drinks."

Lynn folded her arms and paused. "Thirty and I'm in. You gonna hang out here?"

"I'll be in the back lot, green Subaru," Jawnie said.

"I'm shocked," Lynn said and rolled her eyes.

"Yeah, I know. When you're done, there's a diner down the street. We can get something to eat and you can fill me in." Jawnie pulled an additional ten out of her pocket.

"Deal," Lynn said, and they fist-bumped to seal it.

Glad to see, in these times, she's a germaphobe too.

Lynn headed down the stairs, and Jawnie hoped she wasn't putting the girl in any kind of danger. Jawnie knew, in the back of her mind, she was jumping to conclusions. What she fully expected to happen was someone would ask Lynn to leave before she sat down. Jawnie prayed she was wrong.

Ten minutes passed before Jawnie allowed herself some good thoughts and retreated to her car. Lynn emerged an hour later, by herself. Jawnie unlocked the door and Lynn got in.

"They cut me loose when they had church business to discuss. Can I get a burger and fries now?" Lynn said, wrapping an arm around her midsection. "You probably heard the grumbling all the way out here."

Jawnie's mind raced. *Church business? What the hell. And what about making sure Roan went straight home after this?* Jawnie gambled and assumed Roan would be a good boy and head straight home. She needed to hear everything Lynn learned while it was still fresh in her head.

"Let's go grab something to eat. Hopefully, they have a tofu option."

* * * * * * * * * *

Jawnie expected the ride to the diner to be extremely awkward, littered with cringeworthy bouts of long silence, but Lynn had other intentions. She felt the need to qualify that she wasn't homeless. It, instead, was a conscious decision on her part. She had a home with her sister and her husband, but wasn't interested in spending a majority of her time there. She preferred to spend most of her time on the street and away from what had become a toxic environment because of constant conflict.

Jawnie listened and couldn't tell from which side of the divide the toxicity came. Lynn let slip that she had a bedroom at the house, which was in Severn, a small town, eight miles south and she wouldn't return unless absolutely desperate. She defined desperation as needing a shower and access to a washing machine, or cravings that led her to raid the pantry with a takeout bag. The only condition her sister put on the random visits was Lynn receive both vaccine jabs as to not put the sister or husband at risk. *Apparently, we have different definitions of desperate. Sounds like some serious issues with her sister. Was it drugs, or something more?* She shook her head. *It's none of my business. The less I know, the better. The last thing I need is to over-worry about yet another person in my life. But thank God she's vaccinated. Who knows what's stirring down in that basement meeting room?*

Dot's Diner was on the outskirts of a nearby, small industrial area. Commercial warehouses surrounded the small brick diner on all sides. If you didn't know Dot's was there, you'd drive straight past it looking for the closest Burger King. The locals preferred it that way. Chrome covered the inside of the diner except for the red vinyl booths and matching stools at the lunch counter. Rockfish had mentioned the place twice in passing when Jawnie first moved to the area, but an old-timey diner with extra grease listed as a side on menu didn't cause the vegan inside her to salivate.

Jawnie parked in front of the entrance door. Lynn jumped out and held it open. The hostess led them to a booth in the far corner, away from the rest of the customers, and Jawnie handed her a five to say thank you for the privacy. *I need to hit up the petty cash drawer back at the office. I'm handing out cash like it's free government cheese.*

Their bottoms slid across the red vinyl and hadn't come to a complete stop when a waitress pulled up and asked for drink orders.

"I'll have water with lemon," Jawnie said.

"Gimme a cookies and cream milkshake to start," Lynn said, and reached for the menus stacked behind the condiments. She handed one across the table and buried her nose in the other.

"Everything looks very good," Jawnie said, attempting to make small talk. In truth, it all looked bad, very bad to her. *Maybe if they allow a shitload of substitutions, I could Frankenstein monster this cob salad into something that would pass as somewhat vegan.*

Jawnie was mid-substitution in her mind when Lynn asked a question from behind her menu.

"I've told you way more than you need to know about my living situation. How about you tell me why you're so interested in this dude? What's he to you? Family?"

Jawnie peered over her menu and contemplated her reply. She and Lynn had entered into a contract for services agreement, and she felt she owed some explanation before peppering Lynn with questions about the meeting.

"His wife thinks he's cheating, and I'm supposed to find out who the mystery lady is and report back."

"Oh, you're a narc," Lynn said. "Makes sense now."

"Licensed. Private. Investigator."

"Hmm, job seems simple enough."

Jawnie bit her tongue on her own smartass reply as the waitress suddenly reappeared and asked for their orders. After she left, Jawnie restacked the menus behind the condiments.

The women made eye contact for the first time since sitting down and Jawnie let fly. *Better late than never.* "You would think so."

"What?"

"Never mind," Jawnie said, seeing the furrowed brow and quizzical look on Lynn's face.

"Well, anyway, I got good news for you, Dick Tracy. If one hour of one night means anything, I can tell you this guy isn't sleeping with anyone in that place."

Jawnie leaned across the table. "What makes you so sure?"

"He's looking for something more. Bigger, I guess you could say." Lynn said and pulled a couple of folded papers from her bag. "These will tell you what you want to know. Back in a sec, I gotta go use the bathroom. Way too much Jesus Juice at that place."

Jawnie watched Lynn get up and walk towards the restroom. The thought of Lynn ditching her crossed Jawnie's mind, but she discarded it. *Let's see what all this is about.* Jawnie looked down at the papers. They were pamphlets, flimsy, cheap paper, tri-folded. The first was simply entitled, "The Church of the Universal Nurturing II."

That explained the Jesus Juice reference. The other simply asked, "Are You Financially Prepared for the Rapture?" And in a smaller font directly below, "Don't be caught without God's Currency."

"That explains Roan's transformation into Ned Flanders a few times a week," Jawnie said aloud to no one in particular. She'd look them over in the morning, but at first glance, didn't think they added any substance to her investigation. *I don't think Claudia would give a shit if Roan told her he had found God. That bitch would automatically assume God was code for a busty blonde with very loose morals.* She refolded the pamphlets and put them in her jacket pocket, as Lynn slid back into the booth.

"You look at those?" Lynn said.

"Yes, I was sitting here trying to figure out if his wife will believe it when I tell her," Jawnie said.

"I can tell you, first-hand account, whatever they're selling, he's buying wholesale."

Out of the corner of her eye, Jawnie watched the waitress grab their plates from under the warming lights and head in their direction. The Frankenstein salad didn't look half bad, and Jawnie picked up a fork and dove in. On the other side of the table, Lynn inhaled her food. The burger and cheese fries mixing in her mouth did little to stop her from continuing.

"You saw those two circles of chairs? The more important members sit in the inner circle. That's where your guy was. Those of us that looked like we couldn't pay our own way were told to sit in the larger, outer circle."

Jawnie nodded, stabbed a piece of Romaine lettuce and listened.

"Some chick named Sister Lilith ran the meeting, but the whole sermon, or whatever the hell they call it, revolved around someone named Mother Elizabeth. She wasn't there and what I gathered from casual conversation... she doesn't attend these meetings—"

"Okay, Lynn, I think I have enough to work with," Jawnie said. "I can't thank you enough for doing this."

"I did good, then? You got any more work for me? I mean, if it means cash and a meal, I don't mind getting my hands dirty so you don't have to."

Her frankness shocked Jawnie, but the girl wasn't lying. *Have I found my first confidential informant? I think I have. What would Rockfish say?* Deep down, she hoped he would say something. Anything.

"You know what, Lynn, maybe having you sit in on another meeting would be beneficial to my case. I can report back to his wife that we observed him multiple times before coming to our conclusion. If she doesn't like that, she can pay my fee and find someone else."

Lynn finished her burger, grabbed a napkin and then slid out of the booth. "Hey thanks for the dinner, boss, but I have to get going. People to meet, places to be. You know the deal." She held out her hands and shrugged.

"Wait. Give me a second to flag down our waitress and get this in a box," Jawnie said. "I can drop you off wherever you're going."

"Nah, don't worry about it. It's better this way now that we've got a working relationship." Lynn smiled and headed toward the door.

Jawnie spun around in the booth. "I've got no way to contact you," she said.

"I left my number on the napkin, but don't worry, I'll be there next week," Lynn said. "Meet me outside afterwards and we can do this again." She was out the door before Jawnie could get a syllable out.

"See you next Tuesday..."

Twenty minutes later, the waitress asked Jawnie if she needed anything else. She jerked, having lost herself in thought, staring through the salad she had pushed around the plate more than ate.

Jawnie had taken a big step tonight, recruiting what could be her first CI and that alone should be reason to celebrate, but there were too many negative thoughts rocketing around inside her head. Even with Lynn's information, Jawnie knew that her call to Claudia in the morning would not go well. *There's no way I call and she believes a word I say. Don't worry.*

Your husband's not cheating on you. He's born again. Yeah, that would go over well. If I only had a partner who I could run my problems past. Those learning moments are what I miss most right now.

Jawnie concluded she needed to address the other side of this problem. Perhaps if she could talk to Roan, because it was obviously clear Claudia hadn't, then she could get answers that might satisfy the wife. Jawnie needed to put this puppy to bed, with a small asterisk next to Claudia's name in the computer system, so that no one would take her call again. But Jawnie knew better. If Claudia called, Rockfish would pick up or return the message. He rarely turned down business, no matter how busy they were.

Steve. What are you up to right now? I feel like I've been abandoned. Maybe I shouldn't have agreed to have the training wheels taken off so soon? Where are you when I need you?

Jawnie thought it strange not seeing him in the office daily. She wanted to tell him about Lynn and get that shit-eating grin and attaboy from him. How she had looked forward to moments like that. *Had.* Jawnie grabbed a napkin to dab her eyes.

Jawnie pulled out her phone and stared at the number pad. She thought twice and put it back in her pocket. One damp napkin later, she pulled it out and left him yet another voice message.

****

Late Friday morning, the one week—so to speak—anniversary of Mack's medical emergency, found the father and son on the back deck of their house with an empty coffee carafe and two plates littered with breakfast crumbs. Rockfish, lost deep in his own thoughts while Mack worked on the TV Guide crossword puzzle, Zippy curled up at his feet. The men had said little since Mack served his world-famous bacon, egg, and cheese breakfast sandwiches. *I'm thrilled the old man's having one of his better days, but if the past week meant anything, when the roller coaster went up, it was only a matter of time before it rocketed back down. Rinse and damn repeat. I really thought Zippy would have had a greater impact on his overall mood, not just when the two of them walked or played fetch.*

Mack finally broke the silence.

"Seven across, '70s Jack Klugman role, eight letters. Odd Couple doesn't fit. Neither does Oscar Madison. Can I get a little help, please?"

Rockfish looked over at his dad. The old man kept licking the tip of his pencil as if the rush of lead would activate something in the far reaches of his brain. He nodded. Mack wanted some father and son time or plain conversation, but the son half of the equation wanted nothing to do with it at the moment.

"Banyon doesn't fit either. But that series only lasted one episode."

Rockfish gripped the armrests of his chair tighter, and it was almost as if he could feel that little vein in his forehead pop out. He was close to his temper getting the better of him, but he also knew he couldn't project his anger on Mack. Rockfish took a deep breath and held it for a count of ten. But the damage was done. Zippy felt the tension in the air and practically climbed up into Mack's lap. Rockfish loosened the grip on the chair and tried to answer his dad in a calmer voice.

"Dad, we used to watch it together when I came home from high school. It ran in syndication on Channel 29 at 4pm each day."

"He was in a couple all-time great episodes of the Twilight Zone."

"The clue says role, Dad," Rockfish said. "Not the title of a show. Not to mention you're in the wrong decade." Rockfish looked over at his dad and tilted his head to pull it out of the old man. But all he got in return was a vacant stare.

"Quincy, M.E. Lose the punctuation and the space, for crying out loud."

"That fits!"

With one of the world's problems solved, Rockfish reached over and gave Zippy some loving before returning to his own universe, his own hand-held problem.

"... so, if you get this, gimme a call. I did a thing tonight, and you'd be proud..."

"You know, Sonny, no matter how many times you play that message, it ain't gonna dial the number for you."

Rockfish didn't move his chin from his chest, but closed his eyes. *I know he's trying to be helpful. That's what old people do. It keeps them alive. Makes them feel useful, departing age-old wisdom down through the ranks. But it's not gonna help in this situation.*

But what it did was make Rockfish think. His mind traveled back to a conversation they had in the hospital last week. Rockfish had demanded Mack follow doctor's orders and speak to a counselor regarding what was eating him alive from the inside. But father knew best, and Mack had opened the floodgates that early morning to his son. Even the staff said they had seen a difference in him from the day the hospital admitted him.

"Dad, with each passing day, I'm getting worse tunnel vision in finding out who exactly did this to you and getting your money back. I'm ignoring friends and even worse, ignoring some of my other commitments."

"I told you, Sonny, you don't have to do this," Mack said and got up to drag his chair closer to Rockfish. "It was my fault. I was so damn gullible." Mack shook his head and rubbed his temples with one hand. "If I can write off the loss and try to move on, so should you. But I know, easier said than done." His free hand rubbed Zippy behind the ears and they both looked happier to Rockfish.

"I feel I have to do this. You won't file a complaint with the police and after leaving the house on Monday, Iggy's gone AWOL. He seems to do everything possible to not remember any of this happened." Rockfish ran a hand through his hair and down to his neck, where it lingered, feeling the tension.

"As a private investigator, if I can't solve this for you, then what the fuck am I doing with my time?" Rockfish shrugged. "Only yesterday, I was feeling my oats, had a good lead, but the more I worked it, the more I felt as if I was spinning my wheels. I'm obsessed with this case." He let out a nervous laugh. "I can't even concentrate on the smallest piece of shit waiting for me back at the office. Obsession, a bad word and even worse cologne."

"How about we go out to Manny's tonight and get some crabs to—"

"Oh shit, if I knew we were sunning ourselves, I'd have brought my speedo," Raffi said and closed the side gate behind him. Zippy jumped up and bolted down steps, barking.

Rockfish watched as Mack pursed his lips and nodded. He corralled Zippy back onto the deck and the two of them walked back into the house. *To be continued. Like a two-part episode of Quincy, M.E. But seriously,*

Dad's gotta have some faith in me. We're not in high school when I'd be in trouble, because Raffi talked me into doing some dumb shit.

"What's shaking, Ke-mo sah-bee," Raffi said, and sat down in Mack's vacated chair. "You'd think the pup would have remembered me from the other day."

"Who knows? I was having a conversation with Dad. One, a couple of days overdue."

"You want to get started?" Raffi said. "I brought my iPad. We can whip up this Facebook profile, but first I could really use a drink."

Rockfish looked down at his phone. 11:45am. *Gotta start sometime.* "I got an open bottle of Jameson. If you need a mixer, I keep the pleated skirts folded, right next to the fridge." Rockfish disappeared into the house and emerged a few minutes later with the bottle, two rocks glasses, and a Tupperware full of ice cubes.

"Funny that all these years, you had a Facebook page for your business but never a personal page," Raffi said.

"Ain't nobody I wanted to stay in contact with that I couldn't do it face to face. If we're not having a drink or shucking oysters, why the hell would I care you burned down half the neighborhood in a gender reveal fuck up?"

"Okay, last question. Why didn't you ask your young, hip partner for help with this?"

"Less questions, Raffi, more profiling."

It took a good four fingers of Jameson, apiece, for the two men to complete a profile their buzzed selves felt proud of. Raffi then did a quick search on the username *SunnyWest69* in order to add Rockfish's first friend. "Jesus Christ," he exclaimed.

Rockfish looked over and Raffi held up the iPad for him to see. Sunny's profile picture stared back, and Rockfish noticed what all the hubbub was about.

The profile and header pictures reminded Rockfish of Friday nights as a teen trying to outlast Mack so that he could watch those late-night Cinemax movies. Like those movies, these pictures served an obvious purpose.

"What's she see in an old fart like you?" Raffi said.

"Money, the same thing you do."

"Come on, Stevie, we go way back," Raffi said. "Funny, though. She doesn't list any J&J employment."

"Huh?"

"Jamocha Jubblies. I don't know, maybe they fired her after someone saw her coming on to you so hard. Either way, what's our next move?" Raffi said. He slapped his hands together and rubbed them.

Rockfish smiled. *He's open for business and I could use some backup for a change.*

"Next? We send a message, as instructed, and wait. Now how do I do that?"

"You need to download Facebook's Messenger app," Raffi said.

"You've got to be fucking kidding me. I deleted that app along with my marketplace ad when the show launched. I didn't really need the type of traffic the ad brought in anymore."

They came up with a witty opening line and hit send. Each man poured themselves another Jameson and Rockfish got Raffi up to speed on his thoughts since they left the cafe.

"I've come to two conclusions about this scam so far. Sunny and Iggy's gal ain't the brains behind this operation. Second, when either Iggy or Mack mentioned my new-found streaming fame, this group of scam artists immediately began planning how to land a bigger fish. That's why the yellow Xterra was always outside the office, but with me walking into the cafe, it gave them the opening they were looking for."

"Sounds reasonable," Raffi said.

"That's what I think. What I know is less. I sent the Facebook link to my buddy Decker at the Baltimore PD. Nothing came up when they ran the name Sunshine West and got no hits on the picture through their new state-of-the-art facial recognition software. Decker even went one further and checked with the FBI's Internet Crime Complaint Center to see if anyone reported the handle SunnyWest69."

"He come up with anything there?" Raffi said.

"One hit, on a reported eBay auction fraud. Some sucker, err I mean, winning bidder, filed a complaint because he never received the panties." Rockfish grinned and held up his glass before taking a long sip.

"Were they—"

"Don't know, don't care, didn't ask. Although, Decker wanted to know what this was about. I gave him a line of bull. Said it was regarding the Coyne case Jawnie picked up. Wife thinks the guy is cheating and Sunny was one of a half dozen potentials we've identified. He seemed to buy it."

An hour later, the Jameson bottle was nearing empty when the notification appeared on Rockfish's phone.

"Hey, wake up," Rockfish said in Raffi's direction. "Step one's complete. Friend request accepted. Now let's see how long—"

His phone vibrated before he could finish. The new Messenger icon had a red circle in the upper right corner, with a white 7 on it.

"What's she say? Is it dirty talk? I bet it's dirty talk," Raffi said. He got up from his chair and stood behind Rockfish to read over his shoulder.

Rockfish stared at the messages; stone faced. After all, this was work, and Raffi was getting worked up. When he finished, he went through the messages again to make sure he misinterpreted nothing that Sunny, or possibly someone else, had typed.

"Hey are you free tomorrow night to watch me eat dinner with an extremely attractive, alleged scam artist?"

'Mr. Rockfish, are you asking little ol' me out? Raffi said, fanning his face with an invisible fan. "Why, whatever should I wear?"

* * * * * * * * * *

Date night Saturday night found Lana parked on a side street, idling with her headlights off, three blocks north of Jamocha Jubblies. Rockfish turned the radio up and got in the mood for the evening's role. A sudden blur to his right startled him, and he jumped as far as the seat belt would allow.

"Christ, you scared the fuck out of me," Rockfish said, as Raffi opened the door, slid into the passenger seat and shut it. Rockfish lowered the radio's volume.

"Pretty good, ain't I? You know, Rockfish, McGee and Pérez don't sound too bad, if I say so myself."

"And you have, many times. But we're good for now, thanks," Rockfish said, as Raffi slowly shook his head. He gave Raffi the once over and approved of his choice of a disguise. Sunny was already familiar with Raphael Pérez, financier. Now meet Raffi Pérez, human dad-bod, out on the town. Raffi had piled his 'fro under a baseball cap, hid behind a pair of black-framed glasses and dressed in jeans with an Under Armour light jacket. He looked no different from every other middle-aged man out on a Saturday night.

"Perfect," Rockfish said. "She could walk right up next to you and not have a clue, but let's keep our distance. I'm going to head over to the parking lot here in a couple of minutes. Hang back a little. I don't plan for her to be actively looking for a tail, but you never know what shady shit she's done in the past."

"Dude, don't worry about me," Raffi said with a tip of his cap.

"Yet, I do."

"Why are you picking her up here? Seems strange," Raffi said.

"Her story is that someone called in and they needed her to pick up a partial shift. Am I buying it? Not on your life. No way she wants me to know where she lives and have me banging on her door when I realize my money disappeared. Anyway, she said she brought a change of clothes that I'll be happy with."

"I should have asked this earlier," Raffi said, "but where are you taking her tonight?"

"Manny's Seafood Hideaway. I had a hankering for the place since Mack brought it up yesterday, but I wasn't in any shape to drive last night. When we're there, hang loose unless I message you or you see a couple of goons headed my way with ill intentions."

Raffi nodded and headed back to his own car. Lana crept up the street and pulled into Jamocha Jubblies parking lot, which Rockfish noted was extremely busy for a titty-coffee-cafe on a Saturday night.

Sunny came bouncing out a minute later. Bouncing, being the optimal word, and if this hadn't been a work night, Rockfish would have let himself fall heavily into lust before she stepped off the sidewalk. Still, he considered it. Sunny stopped in front of Lana and gave a twirl before opening the passenger side door. She wore a set of heels, a cream blouse unbuttoned enough to leave nothing to the imagination other than the type of lace used in manufacturing the red bra underneath, and a tan skirt that hugged her lower half like nobody's business. Rockfish made a mental note to pick his chin up off the seat before his date noticed.

"Smoking hot car," Sunny said, as she slid in. "I'd love for the tourists on Rodeo Drive to see me in this."

They exchanged greetings as Lana backed out of the spot and headed for the street. Rockfish prayed certain things would settle down before he had to get out of the car.

"It really surprised me when you messaged me yesterday," Sunny said. "I thought you were blowing me off the way you practically ran out of the cafe the other day."

"Even us famous television stars get nervous when we're talking to an attractive young lady." Rockfish wiped his hand across his brow for added effect. "I'm happy we're free today. With my job and the television show still having certain demands, like interviews and public appearances, I don't have a lot of free time. I told my dad about this and he called it kismet."

"You told him about me? That's cute," Sunny said. "I'm glad it worked out for us. Sorry if I smell like coffee, though."

"Nothing wrong with a good potent brew," Rockfish said and wiped his brow again. "Boy, it's getting hot in here."

Sunny giggled and asked where they were going to eat. "Will there be any famous people there?"

"Maybe some local athletes, but I really don't know," Rockfish said. "It's a small, hole-in-the-wall place, a favorite of mine called Manny's Seafood Hideaway. I hope you like fresh seafood. I should have asked first."

"I love lobster."

"Well, then I hope you won't be disappointed, 'cause we're in Maryland, not Maine. I've been craving the best blue crab and oysters the Chesapeake offers." Staring at her blouse, he added, "Don't worry, they'll give you a bib."

Sunny giggled again and gave his hand a squeeze. She coyly moved her hand over his atop the shifter and Rockfish smiled. He guessed she would take it as a nervous smile, but to him, it was an attaboy on a role well played.

The nominations for best actor in a drama are... But don't let your damn guard down.

Rockfish valet parked, and the couple walked into Manny's where the owner greeted them. Manny Jack Schmidt was a recent friend of Rockfish's and a huge fan of the *Pine Barrens Stratagem*. Rockfish had reached out earlier in the day and let him know of his dinner plans and the need to impress the woman that would be on his arm.

"Working on a Saturday night again, huh, Steve?" Manny had said. "No rest for the weary."

"You know me too well, my friend. I'm going to need one of those tables far in the back, but with a straight line of sight to the bar."

The interior decor was more *fair to middling* than *high end*. Manny reinvested in the seafood's quality he bought each morning and the kitchen staff needed to keep those Michelin stars. Those that stayed away because of the tablecloths not being cloth did not know what they were missing. And Rockfish liked it that way.

Manny was a man of his word, and the hostess walked them to a table in the back and removed the reserved placard. Rockfish held out Sunny's chair for her and spied Raffi at the bar. His back was to the table, but he had an unobstructed view of the action through the mirror behind the bar.

The restaurant was close to capacity, but it was only a minute before their waiter appeared and took drink orders.

"I'll have a Jameson whiskey sour and for the lady..."

"Belvedere vodka, neat." Sunny said.

Whoa. That one came out of left field. Better not assume anything else about her and stay on my toes.

After the drinks arrived and they placed their appetizer and entrée orders, Sunny took control of the conversation and fired off a long list of what sounded like to Rockfish, questions that weren't exactly off the top of her head. The topics ranged from handling fame to most memorable cases and concluded with a couple on what his future held. Did he plan on staying in Baltimore or move to Hollywood or even Austin, Texas? Anywhere more exciting than Maryland?

Rockfish answered each as if his life depended on it and he was halfway through his Oysters Rockefeller appetizer when Sunny pulled hard left on the wheel of questions and they entered financial waters.

"I mean, I'm a coffee jockey—"

"Or jubbly."

She wrinkled her nose at his attempt at humor and motored on.

Stick to the role.

"You must do quite well for yourself. I was talking to your friend the other day about investment strategies. I bet you've got some of the best people in Hollywood managing your money."

"Eh, not really," Rockfish said. "I've got a local guy, but I've not been too happy with my funds' performance since the pandemic. Most investors have seen a healthy bounce back, but my money seems to lag. Treading water, so to speak. Not especially optimal for today's markets."

"Those are the same type of problems I was talking to your friend Ritchie about."

Rockfish bit his tongue. *Raffi, Ritchie, whatever.* Sunny continued.

"I have some friends that left their jobs on Wall Street to start their own Investment Fund, but these transactions are outside the box. Stocks, bonds, and mutual funds are yesterday's strategies." She looked to her left, then right, before leaning in. "This group? They focus on Cryptocurrencies, NFTs, and blockchains. Stuff that will blow your mind." Her voice was barely above a whisper, her eyes wide.

"N-F-what's?"

"Non-fungible tokens, but my friends can explain all this better than me," Sunny said. "Huge returns if you get in early and are comfortable with technology. I know they have some free time next week and will be down in the area before heading back to New York. I can hook you up." She winked and leaned in further. Her boobs pushed against her dinner plate.

"I'd love to meet them. Can I bring my friend, Ritchie? He's a big-time investor, always looking for additional revenue streams. Did I say that right? I don't know a lot about this, as you can tell." Rockfish gave her the dumbest look he could and shook his head.

It wasn't long after they finalized plans for a meeting early the following week that the entrees arrived. Then, even before he could dig in, Rockfish felt something against his leg. It took him longer than it should to realize Sunny had slipped her foot out of her shoe and was now rubbing it against his calf. *Has it been that long? Maybe it has.*

"Let's skip dessert and head back to my place," Sunny said. "I've got a couple of bottles of champagne and more comfortable furniture." She winked and Rockfish smiled widely. Sunny was forward, and it wasn't like he didn't expect it. She knew what his answer was.

"Give me one minute, if you don't mind? I need to use the restroom," Rockfish said and stood up.

A minute later, Raffi left his stool at the bar and followed. Rockfish was leaning against the line of sinks when Raffi walked in.

"She wants me to go back to her place," Rockfish said. "You up to hanging outside for a while? Actually, I may need you to hang closer, in case there's muscle there to roll me, but I doubt it. She and whoever she works for are playing the long game with me."

"You plan on spending the night?"

"I want to get some more info out of her about these money-men she wants me to meet. By the way, we're gonna meet them next week. I got you invited since you played rich so well the other day. And your name is Ritchie. Don't ask."

"You didn't answer my question."

"Look, I'm a professional. I'll do whatever it takes to learn who her bosses are. Once we know that, we can pull in the cops."

"You could be a politician with dance moves like that, Stevie," Raffi said. "If you're staying for round two, hit me up. I've got Cialis and some Viagra in my glove compartment."

Rockfish shook his head. "How are we friends?" He said and walked back towards the table, only to find it surrounded by an army of busboys. He cocked his head and looked at Sunny.

"We can eat, too, on that comfortable furniture. I asked the waiter to box everything up," she said and dropped her eyes to the table.

Rockfish watched as Sunny held a pair of panties in her hand. The red color and lace pattern seemed familiar to him. She casually dropped them into her clutch and snapped it shut.

"We should go now," she added.

****

Rockfish punched in the security code Sunny provided and the gate swung open. He nodded to the security guard on-duty as Lana rolled through. He slid his foot off the brake and moved through the parking lot, stopping at a spot Sunny said the complex reserved for guests.

Only then did she take her hand off Rockfish's thigh. Once out of the car, she took him by the hand and led him up to her apartment.

Oh lord, what the hell am I in for tonight? The sacrifices we make for our craft.

"Make yourself comfortable on the couch," Sunny said. "I'm going to get the champagne."

Rockfish ignored her and firmly placed his hands on her hips from behind and the two of them formed a mini conga line shuffling towards the kitchen. Sunny stopped when they reached the doorway and spun around.

"I thought I told you to sit on the couch and wait for me?" Sunny said, her voice dropping an octave.

Red flag.

"Or no dessert," she added, as if realizing she had gone off script and given Rockfish something to question.

He walked back to the couch, sat down, and thought about his surroundings. *How can she afford a place like this, in this neighborhood, hell, in this building by slinging coffee for a living?* Not to mention how sterile the entire apartment was. It appeared meticulously decorated, and not one thing seemed out of place. The topper was what he didn't see. Not a personalized touch anywhere. No pictures of family, or anything of the sort. The living space resembled a model apartment that a building manager would show perspective tenants, as opposed to a young woman's actual living quarters. A little voice in the back of his head whispered, *Danger, Will Robinson.*

When Sunny finally emerged from the kitchen, a champagne filled flute in each hand, Rockfish's mind raced to come up with an excuse to leave before something terrible happened to him. She handed him one of the champagne flutes and put the other down on the coffee table. She leaned down and placed her index finger gently on Rockfish's nose. "Now you hang tight. I'm going into the bedroom and get that dessert ready for you." She licked her lips, turned, and walked down the hallway. Rockfish heard a door shut behind her.

He immediately looked right and then left, to see where the bad guys would jump out from. After a second, no one emerged from a hidden door, and he thought again about the conniption fit Sunny threw in the kitchen doorway. His eyes went to the glass in his hand and then the other on the coffee table.

Swap the glasses, the little voice said. *You've seen how this goes.* Rockfish put his down and picked up Sunny's. The telltale red lipstick smudge on the side of her flute killed that idea dead in its tracks. *Ah dude, you're fucked,* he and the little voice said in unison.

Without thinking the entire plan through, Rockfish chugged Sunny's glass and then poured the contents of his into the now empty flute. He placed her glass back on the coffee table and grasped his own, now empty.

Not a minute later, he heard the door open and then Sunny stood over him in a small baby blue nightie. He held the empty glass to his chest and with a dumb look said, "I'm sorry, I got nervous and drank it without you."

Sunny smiled, and it reminded Rockfish of the Cheshire Cat, but not in a good way.

She leaned over, giving him the cleavage money-shot and whispered in his ear, "Don't be nervous. I'll be gentle." Sunny turned around and went to retrieve the champagne bottle from the kitchen.

When she came back, Rockfish held out his glass and Sunny leaned over to pour. She let Rockfish have an extended shot of the view before sitting on the couch and proposing a toast.

"To a budding friendship and successful business endeavor." They clinked their glasses together and Sunny drained her flute.

She leaned forward and placed it on the coffee table before scooting closer to Rockfish and alternating words between saleswoman and temptress. She rubbed his thigh while espousing the expertise and guaranteed returns of her New York friends. The longer she talked, the more she lost her place in the sales pitch, started slurring her words and gave up altogether on the thigh massage.

Fifteen minutes after putting her glass down, Sunny was out cold. Her mouth hung open and a line of drool stretched from her bottom lip to the arm of the couch.

"Raffi, get up here. Gate code 782902, apartment 803, make it fast."

By the time Raffi arrived, Sunny had slid off the couch and was on the floor, half under the coffee table. Raffi immediately spotted her, walked over and stared.

"Hey, we got shit to do," Rockfish said. Raffi didn't move or acknowledge. "Put your eyes back in their sockets and lose the awkward teenage boner. I need help." Rockfish punched him in the shoulder and Raffi's head finally turned.

"What did you do to her?"

"Me? Nothing more than having her drink the champagne she poured for me. Something didn't smell right and my spidey senses were going off, overtime."

"Dude, you think she was going to date rape you?" Raffi said.

"Hardly. More likely... hell, I don't know what she was planning," Rockfish said. "We need to give this place the once over and then GTFO. Remember, mess nothing up. Everything goes back in its place. You look out here and I'll take the bedroom."

"Stevie, you always get to have all the fun."

Rockfish walked down the short hallway and into the bedroom. Sunny's outfit from dinner lay on the bed. The walls were bare and there wasn't even a phone charger on the nightstand. He opened the closet doors and aside from half a dozen wire hangers; it was empty. The bureau and nightstand drawers gave the same result.

What the fuck is going on in this place? He walked to the far side of the bed and spotted something sticking out from underneath. Rockfish bent over and pulled out a small canvas overnight bag. *Something more in line with a trip to the gym, then a love nest.* He unzipped the bag. Socks, leggings and half a dozen Jamocha Jubblies t-shirts were inside, but nothing that gave him the *ah-ha* moment he expected. He called it a day in the bedroom and walked back out to the living room.

"Don't you even fucking think about it," Rockfish said.

Raffi was in the living room, standing next to a chair where Sunny's clutch purse lay open and her panties were in his hand.

"The last thing we need is her coming to and thinking we rousted the apartment and went through her things," Rockfish said.

Raffi looked at Rockfish, then to the panties, and finally back at Rockfish. In one swift move, he brought them to his nose, deeply inhaled, and then dropped them back into the clutch.

"Jesus Christ, man."

"Don't you kink shame me," Raffi said.

"Aside from taking *weird fetishes for $400, Alex,* did you find anything that could help me?"

"This place is empty. No dishes, silverware, but someone stocked the fridge with that cheap champagne," Raffi said. "It's hard to believe anyone lives here. If you ask me, it's used on a case-by-case basis."

"Fuck," Rockfish said, and shook his head.

"And I'm basing my conclusion on the tiny HD camera over there, hidden on the bookshelf. I'm betting once the roofie kicked in, there'd be some sweet 1080i pictures or video of you in slightly compromised positions. If you turn down the investment scheme, they hit you with the extortion angle. She, or they, were making sure someone got paid either way."

Christ! Raffi's actually making sense and I'm agreeing with him. Better buy a lotto ticket on the way home. "I get it, but then again, I'm not married. Who cares if I fucked her?"

"I'm saying this could be the general scam. Your results may vary."

"Anything else out here?" Rockfish said.

"Only this SD card I snagged from the camera and her cell is still on the kitchen counter."

"Fuck, why didn't I think of that," Rockfish said and retrieved the phone from the kitchen. Back in the living room, he thought aloud. "Let me think about the card, don't lose it. Also, not sure what model iPhone this is, but could her face unlock it, in that condition?"

"Only one way to know for sure," Raffi said. He bent down, without waiting for a reply, and gently turned her head so Rockfish could get a clear shot.

"A la peanut butter sandwiches," Rockfish said, and held the phone as steady as he could. "God damn, it worked." He now had unfettered access to Sunny's digital life.

Raffi moved closer to peek over Rockfish's shoulder, but Rockfish realized he needed one thing from his friend.

"Do me a favor?" Rockfish said and tossed Raffi his keys. "Google the closest Walmart. Take Lana and pick up a replacement SD card. They're open all night, every night. I'd like to plug the one you found in back at the office and see what's saved on it. Make sure you get the same brand and size. I want whoever pulls this out for their first reaction to a blank card be focused on equipment malfunction. Also, on your way back up, grab a pen and paper from the center console. While you're out, I'm going to go through the phone and snap a shitload of pictures with mine of anything that strikes me as interesting."

"Don't you go through her pictures until I get back," Raffi said. He walked out the door without waiting for an answer.

Rockfish took snapshots of Sunny's recent call logs, contacts, emails, text conversations and other social media accounts. He'd have to break down and ask Jawnie for help in exploiting all this information.

Last, he opened the picture app and found 6,237 photos and 366 videos. Rockfish did not know how big that number was, size wise, and made a command decision to air drop the most recent one hundred and fifty photos and ten videos to his own iPhone.

Ninety minutes later, Raffi returned with the replacement SD card.

"Sorry it took so long. There's never anyone in their goddamn Electronics Department, no matter where the store is located. But I got the exact one. You should be good to go. But I gotta ask. How scared were you she would wake up while I was out?"

"A little, but she's tiny and probably drank a dose tailored for someone twice her weight. Now help me get her back on the couch," Rockfish said after returning Sunny's phone to the kitchen counter. "We'll prop some pillows around her, so she doesn't slide off again."

Once Sunny was steady, Rockfish wrote a brief note and placed it under her glass on the coffee table.

Sunny - I'm so sorry that I bored you to sleep. I promise you I'm not this uninspiring. Please give me a second chance to prove this occasion a fluke. And I look forward to meeting your friends that could help me better invest my money. - Steve

"What do you think she'll think when she comes too?" Raffi said.

"Hopefully, she thinks she's an idiot and got the glasses mixed up. Nothing more, nothing less."

CHAPTER FOUR

Rockfish put his extra-large Wawa coffee, black, down on the desk and powered on his computer. The quiet of the office on a mid-morning Sunday was relaxing. Mack and his lost puppy dog face were out of sight and out of mind, along with Raffi's mouth running a hundred miles an hour in all directions. His plan was to come in this morning and get caught up on paperwork, those few cases only needing the last report in order to move their status to closed. Last night's adventures added the additional tasks of getting all the information he captured from Sunny's phone entered in the firm's new case management system.

In the old days, he would have spent a shitload of money on photo paper, printed everything out and dumped it in a filing cabinet. Jawnie had changed that. The office had moved into the current century with technology since she had arrived. Her list of necessary office upgrades had three tiers, red, yellow, and green. The case management system had been at the top of the priority list and came about only because of the influx of cash from *The Pine Barrens Stratagem*.

Jawnie. He owed her some explanation for his behavior the past week, but there would be a time for a mea culpa conversation. But not until he had Mack's cash back in hand and safely into a joint account that Rockfish could monitor. The old man could only buy dog food and toys. *That's it!*

When the photo transfer from his phone completed, Rockfish looked at the large number of photos he had taken. They were screenshots of her contacts, iMessages, emails and call log, all of which someone would need to fat finger into a format for analysis and upload to a wide variety of online data mining platforms to gather additional intelligence. *Thanks again, Jawnie. Shit like this would have taken me months in the past, but we definitely have to hire someone to do this data entry bullshit.* Receptionist, intern, or someone from a temp agency, he didn't care, as long as a warm body could do his clerical work.

Rockfish pulled the SD card out of a small Ziploc bag and put it into the card reader attached to his desktop computer. If Jawnie were here, she would be proud he had remembered to run a virus check on the card on a standalone computer she had purchased for such an occasion. The card reader on his desk recognized the SD card and a separate window opened, showing 109 image files. He clicked to sort them by created date. The oldest was from two months ago and the most recent was two weeks ago. Rockfish clicked on gallery mode and reviewed the images.

The background of the images was all the same. There was no mistaking the couch from the apartment. The same brand of champagne bottle and two flutes always sat in the frame. The only thing that changed with each set of pictures was the girl and old man genitalia.

Rockfish made a mental note to burn the clothes he had worn last night. He continued the review. A dozen photos in Iggy showed up on screen. *Good for him and, obviously, medical science.* What he didn't see was Sunny. He didn't recognize her in any of the photos, even those where the girl had her head down and face obscured.

Was I her first? Explains why she was dumb enough to fall for my trick. Was she being reprimanded at this very moment by the people that hired her? I'd have to give her a D+ for the evening, but maybe her boss would be more forgiving. Had her bosses become aware, or was her message this morning more of an attempt to get this train back on the tracks?

The highly expected message from Sunny came in at 9am this morning. Rockfish was walking out of Wawa with coffee and a breakfast sandwich when the Messenger notification went off, but he didn't bother to read it until he unlocked the office and settled in at his desk.

Oh no, Steve, I'm so sorry for my behavior last night. I'm embarrassed I couldn't hold my liquor and you ended up having to entertain yourself. I promise to make it up to you after we meet with my friends. Deets coming, I promise. Heart emoji, red lips emoji, fingers crossed emoji, heart emoji.

He had yet to reply, and took a moment to grab a screenshot and sent it off to Raffi with his own message attached.

Looks like we're still good. When I get the 'deets' I'll reach out. Also, the couch pictures give off a casting couch video at the Shady Dell retirement home kinda vibe.

Rockfish put his phone back down on the desk, opened Excel, and put on his data entry hat. He renamed one tab Phone Numbers and the second tab Contacts. The phone number tab had a second column to show incoming or outgoing calls. He immediately started cursing the firm's lax hiring practices all over again. The process was monotonous, and it wasn't long before his mind wandered.

Jawnie. It wasn't right to ignore her calls and texts since he took up this impromptu case or act shitty towards her the few times they spoke. She wasn't an intern, or some schlub beneath him on the corporate ladder. When he walked in this morning, the sign out front still read *Rockfish & McGee - Investigative Specialists. She's an equal partner in this business, no matter her level of experience. She definitely doesn't deserve the shit I'm shoveling.*

Mack. The old man hadn't stopped moping around the house in his robe and slippers, eyes glazed over with a where-the-hell-am-I look on his face. Even on his good days. Zippy had helped and the dog being house broken was a bonus for when Mack zoned out. He and the root of all their current problems, Iggy, hadn't spoken since the day Mack came home from the hospital. Mack spent the daylight hours sitting in his recliner, binge watching old episodes of Kojak and Columbo on NikolaTV. The TV Guide crossword helped what few synapses he had left fire off on time and in the right direction. *If I don't get him out of this funk and up on his feet, the paramedics will have a hard time getting him out of that chair once his skin melds with the fabric. He's so happy with the dog when they play. How can I make that happen all day, every day?*

Last, his mind rambled back to his incredible luck at Sunny's apartment. *What the hell could we be walking into this week? Would the luck—*

His phone vibrated on the desk and brought his mind back to the present. He unlocked it and the feed from the front security camera filled the screen.

"Guess I'm not the only one working on the Sabbath."

****

Jawnie unlocked the door, stepped inside, and turned to lock it behind her. She ignored the alarm panel on the wall as she noticed Lana out front. Rockfish was in his office, and she walked back towards hers to drop off her backpack before planting herself in his open doorway.

"Mack mentioned you'd be here sometime this morning. I drove by earlier but didn't see your car. Cute dog. He's a jumpy one."

Rockfish kept his head down and focused on the task at hand. Jawnie wondered what kept his eyes glued to the screen while his fingers worked on what she thought was the numeric keypad side of the keyboard.

"You want me to put on coffee?" Jawnie tried a second icebreaker.

"Yeah, if you don't mind. I'm almost through this one," Rockfish said. "Stopped at Wawa on the way in. I didn't know the entire office planned on coming in today."

Jawnie had his attention and line of sight as he had stopped working and looked up at her.

"Well, the receptionist called out sick today," she said with as serious a look as she could muster.

"Very fucking funny, McGee."

McGee. I've punctured the Teflon armor.

Jawnie walked back and turned on the coffeemaker before heading to her office. When the coffee maker beeped, she grabbed their respective cups, filled them, and walked back to Rockfish's office. This time, she marched through the doorway and sat down in the visitor chair opposite him.

"Here you go," she said, and handed him the Ravens mug. "Careful, I filled it to the brim."

Rockfish slid the keyboard back under the desk and turned off his monitor. She realized she had his full attention at the moment. She shuffled her chair closer to his desk.

"I've noticed that yellow car isn't across the street anymore," Jawnie said, picking her spots to keep the conversation going. "Hasn't been there in five days. I bet they got bored with all the excitement around here."

"It's good to see that you noticed. Being aware of your surroundings is a big part of this business. But, no, they didn't get bored. In my unofficial investigation, I can say they were watching me. They were also part of the group that scammed Mack and Iggy. I assumed that once they learned, through liquor or talkative old men thinking they're going to get laid, that I was Mack's son, all eyes were on me."

"They wanted to rip you off, too?" Jawnie said and leaned in. *He has to know I'm interested in hearing more.*

"Again, guessing when they learned I was on television, all they saw were dollar signs." He rubbed his thumb and index fingers together. "I've met one of their young girls that pulls the marks in, and a buddy of mine and I are meeting with some investment types this week." Rockfish stopped and sipped his coffee before continuing. "The claim is that they can help grow my Hollywood dollars faster, with larger returns than I'm getting now. Once I can identify these clowns, I'll reach out to Decker and see if the PD wants to set up some sort of sting operation. Or I'm leaning towards beating the shit out of them and going through their office space with a fine-tooth comb to see if I can recoup Dad's cash first."

"That's awesome. Not that you're going to fight a couple of guys, but that you put all this together so quickly. Decker will appreciate the nice little evidence package you hand him," Jawnie said. She noticed the way he looked across the desk at her when he broke down how successful his revenge tour was proceeding. *He's in his happy place. He hadn't exactly gotten close to an apology for his behavior towards me the past week. But when had he ever? Rockfish was the type of guy who'd argue with you at the top of his lungs one day but expect everyone to forget and forgive the following day. Whatever it takes to move past this bullshit.*

"Speaking of evidence, I got a dump truck's worth last night," Rockfish said, and leaned back in his chair. "I'm giving it a cursory review this morning, but will need some help with those online public record sites, social media exploitation and that reverse image thing you once showed me."

"Tineye is the reverse image program and all the info you're looking for is on your desktop in a folder labeled Tools."

"I'll check it out and let you know how it goes. There is also an SD card, and you'd be proud. I checked it for viruses before placing it in my card reader to review the contents. I get points for that, right..."

Jawnie was aware her partner was in full pat-myself-on-the-back-mode for getting this evidence haul. *But he sure as hell isn't forthcoming about what his evidence is and where he got it.* It bothered her he continued to play it so close to the vest, but at least today it wasn't as close as it had been the previous week. *Baby steps back to normalcy.*

"... okay, maybe not. So, tell me how Coyne's coming along. Putting that puppy to bed, I hope? I need you to move over to Andrist as soon as you can. That thing is still hanging over our heads and needs to be wrapped up with a nice bow. I'm writing the last reports on the Chaille, Shank and Erickson cases today."

In retrospect, Jawnie should have chosen her words more carefully, but despite being happy for the conversation only a few minutes ago, she now concluded if they didn't address the issues, they wouldn't go away like Rockfish expected or hoped. *He can't buy me a dog and hope to move past all this.*

"Now you have time to listen to what I say?" Jawnie said and hoped he could hear the slight sarcasm in her voice. She had made sure it also contained a heavy dash of heat so he wouldn't laugh it off and move on. "Is it because I'm sitting here in front of you and not sending thoughts and prayers via text into an almost *at capacity* voicemail box?" She leaned back in her chair and crossed her arms.

Rockfish glared back, but Jawnie couldn't get a read on his emotions, so she continued.

"When this started last week, you promised your side gig wouldn't take you away from our paying clients. Now it's like, hey, can you wrap your shit up quick and pick up what I dropped over here?"

"It was my father—"

"I know who and how it affected you," Jawnie said, not fearing the repercussions of cutting him off. She was going to lead this in the direction she wanted. "I'm stating what you said last week is in direct conflict with your actions of the past nine days. Also, I'm a full partner here. While I love to get advice and guidance from you, fuck, I live for those moments. You can't order me around like the support staff we've yet to hire." She scooted the chair back to its prior spot.

They sat staring at each other. Rockfish moved his hand to his mouth and sighed. *Was he thinking of the right words to say? Or was it more like making sure he didn't say the wrong thing that would only deepen the cracks in our foundation? Screw him, I'll cut to the chase.*

"Steve, I cannot and will not accept this behavior from someone I consider a peer, let alone a mentor."

"Jawnie, I'm sorry," Rockfish said. "I'm sorry if my emotions caused me to go all lone wolf over this thing." He sighed and closed his eyes. A full minute passed before he opened them again.

She smiled on the inside, not wanting him to think his two sentences had sealed the peace accord. Instead, Jawnie nodded and tilted her head. She was all ears.

"But going rogue and by myself was an instinct. It's how I've done business, personal business, for years. It's not like we've been partners for decades, and I went sideways out of the blue. Look, I'm close. Real close. Give me this week and if I don't have shit to take to the cops, I'll drop it and pay my father back out of my wallet. That should at least get us out of his funk. Us meaning Mack and I, although it could also include you and I." He stopped for a breath and his eyes seemed to show actual concern. "Come on, cut an old man some slack. Fuck, I don't know any better than to shove every damn emotion down inside." Rockfish stopped and held out his hands in front of him.

Jawnie wasn't sure if he wanted her to climb over the desk and hug him, or was signaling it was over, and that was the best he could do.

"Do better next time," Jawnie said, and she picked up her chair and moved it closer to the desk.

"I will. Try, I mean. I'm not gonna hit the mark every time. Now back to Coyne. Other than the wife being a royal pain in the ass, you figure out who he's banging?"

"Nobody, as far as I can tell," Jawnie said. "He leaves work those two days, does a good deed like feeding the homeless, then attends some wacky religious meetings for reasons only he knows."

Jawnie gave Rockfish the condensed version of Roan Coyne's charity work and then received the much-expected attaboy moment over recruiting her first CI.

"Outstanding," Rockfish said. "How much are you paying her?"

"Right now? Thirty bucks and a meal."

"Not bad. It won't break the bank, but be cautious. And here's how you handle Claudia. Tell her exactly what you've witnessed last week. This church group is helping him get over something. Might not be a woman, drugs, or booze. We don't know, but what we know is he's not cheating." Rockfish took a deep breath and nodded before continuing. "Say you'll give it one more shot. You've got someone on the inside now that can give you firsthand knowledge of what's going on behind that door. Wednesday morning, you'll give her the last report. She can accept the findings and pay us. Or choose to throw the entire thing in the garbage can, but she will still pay us. Totally up to her, but we'll have washed our hands of it."

"Thanks, Steve," Jawnie said.

"Last, if she says she wants to talk to me, let her. I'll back you one hundred percent. Matter of fact, if she does, I'll give her the 4-1-1 on this bimbo I identified the other day. Let Claudia go waste her money and another P.I.'s time tracking that bullshit down."

Jawnie stood up and held her fist out. "Bump it," she said, and he did.

"Best thing COVID-19 ever did was get rid of the handshake," Rockfish said.

Jawnie walked across the hall to her office to call Claudia Coyne and see if she was free to meet later that afternoon.

****

The Dairy Bar lunch crowd had dispersed by the time Jawnie walked in for a late lunch Monday afternoon. The patio was open with standing heaters spaced throughout. Most diners ate inside, despite the sun overhead on a warmer than usual March day. Jawnie liked the privacy and followed the server. She sat down at the table, facing the patio door, her back to the sidewalk. She waited for Lynn and glanced down at her phone.

Mom always said, if you aren't ten minutes early, you're late. And Lynn is now officially late.

Jawnie had remembered Lynn's napkin and had reached out yesterday after talking to Claudia. She wouldn't be able to meet with Lynn prior to the standing Tuesday, Church of the Universal Nurturing II meeting. The meeting with Claudia resulted in a short list of requirements the woman needed to move on from this case. Or at least their firm. *I pity the fool that she hires next.* Jawnie wanted Lynn to know exactly what needed to be accomplished the following evening. A rushed conversation with vague deliverables and a few dollar bills pushed into Lynn's hand, as she entered the alleyway, would not cut it this time.

"Hey boss," Lynn said as she came through the door that separated the inside and outside dining.

One o'clock, on the dot. We'll work on that later. Her eyes widened as Lynn walked towards the back table and Jawnie raised her hand to her chin to make sure it wasn't hanging open. *No way this was the same girl as Thursday night.*

Gone was homeless chic and in its place, well, Jawnie didn't know what to call it, but Lynn cleaned up well. She was rocking a button up, oversized men's blue dress shirt and white jeans. Her blonde hair was straight and bounced off the top of her shoulders with each step.

"Hi, glad you could make it."

"For a free meal, I should have been here ten minutes ago," Lynn said.

"You look great, color me surprised," Jawnie said.

"Well, it's a work meeting, and I mentioned I was on the street, by choice." Lynn shook her head and flipped her hair. "I swung by my sister's last night and grabbed a few things. Also, I feel these people on Tuesday night will be less scared of me and someone might open up in a sidebar, if I don't look like I'd pull a knife on them." She smiled and played with a strand of hair by her ear.

"Excellent call," Jawnie said. She smiled across the table and handed Lynn a menu. "Take your time, we'll talk after we order."

After their drinks arrived and each ordered, assuring some server-free time, Jawnie got down to business.

"I spoke with the wife yesterday and reiterated our stance of one last try to determine if this guy is cheating."

"Gotcha," Lynn said and nodded.

"Specifically, I mentioned having someone on the inside of that meeting room. Now, of course, you were there last week, but she's more excited about it this time. Don't ask me. I told her tomorrow is our last chance. She's already online, trying to find someone else to investigate her delusional thoughts for a reasonable fee. May God have mercy on their soul."

Lynn laughed aloud. "Sounds like this client is a genuine piece of work."

"She is. I thought to give you a small recording device, but who needs two hours of Jesus talk?"

"Maybe this woman does?" Lynn said. "I mean, if she's this much of a pain in the ass, a CD with two hours of her husband praising Jesus and screaming that he can't wait for the rapture might be what she needs. And if not, we've wasted two hours of her life."

"I like the way you think." Jawnie chuckled at the thought of Claudia perhaps being converted during her listening session.

"But seriously, I'm in the back row. If the seating arrangements stay the same, then he's in the inner circle and I'm on the outside. I can use my phone if I can get up near him beforehand, during snack time or try to make small talk with him on the way out, afterwards. But there is a lot of noise, no matter if it's mid-sermon or not."

Jawnie thought about it for a minute. "Do nothing like that. It's not worth the risk. Something about these types of groups always strikes me the wrong way. I don't want your phone to fall out of your pocket and poof, you're gone."

Lynn nodded in agreement and Jawnie held up her hand.

"Food's here," Jawnie said as the server came through the door with two plates. They ate in silence for a few minutes before Lynn restarted the conversation.

"I agree with you regarding not making them mad, or at least that Sister Lilith broad, who I mentioned, did most of the preaching, talking, whatever you call it. There is a guy who sits off to the side who looks like he's been a lifelong steroid abuser and he's itching for a confrontation." Lynn wrinkled her nose and shook her head from side to side.

"As a contract employee, your safety is a concern," Jawnie said. "Especially anytime that I'm not around to help defuse a situation. Along those lines, I picked this up for you."

Jawnie pulled a small bag from her jacket pocket and handed the contents across the table to Lynn. She opened the small box and looked slightly underwhelmed. Jawnie couldn't help but laugh.

"A commemorative key chain for First Alert. You shouldn't have," Lynn said with a big grin.

"Keep it nearby. Put it on your bag's shoulder strap or somewhere easily accessible. You feel something's going down, press it, and I get an alert on my phone. I'll be down those steps and through the door to kick some ass."

"What if the door's locked?" Lynn's eyes grew wide.

"I'll bust one of the glass panes, reach down and unlock the deadbolt," Jawnie said. "Not to mention that I'll be screaming that I've already called the cops. If that doesn't work, I'll start recording with my phone. I'd hope that would cause them to stand down."

Jawnie stopped and tilted her head towards the door. They paused the conversation until the server dropped the check and walked back inside. "Okay, so tomorrow night. Be a little early and be chatty. If you can get some words with Roan, that would be great. Other than that, remember all he does, anything that seems out of the ordinary to you and we'll talk afterwards. I'll write it up, attach those pamphlets for good measure. Case closed." She made a wiping motion with her hands.

Lynn nodded, but the look on her face didn't fill Jawnie with the warm-and-fuzzies.

"Everything okay?"

"Yeah, I'm good. You mentioned possibly finding some other stuff for me to help with. With my lifestyle, extra cash in the pocket is never a bad thing. How long do you think it will be until you have something?" Lynn grimaced and rested her hands on her chin.

"I can always use someone who's got one ear to the street and has no fear of walking into the unknown and observing. I'd have to go back to the office and root through all the open files to see exactly where we could use you as a force multiplier. Speaking of the office, how familiar are you with Microsoft Office..."

****

Tuesday night's rush hour found Jawnie parked, for the third time, on a side street awaiting Roan's car to exit the parking garage. She had double checked the pocket recorder twice before leaving the office and completed a third a second ago, before returning it to her jacket pocket. Her hand wrapped around it, fingers gliding across its face, feeling for the record button. Her thumb found the sweet spot, thanks to Rockfish's suggestion of taping a tiny piece of sandpaper atop the button to make it stand out from the others.

Very old school. I need to put in a purchase order for some voice activated ones.

Jawnie was ready. Ready to track, interact, and finally put this case to bed. She let go of the recorder and reached for the water in the cup holder. She looked up after replacing it, and like clockwork, the exit lane's barrier arm raised, and the Aston Martin crept out and turned right.

Third time's a charm. Jawnie pulled back out onto the street.

Much to her surprise, this evening's path followed last Tuesday's turn for turn, and Jawnie called the right turn into McDonald's long before Roan flipped on his turn signal and tapped the brakes.

Jawnie followed him into the parking lot, but swung wide, going around the back side, knowing he aimed for the drive thru. She pulled around and parked. She glanced at the drive thru line. Roan hadn't crept up to the ordering kiosk. She got out, walked across the parking lot and into the restaurant.

Jawnie found an open table and sat down. She watched the workers behind the register fill orders and noticed an obvious uptick in the coordinated dance routine of those manning the grill and deep fryers. Employees shuttled bags of food out from behind the registers and stacked them on an empty table between Jawnie and the door. When the table overflowed onto the four chairs, a team of employees came and scooped the bags up and headed out.

Go time. Jawnie followed the fast food, enough to feed a small army, out the door. Roan had parked in the same spot as before and stood outside the car with all the doors open. Jawnie walked right up to him, felt for the sandpaper and spoke her well-practiced opening line.

"Sir, that is one heck of a lot of food. Do you have a football team or two to feed? Nah, you're dressed way too nice to be a pee wee coach."

Roan turned and looked at her and smiled. "No, ma'am. I'm neither. Only a good Christian doing the Lord's work."

"I'm sorry if I was intruding. You don't see this volume of take out every day, or year." Jawnie nodded to emphasize her apology.

"You weren't. I'm actually feeding the less fortunate. It is something not enough of us do. If answering your question can get you to look at this situation differently, then you didn't intrude. We should all do our part."

Roan turned away from Jawnie and spoke with the employees. He pulled out his wallet and tipped each one. Having seen prior to how this ended, Jawnie pipped up to draw his attention as the employees turned back towards the restaurant.

"That is incredible," Jawnie said. "Few people think the same way as you do." She reached out and placed her hand on his bicep. It had the expected effect, and Roan stepped away with a strange look on his face.

He's not a cheater. I dressed to slay tonight. No way a man who's looking backs away from this. This is the nail in Claudia's infidelity coffin. She's definitely smoking crack if she still thinks Roan's being unfaithful.

"I'm sorry for being so forward. It's that you don't run across this kind of kindness in the world," Jawnie added. "I had hoped some would rub off. I could actually use some."

Roan seemed to have accepted Jawnie's apology and took a step towards her. "I do it out of love. I owe; therefore, I give back. You might understand it better as penance for previous transgressions. When the Lord comes back, I want him to look favorably upon my deeds. If you'll excuse me now, I'm on a tight schedule tonight and must be going. But if you would like to learn more about giving back and preparing for the rapture, please call me." This time, Roan placed his arm on *her* bicep. "People talk of the rapture like it will be some sort of holocaust, but it won't be if you're on the right side." Roan slid a business card out of his wallet and handed it to Jawnie before stepping back into his car.

"I would love that, thank you very much," she raced to say as he shut the door.

Jawnie turned away as Roan's car pulled out. Her thumb felt for the sandpaper, switched the recorder off and walked back to her car.

No need to follow him now. I know where he'll end up.

Jawnie started her car and headed for Allison's parking lot. She would be early, but it would give her a chance to listen to the recording and begin phrasing her argument for when she met with Claudia. Not to mention she'd have some time to dictate a few other reports she was behind on.

The dashboard clock read 7:45pm when Jawnie's passenger side door swung open and Lynn sat down.

"Ready?" Jawnie said.

"I'm good unless the plan changed," Lynn said.

"No changes here. Hang loose till he gets here, then follow him inside..."

****

Rockfish turned off the projector, leaned back in his chair, and reached for his whiskey.

"That's way more old man penis than I ever thought I'd see," Raffi said. "Next time you see Iggy, buy him a drink and pass along my congratulations. That man has some set of genes on him. My old man sold me short, literally."

The men sat in the office, dressed in their finest suits in an attempt, later this evening, to represent bank accounts neither had.

"Have you done anything with the contents of her phone, or curating your own personal slide show from the hidden camera card? Not judging here," Raffi said, and held up his hands.

"I've been going through it. Trying to enter all the phone numbers, contacts, and email addresses into a giant freaking spreadsheet. This way I can manipulate it, sort it, do something with it."

"You're a regular Steve Wozniak over there," Raffi said.

"I've got no idea who that is, but I'll play it safe and consider it a compliment. But the hero we all need is Jawnie. In a brief time, she's made this job a thousand times easier than pre-Jawnie. Well, with the time I'm stuck in the office. She showed me how to get the computer to do a lot of the work analyzing phone numbers, but what's really cool is this Tineye program."

Rockfish stopped and reached to finish his drink. *Another?* He looked at the time and put the empty glass back on the table. *There is such a thing as being too loose for a meeting.* Rockfish pushed the bottle back, out of arm's reach. Also, away from Raffi's before continuing.

"You upload a picture, and it will search across the internet to see where else that same image resides. I plugged in Sunny's more general, personal pictures and got a treasure trove of information back. I've put off searching the more risque ones."

"Sounds like the perfect time for a demo," Raffi said. He placed his hands on the table and pulled his chair forward.

"We're cutting it close on time as it is," Rockfish said. "The program said many of Sunny's pictures were uploaded to other social media accounts, coincidently not named Sunny West. Her actual name appears to be Kelly Westerly, formerly of Homewood, Illinois. She spent some time in Kilingess, West Virginia, before showing up in Maryland a year ago. Dyed her hair blonde and got an enhancement to go with the new address. Not to mention she worked at the Baltimore Zoo before deciding to sling coffee. Tell you what, I used to hate not being out on the street, but now it ain't so bad." Rockfish placed his hands behind his head and leaned back.

"Imma hold you to that demonstration. You gonna hit her with the Kelly Westerly stuff if conversation heads south tonight?"

"Tonight's not about her. It's about these clowns she introduces us to. Learn as much as we can before coming back here to decipher it all. The Westerly thing is some info to keep in my back pocket and pull out if I need to throw her for a loop."

"When she's on the ropes. Got it."

"Enough about her," Rockfish said. "I need you tonight to go against all your urges to be witty and try to steer the conversation. I'm going to be playing that role." Rockfish held up his hand, anticipating Raffi's counterargument, and he wanted to shut it down before it started. "What I need you to concentrate on is listening, retaining what they say. You should be in record-mode in case I miss something or forget before I can memorialize the evening's events on paper."

"Sounds like it would be easier to record everything," Raffi said. "You got a tape recorder?"

"I do and I don't. Nice little pocket sized digital one. I can't find it. I was showing it to Jawnie the other day, so we'll improvise. Also, look around and see if anything stands out to you—I don't know, like a big box in the corner that says stolen cash. That would be hugely beneficial."

"You got it."

"Let's get out of here."

Rockfish locked and alarmed the office before meeting Raffi out in the parking lot. Instinct caused him to glance across the street, half expecting to see the yellow Xterra, but he was happily disappointed. He unlocked the car and both men climbed inside. Rockfish started the car and entered the address into Lana's GPS. After a second, he burst out laughing.

"Dude, you won't believe this, but it isn't too far away from the coffee place. That shouldn't surprise me." Rockfish dropped her down into reverse and backed out.

Your destination is on the left.

"Stevie, you heard the lady," Raffi said. "You missed your turn."

"I heard her. I like to take a lap around the block and get a gander at what I may walk into before pulling in all willy-nilly. Unless, of course, you want to get out and do some recon for me?" Rockfish pushed the unlock button on his door and laughed as Raffi reached over and relocked it.

Lana had made the third left turn in an unremarkable surveillance square when Rockfish let out a "Jesus fucking Christ, what the hell is going on here?" He shook his head and continued down the road a little before pulling over.

"You said one lap around. Why are you pulling over now? That sign says no parking after 7pm."

"Temporary situation. Don't get your meter maid panties all in a bunch. Wait here, I'll be right back. Tonight just got a lot more interesting."

Rockfish gently closed his door and crossed the street without looking either way. He weaved his way through the small parking lot and stopped at the car that caught his attention. He gave a sharp knock on the window and it partially rolled down.

"What did you forget, Lynn? Oh, goddamn it! Rockfish, what the hell are you doing here?"

Jawnie's voice was higher than normal, and Rockfish could immediately tell she was agitated with a large helping of surprise. Each couldn't fathom how they ended up meeting in the parking lot of

Allison's Adult Superstore after sundown, neither one with a shopping list.

"That Coyne wench hire you to monitor me?" She said. "I knew she questioned my abilities."

"You know what? I could very well ask you if there's a March 29th, after hours fifty percent mark down, marital aid sale which no one told me about. But I won't, because I'm here with Raffi chasing down a solid lead to get Mack's money back." Rockfish turned and pointed over his shoulder in the general direction of where he had parked Lana, only to see Raffi, now standing in the parking lot, shuffling his weight from one foot to the other and back again.

"What the hell? I'm here to watch over my CI as she monitors Roan and this doomsday cult." Jawnie opened the window the rest of the way and Rockfish stuck his head inside.

"What the fuck?" Rockfish said. "You got doomsday cultists in my scammer's investors club meeting."

"No, you got a scammer's investors club in my doomsday cultists meeting." They laughed and could still not believe the coincidence.

Rockfish leaned further into the window. "How did we not know?"

"Going out on a limb here," Jawnie said, "But lack of clear, two-way communication is a good guess."

"Well, my guess is we need to compare notes afterwards and figure out how we ended up working the same set of bad guys from opposite ends."

"Again, it all traces back to communication," Jawnie said. "I really don't have a bad guy, more of a clueless rich one who is probably giving money over to these clowns, hand over fist, but that's not exactly a crime. We can meet up right afterwards?"

"No can do. Raffi and I will stay late for the big smart money pitch, which I'm now guessing is after Sunday school lets out. Can you two meet first thing in the morning?"

"Yeah, we'll be there, or I'll have all Lynn's info for you."

"I gotta get inside before they run out of communion wafers," Rockfish said. "Wait, what's your person look like or wearing? So, I know to steer clear..."

CHAPTER FIVE

Rockfish picked up Raffi on the way into the office. Both were worse for wear, having talked and engaged in a few cocktails after their business meeting. Rockfish had set an alarm and willed himself into the shower, but Raffi looked how Rockfish felt on the inside. Raffi was still in his suit from last night and his bed-head would give Diana Ross' afro from 1975 a solid run for its money.

Rockfish pulled down Lana's driver-side visor to block the morning sun's glare. He flipped on his turn signal and maneuvered into the McDonald's parking lot, only to stop and give a wide-eyed look at the length of the drive thru line.

"Holy crap, don't these people have jobs?" Rockfish said. "This line moves so much quicker at 9:30."

Raffi groaned an inaudible reply. Rockfish looked to his right. Raffi's head leaned against the window. *Well, he's in no shape to be my errand boy.* He released the seatbelt and walked inside, hoping the line there was shorter.

Ten minutes later, he got back in the car, put the coffees in the cup holders, and dumped the breakfast bag on Raffi's lap.

"Don't let that spill, if you know what's good for you."

Lana slid into her usual parking spot, and Rockfish opened Raffi's door and helped him out. He unlocked the front door, and the sensors kicked in, filling the office with florescent light. Rockfish turned to the alarm panel and cursed himself for his forgetfulness the night before. He walked over to the bar and put the McDonald's bag down. "Crash on the couch if you need to, Raffi."

A second later, a woman's scream filled the room, followed by a shout of "Get off of me!"

Rockfish spun to his right, where the cry for help originated. Raffi was on the floor and a woman kicked down at him from the couch.

"Hey, hey, knock it the fuck off lady, that's my friend. Who are you?

Someone grabbed Rockfish's left arm from behind. He cocked his right hand and turned to land a knockout punch when he recognized her. *Jawnie. If that's my partner, then the Intercontinental Couch Wrestling Champion must be Lynn.*

From the looks of Jawnie, Rockfish assumed she had spent the night. *Explains why the door was locked but not alarmed.*

"Whoa, whoa, whoa," Rockfish said firmly, trying to restore some kind of order. He locked eyes with Jawnie and could see she now grasped the situation.

"Lynn, Lynn, it's okay, they're with us."

Each of the partners moved towards their respective guests. Jawnie sat down on the couch next to Lynn, while Raffi remained on the floor, curled up in the fetal position, until Rockfish helped him up.

"I'm guessing introductions are in order," Rockfish said, and reached over for his coffee.

"This is the woman I mentioned to you," Jawnie said. "Lynn, this is Steve Rockfish."

Lynn stood up and held out her hand. "Gwendolyn Hurricane-Tesla, but you can call me Lynn."

"Without a doubt," Rockfish said, and countered with a fist bump. "This is my buddy, Raffi, last name, not as remotely cool or important. You ladies want a minute to freshen up, grab some grub, or should we let Raffi and Lynn pick up where they left off? Two out of three falls and Raffi, you're down one to zero."

"I'm good," Jawnie said. "How 'bout you, Lynn?"

"That couch was better than the local shelter. I'm fine."

"Let me grab some water and snacks from my office and we can get started," Jawnie said.

The four of them eventually made it to the conference table, and Jawnie explained she couldn't sleep after the events of last night and figured she'd burn some energy back at the office. She wasn't keen on dumping Lynn on the street, so they came back and started some serious research on this group. "We ended up passing out at some point and catching a few hours' sleep," Jawnie said.

"Let's lay out all our cards and see what we got. I'm sure it's more than some investment scam and attempts at milking rich, not-really cheating husbands," Rockfish led off with. "I'd like to confirm that the wench that started my, or should I say *our* involvement, Shae La Guardia, was present last night. She placed the food trays out and then took a chair in the inner circle. She dressed more conservatively than the pictures I've seen and was wearing glasses, but no doubt it was her. Sunny, my sponsor, so to speak, was also there and walked me around, introducing Raffi and me to everyone."

"Guessing your dad and Iggy weren't cult-worthy?" Lynn said and tilted her head.

How much had Jawnie filled her newfound friend in? His little two-man team was expanding past his comfort zone, but everyone needed their own Raffi, he guessed.

"More like they knew those two were good for a few small-time hits, but there are bigger fish out there. Such as Roan and yourself," Jawnie said, directing her reply to Rockfish.

"Bingo. This so-called religion—"

"It's the Church of the Universal Nurturing II, a spinoff of the original from the '80s," Jawnie said.

Rockfish choked on his coffee and had a hard time putting his cup back on the table.

"Wait, the Church of the Universal Nurturing, take 2?" Rockfish could feel his face flush and he burst out laughing. By this time, Raffi caught on and joined the laugh track.

"I don't get it," Jawnie said. "This type of doomsday cult is funny to you?"

"No, I mean, I found the Hale-Bopp Comet idiots funny, but I was thinking more of the acronym."

"It's C-U-N, but they pronounce it *Sun*," Lynn said.

"But hold on. Wouldn't Church of the Universal Nurturing II be C-U-N-T and pronounced—"

"See You Next Tuesday. That's how we'd pronounce it," Jawnie said, cutting off Raffi and staring daggers at the two men at the table.

"Yeah, no one clearly workshopped that acronym before choosing to take the lazy way out and stick a two on the ass end," Rockfish said. "Let's hope they put that much effort and thought into everything else they do. It'll make our job that much easier."

"Are we done with middle school recess?" Jawnie said, her arms firmly folded across her chest. "And what exactly is our job now?"

"Find out what their end game is. Get Mack's money back, maybe with some interest. Protect the stupid, like Iggy and Roan. Get enough information on the big grift because its gotta be next-level. Pass that info to the cops. Or Feds, depending on what they're into. Jawnie, you've ridden this ride before," Rockfish said with a nod.

"Yeah, and it got me bound and gagged in the trunk of a police car. One you rammed and pushed into a ditch." Her grin grew wider.

"You're welcome," Rockfish said and grinned. "If we can get Claudia to believe there is no adultery angle, she'll tell us to do what's necessary, short of kidnapping to get her husband away from these lunatics. This assures we're not only doing the right thing, but getting paid for it."

"I'm a hundred percent sure she'd green light a kidnapping," Jawnie said.

"If they gave him the sales pitch they gave us last night, add in whatever issue he feels he needs to repent for in order to come out on the right side of the rapture, and I'll guarantee this: Sister Lilith will start using him as a private ATM. Or, worse, a bank for large wire transfers."

"These cats are all in on cryptocurrency," Raffi said. "Claim to have the only one that will allow you access to your money after Jesus returns to earth and the four horsemen fuck some shit up. They call it SunCoin. It will be the only post-rapture currency accepted by the church and other CUN-businesses."

"Once Raffi and I convinced them we were believers… in at least part of the rapture story," Rockfish said. "They threw around a ton of tech mumbo jumbo that went over my head and I kept nodding in agreement."

Rockfish looked across to Jawnie. She had been quiet the past few minutes and he could see in her face that she was deep in concentration. He thought about stopping for a second, but continued.

"I think the pitch would have played out the same way, even if we hadn't seemed gullible for the end of the world scenario. They focused on this opportunity to get in on the ground floor, an investment worthy of Bitcoin-type growth over the next few years."

"I have a question," Lynn said. "Could this be any kind of legitimate?"

"Cryptocurrencies or only this Cultcoin?" Rockfish said.

"I mean, are these investment types you met with, or anyone associated with the church, in a position to cash investors out at some endpoint, or is it a straight multilevel marketing Ponzi type shit?"

"That's what we need to find out." Rockfish looked over at Jawnie when he finished. She was nodding along with him.

"I agree," Jawnie said. "It's worth our time, even if Claudia doesn't want to back us. And if we're doing this, let's identify the members of this group with an organization chart. Like you see in the movies where they lay out the hierarchy of the particular crime family. Identify them top to bottom with roles. We can put it on the whiteboard now, but we'll want to move it to the computer at some point."

"Excellent," Rockfish said. "You want to cover that when you go over what your research disclosed? I have one more thing."

"Sure."

"Sister Lilith expects Raffi and I to return on Thursday, but maybe if Raffi shows up without me and mentions something came up on my end. I'd like to see how that little wrinkle fucks with their plan."

"Not a problem. I can attend and take copious notes," Raffi said with a salute. "I also suggest mandatory masks when down there. Lord knows what any of these people are carrying, not to mention the DNA from upstairs possible leaking through the floorboards."

"Good points. It's sketchy as hell down there," Rockfish said. "Damp too, bad shit likes to grow in environments like that. And we'll talk added compensation for you later."

Raffi shook his head in agreement, and Rockfish made a mental note to remember before continuing.

"I want to see how hard they'll pursue me, to make sure I'm there the following Tuesday. I'm expecting they'll come at me harder, not wanting to lose a cash cow. Last, I'd like to run into Roan, purely by chance, over the next couple of days and see if I can determine how far gone his mind is. Maybe some background on what the fuck drove him to this."

"I re-listened to the tape I made," Jawnie said. "He stated he's trying to repent for past misdeeds. Get on God's good side before the end comes. Maybe as a guy, you'll get more out of him."

"Agreed on that point. Now the floor is yours. What did you dig up?"

* * * * * * * * * *

Jawnie stood up from the conference table and walked over to where the retractable video screen would normally come down. She preferred to talk from this angle, as it was easier to hide her anxiety by pacing back and forth as she spoke.

"Do you have a PowerPoint you need loaded?" Rockfish said. "I can hit the space bar and forward through the slides."

"I'm good, thanks," Jawnie said. She gave him a look that said cut the shit and listen. Rockfish grinned and Jawnie hoped he got the message.

"Most of what we know about the group came from the pamphlets Lynn received after her first night attending services." She held up the two pamphlets and handed them to Rockfish so he and Raffi could look them over. "The first one is *The Church of the Universal Nurturing II* and gives a high-level overview of this church and paints a broad stroke on why you need to jump on the CUN II bandwagon to come out the other side unscathed."

Jawnie stopped and waited for Rockfish and Raffi to look back up at her. *I should have handed those out after I finished talking. It will be like pulling teeth to keep their attention now.*

"The first pamphlet appears, at least to me, that the group updated it recently. Right off the bat, it states only Mother Elizabeth and Sister Lilith can help you successfully navigate the rapture, and everyone will need to atone for their sins before the tribunal period begins."

"And that's why you've seen Roan feeding the poor twice a week." Rockfish said.

He does listen! "I believe so. Also, despite it not being written anywhere, monetary donations to CUN II will accomplish the same thing. I think Roan's playing both ends by giving back with his time and also donating cash from the account his wife's accountant uncovered." Jawnie walked over and picked the first pamphlet off the table before continuing. *Eyes up here, gentlemen.*

"The rest of this thing is more of a scared straight deal."

"And looking at those attending the service," Lynn said, sitting up in her chair. "It's working. Many of those sitting in the inner and outer circles worry they'll be left behind, no matter how hard they work to flip that balance sheet in their favor."

"The pamphlet lists five signs of the second coming. I think someone put this together in about ten minutes after going online to look for recent scary events to shoehorn into each category in order to fit their narrative. Let me go over them:

False Christs - Mentions are made to the former President and the MAGA followers.

Wars and rumors of wars - Destabilizing events in the Middle East, the decision to move the United States embassy from Tel Aviv to Jerusalem, and assassination of Iranian Major Gen Qasem Soleimani.

Famines - Recycled pictures of African kids with distended bellies and covered in flies, alongside images of skyrocketing supermarket prices.

Pestilence - Ebola, COVID-19 and the always popular boogeyman, AIDS.

Earthquakes in diverse places - This isn't more than a cut and paste from a CNN article about recent earthquakes and tsunamis.

"Sound scary to you? I'm betting it does to a lot of vulnerable people," Jawnie said.

"I'm surprised they're not shoveling this stuff at the Iggy's and Mack's of the world to scare the cash out of them. Old people frighten easy," Raffi said.

"Maybe that was Plan B, if Operation Boner hadn't succeeded," Rockfish said.

"Good point."

Jawnie cleared her throat. "Can I continue?" Jawnie said. *It's like herding cats with these two.*

"By all means," Raffi said.

"Thank you. Curiosity got the best of me last night after reading the pamphlet for the tenth time and I wondered since we're dealing with CUN II—Don't even think about it, Raffi—if there was, in fact, an actual original entity. Lo-and-behold, in 1981, Alphie Richards and his wife Elizabeth broke away from the Pentecostal Church of God for reasons not very clear and formed the Church of the Universal Nurturing."

"Snake handlers," Rockfish said. "I saw a documentary on the History Channel on the Pentecostals. Crazier than shit house rats."

Jawnie continued with the timeline she had put together on the original church. "By 1986, Alphie had grown his ministry into a popular traveling revival show with a growing following across Appalachia. News stories from then reported Alphie suffered many snake bites, often requiring hospitalization, but nothing that kept him out of commission for any lengthy period. Come the early '90s, CUN had grown so large, the Richards no longer needed to travel, but eventually built their own church in Kilingess, West Virginia."

"Stop there," Rockfish said. "The chick with the date rape apartment, Kelly Westerly, aka Sunny West, aka God knows how many other aliases, has a digital footprint in Kilingess. She geo-tagged some pictures there and posted them to her real Instagram account."

Jawnie smiled, and deep inside patted herself on the back for a teaching job well done. *A couple of months ago, that would have been a task he begged me to do for him.* Progress made her happy.

"That's something we should keep track of. If this Mother Elizabeth is recruiting people from her former base of operations," Jawnie took a sip of coffee before continuing.

"October 1993. There was an accident and Alphie didn't recover. The article described an off-day freak accident, where two snakes bit Alphie and Elizabeth. Alphie passed away before an ambulance arrived and Elizabeth suffered a stroke, leaving her mute and unable to walk. With no relatives to assist in care and being forty years old, she's placed into a state rehabilitation home in Kermit, West Virginia."

"Alphie wasn't the chosen one?" Raffi said.

"Spoiler alert. Clearly not," Lynn replied and grinned.

"Okay, she's not talking and can't walk," Rockfish said. "Did she buy a motorized wheelchair one day and decide to make the trek to Baltimore at three miles an hour?"

"Here's where your Sister Lilith enters the picture, or at least the earliest mention of her I can find. Fast forward to 2017, when a Lilith

Highchurch appears at the state home and requests guardianship of Elizabeth. The article claimed Lilith presented herself as a distant relative who only recently realized her great aunt's predicament."

"I'm guessing she showed up with some paperwork to prove the relationship," Raffi said. "Not to mention it must have been a slow news day."

"Or not. It is West Virginia," Rockfish said. "I would think any offer to take an elderly woman, with who knows what kind of medical problems, off their books is rubber stamped. I'd bet they didn't even review any documentation Lilith presented. Some bureaucrat approved it and pushed Elizabeth down the ramp."

God, I hate when he stereotypes. Although he's probably right with government employee's eye on the bottom line. I'll agree with his assumption this one time.

"By mid-2018, Lilith and Elizabeth moved to the Baltimore region, and you can find the first mentions of the Church of Universal Nurturing II online."

"I've not seen one snake in either of the sermons I've attended," Lynn said.

Raffi smiled and slapped the table. "It's Baltimore, sweetie, that hillbilly shit won't work here," Raffi said. "We're dumb, but not white trash dumb."

"If this reincarnation is all about the grift, I have to somewhat agree with Raffi," Jawnie said. "You play to your audience and twirling snakes above your head while you pretend to talk in tongues wouldn't fly anywhere along the East Coast. But here's what you'll find interesting. In June 2019, the twosome reportedly fled Towson ahead of fraud allegations. Now we find them here in Anne Arundel County and no one seems to care."

"Good. At least some entity of law enforcement has seen them for what they are," Rockfish said.

"Or they did and wanted them the fuck out of dodge," Raffi said. "I don't care where you do it, don't do it here." He jerked his thumb over his shoulder for emphasis.

"And that leads us to today, where Sister Lilith leads a small congregation of twenty, meeting in the basement of an XXX adult bookstore, with no visual sightings of Mother Elizabeth in over a year."

"Twenty is a safe estimate," Rockfish said. "If they are milking these people, where's the money going? I mean, Allison's can't be charging them some astronomical rent."

"Actually, I think the dildo lady has one of those seats in the inner circle," said Lynn. "Lilith recognized her in front of the group my first time there, for donating the meeting space, until they can move to a more secure location."

"Okay, let's move on to the other, most likely outdated pamphlet which simply asks, Are You Financially Prepared for the Rapture?" Jawnie said. "You know the old saying, you can't take it with you? See You Next Tuesday—See what I did there, Raffi—actually claims you must, because heaven isn't a socialist utopia. Mother Elizabeth's teachings can help you exchange your sinner's dollars for God's currency prior to the second coming."

"I agree. Someone came up with this pre-SunCoin investment scam idea," Rockfish said, placing his hands flat on the table and leaning forward. "But it's the same M.O. Gimme your cash and I promise you can withdraw it, in a unique form, on the other side. Don't listen to me and you will be left behind on earth to starve. You can't eat your dollar bills." Rockfish said.

"I think that sums it up nicely." Jawnie walked back to her seat and sat down. *Well, that went as well as I expected. Rockfish seemed happy with everything I researched on my overnight shift and smart-ass comments aside, it drove our discussion. I'm good with it.*

Rockfish stood up and stepped back from his chair and waited until everyone looked over at him.

"We done, Stevie?" Raffi said. "This hangover needs some tender loving care. Or hair of the dog." He raised his eyebrows with the last word. "Speaking of which, you've got some of Zippy's on the front of your shirt."

"Thanks, Raffi. We're almost done. Jawnie, I think instead of me running to Roan, you and I need to go visit Claudia Coyne. We can play your tape for her, and I can tell her what Lynn and I have witnessed firsthand during these meetings. She can believe us or not, it's her choice." Rockfish slapped the table with his right hand. "But if she remains in her little fantasy world, she can count on her bank accounts, not only that one, to drain at a faster rate. The potential loss of her current lifestyle will bring her around. Bet on it. Bottom line, we'll be more than happy to continue working for her, barring any kidnapping requests. We'll deliver Roan back to her and shut off the faucets. Keep it out of the papers and social circles. She'll like that." He brought his left hand down on the table as loudly as the first.

"I'll reach out to her and see when she's free," Jawnie said. "I'll get that last report for Andrist over to his office this afternoon after I clean up. That will free up some time."

"Raffi and Lynn, stay out of trouble, show up on time Thursday night and take it all in. Let's plan on meeting back here, first thing Friday, to get a readout on Thursday night's festivities. Everybody good?"

"Is anyone going to stay in the office the rest of the day?" Lynn said. Jawnie noticed Lynn's eyes hadn't left the tabletop when she asked the question. *Embarrassed or hiding something?*

"I only ask because I'd like to make up for my time on the couch last night and get working on this organizational chart. I've got a bunch of names, whether real or not, rattling around in my head."

"What about that big 'roided out guy in the black leather duster?" Raffi said. "Do you know who he is, I mean, other than the apparent See You Next Tuesday bouncer? He looked angry as fuck, sitting there hoping someone starts some shit."

"That's Brother Lamb," Lynn said and giggled. "Word on the floor is that he and Sister Lilith are a thing."

"Alrighty then," Rockfish said. "Can we all get to work now before this turns into a recap of As the World Turns? Lynn, I can hang around while you get started."

"I'd like to go home," Raffi said.

"Uber's on the way, buddy. You can invoice it and I'll reimburse you."

****

"Mrs. Coyne will see you now."

Rockfish's eyes went from the exquisite brick exterior to the man who opened the door. *Gotta be a butler, right? With that outfit and the size of this place? Has to be.* He extended his arm and said, "Ladies first."

He followed Jawnie through the large double doors and into the Coyne's home. Home was probably the wrong word for the structure. Manor or estate was probably better served, but at the moment, he was in awe and not thinking straight.

The butler led them down a hallway, through a great room and then into a kitchen before opening the doors out to the patio.

Now I know why See You Next Tuesday targeted Roan's mental issues.

Claudia greeted them poolside, reclined in a chaise lounge on what was a chilly last day of March. She dressed in a Russian ushanka fur hat, complete with ear flaps. Below her neck, a dark green comforter obscured her clothes. The butler walked past her over to a large flat screen TV and muted the volume. Rockfish glimpsed Drew Carey and an energetic contestant on the screen. *Gertie used to love that show.* He reflected for a second on how his old friend from his previous adventure in New Jersey was holding up. It had been too long since he reached out to her. Despite his current problems, he made a mental note to find time to call her.

By the time Rockfish's consciousness made it back to the present, he had missed the first part of what Claudia had said.

"... and the view is too nice to let the weather dictate when I enjoy it."

"We don't mind at all," Jawnie said.

"Please sit down and, Ms. McGee, I see you brought the big guns with you this time. I apologize I could not meet sooner, but this Thursday time frame was the only one I had available," Claudia said. Pookie poked his head out from under the comforter and jumped down onto the patio.

"That's not a problem, Claudia," Jawnie said and prickled at being thought of as a small gun. "This is my partner, Steve Rockfish." They sat down at a small patio table under an umbrella, a few feet away from Claudia.

Rockfish nodded and wondered how crowded her calendar was with game shows and afternoon soap operas. He looked down as Pookie circled his feet. *Not my type. Go hump someone else.*

"James, please get these fine people their choice of refreshments. He makes a mean Negroni, If I say so myself." Mrs. Coyne lifted her own glass as if to prove her point.

"I'll take a whiskey sour, Irish, please, and if I know my partner, she'll take a sparkling water," Rockfish said and watched the butler disappear back inside without so much as a nod. "Now, we have some interesting information—"

"I'm sorry, Mr. Rockfish, but I refuse to talk business until your libations arrive. Please, tell me how your drive over was. No trouble getting in through the front gate, I assume?"

"No issues. The code you provided worked fine," Jawnie said. The threesome made odd small talk until James arrived, three glasses and a tray of cucumber sandwiches in hand. He placed the tray on the table.

"Um, what proteins—?" Rockfish said. He hadn't finished the question when he received a swift kick under the table. Jawnie furrowed her brow and tilted her head. *Message received.* The jolt scared Pookie, who leaped up and returned to the safety of Claudia's comforter.

They drank and nibbled on the finger sandwiches as Jawnie briefed Claudia on her husband's case since they last spoke. Finally, she played the audio of the conversation with Roan, outside the Camden Yards' McDonalds.

"I'd like to add, we had three people observe him after Jawnie made that tape, and I was one," Rockfish said. "Mrs. Coyne, to be honest with you, the only thing close to your husband's junk that night was the seat of a cold steel chair."

She placed her glass down on the patio next to her chaise and tugged on the ushanka's ear flaps with her hands. Her eyes closed and a deep humming noise filled the patio. Rockfish looked over at Jawnie and shrugged. She returned the favor with pursed lips and a shake of her head. She mouthed the word *Meditating*, but Rockfish shrugged again.

Mrs. Coyne stopped after a few minutes, opened her eyes and picked back up the conversation as if nothing happened.

"I've been wrong from the start? They've brainwashed him?"

"While we can prove he's not cheating on you, we came today because we think he's in trouble," Jawnie said. "I don't think he's brainwashed to the point of no return, but he's headed that way. How fast and how far from the edge, I couldn't tell you at this point."

"I don't know what to say."

"Hmm, can I get another whiskey sour?" Rockfish said.

Mrs. Coyne nodded and pushed a button on the armrest of her chaise. *The same as Trump's Diet Coke button.*

"What you're telling me is that instead of some floozy having a firm grip on Roan's manhood, this group has gotten inside his head and is looking to rob me, I mean, *us* blind?"

Jawnie let out an audible sigh, and Rockfish was glad the woman finally got it. *Was it his voice that finally did it? And how long until she drifted back out of reality?*

"That's exactly what we're telling you," Jawnie said.

James walked out onto the patio with a small tray containing three refills. *Goddamn, this guy is good. A push of a button. I need my own James right after we hire that receptionist.*

"What about tonight? Will he be there again? Will you be watching him?"

"We'll have two people there, observing," Rockfish said. He hoped his tone was calming. "They're instructed to stay close and make sure nothing happens to him."

"I need to call the police."

"Ma'am, certainly that's your right," Jawnie said. "But take a breath and think about how that call would go. Would you tell them your husband is attending a nonconventional religious service and donating money?"

Rockfish leaned in and folded his hands on the table as Ms. Coyne contemplated Jawnie's words.

"They'll turn around and ask you if they should arrest him under the clueless charitable donations statute?"

Claudia pulled harder on the ushanka's ear flaps. Rockfish turned and looked at Jawnie. This time, she shrugged. Rockfish considered leaning over and pressing the James button to see if he could help when Claudia spoke.

"Then, by all means. I cannot have you close your investigation. I would like to extend it. Spare no expense and hire some Green Delta Special Rangers to get him out of there. If we do that, you two can talk some sense into him, can't you?"

Jawnie was right. Claudia would green light a kidnapping and open her checkbook to accomplish it. He shuffled his chair closer and leaned in to see if he could get through. He reached for Claudia's right hand and held it between his.

"Now something like that could be very costly, not to mention very messy. If even the slightest thing went wrong, we could lose our licenses. And since Blackwater rebranded and changed the company name, I wouldn't have the first clue where to go in order to hire a band of mercenaries. Plus, when you do that, one person is always a wildcard and shit goes sideways."

He stopped and squeezed her hand a little harder. He needed her to look deep into his eyes and connect with what he was about to say.

"Let us continue to do our thing, minus the small mercenary army. We can build a strong case of fraud against these people, and then we'll present all the evidence to the police or even the FBI. Give us a bit of time to gather it and keep your husband safe. I promise you they'll all go to jail and your husband can get the help he needs to get back in his right mind." He leaned further in, trying to will the right answer out of her.

"What if it's too late?"

Rockfish could see the pools of water welling up, but the waterworks hadn't flowed. Yet. *Crocodile tears? Or does she have a heart under all that crazy?*

"We've got enough eyes on him. If something is coming down the pike, we'll physically remove him for his own safety. At least that way, we've got a legal leg to stand on. But when he's here, you need to talk to him. Listen to what he says and try to sprinkle in some of your concerns that might cause a crack or two in his current belief system. And by all means, try to shut off that money spigot. If we're lucky, that action, right there, might cause a little desperation on this group's part and give us the advantage we need."

When all parties came to an agreement, Mrs. Coyne pushed the button and James opened the patio doors and asked the visitors to follow him back to the front door. As they walked through the great room, Rockfish reached into his wallet and pulled out a twenty-dollar bill. He nonchalantly handed it to James as the partners headed out the front door.

They walked down the stairs and sat in the car. Jawnie looked at Rockfish. "What was that about? Not that I've come in contact with many butlers, but I'm pretty sure you don't tip them."

"Kid, you still have much to learn. You never know, we might have to call on James for something and you want him to take your call."

* * * * * * * * * *

Lilith turned off the water and the rain shower head slowed to a drip. She stood there, enveloped in steam, before reaching for the glass door. The Sagamore Pednry Hotel was $1,110 a night. *And worth every penny.* The pampering served as the perfect getaway from the grind of the grift.

She reached for a towel to put up her long brown hair and then slipped on the luxurious white robe. Check out days were the worst, but once back at the townhouse, Lilith would begin planning the next escape to the life she was destined to lead. She reached for her toothbrush when there was a knock on the door.

"What do you want, Earl? I'm trying to get ready as fast as I can."

Earl, otherwise known as Brother Lamb, poked his head through the door.

"We're running up against our late check out and you've got that 2pm back at the residence with DiT West."

She could see Earl through the mirror without having to turn around. *Look at that hair. Too long, and he's going to have to dye the premature gray in that damn five o'clock shadow. He isn't a biker anymore. West? Ah shit, I forgot about the DiT meeting.* DiT started as a joke between Earl and herself, calling a recruit a Disciple-in-Training. They shortened the title to DiT, which was their personal shorthand for DiT wit. It showed what they really thought of the people they conned. Both the marks and those within the church.

"How much do we have left in the Towson account?" She said. "I'd like to come back here sometime mid-next week for a couple of days. It's so refreshing. I, I mean, WE deserve this."

"Off the top of my head, I'm not really sure. Maybe slightly north of fifty thousand? Regardless, we need to get moving."

She shooed him away with her hand. *No bad news.*

This was her happy place. She'd deal with Sunny's failure in a few hours, but right now, she needed to breathe in this place and bottle it up if she could. Despite dragging her feet to leave the hotel, Lilith knew Earl was only doing his job. And that had turned out to be a bonus. Originally, she had picked him out from all the others because of the way he looked and carried that body. *Oh Lordy, that body.* Earl was muscular, with tattoo sleeves covering both arms. Who would have thought the man was even better at organization and had less of a moral compass than her? *The Lord works in mysterious ways, but I sure as hell am not rushing to leave.* She reached for the toothpaste and then proceeded with her makeup routine. Her flowing brunette locks were last, and an hour later, she was ready to return to the actual world.

Later, Earl pulled up in front of the two-bedroom brick townhouse and dropped off Lilith while he circled the block, looking for available street parking. The house was small but gave the marks the illusion of a simple life. She had stepped out of the Lincoln Navigator, half expecting to see Sunny on the stoop waiting, but the steps were empty and a quick look up and down the street gave Lilith the all-clear. She jogged up the stairs and unlocked the door.

By the time Earl knocked, she let him in and relocked the door. The small foyer opened to a living room on the right and a small dinette area on the left. The stairs to the second floor separated the two.

"She'll be here any minute. That one's always early," Lilith said. "You stay down here and let her in. I'll run upstairs and put on my great niece of a prophet hat. And lose that Coach bag. The last thing we need is a young girl asking why we're spending money on an expensive travel bag."

Lilith heard Sunny greet Earl when he opened the door, and she retreated to the small chair in the loft area outside her bedroom. *Sunny can wait. I'm in no rush and we're definitely not running on Sunny-time, the last time I checked.* Fifteen minutes later, Lilith rose and headed for the stairs.

"Thank you for coming on such brief notice," Lilith said as she reached the bottom step. Sunny sat in the living room on a small love seat, dressed in her Jamocha Jubblies uniform. Lilith presumed she was headed directly to the cafe for work when they finished.

Sunny stood up and met her halfway. They embraced and retreated to their respective chairs. Earl stepped into the Brother Lamb role and leaned against the gas fireplace. Lilith didn't expect any trouble, especially with Sunny, but after dropping her guard in Towson, she didn't consider anyone above trying to screw her.

Lilith cleared her throat before speaking. "I wanted to talk with you regarding prospect Rockfish. I'm hearing things about you dropping the ball and then I'm seeing things, well, not actually seeing things as he no-showed last night's homily." Lilith started off accusatory, but knew if the girl fumbled with excuses, anger would be next.

"Sister Lilith, I mentioned before that his schedule would not allow—"

"I don't want to hear it," Lilith said, and smacked the arm of her chair. "No excuses!"

"You must understand, this isn't my fault. I reached out to him half a dozen times, by phone, text, and even tried to catch him at his place of business—"

"Yet none of your efforts supported the church's mission? I could not be more disappointed in you at the moment. Even if you had come today to tell me of your leaving. I have such plans for you, but I'm wavering."

"If I contact him, I'm sure he would be apologetic. What I need to do—"

"Is absolutely nothing more on this assignment. I'm relieving you and I will deal with Mr. Rockfish from this point forward. Do I need to revisit your major screw-up last Saturday night?" Lilith gripped the chair's arms tightly and leaned in towards Sunny. "If you had done as you were told, as I had told you, we would have this sinner over a barrel and be well on the way to saving his soul by now." Lilith sat back up straight and stared into Sunny's eyes.

Lilith stopped and looked. Sunny's head was down, her eyes closed. Her fingers interlaced on her lap. *Tough love wasn't easy. If I didn't care, I wouldn't have plucked her out of that hollow in West Virginia, where her only hustle was to figure out where the next OxyContin came from.*

"Look, Sunny, you didn't do that bad, but those new tits aren't ready for prime time. Working with these sinners to either save them or use their ill-gotten gains to support our mission is difficult. I'm going to take over the Rockfish deal and transfer you to assist with assessing the worthiness of the new arrival, Lynn. Show her the ropes, educate her on the benefits of working with the flock to help secure the funding we need to move to the compound. Wait, wasn't she that girl we would step over in the alley from time to time?"

"Might be. I don't really know."

Lilith stared at Sunny, willing the girl's head to rise from her chest. Sunny needed to learn that, while Lilith was disappointed, she wasn't giving up on her. "Look up at me, Kelly. We don't need you to get down on yourself. Pick yourself up. Get this girl up to speed and I'll let you work Rockfish-adjacent on his buddy, this Mr. Pérez."

Sunny picked her head up and stared back with wide eyes, giving Lilith the feeling the girl listened intently.

"You must never forget; these types of men are leeches. Never fear separating them from their ill-gotten gains to further the church's goals. Do you not want to be ready when *He* comes? Would you rather be led to the kingdom of Heaven and not have a SunCoin to your name, or show up at the gate, pockets loaded and ready to live your best afterlife?"

"I want to be there, at your side. At Mother Elizabeth's side."

"Then do as I say. Your endgame is to get a check from Mr. Pérez to lay that foundation, proof he's a genuine believer. If not, get a slightly bigger check out of him and move on. You know, try to drink your own champagne this time. Remember, we can't save 'em all. The church has expenses, and the Lord won't delay his plans because we've not prepared properly or in a timely fashion."

"I understand, Sister Lilith. Thank you for not banishing me. I won't fail you again."

Lilith smiled. "I know you won't. Tuesday night, make sure you converse with Lynn. Sit next to her during the sermon. I watched her last evening and her behavior seemed to me she would want to help where she could. After her opening up about her past-issues with addiction, family troubles, she needs our direction and support. Someone or something will fill that hole in her soul, and it needs to be you, and then us."

"Will I still be able to meet Mother Elizabeth?" Sunny said. "Will it be soon?"

"The same time all the chosen ones do; once we've secured our own place, free of outside prying eyes and influences. Only then will she allow me to bring her to all of you."

Sunny let herself out and Earl took her spot on the loveseat.

"She seemed okay with it," Earl said. "I don't think she'll be a problem we'll need to deal with again. But if so, I can handle her."

"I'll start on Rockfish and close the deal. If we can get him into the flock, imagine the Hollywood types he could attract. If we pull that off, we'll have enough to begin renovations on the farm out in the sticks."

"Avila, I grew up there, remember?" Earl said with a tilt of his head.

"Whatevs. That place will give us a base of operations away from nosey neighbors and far enough out that the cops won't care what the hell we do." Lilith shrugged her shoulders. "How are the current conversions towards a down payment coming along? I don't want to touch any of the funds already moved overseas. Only what we have here and expect to collect over the next week."

"We're currently at forty-eight percent of projection. I spoke to Coyne last night and reminded him how important it is that he produces a large tithe. He's promised and I reinforced we're counting on him to put us over the top. He was a little sketchy, but promised we'd have it by Tuesday at the latest."

"Excellent. When the cash comes, transfer it to the account in the Seychelles Islands," Lilith said. "Use the Bank AL Habib Limited account, but make sure it's well washed before landing there. Clean that shit, good, but fast. We'll need it for closing on the seventh."

Earl sighed. "I know the routine. What concerns me is pushing all-in on this Hollywood deal." He shook his head in disagreement. "It would be smarter to hit and run here. Set up shop somewhere else to grease the rest of the rubes out of what they have left."

"Patience, Brother Lamb," she said with a sly smile. Earl wasn't aware of half the actual plan, and Lilith wouldn't have it any other way. The less he knew, the better the odds for success. "We'll be sipping champagne coolies on the French Riviera when this is all said and done. Or if we can make this Rockfish-Hollywood connection, it will be on our own beach, on our own private island." Lilith quietly clapped. *If Earl doesn't stop questioning my every move, I might be looking for a new towel-mate on that island and he'll be back making bathtub meth before he knows it.*

Earl nodded and stood up. "One last point on this whole Rockfish thing. Are you positive that he doesn't think we're the ones that ripped off his old man?"

"Despite Sunny's screw up, my conversations at mass with him lead me to believe not. Don't worry over something that doesn't need the energy."

"Be cautious around that dude," Earl said.

"Honey, I work people, I don't get worked. In that vein, make me a reservation for two, tomorrow night, Sunday, or Monday, at Cucina Magdalena. Whichever day is their least busy. Then reach out to Mr. Rockfish's secretary and advise them I respectfully request his company for dinner."

CHAPTER SIX

The Saturday morning meeting of *Rockfish & McGee - Investigative Specialists*, along with Lynn and Raffi, began on the back deck of Rockfish's house. Rockfish emerged from the sliding glass door with glasses, champagne, and a carton of orange juice.

"Who's up for a mimosa?" he said. Two hands went up. "What's up Jawnie, no morning go-go juice for you?"

"I'm going to pass. That's Tropicana Healthy Heart orange juice. It's not exactly vegan friendly. The label says the container is chock-full of omega-3 fatty acids."

"Sounds super healthy. All I see on television is that we all need more omega-3s in our diet," Raffi said.

"Okay, learning moment. Listen up. Omega-3s are usually derived from fish, primarily anchovies. Here, let me read the label for you, so you don't need to pull down your readers," Jawnie said. She gave Rockfish a shit-eating grin before continuing. "Contains tilapia, sardine, and anchovy. Case closed. I'll stick with the coffee I brought. Thank you very much."

"Your loss. Also, Mack's whipping up breakfast if anyone's interested," Rockfish said. "Go inside and put your order in if you want anything. Careful with the sliding door, Zippy tries to sneak out and let's refrain from rehashing the omega-3 argument again."

"Yeah, you heard the man," Jawnie said. "I'll add that, if I ate eggs, I'd be an ovo-vegetarian and not truly vegan. You know that I have to bend the rules a lot, especially in this town, if I don't want to die of hunger. But enough about my dietary issues. I know Raffi and Lynn wanted to meet yesterday to discuss what went on during the Thursday sermon, but another case needed our attention down in D.C. Apologize for that, but we've still got other paying clients that need our attention."

Rockfish finished pouring three mimosas and pulled up his chair. "What did I miss? How'd they take my absence?"

"I'll take that one," Lynn said. "In the beginning, when everyone was milling around and making small talk, I was in the middle of the room, trying to start up a conversation with Roan. To see if I could wiggle my way in and eventually get him to open up. But your girl Sunny kept coming up to me. She's annoying as shit and I ended up slowly shuffling to my left, so I could better eavesdrop on what appeared to be a heated discussion between Sister Lilith and Brother Lamb." Lynn stopped and took a sip of her mimosa. "They were pretty hot you weren't there. He kept pushing the fact that every sermon you missed it would be that much harder to pull you back in. Lilith said she didn't have the time to berate Sunny right then and there and figure out what the hell went wrong. At that point, they noticed I had made my way closer. They shut up and Brother Lamb stomped off. I'm sure Sunny's gotten an earful by now."

"Hmm, I could reach out to Sunny and test the waters," Rockfish said. "Or I can show up out of the blue on Tuesday and see the reaction. How about you, Raffi? You look like you're holding back on some good shit?"

"Stevie, you have no idea. While Lynn was off doing her thing, I was working the room, too. But when the bell rang for everyone to take their seats, I had to hit the head. You know they offer a lot of snacks and punch beforehand."

Raffi was animated, and his hands talked faster than his mouth. Rockfish took a sip of his drink and was afraid to comment and interrupt the show.

"Now, I head down the hallway and before I turn and open the bathroom door, I see a blur down the end of the hallway. You've got me there to observe, so I did. Brother Lamb had either come out of a door or was ready to go in. I couldn't tell. But he stopped and stared down at me. He froze and closed the door behind him. I couldn't completely make out his face in the dark in the piss poor lighting, but he kind of reminded me of a kid caught with his hand in the cookie jar."

"Or in this case, a kid coming out of his dad's closet with a dirty magazine or who knows what if that's one of Allison's storage rooms," Jawnie said.

"Exactly. She gets it, am I right?" Raffi turned, raised his hand, and Jawnie left his high five hanging.

"Anyway, he gathered himself and walked towards me. That dude gives off some weird vibes, always wearing that leather duster. Creeps me out. I threw open the bathroom door and went in, praying he didn't follow me."

"Did he?" Rockfish said.

"Nope, and I didn't see him the rest of the night."

"Well, glad we all gathered here for that."

"Stevie, you ain't listening. I came out of that bathroom, and with the opening hymn in full verse, I tiptoed down that hallway and tried the door. Lamb must have locked it behind him. I'm betting there's something in that room. Something big that could help us out. Now that ain't nothing but a plain old doorknob lock. No dead bolt. A couple of old pros like us should be able to get past it in no time flat. One late night, in and out."

Rockfish grinned. *God bless him. Raffi is stuck in the old days before the new office, clientele, and the notoriety of being on a hit streaming service brought.*

"Raffi, those days are long gone. I can't get away with a lot of the chances I used to take. I trip an alarm now, or get seen sneaking into somewhere I shouldn't, I'm in the paper. That's bad for business. I have to do things more legit now. Or at least keep my actions at the misdemeanor level." Rockfish watched as Raffi's shoulders slumped and he dropped his head slightly. "I'll tell you what I'm going to do. I'm gonna let your idea marinate. We need to put our heads together to see if we can figure out a better way to get the information we need. If not, well then, I've still got my lock pick set and we can, as they say now, circle back to your idea."

Raffi looked up. But Rockfish could tell the answer bummed out his old pal.

"There is one more point from Thursday I would like to mention, but I didn't want to cut off Raffi," Lynn said. She paused and looked around, as if asking for permission to continue. Rockfish nodded his head.

"From my brief conversation with Roan and watching him the rest of the night, he definitely wasn't his normal enthusiastic self. He appeared withdrawn and at one point got into what looked to me, like a heated sidebar conversation with Lilith." Lynn shook her head and bit her bottom lip before continuing. "It wasn't long after he got up and paced around the back of the room before eventually leaving early. Whatever they spoke about seems to weigh heavily on his head."

Rockfish turned and looked toward Jawnie, as the Coyne angle was more her deal than his, but her chair was empty. He found her over on the far side of the deck, phone glued to her ear.

"Hmmm, it might be worth reaching out to the wife and see if she's learned anything or been riding his case extra hard lately," Rockfish said. "You should mention it to Jawnie when she finishes whatever she's doing."

The three waited until Jawnie walked back to the group and sat down.

"Lynn was telling us—"

"Did you bother to check the office voice mail yesterday?" Jawnie said, interrupting.

"No, I was rather busy," Rockfish said. "You might remember, as we were together."

"I get it. This isn't a gotcha thing, but I didn't have a chance either and it just crossed my mind. I checked before telling myself I would do it later and never get around to it. Another reason we need a receptionist, but I hope I'm preaching to the choir."

"You are."

"Remember how Lynn said Lilith was unhappy with Sunny's poor performance concerning your absence?"

"Ah yeah, only a few minutes ago. I'm still able to hold off the dementia, despite my age."

"Well, it appears Sister Lilith demoted Sunny. Brother Lamb left a voicemail. Lilith would like to have dinner with you, Monday night at Cucina Magdalena. Better get a suit cleaned."

Rockfish ignored Jawnie's sarcasm, and Raffi leaped at his chance.

"Stevie, you need back-up on this too? If I need to work another night, it's gonna cost ya extra."

"No, Raffi. I'll be solo on this one. I should be okay. If things get hot and heavy this time, I'll bring her back to my place," Rockfish said with a wink.

****

The meeting adjourned shortly after lunch, and Rockfish and Jawnie walked to the far side of the deck to continue their conversation. Lynn assumed it wasn't for her or Raffi's ears. She put her empty glass down on the small table between two chairs and walked over to the steps that led down to the side yard. Raffi stood on the inside of the sliding glass door, carrying on an animated conversation with Mack. The silver Labrador sat at attention between the two, oblivious to the conversation and enjoying the attention Raffi was giving the area behind it's ears.

Lynn was the odd man out. *Not the first time, not the last time.* She leaned against the railing, her arms folded in front and her upper body twisting to the music that played in her head. Jawnie had picked her up this morning at the Super 8 Motel in West Baltimore. All the cash she earned from her newfound contract work went to maintaining this semi-stable living environment. She would obviously need a ride back, but Jawnie's conversation with Rockfish didn't look casual or like it would end soon. Lynn hated having to beg and rely on other people to get through her day. But here she was, hoping Jawnie would look over in her direction and remember their ride over together.

"Hi, little lady. You look like you're searching for something?"

Lynn glanced to her right and saw that Mack had come outside. He was bent over, loading the dirty dishes and glasses onto a tray. "Anything I can do?"

Lynn walked back over to where the chairs were and held out her hand.

"Hi, you must be Mack. I'm Lynn. I don't think we've been officially introduced."

"Do you work for Stevie?"

"Something like that, but right now, I'm hoping Jawnie remembers she was my ride over here." Lynn reached down and it was her turn to scratch Zippy behind the ears. She followed Mack's eyes as he put the tray down and scoped out where Rockfish and Jawnie remained in deep conversation.

"They look pretty serious," Mack said. "It might be awhile. Would you want to come inside and have a seat? I can brush off a chair, so you don't get dog hair all over your pants."

"That's nice of you, but I'm fine. I'm going to stand here until she notices me. Maybe if I pace back and forth, it will get her attention?" Lynn raised her eyebrows.

"I've seen these two get deep into it and lose track of time. I don't drive anymore, or I would offer, myself."

"Thanks Mack, but—"

"Raffi, get your ass out here," Mack called out, and Raffi slid open the screen door and stuck his head out. Mack waved him back outside to where he and Lynn stood.

Lynn cringed as Raffi walked over. Dependence on others wasn't her thing and one reason she had left her sister's house. *I'd rather be out moving from shelter-to-shelter or an alley than feel like I owe someone for helping me. My demons are just that, mine. At least with Jawnie, I'm kind of earning my keep.*

"Raffi, do me and Stevie a favor. Give Lynn a ride home. Looking at those two over there, I don't think they're going to end soon and she's got somewhere she needs to be."

"Come on, Mack, I got places to be, too."

"Thanks, Raffi. I knew Stevie and I could count on you," Mack said. He picked the tray back up and headed inside the house, Zippy hot on his heels.

Great. He's going to hate me now for this. Should make for a wonderful working relationship however long this thing lasts. And I need it to last. "You don't have to," Lynn said and shook her head.

"No, no, no, I actually think this might be a good thing," Raffi said.

Lynn noticed a weird look in Raffi's eyes. *Should I push back harder? Fuck it, I'm a big girl and know how to take care of myself better than most. I'm probably jumping to the worst conclusion.*

"Hey Stevie, we're out of here. I'll drop off Lynn. Don't you two worry about it," Raffi said with a wave.

Lynn waved too and followed Raffi to his car.

"I have a proposition for you," Raffi said before Lynn even grabbed the seatbelt.

"Yeah, that's not gonna happen because you're giving me a ride and the endpoint is a Super 8." Lynn buckled herself in and reached up to pull the sun visor down. *Christ, I'm not even showing any skin. I couldn't be dressed more like a tomboy if I had tried.*

Raffi laughed. "Oh, God no. Not like that at all. I'm talking about earning our keep around here, on this case. I mean, I'm not speaking for you, but I'm bored as shit sitting in a glorified bible study meeting while people keep grabbing at my wallet. We need to get a better view of what exactly is behind that locked door."

"I can already see. It's dildos, or Fleshlights, maybe butt plugs of various sizes and shapes. You name it," Lynn said. "When some weirdo walks in and asks for the Donatello, from The Teenage Mutant Ninja Turtles butt plug line and there aren't any on the shelf, where do you think the clerk goes to check?"

"Lynn, that's a gigantic leap. I saw Brother Lamb come out of that room and he's not an employee."

"How do you know what he does with the other twenty-one hours of his day?"

"Because... I've never seen him work the register."

Lynn let that one pass. She didn't need to know Raffi had a rewards card for Allison's Adult Superstore.

"Enough of the funny riffing back and forth," Raffi said.

She nodded and let him continue.

"Look, I'm a scammer. Not very proud of it, but it is what it is. And I can tell you I know my kind. Why do you think Stevie brought me on board? I'm here to pull a scam over on the scammers. I can't do that sitting with the audience. If I feel something in my gut, and I do, I have to trust it. Act on it. Been that way my entire life. Again, not proud of it, but I excel."

Lynn nodded in agreement as Raffi spoke. *I get where he's coming from.* After meeting Mack, she too felt the need to go the extra yard to help him get his money back. *Hell, even I'm questioning how sitting and listening to a bunch of bull twice a week is accomplishing anything. Working for Jawnie means a lot. Am I fucking it up by entertaining this idea of Raffi's? That's the last thing I want. I want to help and get some praise. Maybe this is my one shot or one opportunity to seize everything I ever wanted?* As the rest of Eminem's *Lose Yourself* lyrics flashed across the screen inside her head, Lynn was ready to dip her toe in and test the waters.

"You saw me today shoot my shot. I said, Stevie, you asked for my help for a reason. Then let Raffi do what Raffi does. I'm telling you, these people have that back room loaded with God knows what, but whatever it is, it's important to them. If it's important enough to lock up, then it's important to Stevie's case. Our case. Now if he's sitting up on some moral high ground now, I get it. But again, he hooked my wagon to this case for a reason. Let me take the chance he can't anymore."

"Go on, I'm listening," Lynn said, and smiled. A toe had become one foot.

"How I see it going down is we wait till Tuesday night. After the meeting ends, you go your way. I'll go mine. I can fake some car problems so I'm stuck in the parking lot, long after Lilith, Lamb, everyone leaves." Raffi glanced over at Lynn and then back at the road. "You double back, then we go in. I already checked out the door at the bottom of the steps. No alarm, I can see. All you gotta do is be the look-out. I'll do the dirty part. Rockfish ain't the only one with a lock pick set. I got tools and I'm itching to use them."

"To clarify, I'm hanging in my old alley keeping an eye out?" Lynn said. "That's it for me?"

"That's it. Your old alley. You said it yourself, plausible deniability if anyone walks up."

"I'll play the part. But if I see a black duster come around the corner, I'm screaming and running. Not necessarily in that order."

"Whatever. He won't be around. Once I'm in, I'm taking photos," Raffi said. "If it's filled with cases of Donatellos, then I back out the way I came in and no one is the wiser."

In her mind, Lynn knew she should waiver more, but this was his expertise. *And, and he sounds so goddamn sure.* "Okay, I'm in."

"Great. Wear some dark clothes and hang out a couple of blocks away from the building when everyone leaves. I'll tap my horn when the coast is clear. Remember, I'm in and then I'm out, and we'll be on our way to Rockfish, McGee, Pérez and..."

"Hurricane-Tesla."

"You're kidding me, right?"

Lynn turned her head and gave an Oscar winning resting bitch face to the man. Raffi pulled up under the Super 8's awning and Lynn got out of the car. When she shut the door, Raffi lowered the passenger-side window.

"See you next Tuesday!"

****

As per his normal routine, Rockfish shit, showered, and shaved a good hour before he had to meet Sister Lilith for dinner. He skipped the tie. The maître d' could always force one on him if the conversation got to that point. *Slacks and a dress shirt should get me a seat at the table.* He hung his favorite blazer by the garage door. He'd hang it on the hook in the backseat until he got to the restaurant. From the message, he assumed the good sister would meet him there.

Rockfish sat in his recliner, and with time to kill, grabbed the remote. The red light on the front of the television blinked a few times, and a couple of seconds later, Lieutenant Joe Kenda stared back.

TMC. Rockfish knew who had watched the boob tube last. *Discovery ID*, or *The Murder Channel*, as Jawnie referred to it, had been an evening staple since Mack moved in. Rockfish wouldn't lie. There were serious concerns about Kenda's face burning into the flat screen.

"Hey, hey, don't you dare change that," Mack said. Rockfish twisted around to see his dad and new found best buddy coming down the stairs. *He's moving faster than he had in a couple of weeks.* He chalked it up to the old man's fear of the channel changing, as opposed to a miraculous recovery. Mack's depression and anxiety had hung over the house like an albatross since the weekend in the hospital. Not every day, but the majority. Zippy had helped, but the old man had a ways to go.

"This guy solves all the best cases," Mack said, and plopped himself down on the couch. "Every single last one of them. No offense, Son."

Rockfish wasn't sure how to take that insult. He was definitely sure it was an insult. *Was Mack insinuating that Kenda could have gotten his money back for him already? Or did he have a thing for old men who can wrap shit up in a nice shiny bow in an hour, excluding commercials?*

"I'm going to say, none taken, Dad. Even though I'm really not sure."

"Geez, someone's wound tight. Relax. You're dressed like Danny Terrio when he came out at the beginning of Dance Fever. When was the last time you had two dates in ten days? By the way, did you know his given name is Denis Mahan? Everyone wanted to be fake Italians in the seventies. I bet Kenda could tell us why he changed his name. Do it in under an hour, too."

Rockfish looked at his watch again. Still too early to leave, but now, a drink or three at the restaurant bar sounded a hell of a lot better than remaining here with Mr. Bipolar. The constant lows and continued moping around were bad enough, but the sudden shifts to manic highs would end up driving Rockfish to drink. And tonight, it did.

"Alright, Dad. Enjoy your evening. I'm going to stake out the place before my date shows up." Rockfish got up from the recliner. He hadn't yet reached his blazer when Mack fired off another statement from left field.

"It was nice to see your friends over here the other day. You all seemed to enjoy yourself."

Rockfish said nothing, pressed the garage door opener, and walked over to Lana. *The doctor said it would be a little while before the meds started working their magic, and even then, they might need to be adjusted in order to keep Mack on an even keel. By that time, would he even care I got his money back? What I went through to do it? Maybe I should get out in front of this mess and change my name to Kenda?*

Rockfish shook his head, pressed the ignition button, and backed out of the garage.

* * * * * * * * * *

"Fucking make sure he keeps it in his pants!" Earl shouted in Lilith's general direction and slammed the front door behind her.

She ignored his parting shot, as she had the previous dozen while getting ready for dinner. *Why does jealousy always show up after you fuck a guy? Fuck a stifling relationship, both professional and personal. He's not even the one, is he?*

Lilith ambled down the front walkway as fast as she could in these heels, wanting to avoid one last audio salvo from an open window. The Uber driver waited in front of the townhouse, and Lilith said a quick prayer thanking his promptness. Earl had worn on her last nerve with his verbal abuse and this afternoon's final straw was his refusal to drive her.

Lilith looked like a million bucks, but on the inside, he had mentally worn her down and, uncharacteristically, she wasn't prepared for what lie ahead. *Get your shit together, kid.* She slid into the backseat of the Dodge Charger and met the driver's eyes in the rearview mirror. *Damn, is he even old enough to drive? Is that a Pokémon hat?*

"Alrighty, looks like we're headed to Cucina Magdalena," the Uber driver said.

"Yeah."

"You look dressed for it. Hot times at Baltimore's newest hotspot."

"Cut the shit, Romeo, and drive. I'm not in the mood." The driver's eyes dropped from the rearview mirror and he moved to fiddle with the radio.

Lilith, for a moment, thought about changing her destination. The Spa at The Sagamore Pendry Hotel was what she really needed. But a rubdown by Roberto wouldn't fill the coffers nor get her any closer to hiring Roberto to give the same service on her private beach. *That would really piss old Earl off. So would grabbing an Uber back home drunk off my ass. Then I can give him the silent treatment and let him stew in his own thoughts, wondering what happened.*

"Jesus Christ, I need a drink," Lilith said before realizing it was out loud.

"There are water bottles behind the passenger seat, ma'am."

Lilith sighed.

* * * * * * * * * *

Rockfish had drained the remnants of his second whiskey sour when he spotted Lilith from his seat at the bar coming through the doorway. She was alone, as he expected. But it wouldn't surprise him if she had come in with an entourage. Intimidation, aka the hard sell, was usually part of the religious grift handbook. But with only one look as she walked towards the maître d, he knew she carried herself as an army of one.

Lilith wore a red, body-hugging dress. *Devil red.* It was knee-length and off the shoulders, with loads of cleavage. Enough that he wanted to hang an *oversized load* sign from her white gold necklace as a warning to other diners as they squeezed by on the way to the restrooms. She had taken the Sunny route to another level. *Good thing there's a neutral bartender at this place.*

Lilith walked up to the maître d', and the man pointed towards the end of the bar. Rockfish raised his glass and stood up. He followed them to a small table off to the side and sat down while the young man in the three-piece suit held out Lilith's chair. A waiter appeared out of nowhere, dropped off menus and scribbled down their drink orders.

"An Irish whiskey sour and a dry Manhattan for the lady," the waiter repeated back. "I'll be back with those."

Rockfish took a sip from his water, put the glass down, and broke the silence. "Well, Sister Lilith, to what do I owe the honor of this invitation?"

"Please, call me Lilly. After all, I am off the clock."

"I can see. That dress is about as far from the pulpit as you could get."

"Mr. Rockfish, it's not a crime for a woman to dress in a way that makes her feel empowered without worrying about wolf whistles."

Did she catch me staring? Eyes up here, asshole.

"And if we're going to critique, you need a tie. But we aren't here to discuss the social issues of the day. We missed you Thursday night," Lilith said with a stern look.

"And here I thought you said you were off the clock," Rockfish said. "Look, I can save us boatloads of time. I'm no rube, but I am all about padding my retirement account. The rapture deal doesn't really do a thing for me and the only four horsemen I care to know were led by Ric Flair and Arn Anderson." Rockfish stopped as the waiter dropped off drinks and took their dinner order.

"Clock or no clock, that's disheartening to hear. My followers are not rubes, but souls lost and searching for direction, needing the stable hand of a guide through troubling times. All they wish from this life is a hand to enlighten and assist in order to come out unscathed, to enjoy all that heaven offers. All of which *I* provide for them." Lilith reached for her Manhattan, finished it, and waved the empty glass to get the waiter's attention.

"Another for you too, Sir?"

"I'm good right now, thanks." Rockfish was content with nursing his drink and paid more attention to the refilled water glass. *So much for the lecture I sat through and all those handouts. Mother Elizabeth must be the draw, but the ego with this one... Is it the thought of Mother Elizabeth that brings them in? And once Brother Lamb bars the doors, Lilith turns the sheep's pockets inside out before leading them to slaughter?*

"Like I said before, Lilly, you can leave the Jesus stuff on the stoop. I won't exploit my Hollywood associations to help you recruit on that angle. I'm here because you appear to have a money-first business plan. Not that there's anything wrong with it. We all do what we do for the almighty dollar. I'm a slave to it, as much as the next man." Rockfish picked up his drink, gave a slight nod with his head, and completed the air toast.

Lilith stared back and didn't follow suit.

"Steve, if you're insinuating that I'm after these poor souls' money, then you wouldn't be too far off. After all, how many prominent, up-and-coming religions do you know of that meet in the basement of a porn shop?"

"Superstore. Don't sell yourself short."

Lilith pursed her lips, and Rockfish wondered if he was wearing her down or pissing her off. She reached for her drink before saying another word.

"Is it a crime? I want a mega-church, a compound type environment where I can sermonize without prying eyes. Why should I hide it?" Lilith held her palms out. "Because I'm a woman? If I am to lead these individuals through the rapture and into heaven, I cannot do it with the instruments currently in my tool chest. I mean, seriously, what the fuck is your concern if I'm guaranteeing you a thirty-five percent return on your investment?" She tapped her forehead with her fingertips and looked straight across the table.

"Ha! Now you've got my attention," Rockfish said with a shit-eating grin. *Eyes up, eyes up.*

A minute later, their salads and another Manhattan arrived with entrees not far behind. They dug into their food, and some time passed before the conversation picked back up. Rockfish ordered a Diet Coke when the waiter stopped by to check on the food.

"Don't give me that look. I drove here," Rockfish said. "I'm not a big fan of the local taxi scene and having to retrieve my car in the morning."

"Better you than me," Lilith said, and reached for her most recent Manhattan. Rockfish, officially, had lost count.

"Okay, back to the reason we're here," Rockfish said. "If this cryptocurrency you created—"

"SunCoin."

"Yes," he replied, stifling a laugh and imagining Jawnie's swift kick under the table. "Excuse me, my cola must have gone down wrong. Damn bubbles. If SunCoin is all you represent it to be, with appreciation and some serious capital gains, then I'm interested. The same for my Hollywood buddies. But they might want to meet the elusive Mother Elizabeth. Isn't she the real driving force behind this movement? I bet my old producer and friend, Angel Davenport, could whip up a documentary on her life if he had the chance to meet her. No such thing as bad press."

"That old bag? Please. She's part of the marketing materials, no more, no less," Lilith said, and lifted her glass again. "All part of the window dressing that will get you that thirty percent return on your investment, my friend. But the actual story here is me. Remember that." She returned the now empty glass to the table.

"Thirty-five," Rockfish said, correcting her. "You said thirty-five percent earlier." Her dismissal of Mother Elizabeth came as a surprise. *I'll chalk it up to the alcohol.*

"You pay attention too much. Anotha r—round?" Lilith said.

Wait, was that a slur? Had I missed that before? Rockfish shook his head. *Was I too busy with the two jumbotrons in my face? Am I being cancelled? Damn cancel culture. I sneaked a peak, I admit it. Is it possible to cancel a onetime docuseries part-time star? Eyes up, asshole. Pay better attention.*

"I think we're good for now," Rockfish said. "You're going to get me that prospectus, and I'll speak to Angel about doing a joint investment to test the waters. Based on the return, we can go from there."

"D—Deal."

Rockfish could see her eyes light up with what her buzzed brain saw as a win. Lilith puffed out her chest proudly and literally. For the first time this evening, he didn't take the bait.

"Night cap at a bar, then? Your choice."

It wasn't what he expected her to say, and the little man in the back of his head was giving Rockfish the wrap-up sign. He pondered for a second and ignored the man. There was a dive bar within walking distance of his house. *Less of a hassle if I have to retrieve Lana after sunrise.*

"I know a place."

Rockfish refused Lilith's fumbling attempt to pay and then sent the valet to retrieve Lana. When Lilith secured her seatbelt, he pulled out onto the street and came to an immediate stop at a red light. Headlights from behind lit up Lana's interior and the glare off his rearview mirror was blinding.

"What the fuck?" Rockfish said and turned around to see who had lit him up with high beams. He couldn't make out the car, other than by the lights streaming straight in through his back windshield. It had to be an SUV. He rolled down the window and gave a one-finger salute as the light turned green. The SUV remained on his ass and Rockfish's mind raced through his recent case load to identify the person with the headlight hard-on for him. He came up empty, jerked Lana's wheel hard right, and barreled down a side street.

By the time he straightened the wheel, Rockfish was aware of two things. A moan from the passenger seat let him know Lilith didn't take the sudden turn as well as Lana, and a peek into the now clear rearview showed a large white SUV lumbering to make the turn. *A Lincoln Navigator. If I know my shit.* He pressed down on the accelerator and kept the blinding light far enough back so he could think and not have his dashboard whited out.

"W-w-what are you doing? Stop with the r-r-rollercoaster."

"Puking on these seats is prohibited," Rockfish said. "Don't even think about it." He hit the brakes last minute and made another quick right. A moan came from his right as the Navigator lumbered to follow suit.

"Do you know anyone that drives an insanely tricked out Lincoln Navigator?"

"White?"

"Yeah."

"Nah."

"Well, someone's trying to tail us and doing a shit job of it," Rockfish said. He glanced back at the Navigator. The SUV had trouble staying between the lines, but for each maneuver Rockfish put Lana through, the SUV kept pace. *Some jealous clown or an unsatisfied investor? Probably the same.* He pressed down on the accelerator.

Rockfish hurriedly glanced left, then right, and without stopping, made a left on red. Lana's tires lost traction, and she fishtailed through the intersection. Traffic prevented the Navigator from following suit, and Rockfish gunned it. Up on his left was an abandoned gas station. He killed his headlights and pulled in alongside the second row of pumps. Hidden, but with an unrestricted view of the road.

A minute later, the Navigator zipped by at an unsafe speed. *Yup, a white Navigator.* Rockfish slipped Lana into drive and eased out onto the street in the opposite direction. When his passenger didn't compliment him on the now improved and smoother ride, Rockfish looked over. Lilith was out cold. *Please don't drool on my leather seats. What a fucking mess. And you want to handle my retirement account?* He felt disgusted with how the evening had played out.

Rockfish street parked on the side of Frank's Tavern and called a taxi for his date. He never considered waking her and asking what the hell that was all about. Conversation at this point would be fruitless. Lilith would not be answering questions on their chase partner, and Rockfish doubted she would, even if sober.

He gently roused her when the car pulled up and helped the driver get her into the backseat. Lilith mumbled an address and Rockfish walked into Frank's alone.

Familiar territory. Rockfish pulled up a stool. Frank nodded a silent hello and an Irish whiskey on the rocks magically appeared on the cardboard coaster in front of him.

Who was that driving? What was Lilith's end game tonight, and what the fuck did either of them accomplish? Whatever it was, it was an epic fail by both of them. What if Raffi was right about how to handle this? The questions raced through his head, and he asked Frank for a pen. He needed to write these down because if the rest of the night went to plan, he wouldn't remember them in the morning.

CHAPTER SEVEN

Jawnie knocked on the partially open office door and hoped Rockfish hadn't fallen asleep. He waved her in and Jawnie pulled up a chair. In between sips of coffee and chews of greasy breakfast sandwiches, Rockfish recapped the previous evening. He let her know he had already decided to call for help before it came up in their conversation.

"I called and left Decker a message this morning. Hopefully, he's got some free time today. If I can get Mack's money back, great. But even if the police can't recover it, as long as they take these ass clowns down, well, that's all that really matters. We're officially stepping aside."

"Maybe we should touch base with Raffi and Lynn? Not have them attend the evening mass?"

Rockfish waved her off. "After last night, let's not give Lilith any reason to get suspicious. Let them go, keep their ears open and do nothing else. Until Decker tells us to stay clear. Never know what tidbit those two might overhear."

"Okay, I agree, but that doesn't solve my Claudia Coyne issues."

"Maybe I finally get off my ass and talk to Roan," Rockfish said. "Swing by his house this weekend. A place and time where he's comfortable. Even better if his wife's not around."

"But what if she is?"

"I explain to her that if the police are now involved, I cannot be. We don't work active cases."

They agreed on the path forward, and each retreated to the quiet of their individual offices. It wasn't until Jawnie dug up a little something based on Rockfish's retelling of his date that she knocked.

"Come in," Rockfish said.

Jawnie walked in and Rockfish had nestled his head atop his folded arms on the desk.

"Do you remember Regina, the girl I dated from the DMV?"

"The one with the Orioles season tickets?" he said and raised his head up off the table. "I liked her, but it didn't end so well, if I recall."

"Right, I took one for the team and reached out this morning about your race buddy last night."

"What it cost ya?"

"Dinner and a movie. Don't start with me. There's a Navigator Black Label registered to Elizabeth Richards."

"Can't be. This one was white," Rockfish said.

"No, the Black Label is the name of the top-of-the-line model. It comes in Pristine White. Would have been easier with a tag number, but we made do."

"Motherfuckers," Rockfish said. "That Lamb clown had us staked out and maybe watching her slide into Lana when we left didn't give him a warm and fuzzy feeling."

"Remember, Lynn said there were rumors those two were chummy. His driving and emotional reaction to last night probably confirms Brother Lamb is a moniker and not a blood relation. The man's caught feelings."

"All the more reason to bring in Decker. Before someone gets hurt." Rockfish said, and he gently lowered his head back down. *Hangovers at my age are too damn dangerous.*

* * * * * * * * * *

"Peace be with you and may the good Mother keep watch over us until the next time," Brother Lamb said, as the last of the parishioners exited and climbed the stairs up into the alley. He closed the door and walked back to the center of the room.

"I noticed your boyfriend didn't make it after the party last night."

Well, that was a world record for transition from Brother Lamb to green-eyed monster Earl. He had been moody with her throughout the day. She had tiptoed around him, knowing it would be only a matter of time before he would blow. She didn't expect it to be almost a full twenty-four hours later. *I need to get the hell out of here. Head home and run a calming bath. But business before pleasure. Someone needs to be put back in his place.*

"Earl, what the fuck is up your ass? Dinner, drinks, and I ended up not feeling well. It's not that hard to understand." Lilith stepped closer to Earl, hands on her hips. "He would have driven me home if you had stayed put like I told you. But no, you had to try and out private-dick the man. After your little stunt, it's going to take a lot of work to bring him back around to agreeing to make that initial deposit."

Earl stepped forward, their noses inches apart. "Yeah, Rockfish would have deposited *something* last night if I had stayed home."

"What are you, twelve? I didn't ask you to follow me last night. There was no need for a white knight to swoop in. The meeting was strictly business." Lilith poked Earl in the chest with her index finger. "Hell, I let you wine, dine and whatever else to the Dildo Queen for these luxurious meeting digs and her donations. I didn't ask one question. I understood it was for the good of the order."

"Goddamnit, leave Allison out of it—"

"Oh, I will. Now be a good little assistant and drive me the fuck home," Lilith said, and walked out the door. She made a point of slamming it behind her before he could catch up. At the top of the stairs, Lilith noticed a car remained in the parking lot. As she walked closer, she could see Rockfish's friend, what's-his-name, standing next to a car with the hood up.

"Kind sir, is everything okay? This isn't a safe neighborhood."

"Ah, stupid old thing won't start. No worries, AAA is on the way," Raffi said with a wave. "Great sermon tonight. I really enjoyed it."

"Are you sure? Brother Lamb is quite the mechanic. He could look at it. Isn't that right, Brother?" Lilith turned and beckoned Earl to join the conversation.

"Yeah, maybe if we could push it under that streetlight, I could get a better look."

"You know what? Let me try it one last time. I don't want to be a bother," Raffi said as he slid back into the driver's seat.

Lilith was thinking the man seemed nervous about something when the engine roared to life.

"What do you know? It started." Raffi jumped out and slammed the hood. "Thanks for the offer," he said, before driving away.

Lilith looked over at Earl, and he shrugged his shoulders.

****

Lynn looked down at her phone again: 10:23pm. Another minute had passed, and she still hadn't heard the horn. *Come on, Raffi, how hard is it to beep when everyone's gone? Did he run into problems?* She was already betraying Jawnie's trust. There was no need to let her mind go full negative.

A horn finally sounded, but it came from behind and not toward Allison's. She turned to see Raffi pulling up alongside her. The passenger window came down, and she looked at him strangely.

"Change of plans. Get in," he said. "You hungry?"

They ended up at Dot's Diner to deal with Raffi's nagging feeling that Sister Lilith or Brother Lamb might think something was up and decide to hang around for a little while or circle back.

"Who the hell knew that Brother Lamb was a certified Mr. Goodwrench?" Raffi said and wiped his mouth with the napkin. "The guy gave me an awful weird vibe. Like the slightest thing would have set him off. I want to make sure I do my thing when they are in bed and far away."

Lynn wasn't sure what to believe. The time killer became diner food and coffee to fuel the mission. "I don't know who this Goodwrench character is and how he fits in to all this," Lynn said.

"Before your time, and it doesn't matter. Let's finish up here and head over. I'll drop you off on Richwood Street and I'll park on Hempstead. We'll meet at the steps."

Lynn arrived in the alley before Raffi and took up a familiar spot next to her old dumpster. *Hey buddy, long time no see. I do? Thanks. I've been taking better care of myself, although I might throw it all away tonight, in a poor attempt at levelling up. You're right, I know. I can't afford to blow this and go back to my past life.* Lynn wiped the sweat from her hands across the front of her jeans. She shifted her weight to her left foot. A second later she leaned back to the right. The alley dance continued until beads of sweat formed across her forehead.

"Hate to break up the reunion, but I'm going in. No time to waste," Raffi said as he walked up behind her. He had a backpack slung over one shoulder and disappeared down the cement steps. *I guess burglary tools aren't as compact as they show on television.* Lynn stepped out from the side of the dumpster and tried to casually glance from one end of the alley to the other. It wasn't her first time as a lookout for nefarious means, but it sure as hell felt like it. *Another lifetime.*

Lynn's phone vibrated in her back-pocket and she looked each way before pulling it out. Raffi's text was one word: *in*

Lynn assumed he was through the door at the bottom of the stairs, and she kept the phone in her hand, anticipating another text when he made his way into the back room. *Yeah, he's pretty chill. No big thing for him. I guess this is an everyday occurrence in his other life.* She tightened her grip on the phone to make sure she didn't miss the next notification or let it slip through her moist hands.

The notification came a second later but as audio. A loud crash and what sounded like muffled curses filled the night.

Lynn bounded down the stairs without really thinking. She reached for the door to find it slightly ajar. She pushed it open and stared into the dark room.

"Careful, watch out for the chairs," Raffi said.

"Are you okay?" Lynn said and took a couple of steps inside and turned on her phone's flashlight.

Raffi stood in the middle of the room, surrounded by overturned folding chairs.

"Fine. Too full of myself after getting through the door so quickly. I made a beeline for the hallway but forgot about the chairs. Back to your post."

Lynn watched as Raffi used the light from her phone to navigate the remaining obstacles on the way to the hallway. At that point, she turned, walked back up the stairs and repositioned herself.

Fifteen minutes passed when a hand touched her shoulder and Lynn jumped. She bit down hard on her tongue and stifled a scream before turning around. Raffi stood there. He gave her a thumbs up and, as prearranged, they headed off in different directions. Neither worried about walking past businesses with outward facing security cameras. Other than a hat for him and a hoodie for her, neither hid their identities under the assumption criminals would never report a break in. Thus, the police would never be asked to pull and review the footage.

Three blocks later, Lynn continued to move her tongue around, feeling the left side swell, when she heard a familiar engine roll up. She slid back into the passenger seat and Raffi pulled out into traffic.

Neither spoke nor looked in any direction other than straight out the windshield. Raffi concentrated on appearing as nonchalant as possible for a man who picked up a woman on the side of the road at 1:00am. Also, that woman couldn't stop thinking. *Goddamn this active mind. I can't shake the feeling someone somehow watched us the entire time. I want to get back to my room and under the covers before someone drops the hammer on us.* Her tongue continued to annoy and would no longer lie comfortably in her mouth. *Nothing I hate worse than mouth pain. Mush mouth.*

After a handful of turns, Lynn recognized a few landmarks. *Speaking of the Super 8.* The neon sign appeared in front of them. Now she understood where the after-action discussion would take place.

Once inside the room, Raffi dropped his backpack at the foot of a chair and sat down. Lynn sat on the edge of the bed directly across and waited. Raffi grinned back and reached down into his backpack. He pulled out what at first glance resembled a shoebox, but with a closer look, Lynn could tell the box was metal.

"You know what this is?"

"It's a cash box. We used one at the roadside farm-stand I worked at as a kid."

"Yup, with a cheap lock, anyone could bust open with a screwdriver," Raffi said. "Based on the weight, it feels like it's got something in it worth checking out." He shook the box, but Lynn didn't hear any rattle.

Raffi moved the box to the nightstand and pulled the lock-pick kit from his front pocket. He knelt on the floor and stared straight into the keyhole.

"Wait," Lynn said. "Maybe we should wait to open it. Bring it into the office tomorrow?"

Raffi turned to his left and shook his head. "Not going to be embarrassed if it's filled with shit." He turned back to the cash box. "If it is, I'll toss it in the dumpster on my way out."

"Was that the only thing in the room?"

Raffi stood up and sat back down in the chair and let out an enormous sigh.

"Okay, let's get these twenty questions out of the way so I can open this damn thing in peace. No, it wasn't the only thing in there, but it was the only thing that stood out to me, shoved down in the bottom drawer of a desk. The only other thing in the room was a bunch of boxes stacked in the corner." Raffi stopped for a breath and rubbed his temples before continuing. "I didn't have a knife to open them nicely and didn't want to tear them open with my teeth. Bunch of chemicals from what I could tell from the labels. Don't worry, I took pictures."

What a condescending little man. But if I call him on it, it will only prolong a night that has gone on way too long as it is. "What did you make of the stuff?"

"Could be where they store the cleaning shit for the jack booths on the main level. I don't know. Like I said a second ago, I got pictures."

"Maybe Jawnie can look at them and figure out if its Allison's stuff or something more," Lynn said. "But to me, cash and chemicals behind a locked door? It doesn't pass the smell test."

"I told you I didn't open the boxes, only snapped some photos. Let me open this thing." Raffi got back on his knees and focused on the lock.

"Bingo."

Lynn had gotten up off the bed and stood over Raffi, wanting to catch the first glimpse of the contents. While it wasn't the gold light from *Pulp Fiction*, what she saw elicited the same response. Stacks of bank banded hundreds lined the box, and Raffi snapped it shut.

"Holy Shit, how much do you think is there?" Lynn said.

"Based on my expertise, enough to at least pay back Mack, his friend, and then some. We're gonna pull into the office tomorrow as heroes. Wrap this one up in a nice bow for Stevie."

I'm not sure that smile of his can get any wider or if his head can bob any faster. Lynn raised her hand and they high-fived.

"Of course, we'll have to attend a few more of these meetings," Raffi said. "If we bail now, we're gonna be the first people they suspect."

They spent the next ten minutes soaking it all in, what they thought was their first big win in the case. Each imagined the kudos and compliments that would rain down upon them the next morning. The only thing that soured the victory celebration was when Lynn noticed the time, and each realized it would be better if they had a couple of hours of sleep come morning.

"I'll be back at 7:30 to pick you up so we're in the parking lot waiting when Rockfish or Jawnie show up."

"But we're waiting until they are both there, right?" Lynn said.

"Of course."

Lynn shut the door behind Raffi and realized with the contents of the cash box dancing in her head and the dull throbbing in her mouth, it would be a long night with little actual sleep.

****

Lilith sat up in bed. The glow from Earl's phone lit the small bedroom in an eerily green light. The light shone on the three beer cans on his nightstand. *Were they all from tonight? A fight for another day.* The chime notification had woken her and gone off a second time as she had fallen back to sleep.

"Earl, the motion alert thing on your phone keeps going off," Lynn said as she tried to nudge him awake.

"All good. Don't worry," Earl said without opening his eyes. He rolled back over and pulled the comforter up over his head.

"It went off. I woke up. I fell back to sleep, and it woke me up again. Doesn't that mean anything to you?" She jostled him harder until he twisted his neck to look back at her.

"Cut the shit, Lilith. It's nothing. It goes off all the time and you always sleep through it. What I need to do, and not at this moment, is find a better spot for the jimmy-rigged camera. I half-assed a Ring doorbell into a basement drop ceiling, not exactly as the manufacturer intended. I think it needs to be attached to something more stable." Earl rolled over and faced Lilith before continuing. "Maybe closer to the bathroom end of the hallway. Right now, when the HVAC vent next to it blows, sometimes the panel rattles, causing the motion sensor to go off. Not to mention when a fat mother fucker goes into a booth and jacks it too hard. The floor above vibrates, so the shitty drop ceiling below wobbles a bit. Now go back to sleep. I'll show you the uneventful footage in the morning." Earl reached over to the nightstand and turned the phone over.

The eerily green light faded.

"But it went off twice."

"No law against how many fat people Allison allows in one booth at a time. Let it go, woman!"

"Okay, but you had the rest of the Towson cash in your room. Tell me you took it out of there like I said."

"I did," Earl said. "I put it in the safe deposit box. You calling me a liar?"

"What about the other stuff? I never understood why you wanted to keep it all. With the vaccine readily available for over a year now, it's not like we're finding marks to line up and donate for an opportunity to take Mother Elizabeth's Elixir for the Cure. The SunCoin angle is what we need to get them to focus on and admit we missed the boat with the fake Covid cure."

Earl quickly turned over in the bed and grabbed Lilith's left arm. She winced under the vice-like grip and knew that it would only get tighter until she conceded the point.

"Look, I moved the fucking money. Who cares about some boxes of chemicals? Ain't nobody gonna look twice at that shit. I'll move it when we have some-goddamn-where to put it. I planned on driving it out to the farm, but we lost the pre-approved mortgage and the shot on the Avila compound. Need I fucking remind you Coyne didn't come through with the cash he promised—"

"I know, I fucked up and didn't press the issue with him—"

"I don't care if he shits it out now. That opportunity came and went," Earl said, tightening his grip and giving it a twist. "I'm going to advise you to stop questioning every goddamn thing I do. I'm done here, not another word." He let her arm go, rolled over, and tugged on the blankets.

Lilith didn't scoot back down, but continued to sit upright. She ran her right hand over the sore spot on the other arm. Tears streamed down her cheeks. She pondered how much it would cost for Brother Lamb to go the way of Brother Zed. Her taste in men never seemed to improve, despite the hope of them outgrowing the bad boy phase that initially caused her attraction. Lilith was a dominant woman in all aspects of her life but one, and she regretted every minute of her choice.

A few minutes later, another word did come. Not from Lilith, but from the room next door.

"Great, you woke it," Earl said. "Go fucking deal with it."

Their argument had woken Mother Elizabeth, and Lilith pushed the comforter aside. She got out of bed to see what the loud groan was all about. *If only the old woman could talk, this could be so much easier.* Lilith could handle an angry Earl or a mute, decrepit old woman, but not both. Not for much longer.

Lilith walked into the townhome's other bedroom, and the smell of urine overwhelmed her. She turned on the overhead light and grabbed an adult diaper from the stack on the floor next to the bed.

Probably need to turn her body, too. Bed sores weren't a good look for the one who was going to lead the flock to heaven. Lilith wondered if the old broad would make it to the end of their last act, or would she have to wing it alone?

CHAPTER EIGHT

Rockfish stared at the olive-green rectangular metal box in the center of the table. Raffi had met him at the front door, bright and early this morning, grinning ear to ear. Rockfish hadn't bothered to ask about the contents. Oh, he could imagine what was inside and take a few guesses that would either land close or be dead on. But the more he knew for a fact, the closer he was to being named as a co-conspirator.

They sat around the conference table, Rockfish on one side and Raffi and Lynn across from him. He glared at the two who had taken what he said and ignored it. Raffi sat absolutely glowing and oblivious, while Lynn kept her eyes down, trying to avoid Rockfish's livid gaze. Jawnie had already given her a piece of her mind before retreating to her office to print off eight-by-tens of the pictures Raffi had taken the night before.

"They are going to come after me, even if they only remotely think it was you. You're tied to me. We rolled into this whole mess side by side."

Raffi lowered his head a little, closed his eyes, and nodded. "I know you said don't do it, but I was in and out. No cameras, no alarms. I knew there was something there worth the risk. They'll blame some homeless person from the alley before thinking of us. No offense."

Lynn didn't answer Raffi, but rolled her eyes and looked across at Rockfish.

"I had a feeling that someone watched us the entire time. I couldn't shake it. Still can't. I don't have a damn thing to back it up, though." She shuddered and Rockfish caught the shake in her shoulders.

Rockfish took his turn and shook his head. *This is all my fault. I gave him enough rope and he hung me, too.* He lowered his head into his hands and took a deep breath. *If Raffi was even close to his previous stealthy self, then this could be free money, with only a heavy guilt charge. If his ego got the best of him and he was careless, I can expect someone to break in here, or at the very least, my house in a matter of days.* He sighed again.

"So, how much is in there?" Rockfish said.

"I didn't count it," Raffi said.

"Bullshit."

"He didn't," Lynn said. "At least when I was around."

"Stevie, I didn't. I mean, I opened it and took a gander. Which resulted in a professional estimate, but no, I didn't physically take it out and count each bill."

Rockfish raised his eyebrows and tilted his head. Raffi got the point. *Christ, if he keeps rubbing his hands together, the smoke alarm above is going to go off.*

"Probably a little more than 50k, give or take."

Rockfish had kept the dilemma rattling around in the back of his head, at arm's length, until this point. Once Raffi threw a figure out there, it became more physical and less hypothetical. All the bad choices came to the forefront.

"Lynn, do me a favor. Can you go back and see what's taking Jawnie so long? I want her input on how this company moves forward with this. Printing off half a dozen pictures shouldn't take that friggin long."

Lynn walked back to Jawnie's office, and silence settled over the conference area. Rockfish couldn't help but think how much easier his decision would have been a year or two earlier. *Shit, would have been easier if I were still alone working out of the trailer. The box would be somewhere safe and I'd give it a couple of weeks to see if Lilith had a clue, or Brother Lamb the balls to come collect. Then I'd call Mack and Iggy over and play the part of savior. There would be no partner to worry about or to agree with on a way forward. More importantly, no real reputation that would have taken a hit if Raffi's little midnight raid came to light.*

Rockfish looked back at the box in the middle of the table. He got into this mess to recoup his dad's bogus investment and it appeared, he had done exactly that. Depending on how far Iggy was in the hole, their company could turn this total mess into a break-even learning experience. Well, everyone but the Coyne's. But Claudia had originally hired the team to determine where her husband dipped his wick, not to deprogram the man.

"Stevie, I—"

"Don't you say another goddamn word. I need to think."

Raffi slumped back in his chair and, for once in his recent employment, did as he was told.

Rockfish stared into his coffee mug and tried to look at what he should do with the cash from all sides. In his eyes there were only two options: keep the money and pray no one spotted Raffi, or follow up on his call to Decker and go to the police with everything he knew about this bunch of grifters. Get his father out of his funk and spend time looking over his shoulder, or turn over everything and hope the slow, squeaky wheels of justice caught up to these clowns and their fake cryptocurrency. *Speaking of squeaky, 50k would buy one heck of a lot of dog toys.* Zippy was growing on him.

In the end, Jawnie and the particular skill set she brought to the job decided for him.

"You need to call the cops. Decker, the front desk, someone in charge."

Rockfish looked up and immediately saw the concern in her face.

"After I started printing, I started doing my thing and fell down a pretty scary rabbit hole. If you take the contents of three of the boxes, sodium chlorite, lime juice and hydrochloric acid, you have the recipe for a fake and possibly deadly COVID-19 cure. Last year, the State Police in Florida busted a group out of Clearwater, the Eden Church of Holy Healing, for selling this same concoction as a cure, long before the CDC approved the vaccines."

"Do tell," Rockfish said and leaned in. Jawnie sat back down before continuing.

"What they were selling was a two-part kit. The first, a liquid being twenty-eight percent sodium chlorite, dissolved in distilled water. The second part was an activator agent. An acid, either citric, like lime juice, or actual hydrochloric acid. When the two parts of the kit are mixed, you've got chlorine dioxide. It's a powerful bleach."

"Was that around the time the former president told everyone to drink bleach?" Raffi said.

"Bingo. He was the Florida church's primary marketing tool. I'm going to guess Lilith was attempting to duplicate the same and whether it was lack of sales, or the vaccine push, they never got this part of their scam off the ground. Hence the sealed boxes. But with See You Next Tuesday, there's one additional element."

"The fourth box Raffi saw," Lynn said.

"Yes. A box of banned Chinese candy called All-Natural Super Colossal Happy Dunking Snack. Huge with kids a few years ago. It comes with one of those candy sticks you lick and dip into what's supposed to be some flavored sugary goodness. Kids eat that shit up and they did. And then a bunch got really sick around Halloween."

"That is scary," Rockfish said. "But unless these cunts, sorry, See You Next Tuesdays, were planning on using the powder as some new communion ritual, I don't see the problem. Who cares if they bought this candy from some sketchy webite and were going to feed it to some rubes? It's not like you said people died."

"But people were *going* to die. *Are* going to die." Jawnie said. "Have you ever heard of The Divinators of Hidden Extinction?"

"Let me guess, more Appalachia snake handlers?"

"Not even in the same ballpark. They're an offshoot of Santeria and per a VICE expose, aligned with the Chucho Cartel in Mexico. They somehow found out if you whip up a batch of your fake COVID-19 cure and pour in a couple packets of this tainted candy, you get Vypadium gas. It's deadly."

"Holy shit, I get it. A tandem on a motorcycle can take out a Cartel target or two, but when you need a shit ton of people whacked in one fell swoop, with little risk to your own..."

"The article said it nukes your lungs and you bleed out of every orifice. I couldn't think of a more painful way to go."

"This gas is Lilith's rip cord?" Lynn said. "She pulls it when the financial well runs dry?"

"I don't know. She might be full on Hale Bopp or Jonestown," Jawnie said. "Or maybe Brother Lamb is, but this whole thing has outgrown getting Mack and Iggy some payback."

"Well, that mission is already accomplished," Raffi said.

"Shut it!" Rockfish said. "Jawnie, gimme like three sets of those pictures. No more voicemails. I'm headed downtown to find Decker or whoever his boss is. Let's go. Raffi, you'll need to go home and don't fucking move until you hear from me. Jawnie, toss the cash box in the safe, I'm still marinating on that."

* * * * * * * * * *

Rockfish wasn't two sips into his coffee when the rain started dotting Lana's windshield. *Perfect start to the day.* Thursday morning, the day after he had spoken to Lieutenant Dan Decker, found Rockfish and Jawnie sipping coffee in the Wawa parking lot down the street and out of a direct line of sight to Allison's Adult Superstore. When asked if they could observe the execution of the search warrant, Decker had requested the two civilians remain at the staging area, until his men could make entry and give the all-clear. Rockfish agreed, because he didn't have a say in the matter, not to mention if it wasn't for his old friend, none of this would be happening.

The previous afternoon, they had locked the office door, dropped Lynn off at her motel and the partners traveled down to the Baltimore Police Department-Southern District building, off Cherry Hill Road. Decker had ushered them into his small office and shut the door.

As Rockfish recounted the sordid tale from the beginning, Decker seemed as disinterested in the fraud as the first time Rockfish had somewhat run the scam's details past him a few days prior. Even the additional details on the SunCoin scam and victim information, such as Roan Coyne and Allison of the SuperStore, failed to get a reaction or increase his interest in the case.

Jawnie and Rockfish had a rumbling in the pit of their stomachs as she stood to talk. Based on the conversation on the way over, Rockfish could tell the little white lies which held their circumstantial case together didn't thrill Jawnie. Since becoming a partner, Jawnie spent an extensive amount of time learning the law, as any good private investigator should, but how Raffi got the photos continued to concern her.

The agreed upon story was a CI working for the firm attended the Tuesday night See You Next Tuesday service and happened upon the boxes while looking for the bathroom. The door was unlocked, and as a concerned citizen, he took some pictures. All parties agreed no one would mention the cash box for the greater good, but to Jawnie, the photos were the proverbial fruit of the poisonous tree. But after much discussion and some pressure from Rockfish, Jawnie's ethics took one for the team and she sold it like a pro. Rockfish knew it wouldn't be the only time in her career a slight bending of the truth for the greater good would not sit well with her conscious. *She'll get over it. Sometimes a stiff drink is needed to help get over the hump.*

Decker only came around when she hit stride during her presentation. She spun an attention-grabbing tale comprising of the cellphone pictures of cardboard boxes, the labels and her research up to that point. The alleged replication of the Eden Church of Holy Healing's COVID-19 cure scam raised Decker's eyebrows. But the potential *what if*, involving the fake cure, the banned Chinese candy, the combination of the two, and the long history of its use by the Cartel's death squads, raised the stakes. However, Rockfish's keen eye and a knack for history sealed the deal with Decker and helped him gloss over some of the larger holes in their group's story.

This visit wasn't Rockfish's first time in Decker's office, and the small bookshelf behind the desk hadn't changed over the years. One book, the 9/11 Commission Report, had always stood out and Rockfish used it as his closing argument.

"You don't want to be the FBI bureaucrat back in Washington that ignored the Phoenix Memo." Rockfish pounded the desk as he drove his point home. "No one wants to be the guy who could have prevented 9/11 but chose not to. For whatever reason."

Decker excused himself and walked down the hall to his superior's office. A little over an hour later, he sent Rockfish and Jawnie home as he shopped for a magistrate that would sign off on a search warrant for Allison's basement and the date-rape condo.

Back at the convenience store, Rockfish reached behind the steering wheel and turned on Lana's intermittent wipers. The bottom third of his coffee was cold, and he contemplated going back inside for a second cup while they waited. At that moment, Jawnie brought up what he was thinking.

"Are you worried yesterday evening's goose egg at the townhouse will carry over into today?"

"Not a chance," Rockfish said. *I hope she can't make out the lack of confidence in my voice.* Decker had called last evening, letting Rockfish know he had secured two warrants for the following morning. They identified the location of Lilith's townhouse from the Navigator's registration, but with not a single piece of probable cause, the magistrate refused to include it in the warrant.

Rockfish had informed Decker that his people would check it out, and he had sent Jawnie and Lynn over to scope out the townhouse situation. It wasn't five minutes after her *we're here* text that she followed it up with another, detailing the piles of trash left behind, easily observed through the windows. Someone had packed the blinds and curtains along with all their belongings. Based on the scene, they had left in a hurry.

Rockfish's hope was down to the basement office and the date rape condo. But even that faded as the Baltimore PD executed the search warrant.

Lilith was obviously aware of the break-in. It explained the townhome being evacuated. How, though? Was Lynn right? Had someone observed them? But then why not stop it while in progress and confront them? A million more questions fired off in his head, but he was no closer to answering a single one. He only knew what might have tipped them off. That *something* remained in his office safe, at least until he could think of a better place and use for it.

ALL CLEAR, the text from Decker read and Rockfish dropped Lana into drive. He pulled into the now very familiar back parking lot of Allison's, alongside the vehicles of the entry team, and turned off the engine. The windshield was clear enough from the last wiper pass he could make out Decker standing in the alley, talking on his radio.

"The man does not look happy," Rockfish thought aloud and Jawnie agreed. He opened his car door and stepped out when he saw Decker walking and pointing towards him. Stay there, his lips read. *That's not good. But at least I'll be dry.* He got back into the car and timed rolling down his window with Decker's approach.

"Steve-O, can you kindly remind me why I listen to what you say? Or even better, why I continue to put my ass on the line, time and time again, for your harebrained ideas?" Decker's face was flush and there was a facial tick Rockfish hadn't noticed before.

This is gonna be bad.

"We've run fine tooth combs over this *park and pull* and that risque rendezvous condo based on the information YOU provided. You know what I got here? Shit. Take a guess at what Rodgers found over at the condo."

"Shit?"

"Absolute fucking dog shit," Decker replied. "Not one goddamn thing you told me yesterday panned out. And I've got a sneaking suspicion that somehow you're the reason."

"Dan, I didn't do a thing. Swear. I'm trying to do the right thing here."

"Oh, right. How about little miss innocent too in the passenger seat? I'm standing here in the goddamn rain, catching flak from my Captain who's catching the same shit from the Commander. Shits running downhill fast and guess who's next in line?"

"Me," Rockfish said, finally getting an answer right.

"Goddamn right. As soon as I walked into that place and my men said it was empty, I knew you fucked me on this goat rodeo." Decker gritted his teeth and shook his head. "I could feel it down in my taint. But then one of my men solved the mystery of my sore asshole. He found a hole in one of the drop ceiling tiles. Wires were sticking out of it as if someone had ripped something out. My tech guy said the cut-out is the perfect size for one of those motion doorbell things. Smile, you were on Candid Camera." Decker smacked Lana's roof hard with his hand. "Somewhere, Steve-O, someone watched you. I know it and, now, so do you. Did they watch you break the fuck in here, live, maybe streaming on YouTube, and then they hauled ass over here to empty it out when you were begging me to believe your cockamamie CI wrong door to the bathroom story? How the fuck long have we known each other? This one takes the cake." Decker threw his arms in the air, turned in disgust and walked back towards the alley.

In and out, easiest job I ever did. Rockfish punched Lana's steering wheel time and time again. Raffi's words hung on him like an obese albatross with a broken wing and one leg in a cast. *They watched him go in. Saw it was Raffi, knew he was a friend of mine, and with what was in those boxes, they knew we'd immediately go to the cops. They rush right over, move it out and are in the wind before anyone knows any different. Motherfuckers!*

"Dan, can I get a copy of your report for my case file?" Rockfish shouted across the parking lot. He knew the request would land horribly, but he had to at least ask.

Decker stopped dead in his tracks and turned around. He was back at the open window in a matter of seconds. The rain continued to run down his face and POLICE windbreaker.

"You know, Steve-O, telling you off felt pretty damn good and long overdue. I highly recommend it to any of your future clients." This time, Decker smacked Lana's roof a few times, but softer than before. "I'll do your hippy partner a favor and save the environment. Here's the official Baltimore Police party line on the execution of this warrant. We made entry at the bottom of the outdoor stairs. The room in question was unlocked, with only a small desk in the center and no chair. Nothing else. My officers matched up the walls to the background of the room in the pictures. The same, but no boxes and no chemicals. No imminent dirty bomb threat. Not one piece of the information reported by an unreliable source to the Baltimore Police Department on Wednesday, April 6th was corroborated." Decker formed a zero with his thumb and index finger. He held it in the open window while he took a breath and took a step back. "Oh wait, you got something right. The metal folding chairs? Strewn about. Exactly as you said. Congratulations. If this was the WWF, we'd have found the missing weapons of mass destruction. News flash, this is not the WWF." Spit flew from his mouth. A piece landed on the door.

"The WWE. The F went back to the World Wildlife Foundation years ago," Jawnie said, leaning across the center console. "There was a big lawsuit over the acronym."

Rockfish shot her *the look*, but it was obvious she had spent too much time around him and was equally unhappy with Decker's tone.

"Don't look at me that way, I grew up watching the stuff with my granddad."

Rockfish pulled his right hand off the gear shifter and held his fist low. Jawnie immediately bumped it out of Decker's sight. Or at least, Rockfish hoped.

"Enough of you two. I'm fucking out of here. Thanks for the hot tip, Steve-O. Do me a favor, lose my number. But seriously, stay the fuck away from whatever this is. Baltimore PD will figure it out and my men will handle it. If, and that's a big if, it actually turns into something. You cost us the element of surprise and now this shit, if it's what you say it is, it's out god knows where and we're losing valuable time trying to track it down. My superiors will want the Feds brought in ASAP, too. All the more reason for you to drop it." Decker paused and lowered his head through the open window. "It's now an active case, and remember, you don't work active cases." Decker turned and walked away.

Holy fuck, I haven't had my ass chewed like that in, I couldn't tell you how long. Hundred percent deserved. Raffi fucked me good, and I'm an idiot for trusting his word. Also, not questioning what Decker said, but the amount of venom behind it. Rockfish punched the steering wheel with his left hand. His knuckles still ached from three weeks ago.

Rockfish put up his window, but like before, Decker spun around. He held out his index finger and moved it up and down. Rockfish lowered his window again.

"Cheating husbands. That's your lane. Stay the fuck in it."

* * * * * * * * * *

Jawnie braked and swung her Cannondale Quick 3 into the strip mall's parking lot. Her decision to ride in this early Friday morning, for the first time in almost a month, represented a return to normalcy for her. Or so she desperately wanted to believe. She prayed her actions would help her mind willingly kowtow to this line of thought.

Rockfish had parked Lana in her designated front spot and it surprised Jawnie to see him in this early. After all, she was early, even for her, having skipped breakfast because of the knot in her stomach.

Three and a half weeks, I've ignored this. It's been a slow build since Mack's hospitalization, but this is really starting to get to me. Jawnie walked her bike up to the front door. *Long enough to cause concern and have a professional look at it. Would I appear weak? What if it was another Mack-like wrong self-diagnosis? Stress and anxiety are as common as breathing with me.* She always joked they came standard on the base Millennial model. But no matter how Rockfish claimed he understood the topic better, after watching what it did to his dad, she doubted he would award her the same newfound sympathy or make a trip to the pound for her. She swung the door open and pushed her bike inside.

"Oh, my God. Kathryn Bertine rides again," Rockfish said.

"How the hell do you know anything about Kathryn Bertine?" Jawnie said.

"You mean the former professional figure skater, triathlete, and road cyclist? Not to mention frequent guest on The Doug Stanhope Podcast."

"Who?" Jawnie said with a grin.

"Never mind."

After yesterday's disaster, the partners agreed to postpone the normal Thursday state of the partnership meeting until the following morning. Neither one felt like putting on a fake smile, providing updates on their other cases, and discussing upcoming business. The push in the meeting was the first continuance since they started almost nine months ago.

Jawnie parked her bike by the door and headed back towards her office. She noticed a rocks glass on the coffee table, filled with a familiarly scented brown liquor as she walked by the common area.

"A little early. Even for you, isn't it?" *Damn, I worry about him more than myself.*

"Only trying to lighten the mood a little. Nothing wrong with going into the day with an artificial outlook. Hey, don't keep walking. I'm sorry I ignored your message last night. Grab a seat, fill me in. It's probably our last hurrah with this case. Let's close it out with a whimper." Rockfish raised his glass and Jawnie took up her normal position on the couch.

"Speaking of closing it out, I'll have to meet with Claudia Coyne and tell her we're officially off the case."

"Have the receptionist set up the meeting," Rockfish said.

"Hardy, har. Regarding last night, there's not much more to report," Jawnie said. "Lynn showed up a few minutes before eight and found the door locked. She hung around, trying to act as if it was business as usual.

But it wasn't. No one had removed a bunch of the police tape, so that was still flapping in the wind. A handful of schlubs showed up and milled around for some time before they slowly peeled off. We stuck around for a few more, then left."

"Lynn received nothing from them, showing they moved the meeting?"

"Two things about that. One, if she had, we wouldn't have gone back to Allison's last night. And two, that was our last hurrah. You heard Decker. We're off the case. I will not risk everything we've built over the past year and the firm's license to keep chasing your great white whale."

"I get where you're coming from," Rockfish said and took another sip from his glass.

"I don't think you do." Jawnie leaned in closer. "I get that a lot of what Decker said probably still stings. I'm not sure if you two have had worse arguments in the past as friends or business associates, but it's time to move on. Time for us to move on."

"I'm here ready to work, aren't I?"

"The glass in your hand tells me different. You've got a safe full of twice stolen money. I'm not thrilled with having it, but if it can make your dad and Iggy whole again, then I can force myself to move past my ethical issues. From a corporate standpoint, the distribution of those now twice stolen funds is our last outstanding task. And if you think differently, I'm prepared to fight you every step of the way." Jawnie stood up and watched her partner for any kind of reaction. His head was down, and she added one last point. "I don't care what mental gymnastics you need to do in order to get over this, but I'd suggest you start."

"I'll get right on that, Chief."

"I also wanted to mention I dropped Lynn off at her motel last night and told her we'd be in touch," Jawnie said. She watched as he reached for his glass and then withdrew his hand. *Attaboy.*

"To be honest, I did the same with Raffi, but I chewed his ass and there was a shitload of venom behind what I said," Rockfish said. "I'm not sure how he took it, not sure I really care."

"I was nicer, but when I dropped off Lynn last night, she looked as bad as you do now. She blames all of this on herself for letting Raffi talk her into his scheme. If she hadn't agreed, he might not have done it solo."

"Yeah, but as pissed as I still am, if that were the case, then shit would still be unknown and no one would be the wiser if these clowns use it."

"I agree," Jawnie said. "At least Decker has something somewhat tangible to chase. I hope they're giving it the attention it needs, despite yesterday. Again, our last task in the matter. What do you want to do with that box?"

"Is it still in the safe?"

"Yup. For two entire days now. But I can double check." Jawnie tilted her head towards the bookshelf that doubled as a hidden door to a small closet.

"No. Leave it there. At some point. Perhaps when there's not a potential doomsday cult with some WMDs running around out there, that we can't do anything about, I'll open it."

"The sooner you open it and have a sit down with your dad and his friend, the better. My opinion, nothing more."

"Maybe, once the case is over," Rockfish said and this time reached for and secured the glass.

"GODDAMNIT!" Jawnie said and smacked the back of the leather couch. "Again. As. Of. Yesterday. We. Don't. Have. A. Case. Fuck, we didn't have a client for a good portion of this mess. And with the *hidden in the wall, again twice stolen money*, you can at least do right by a couple of old men taken by fraud. You think it's your choice, but newsflash, we're partners. The sooner we move on, the better it will be for the business, our relationship and your—"

Jawnie's phone chimed. She spun around and looked at the front door.

Claudia Coyne squeezed through the narrow doorway, dressed in the same green comforter as their previous poolside meeting, topped off with a hat that was better worn at a royal wedding or the Kentucky Derby. This time, Pookie walked alongside her, sans leash.

"Mr. Rockfish, Mr. Rockfish," she yelled as she graced the foyer.

He turned to Jawnie and mouthed, *if we only had a receptionist...*

Claudia didn't wait for a response to her shouts and continued past the vacant receptionist's desk and into the client meeting area. Pookie raced ahead and jumped up into Jawnie's arms. She gave him some loving and then placed him back down on the floor. The dog then circled Rockfish's legs and appeared to be on a sniffing mission.

"Zippy," he said and Jawnie nodded.

Jawnie walked over and steered Claudia to the conference table, while Rockfish palmed his glass and disposed of it before sitting down with them. Claudia was out of breath and had trouble catching what little she had, so Jawnie grabbed a cold bottle of water for the woman. Jawnie prepared herself for the hysterical vitriol that was only a moment or two away. She glanced over at Rockfish, who managed a small shrug of the shoulders.

Claudia struggled to put the water bottle back on the table and managed to eek out a short, "He's gone. YOU SAID YOU WOULD WATCH HIM!"

Jawnie glanced across to Rockfish, and he repeated his shrug. They watched Claudia reach with two hands, and bring the bottle to her lips. Jawnie made the command decision to steer the conversation when the water bottle returned to the table. In the end, she didn't have to, and over the course of an hour Claudia calmly weaved a tale of a phone call, a missing husband, and a completely empty joint checking account.

On Wednesday afternoon, Roan's secretary at *Wilhelm, Gicobe and Stottlemyer*, observed him taking a direct call in his office. To her, it was strange, as they normally route incoming calls through her. She watched through the glass as he appeared extremely animated and agitated. Roan hung up, placed a few items in his briefcase, and left. No one had seen him since, nor had he called his wife. Claudia had received a phone call the same afternoon, but from her accountant. He informed her that Roan had liquidated their primary checking account at a branch around the corner from his office.

"I want you to find my husband. I don't care about the cost, but I do expect you'll do better than when you were supposed to be watching him." Claudia signed an updated client agreement and left.

Rockfish waited for their newest client to make it through the front door and out to her waiting car before he let his emotions show. He turned to Jawnie with what she would argue was the world's largest shit-eating grin.

"We're back on the case! Hell, I'm back, baby!" He punched at the air.

"But Decker said... we need to at least pass along this information." Jawnie could see the disappointment in Rockfish's face before she even finished.

"I'm going to pull senior partner rank here. We've a paying client, a signed contract on the dotted line, with a missing spouse and possibly additional emptied bank accounts. It so happens we have some background on the situation. We're more familiar with Roan than another firm she could have approached. You or Decker can't hold that against me. Let's get out there and find that man," Rockfish said with a wink. "You can fill Decker in when I flush out a few more pertinent details in the disappearance of one Roan Coyne."

Rockfish stood up from the table and picked up his jacket from the back of the recliner.

"Where are you going and are you in any condition?" Jawnie said. She hoped the *senior partner* could make out the concern in her voice.

"I feel like a cup of coffee with a side of side boob."

"Um, if you remember, Roan didn't show up in any of the pictures on that SD card. And I know you do because I watched you review that digital evidence multiple times."

"Neither here nor there. I'll bet you either Shae La Guardia or Sunny West have an idea what or where these people are headed to. I'm betting they're still slinging shit at that place. And if they aren't, that's more circumstantial evidence for our case."

"Wait. I have a better idea," Jawnie said. To her, his idea wasn't half bad, but with worse execution.

"I'm listening." Rockfish sat back down and appeared to be all ears.

"Let me go get Lynn. Let it be her redemption moment. As far as we know, she wasn't on the video that outed Raffi. Even if she was, either of these two women wouldn't be knowledgeable. Especially if they're still slinging shit, as you so quaintly put it. They're the proverbial *Left Behind*. One of them would probably open up to her, over you. No offense."

"None taken," Rockfish said.

"Excellent. Let's meet back here in a couple of hours. I'll keep you updated." Jawnie stood up and grabbed her jacket. "If we get a strong lead on where they went and find Roan there, then we call Decker and he and the Feds can ride in on their white horses."

Rockfish's disgust was clear on his face, but he pursed his lips and nodded. "Deal."

CHAPTER NINE

By the time Jawnie and Lynn concluded their game of phone tag, it was late Friday afternoon. Lynn stood outside her room at the motel and waited. The sun would not begin its descent for another two hours, but it was a tad brisk outside. Her favorite UMBC hoodie kept her warm. Jawnie told Lynn to dress casually for what they hoped Sunny or Shae would think was a chance encounter.

Jawnie drove slowly and they went over the scenario. Lynn was about to play the little lost sheep, scared, wondering why the flock moved on without her. Her mission was to get any type of lead on where Lilith might have gone with Roan in tow. She wouldn't force the conversation and walking out of the coffee shop with nothing gained was an acceptable outcome. There would be other opportunities.

The Subaru pulled to the side of the road, three blocks away from Jamocha Jubblies, at 5:30pm. Jawnie kept the car running and Lynn reached to open the passenger door.

"Hold up. I know I ask you this every time, but you've got that First Alert with you?"

Lynn smiled and held up her bag. "You think I'd toss the first gift you ever gave me?" The small silver tchotchke-like item blended in well with the other doodads hanging from the strap. "I'll be fine. The actual bad people left town, remember?"

"I do, and they have our client's husband with them. Remember that. And here's a twenty for some coffee and a bite to eat. Think you'll need more?"

"I'll be fine," Lynn said and got out of the car. She shut the door and started down the sidewalk.

There was a part of Lynn that wanted to turn the tables on whoever she encountered at the coffee shop. Shae or Sunny. It didn't matter. One of them needed their head in a vise until they gave her what she needed. She wanted to kick off her redemption tour with a home run.

She walked up to Jamocha Jubblies' front steps and reached for the door. *You got this.* She walked in.

Despite almost being dinner time for a coffee place, Jamocha Jubblies was hopping. There was a man standing in front of her, and Lynn looked over his shoulder, spotting Shae. There was something about the woman that seemed different. She still wore the breasturant's chest emphasizing uniform, but then Lynn realized the difference. Shae had gone from blonde to brunette and from long extensions to a straight bob. *Looks a hell of a lot better on her than that peroxide. If I hadn't known better, I would've never recognized her.*

The woman who had taken Iggy and Mack for a good-sized portion of their respective saving accounts was playing hostess this early evening. *I've never seen a coffee shop that needed a hostess. Then again, who's ever seen a coffee shop with a clientele made up of mostly middle-aged men in jorts and New Balance sneakers?* Lynn patiently waited her turn.

"How many in your party?" Shae said without looking up from the podium.

"O-M-G, Shae, you work here?" Lynn said, hoping she didn't apply the airhead too thick, but her orders were to play the victim. Slowly gain their confidence and then become the inquisitor was the order she gave herself. "I stopped by for a caramel macchiato. One of those cravings, you know, I couldn't shake this afternoon."

"Hey, Lynn. It's great to see you. How are you doing? For the macchiato, you came to the right place. I've got a small table on the side, if that's okay with you?"

"Sure," Lynn said, and followed Shae towards the side of the cafe that overlooked the parking lot. Lynn sat down and shot her shot. "Shae, you wouldn't have a couple of minutes to help me out, would you? I don't know what happened and I'm kind of floating lost. I don't know what to do, where to turn." Lynn sniffled.

"I'm actually off the clock now and covering for a co-worker who's running late. I've got some time. Need to text my ride and let them know when to pick me up. And I'll put that macchiato order in for you."

Lynn watched as Shae placed her order and then wandered back to the podium and interacted with the next guest. Lynn pulled out a book from her bag and read. *I'm probably in the minority as to customers with their eyes not on the waitresses.* Her drink came soon, and she ordered a chocolate chip muffin, and hoped it hadn't been in the case since the morning rush.

Fifteen minutes later, Shae pulled out the other chair and sat down across from Lynn.

"The noise level is crazy in here," Lynn said, glimpsing at all the diners.

"It's gotten worse since we got the liquor license," Shae said. "Things were quieter and not so handsy before we began serving beer. So how are you holding up?"

Lynn looked across at Shae, then down into her drink. "You mean since my support group abandoned me? Too early to tell. My anxiety's skyrocketed and cravings to return to bad habits ring though my head on the hour." She looked up at Shae and could tell the woman didn't expect that flood of emotion, so Lynn rode the wave. "Everyone has left. No note, no goodbye, nothing. You're on your own, kid. Good luck." She kept her head down until she felt a touch on her left wrist and raised her head.

Shae had reached out and lightly held Lynn's wrist. "You're not alone. Not all of us were whisked away to prepare for the second coming."

"The second coming?" Lynn's eyes grew large.

"That's what Sunny told me. Lilith chose some and others will need to find their own way."

The old DIY plan. She took a second and assessed the situation. *Surely Shae has some inkling of what happened, but despite being one of the more dedicated members, they left her behind, too. It's like a bad Kirk Cameron movie.* Lynn reached out with her right hand and covered Shae's.

"How could they leave without you? You did so much for them and were so integral to the meetings. It doesn't seem fair."

"That's exactly what I said to Sunny when she told me she was leaving, and I'd have to cover the rent on my own. She drove off with that damn Diane Caruso."

"I don't remember meeting a Diane," Lynn said, recognizing the venom in Shae's last few words.

"That doesn't surprise me. She was the Church's webmaster and wasn't around much. Her and Sunny had this little competition. Who could be Earl's, I mean Brother Lamb's plaything of the week. I looked past it. We all have our faults, but now I'm going to be kicked out of my apartment and move back in with my mom." Shae dropped her head into her hands and Lynn could hear the sniffles. "Those bitches. That's a dirty word to use, but I feel so betrayed! I did so much for all of them!"

Lynn handed Shae a tissue from her bag. The waterworks came full force, and Lynn realized Shae had flipped the script. She had taken on the role of the lost sheep and ran with it. Lynn decided to only play the role of an attentive friend for a few more minutes before excusing herself and texting Jawnie to come pick her up. *I'm not holding her hair while she pukes later. I've got one and a half names to go on and it's not like she's leaving town anytime soon.*

Lynn soon said her goodbyes and left. She drove back with Jawnie to the office. Back on familiar territory, Lynn regurgitated the high points of the conversation she had with Shae and her own opinion of why Lilith left the woman behind.

"She's annoying. Me, me, me, what about me? That was the vibe I couldn't shake. I doubt she had much more substantive to say."

"What's this website again?" Rockfish said. He pulled a pad from his pocket and licked the tip of his pencil.

"*CUNtwo.net.* I'm familiar with it," Jawnie said.

"Funny, I don't remember you ever mentioning it," Rockfish said. "And another dumb acronym these chuckleheads couldn't workshop before putting in motion."

"It came up early in my initial research," Jawnie said with a wink. "Nothing spectacular. A cut and paste of the information on the pamphlets we already had. This Caruso chick didn't do a great job building the site. It always gave the impression that not a lot of effort was put into creation, let alone maintaining the site. I had forgotten about it."

"Now that Lynn's helped identify this Diane lady as a paramour of Brother Lamb, or Earl," Rockfish said. "I guess it depends if he's got his leather duster on or not. Either way, is the site worth looking back at?"

"Let me pull up the register information. Most hosting services offer to anonymize that information for their customers, but since this site looks like a middle-schooler built it, it's worth a try. Gimme a sec." Jawnie picked up her phone and pulled up the site's WHOIS result. "Yup. Here it is. Diane Caruso, 9833 Whiskey Run, Laurel. My bad," Jawnie said and raised her hand.

"That's a lead worth checking out. Maybe Sunny and Diane are still holed up there, not wanting the others to know pillow time didn't reserve them a seat on the redemption express like they thought it would."

Lynn nodded in agreement. "I'd be willing to ride out there with either of you."

"Thanks, Lynn," Jawnie said. "I can head out that way in the morning. The more the merrier."

"Okay, that leaves Brother Earl, or whatever the fuck his name is," Rockfish said. "I mean Lamb isn't his government name? I'm shocked. Tells you a lot about the state of the mega-church wannabe grift these days. I'll run with that angle and see what pans out."

"I've got a question. Not sure how important or if it's worth spending any time on," Lynn said. She glanced at the other two and hoped she wasn't making a fool of herself, but it was something that bugged her, and maybe important.

"Shoot, kid," Rockfish said.

"Well, Steve, you were at those meetings with me. There were always two circles of chairs. We were in the outer ring and the sermons went on about working hard and moving to the inner."

"I remember."

"Well, since we learned Lilith and Earl got out of Dodge, it appears there were three groups. The first got the call and were whisked away. Your client's husband is the example here. Then there are the Shae's of the world. They got the call, knew not to show Thursday night, but still were left behind under some illusion of being picked up in a second wave. Last, there are me and a handful of others that didn't get a call or a future promise. Does this mean anything, or am I spinning my mental wheels here?"

"I'll take this one," Jawnie said. "The last group gave the church the illusion of legitimacy. Sure, some of those that sat next to you could have been groomed to become future Shea's or Sunny's, but for the large majority, this group was for show. From the outside, it all looked authentic. Come on in, we're open to all, kind of vibe."

"What separates the first group from the second?" Lynn said.

"Access to sizable sums of money and, to a lesser extent, those which denied Earl an opportunity to lay those healing hands," Rockfish added. "Jim Baker will always need his Jessica Hahn. Wouldn't expect it any other way."

* * * * * * * * * *

Lilith stared through the window at Earl. The single lightbulb illuminated the house's small back porch and attracted every mosquito, gnat, and moth in the hollow. Their second day back in Kilingess, the small Appalachian town built years ago on the sermons of Alphie and Elizabeth came to a close the same as the previous evening. Porch beers for him, two unique plans of action with neither moving forward, and the divide between the two strained partners and sometimes still lovers, expanding exponentially.

Lilith reached to open the back door and that old saying, she couldn't place who said it, rang in her head. *Insanity is doing the same thing over and over and expecting a different result. I know how to fix this and how to not only get us out of this place but out of the country and reunited with the money we've secured. He needs to listen.* She stood there staring through the screen, out over the small backyard pond and into the woods. Crickets and frogs made the only noises until the cheap, flimsy screen door slammed shut.

"I know you don't want to hear this, Earl, but I feel I need to explain to you exactly how dire our situation is and how, if you'd listen, I can rectify this hiccup." Lilith chose her words carefully as to not light the fuse again. She leaned against the door frame and waved at the bugs with her right hand. "I'm not sure how long we can hide out here. Short term, yes, this is a good place. We've bought protection and along with those that remember Mother Elizabeth or heard the stories, we can essentially hide in plain sight in Kilingess. No one will rat us out, but you and I know it won't last. Someone always rats. The sooner you and I are on the move, the better."

Lilith paused, not for dramatic effect, but because she swallowed a gnat. She coughed and looked down, half expecting Earl to have met her gaze, asking with his eyes if she was alright. It didn't happen. *I didn't think it would, but a girl could hope, right?* What Earl did was toss his empty over the railing and into the yard. He reached down into the small cooler at his feet and grabbed another Milwaukee's Best Light.

"That's why, if you listen, I can clean this up and get us on the path to that beach or island," Lilith continued. "Your choice at this point. I have the contacts that would effortlessly get us across the border, safely into Canada. They're waiting for my word. Our next stop would be to catch up with those to forge our documents and then we take our money to a paradise where no one can touch us." Lynn frantically waved at the bugs floating around her head.

"Let me tell you how this is going to go," Earl said. He didn't turn or look up at Lilith, but stared out at the overgrown backyard and the handful of broken-down lawnmowers that littered the landscape. He took another large swill from his can.

What the hell is he focused on out there? Lilith thought. She didn't have time to contemplate an answer as Earl's left hand shot out and grabbed her wrist. His grip was tight and unforgiving, and for reasons she never understood, he gave it a little twist. Instinctively, she tried to pull away, but it only made him squeeze harder. After a second, she relented, but he did not. She knew better than to beg, and her mind immediately went to her thoughts of a week ago. *Why didn't I go? He never would find me or where I'd move the money.*

Earl shifted in his chair and turned to face Lilith. His brow furrowed, his eyes bloodshot. With his free hand, he drained, then crushed the can. It flew over the railing to settle in next to the others. He reached down into the cooler for another.

"I will not leave easy money on the table. You said it yourself, we're safe here."

Temporarily. Nothing lasts forever.

"There's a reason we brought these whales with us. It would have been easy to drop the old bitch in a ditch on the side of some road, hit the gas and not stop until your underlings got us across the border. But I trained these folks to follow you around like lost puppies, hoping for a passing glance or touch from the vegetable. I brought them along for the ride because they have access to cash. The money is still flowing from those two. I don't know how many times I have to tell you, but if there's some meat on the bone, I ain't tossing that chicken wing in the garbage."

Lilith tugged instinctively at her left arm to flick away the moth in front of her, and Earl, in return, tightened and twisted. She used her free hand to swat it away.

"I said that we could—"

"I know what you said. We came here to chill out. We're chillin'. Hidin' in plain sight. Lettin' the trail grow cold. It's all happening like you said. That doesn't mean I agree with or plan on obediently following along for too much longer. Coyne and the dildo queen? They're fucking giddy that Elizabeth has signaled the beginning of the end. The second coming is a comin'." Earl slapped his thigh with the beer can and let out a laugh. Beer soaked into his jeans. "Those two can't get to an ATM fast enough to withdraw as much as they can or wire it wherever I tell 'em. Sorry about that, Brother Roan and Sister Allison. We did not know she was going to signal judgement day so soon. Her previous signs and visions all pointed to Christmas. But we should feel lucky, right? Who likes to sit around and wait? Praise the Lord."

Lilith clenched her teeth, said nothing, and hoped her face said even less.

"Neither one of them has an original thought in their heads. They gonna be desperate for someone to give them, hell, tell them what direction to go in. They want to fork out as much as they can in order to pander to her. And I, for one, plan on taking advantage of this until my pockets can't hold no more cash. Then and only then will we run for the border."

Earl stopped for a second, spit over the porch railing, and put down his beer. His right hand ran though his now shoulder length hair. All while never relinquishing the grip on Lilith's wrist. She hoped he was done, so she could soon retreat inside.

"You know, unless you want to be a martyr. History will remember you and all that stupid shit when it's time to *cross over*," Earl made singular air quotes with his free hand, "you can go with the rest of them. One more body to a pile of people that can't testify ain't gonna matter. Either way, I'll be long gone and sipping one of those umbrella drinks and ordering another. You can choose to be on the towel next to me or not."

"Don't question the way I feel, Earl. You know the answer." The answer escaped Lilith's lips before her brain could stop it.

"The stupid fucking shit that comes out of your damn mouth. I'm stuck here in bumfuckville, because of you!" Earl's voice grew louder and more strained. His fingernails dug further into her skin. "YOU wanted to chase Rockfish and his Hollywood money. His friend ripped us the fuck off. YOU saw the footage. That choice of YOURS has had a ton of terrible consequences, ending with us holed up here."

Earl released her wrist and stood up. Lilith held it with her right hand and tried to pray the pain away. She was afraid to move until she knew what he was doing, so she stood against the door frame, bugs swirling around her face.

"Now if you'll excuse me, there are a couple of female followers that need to confess to some sins happening later tonight. Pretty deviant ones, at that." He stepped off the porch and walked over to the old Chevy pickup in the driveway. The engine turned over on the second try and the rear tires kicked up dirt and dust as he pulled away.

Lilith waited until the taillights vanished over the hillside. She looked down at the ragged folding lawn chair. She sat down and grabbed one of the remaining beers for herself.

How the mighty have fallen. Or you can take the girl out of the hollow, but... Seriously, pick one. Either statement fit how she felt. Lilith took a long swig of the lukewarm beer and tried to clear her mind.

How the fuck am I the bad guy for wanting to cut our losses and run? There is more than enough money set aside overseas, and I know when it's time to cash in. For Christ's sake, I'm the one that taught him. And fuck that guy. We both need to be present to withdraw. Unless he knew the one workaround, I made a point of never ever telling him.

She sighed and took another sip. Shit had been sliding downhill between the two of them for some time now, but it only snowballed the past two weeks. When he questioned her fascination with Rockfish and brain washing him and his Hollywood friends, she threw the fake COVID-19 cure back in his face. Earl had sworn up and down that they could find the right set of rubes to cash this scheme out on. But by the time he got around to securing everything needed, the idea had run its course and the media was alerting the public to the scam.

When Earl came to her beaming that he had found a conduit for the banned Chinese candy—a vendor off the dark web—he swore their endgame had gotten that much better. He claimed when the authorities eventually found the bodies, they would automatically recognize the vypadium gas, the calling card of Cartel hitmen. The police would look at the local Mexican population and further south for affiliations in this dastardly crime. All while, the two of them slipped silently across the northern border to begin their journey.

And all I could ever dwell on was how long until the FBI or DEA broke down our door. Leave it to Earl to get caught up in some sort of international dark web take-down. That was the one time Lilith was happy to be wrong.

But soon after, the thought of slipping away in the middle of the night, while he diddled the recruit of the week, took traction. All it would take afterwards was an anonymous tip to bring the heat down on old Earl. Lilith laughed aloud. She reserved the right to make that call, when she wanted, on her terms. If anyone would sip an umbrella drink solo, it would be her. *Yet, here I sit. Why? Yeah, why?*

Lilith had no answers.

****

Jawnie swung the Subaru into the Super 8 and picked up Lynn a little after 10am, Saturday morning. It would be a half an hour ride to Laurel. Jawnie let her partner know they had an 11 o'clock appointment.

"Once you said that Diane Caruso skipped town, I conducted a couple of open-source database checks and determined the owner's name and his contact information. The landlord is Andrew Baker. I cold-called and played dumb, with a dash of desperation for a place to live."

"Nice," Lynn said.

"I didn't let the man get a word in. I said I understood he had a tenant abruptly leave, and I'd be interested in looking at the property. I didn't care it hadn't been professionally cleaned yet, and still contained some stuff the previous owner left behind. All the better for us, but I didn't tell him that. I reiterated my friend and I really wanted to see the space. He jumped at the opportunity."

Jawnie hit the Starbucks drive-thru before heading to Laurel and then a couple of miles down I-295 when she noticed Lynn occasionally turning and looking into the backseat.

"If there's someone hiding back there, touch the tip of your nose," Jawnie said. "We've got our belts on, I'll slam on the brakes."

"No, no, nothing like that. What's the plastic suitcase-type thing? It's Laurel, not like we've got to find a motel halfway and spend the night."

"It's called a Pelican Case. Easiest description is a toolbox for computers. Back when Rockfish and I met, I was running a computer repair shop. Successfully, I might add. By the end of his case, I took my talents to Linthicum Heights and joined his team. As a P.I., I can use my previous skills to enhance a lot of what the firm now does."

"Okay, you'll use those tools to examine any electronic devices we find?"

"I would only need to make a copy, with the landlord's permission. Diane Caruso left with little notice. I'm hoping she was a piss-poor packer and might have forgotten or left behind something that will benefit our investigation. I'm equally hopeful the police haven't identified Diane and scoured the place. The landlord mentioned nothing about police tape, that's a good sign. Keep your fingers crossed."

"What am I looking for as we go through this place?" Lynn said.

"Webmasters work on a computer. I'll take an old laptop, a USB-drive, or even some CDs or DVDs. Anything I can make a forensic image of onsite. We leave the original where we found it and no one is the wiser. Once back at the office, I load the copy into a program called Forensic Toolkit and do my analysis."

"And solve the case."

"I'd settle for finding any piece of information which points us in the right direction."

9833 Whiskey Run was tucked in the back of a development full of townhouses. They ran six to a row and each set of homes seemed to be laid out with little to no reason or forethought. The 1980s brick-face needed a solid power washing. Jawnie followed the road as it wound around and slowly snaked back towards the last group of houses. She parked at the opposite end of 9833's line of homes.

"What about the Pelican?" Lynn said as the women exited the car.

"Do you want to lug it up there? Wait to see if we find anything first."

Lynn nodded in agreement, and they walked towards the man standing atop the stoop of 9833.

Andrew Baker smiled and gave a wave as the women approached. Jawnie wasn't sure if he was the landlord at first or the super. He dressed in beige pants with a matching shirt. An oval patch across the breast pocket spelled out: Andy. Neither article of clothing looked to have been recently washed. Jawnie spotted the man's extreme comb over but bit her tongue. *Best not to judge.*

"Hi, Andy. I'm Jawnie and this is my friend Lynn."

"Good morning, ladies. My friends call me Hack," he said, giving another small wave.

"But your shirt says Andy?" Lynn said.

"It's a business shirt. I'm on the clock and I didn't think a nickname would look professional. You ladies hoping to share the place? Three bedrooms, you could each have an office to work out of. I know working from home is still all the rage. Plenty of natural light through those windows." The man's smile, if possible, got wider with each word.

Jawnie wondered if Lynn had caught Hack's innuendo.

"Fucking creeper," Lynn said under her breath and Jawnie got her answer. *We are now free to judge.*

Hack led the women up to the front door before stopping. "Ladies, only two rules once we go inside. I can open her up, but I'm going to have to stick with you."

Jawnie heard Lynn gag a little and didn't blame her.

"Ms. Caruso left enough shit in there that I can't legally toss it in the dumpster, on account of if she comes back. Thirty days from now is another story. And obviously touch nothing. Technically, this is all her property. For the time being."

Jawnie gave Hack a thumbs up and he unlocked the door.

"Oh wait, let me save you some time. The rent is $1599 a month and includes internet and electric. Water, sewer and gas are your responsibility. I wanted to throw that out there in case it's a deal breaker for you."

"For the love of God, Hack, can we just get inside?" Lynn said. Jawnie elbowed Lynn in the ribs.

"After you, ladies. I'll follow along," Hack said and threw open the front door.

The house was larger than it appeared from the outside. There were stairs on the right leading to the three bedrooms. The tiny foyer opened into the living room, which wrapped around to the right and led to a small dining area and kitchen.

Jawnie noticed four nylon bags, the kind you pack your own groceries in, were filled and left next to the front door. A loveseat sat against the far wall, with a coffee table. She grew sour with the escorted tour. They'd have to rely on finding something out in the open, obvious to all. *This will not end well for us. Maybe I can get Lynn to move Creepy McCreeperson into the kitchen and I can quickly rummage through these bags?*

The tour followed the carpet around to the kitchen, which was as underwhelming as the previous rooms. Before Jawnie could come up with an excuse to slip back into the living room, Lynn piped up.

"What about those doors?" She said, pointing towards two closed doors at the end of the narrow kitchen.

"You've got a full bath on the left, with standup shower, and the right leads to the partially finished basement. The washer and dryer are in the unfinished part."

Lynn moved ahead, opened the basement door, and headed down the stairs as if she was on a scavenger hunt. "Can we go down here? Hey, hun, maybe it could be our sex dungeon," she shouted back over her shoulder and kept descending.

Jawnie bit her lip and followed Hack. *So much for rummaging through those bags.*

The finished half of the space was empty, but when Jawnie opened the door to the laundry room, a low hanging ethernet cord brushed against the top of her head. The blue cable dropped through the ceiling on her right and ran the length of the basement, tacked to a two by six beam, every so often. Jawnie followed the cable until it disappeared between two slats of a louvered closet door. She turned on her phone's flashlight and strained her neck to look inside. Blinking lights and the tell-tale whirl of a computer fan triggered two of her senses.

BINGO. Jawnie gave a low-key fist pump. She pulled on the small circular doorknob. It didn't budge.

"Hey Hack, what's behind this door? I'm not renting space I can't get into."

Hack and Lynn followed the voice and walked into the unfinished section of the basement.

"That's Ms. Caruso's computer. She asked me to leave it be, for the time being. I'm willing to knock fifty off the rent since you can't use that small closet space. That's still a damn good deal." Hack smiled and raised his eyebrows.

"Tell you what, Hack," Jawnie said. "I'm going to need you to open that door." She reached into her pocket, pulled out her private investigator's badge and license, and flashed it to reinforce her official status before quickly pocketing the credentials. She had seen Rockfish use the trick successfully on multiple occasions and gambled that Hack didn't have the best attention to detail.

"We're investigating a missing child's case and my training tells me there's evidence on that computer."

"Whoa!" Hack said and held up his hands. "I don't know nothing about no missing kid. What are you talking about?"

"That's clearly on a need-to-know basis," Jawnie said. "And you know the rest."

"But Ms. Caruso handed me three hundred dollars and her Snapchat username as she went out the door. Asked me to keep that there, powered on and connected. She said if it goes down, she'd come back looking for her money. But if I do good, she'd send more. Nobody's missing that I know of. You gotta believe me."

Cash or snapshot pictures? Webmaster's has to keep the website up. What other data would she need 24/7 access to?

"I'll be honest with you, Hack. You seem like a reasonable guy. A smart guy. I'm not looking to take the computer. It can stay right where it's at and the same goes for those three hundred dollars she gave you. But I need you to do the right thing here. Give me a couple of hours to make a copy of the hard drive. I'll compensate you well for your time."

Jawnie paused to determine if Hack was keeping up with the conversation and the severity of the situation she implied. He didn't say a word, and his eyes were as bloodshot as when they arrived. *Act like you belong here and have the authority. He'll roll over.*

"Your decision should also factor in this person's family. They deserve answers. I need you to put yourself in their shoes. You wouldn't want to go through the rest of your life wondering what happened to your loved one. I will not take the computer and jeopardize your agreement with Ms. Caruso. It's not even going to be turned off. All I'm going to do is live capture the hard drive. Make a copy. Depending on its size, it could take a couple of hours. And maybe we'll find little Jacob alive."

Hack crossed his arms and turned to his left. There was a minute of awkward silence before he spoke. "Hundred bucks an hour."

Jawnie took a mental step back and looked at Lynn. She thought the child endangerment would have cracked him. Instead, he doubled down. *Those must be some snaps Diane's sending. I don't have cash on me. Lynn would have to drive back to the office and get it from Rockfish.*

Jawnie countered Hack, but not in the way he or her partner expected.

"Two hundred and we were never here. The connection doesn't go down, you keep your original three and the titty pics keep flowing."

They shook on it, and Lynn handed Jawnie a small bottle of hand sanitizer. She squeezed a few drops into her palm and handed the bottle back.

"Lynn, can you do me a favor and grab the Pelican Case? Hack and I are going to stay here and make sure nothing nefarious happens to this box."

* * * * * * * * * *

Tuesday morning found a familiar threesome seated around the conference table.

"Whoa, the prodigal son returns," Jawnie said, as she walked in and sat down. "I for one did not see that coming."

The ice breaker drew a chuckle from Raffi and Lynn.

Rockfish interlaced his fingers on the table in front of him and leaned forward. "Look, I could say we all make mistakes, but I won't blow smoke up anyone's ass. I'm currently persona non grata in the Southern District. No one would argue with that. Decker's letting every call go straight to voicemail, on the slim chance that it could be me. Same goes for all of his men and any other contacts I've developed working out of that precinct."

Rockfish paused as Jawnie and Lynn nodded their heads in agreement. *Fucking Doublemint Twins. It's too early for this shit. Bad enough I had to mea culpa with Raffi. Now I've got to explain to these two my reasoning for letting him back in the fold.*

"I can only get so far with Jawnie's public databases if my only search term is Earl. It would take me days to get through all the *My Name is Earl* YouTube clips." Rockfish paused for the laughs that never came. "Odds are the cops might have some additional qualifiers that would enhance my process, but all I get from them are voicemail greetings. Enter Raffi. He's got the contacts. While not directly working for Decker, they answer his calls. Why? He's provided that police department with a ton of actionable intelligence over the years. There's a reason he's not behind bars and hasn't been for a very long time. Long story short, I called, and he answered. Not to mention, he came through in the clutch."

"Yeah, I called in a handful of favors I had been saving for a rainy day, which I sure as hell pray doesn't come soon," Raffi said, and pulled a small pocket-sized spiral notebook from his front pocket. He flipped through a half a dozen pages before stopping.

"Earl Porbeagle, aka Brother Lamb, is a local boy. Well, somewhat. He's from Avila, Maryland. A small podunk town an hour south of the city. Farms, trailers, but a new winery has opened up recently, so it might be on the upswing." Raffi closed his notepad and returned it to his pocket.

"With a last name, I created a small biography of this clown, something the cops probably did days ago," Rockfish said. "Porbeagle, born 10/27/87, grew up in Avila and graduated South River High in 2005. Arrested for various petty crimes as a teen, and soon after graduation, washed-out as a prospect with the Killer Termites outlaw motorcycle gang. Did a short stint upstate for armed robbery back in 2014 and paroled in 2017. His rap sheet ends with an aggravated assault and DUI in 2019. After that, I'd guess he ran into Lilith and saw the light."

"Shocked he wasn't a saint before they hooked up," Lynn said.

"Definitely the meathead we all pinned him for," Jawnie said. "Raffi, did your handlers over at the PD give you any insight into Decker's investigation?"

"My guy said Decker reached out to his liaison over at the FBI's Baltimore Field Office, but the JTTF took a hard pass."

"JTTF?"

"Joint Terrorism Task Force," Rockfish said. "Composed of State, Local and Federal officers, formed after 9/11."

"Yeah, what he said," Raffi said. "The Maryland State Trooper on the JTTF told Decker to come back when he's found some hard evidence. Not hunches based on the word of a two-bit private detective and his street hustler informant."

"Raffi didn't mind the slight, but this firm's worth well over two bits," Rockfish said. He dropped his head and ran his fingers through his hair. "It pissed me off, but knowing they're barking up the wrong tree and ignoring the Porbeagle angle made me shake my head in disgust. Sorry to keep interrupting. Go on, Raffi."

"My guy says Decker's not even looking at the white-collar angle. They're reviewing all Districts' drug cases that have Cartel or even the weakest ties to Mexico. They're all in on the WMD aspect. He sees the shiny promotion light that comes with marketing this case as international terrorism. Any ongoing investigations with even the slightest mention of that one group..."

"The Divinators of Hidden Extinction," Jawnie said.

"Yeah, those guys," Raffi said. "Those cases are getting extra scrutiny and the cops are pulling guys off the street to sweat them for any information. So much so, people's lawns are overgrown."

"That's enough of the schtick, Raffi," Rockfish said. "They're totally falling for a red herring. Earl and Lilith are one hundred and eighty degrees off in another direction. Probably laughing their asses off."

"You say a hundred and eighty degrees. I say four hundred and thirty miles," Jawnie said. "Kilingess, West Virginia to be exact."

Rockfish watched as Jawnie reached for the remote to bring the screen down and Lynn jumped up and lowered the lights. *Jawnie still has a thing for the dramatic.* Rockfish leaned back in his chair. *In my day, I'd have one piece of graph paper and everyone passed it around.*

"I've spent the last two days going through that hard drive. Without a doubt, I can say Diane Caruso used it for three things: an active web server, an active but not recently used exchange server, and her personal web surfing. Her personal use was for Yahoo email, accessed through a browser, Amazon, and The Hub, as the kids refer to it today."

Jawnie clicked the remote for her first slide, and Rockfish grinned. The screen filled with a screen capture of an email from Diane Caruso to the Internal Revenue Service.

"The biggest takeaway is that she and Sunny took off for Kilingess. You can see from this email exchange, four days ago, she emailed to confirm a change of address with the IRS. They will mail her next stimulus check to 629 State Road 611, Kilingess WV."

"It makes sense since Sunny's with her," Rockfish said. "I said before, Sunny previously posted Instagram pictures from that town before she arrived in Baltimore."

"And the next email received was also the last web-based email viewed on this box. It came in the following morning, coincidently, hours before Diane packed her shit and left." Jawnie clicked the next slide.

To: diane.caruso@yahoo.com
From: onyourknees@hotmail.com
Subject: here now safe secure get moving if you ain't already

"On Your Knees. That sounds like the ego of Porbeagle. The balls on this guy," Rockfish said, slamming his hand down on the table.

"When you are on the run, run to somewhere you're familiar with. And where the general population is stupid enough to hide and protect you, not to mention believe in your doomsday voodoo. I looked at the full headers on that email and someone sent it from Kilingess."

"They're all there," Lynn said.

"Now I didn't make a slide for this, but that computer hosts the official See You Next Tuesday website. I checked and found the only site it hosts is *CUNtwo.net*. I'm not sure why they want the site up and running, or what illusion that is supposed to project? But there is a new post from Friday when I pulled it up on my phone. The post is in Spanish and a regurgitation of what's already there, but to me, it's more smoke and mirrors on their part."

"More of the same old, to push the focus on the Cartel angle and to keep the cops chasing their own tails," Rockfish said.

"Couldn't agree more," Jawnie added. "Of course, that's assuming Decker's even come across the website." She clicked her slide show one more time before continuing. "They also used the computer as a mail server for the domain *CUNtwo.net*. Multiple users had logins for this mail server and would login in to read new messages and send email via remote access. The address *Lilith@CUNtwo.net* could be used on her phone or personal computer to send or receive mail using the mail server on Diane's box. Like I said, someone created multiple accounts on this server, but the only two used were Lilith's and one for *Mother.Elizabeth@CUNtwo.net.*"

Rockfish stood up and walked over to the screen. The example Jawnie picked for today's lesson showed detailed instructions from the Mother Elizabeth account to a manager at Bank Al Habib Limited regarding an incoming USD $125,000 wire transfer. *Christ. They've moved it all overseas to some Al-Qaeda, Hezbollah, or Taliban bank. Maybe Decker is attacking this from the right angle, but the wrong goddamn side of the globe!*

"Odds that the old woman actually sent this?" Rockfish said.

"Slim and none. I'm betting if we delved into the thousands of emails on that server, we'd find it was Earl and Lilith behind the keyboard on all the banking related emails. There are so many, someone could spend some serious time on the analysis. And someone should. There's a goldmine of evidence for any kind of historical conspiracy case, but I only had time to do keyword searches."

Rockfish paced in front of the screen. He could feel his blood pressure rising.

"Steve, sit down. You're reading too much into this. I can tell by your facial expression and you've clinched your fists. This is straight up money laundering, nothing more. Bank Al Habib Limited is well known for washing dirty money and making it available to their clients whenever and wherever they need it."

"That may be so," Rockfish said. "And I appreciate you looking out for my heart's health. But Claudia called me yesterday, more pissed than ever. Roan moved another forty-five thousand to this same bank. Where I now assume Lilith or Porbeagle can get their grubby little hands on it."

"Yes, but not until they get out of the country. Do you guess Roan's in Kilingess with them?" Lynn said.

"Can't kill the golden goose yet when he's got more eggs to lay."

"What do we do?" Jawnie said. This time, she stood up. "I can talk to Decker. He might listen to me."

"No. Not until one of us lays eyes on Roan," Rockfish said. "That's what his wife hired us to do. And goddamnit, that's exactly what we're going to do."

"How do we do that?"

"We flip for it," Rockfish said. "One partner stays here and minds the shop, the other hits the road."

CHAPTER TEN

In the end, the quarter landed on its edge and they each packed a suitcase. Raffi and Lynn stayed behind on standby.

Rockfish knew Lana would stand out among 4x4 pickups and the Subaru had spent too many nights sitting in Allison's back parking lot to be considered anonymous. They would need something nondescript to fly under the radar as they crossed into West Virginia. A former client, Marvin Trotter, owned Baltimore Pike Motors and set Rockfish up with a 2005 Dodge Caravan that more closely fit the role. To finish the look, Rockfish took the long way back to the office, along some dirt roads to acclimate it more to their destination.

Jawnie flipped the door sign to closed. Rockfish brought the van around to the front and they loaded the back with work gear and personal luggage.

"Ready?" Rockfish said.

"Let's go," Jawnie said. He slipped back behind the wheel and punched the destination into the GPS.

Seven and a half hours later, they crossed the city limits into Scrumsville and checked into The GearJammer Inn. The small town was west of Kilingess, a thirty-minute drive down a windy road, with no room to pass, and an hour if you ended up behind a coal truck. At fifty-nine dollars a night, The GearJammer was cheap. They'd reserved two rooms, as Claudia Coyne would eventually reimburse them via the expense report. According to Rockfish, the Waffle House across the street provided the only dining option they would need. Jawnie immediately questioned his call, but a check of Google Maps told her he was probably right.

Jawnie knew there was no chance of going vegan in this state. She did a quick search on *nogluten.com* and learned that the Waffle House had no gluten-free options, although they cooked the eggs, meat, and hash browns separately. Jawnie instinctively crossed herself and said a silent prayer for her insides.

After dinner, they met in Jawnie's room to game plan for the next day. The standard GearJammer room had two twin beds, an armoire and a small sink in an alcove in the back of the room. To the right of the sink was the door to the bathroom. Rockfish pulled the desk chair over to the bed, where Jawnie had thrown the pillows to the floor and sat with her back to the headboard. Rockfish complimented her on being flexible enough to sit Indian-style, as it had been years since he could. By the frown on her face, he instantly knew he'd fucked up.

"You don't say that, like that. Someone could interpret it as racist. I know you're not. Old and clueless maybe. But it doesn't mean someone won't call you out."

"Not in Scrumsville, they won't."

"It's called Easy Pose, or Sukhasana. I don't expect you to remember either, but the fewer racial stereotypes, the better." Rockfish couldn't see the harm in what he'd said, but knew dropping that line of conversation was for the best.

"Speaking of Scrumsville, we're far enough away. I don't think we'll have to worry about being spotted by anyone," Rockfish said. "I get it, traversing back and forth to Kilingess will become more of a pain in the ass the longer we're here, but I'm not taking any chances. Bright and early tomorrow, before anyone's up and about, I'd like to drive out there and take a couple of passes in front of Diane's property. Best to see what, if anything, has changed since the last Google Maps satellite image."

"I'll make sure we've got one in the van tomorrow," Jawnie said and held up the folder where she had stored the printouts. "These are pretty dated, so I'll snap off pictures as we pass and print if needed."

"What we're looking at is a single wide trailer, set roughly a hundred feet off-road." Rockfish said. "The front and back yards are clear, except for a trampoline behind the house. Open fields bookend the trailer. This time of year, I do not know what could be planted in those fields. We'll deal with it when we get there."

"Based on the satellite pictures, the crop looks to be soybeans, definitely not tall enough to give cover. But the images are three years old and no way of telling what time of year Google took them."

"Now the field to the east is our best chance," Rockfish said. "It's the smaller of the two, and it appears like it slopes upward and ends at this tree line. If it's not too far away, that would be our best location to set up camp. There's a dirt road leading up that way. The only problem is, if there's no place to stash the van, we'll have to find somewhere else and hike up to the tree line. I agree with snapping off some new pictures during the morning pass. This way, we'll get any license plates, and if someone is really looking down on our behalf, there will be a Lincoln Navigator parked in the driveway. And we can wrap this up in a nice bow."

"Steve, no way in hell you think things are going to fall into place that easily for us?"

"I can dream, can't I? But based on those emails you dug up between the two, she is meeting Earl somewhere, or he's driving to her. Fifty-fifty chance, I suppose."

"The first scenario is best. I mean, we know little about Diane, but I doubt she'd pick up on us following her in this van, and once we identify where Earl's at, we'll keep eyes on him. If he drives to her, we'll follow when he leaves. Probably need to be a little more careful at that point."

Rockfish nodded, and their brief history together told him she had more to say.

"Here's where I throw in the monkey wrench..."

He chuckled and nodded for her to continue.

"What if either of them pulls out of Diane's driveway and we have to hike back to where we stashed the van and lose sight of where they went? I can see one of us hoofing back for it, while the other tries to watch, but the most I'll be able to relay to you is in what direction they went down the road."

"Very glad you asked that question," Rockfish said. "That's what these puppies are for." He got up and walked over to the desk, where he had draped his jacket. He pulled two small rectangle-shaped objects from the front jacket pockets and dropped them onto the bed.

"Oh, I know what they are. I pay the bills, remember? I'm all for technology, you know that. The problem I see is we'd need to figure out a way to get close enough to a vehicle, without being seen, and secure that GPS tracker somewhere on it. Why are you carrying them around, to and from dinner?"

"You never know what a town like this will throw at you. I know I said we're safe, but we might walk out of the Waffle House and Lilith is headed down the other side of the street. It's better to be prepared." *It's one of the few good goddamn things that came out of that television show. I can complain about a shit-ton of things associated with that endeavor, but the ability to afford the tools that allow me to work smarter and not harder will never be one of them.*

"Also, the magnets," Rockfish said, and pointed to the two silver circular spots atop each tracker. The devices were small, three inches long by only an inch and a half wide. "Walk up, slap it on, somewhere underneath, and keep on walking. Won't take much to secure to any part of the undercarriage. Battery lasts two weeks, and it sends all the data points to an app on my phone."

"If we are still in Scrumsville in two weeks, you are going to be short one partner."

Rockfish ignored Jawnie's lighthearted but veiled threat and kept to the selling points of the Optimus 2.0.

"They were fifty bucks apiece. You know what it would take to do this job years ago? How the hell I never threw in the towel and went back to the refinery, I'll never know."

"I get it, you like your toys."

"Speaking of new toys," Rockfish said. "You sure we're going to be okay with Lynn handling the office for us?"

Jawnie raised her eyebrows and tilted her head. "You better have not implied what I think you did. And it's not like I gave her a key and alarm code to have a free run of the place. All she's doing is calling in and reviewing voicemails a couple times a day and then summarizing them for me."

"Does this mean we finally have a receptionist?"

"More like a temp. But we'll see how this works out. Again, as a receptionist. Don't make me put you in the same column as Raffi."

Rockfish had a hearty laugh and refocused the discussion on rehashing the following morning's game plan and any contingencies should someone spot them. When they felt comfortable, Rockfish stood up, grabbed his jacket, and stopped at the door.

"Get some sleep. Sunrise is 6:35am and we should make our second pass by then."

****

After a couple of early morning passes for Jawnie to grab a handful of fresh photos, the team backtracked to an abandoned gas station they had passed on the way in. Rockfish parked the van behind the dilapidated building. Jawnie bundled their supplies and they headed out with backpacks bursting at the seams. It would be a two-mile trek to the edge of the woods overseeing Diane's trailer.

The route would take them along the main road for half a mile and then a diagonal cut across fields littered with large, round hay bales before entering the woods for the rest of the hike. As they veered off the road, Jawnie wanted to pick up the pace so that they weren't visible to any curious drivers coming down this open stretch of highway. But one glance at her partner told her he was already looking forward to the first rest stop.

They arrived at their vantage point an hour and fifteen minutes later. Rockfish dropped his backpack and took up position on the ground. "Let me sit here for a minute and I'll be okay, I swear."

Jawnie slid off her pack and patted Rockfish on the shoulder as she walked over to get a better view of their target. The line of sight was perfect. She could use her telephoto lens and look down into the trailer through a window. They were close enough to watch what went on in the backyard without the help of her camera. The field between them and Diane's was also littered with the large round hay bales. *They'll provide more than ample cover if I need to get closer for any reason.*

"Nice job picking the spot, boss. I hope you live to walk another day."

"Fucking Bataan Death March had nothing on this hike," Rockfish said and Jawnie could tell he had yet to catch his breath.

They set up their gear and took turns peering through the camera's telephoto lens, down onto the property and sometimes straight through the uncovered window. It wasn't long before Jawnie concluded that the only people at home were Sunny and another woman who she assumed was Diane.

"No sign of Roan unless they're keeping him in some back bedroom and not letting him out. But all these two are doing is eating cereal and watching television. *The View* was on. Now it's turned to *The Price is Right*."

"See, now you're experiencing the glamour side of being a P.I. Not all of it is meeting with Mafia Dons and car chases. I used to love this grunt work, but this old body sure doesn't want to keep up."

"Sit tight," Jawnie said. "You keep providing that wit and wisdom and I'll take care of the physical stuff. Partners, remember?"

The quiet morning hours slowly turned into an equally uneventful afternoon where Rockfish spent way too long bitching about the Nature Valley pressed cardboard bars that Jawnie had packed for lunch. And she, without hesitation, returned fire. "If you hadn't done takeout from the Waffle House this morning, you could have spared us all, and not had to keep making that twenty-minute hike back into the woods every hour on the hour. That stuff isn't meant for anyone's stomach, and those cardboard bars are binding. We should all be thankful for that."

"Maybe it's the water?"

She looked down at the Dasani bottle at her feet. *Yeah, it's definitely the water and not seventeen grams of pure grease. I'd better change the subject before this goes any further.*

"We're going to want to get one of those trackers on that Jeep down there."

"Yup, hopefully once it gets dark, we'll draw straws," Rockfish said.

"I'm letting you know I'm going to do it. I'm quicker, a smaller visual target and won't need CPR upon my return."

Jawnie was into the last hour of her shift on the camera, a little after 2pm, when the back door to the trailer opened. The women emerged and walked across the lawn towards the trampoline.

They're not going to jump on this thing, are they? She watched them crawl through the netting and lay in the center. *Now they're not dressed for sunbathing, not to mention the sun isn't cooperating this afternoon and it's freaking mid-April.* Jawnie hunched over the camera's tripod and swung it towards the trampoline. A flash of light caught her attention, and she zoomed in. The flick of a lighter and a hand rolled joint passed between the two. Jawnie wouldn't need to wait for the cover of darkness when a THC haze would do the trick.

Jawnie turned and waved Rockfish over. "Look at this."

He glanced through the telephoto lens, and she relayed her plan. Rockfish kept nodding as he agreed. *Or is he enjoying the view? I'm going and won't take no for an answer.*

"Okay, no dillydallying. Down and back," Rockfish said. "Put your phone on vibrate in your back pocket. If it goes off, turn around and head back. That means they've moved off the trampoline and I don't want you taking any chances. You got me? Vibrate equals full stop and start working your way back. No hesitation, get back here, moving from bale to bale to bale."

"Got it."

"Come back as careful as you went down. If you hear my voice, then you know shit's gone sideways. Time to put on your track shoes."

Jawnie took one of the GPS trackers and carried it in her right hand. She serpentined from one hay bale to the next until she had made her way down to where the field met Diane's property. Jawnie peeked out around the large bale and could see it was a diagonal sprint, twenty yards to her left, to where the Jeep Wrangler sat in the driveway. She peeked around the other side but could not see past the trailer's back corner. Back on the left side of the bale, she knew her best shot would be to aim for the passenger side rear wheel. *Snap this puppy on and then slide around the back to reassess. Fuck, I hope no one drives down the road at that point.*

Jawnie inhaled deeply and took off. If she were wrong and there was a third occupant, who was in the front living room, she'd be fucked before she got halfway. She reached the Jeep in six long strides and the driveway gravel gave way as she slammed on the brakes. Jawnie landed on her ass and popped right back up. She slapped the tracker up into the wheel well and heard the satisfying *clunk*. She pulled her hand back. *Well, it didn't fall out. That's a bonus. No buzz from Rockfish yet. Time to press that luck he told me not to.* She presumed that if no one had fired a load of buckshot over her head by now, no one was sitting in the living room, looking out over the front yard.

She worked her way around the back end of the Jeep and then forward, along the driver's side, towards the set of double windows next to the small front porch. Jawnie reached up and stood on her tiptoes to peek inside. The stench of cigarettes hit her senses from the open window before her eyes focused on the inside. A second later, when they did, she wished they hadn't. The place was a disaster. Domino's boxes and Big Gulp cups littered any flat surface. And then she saw it. Someone had draped a black leather duster over a wooden chair next to the small dinette.

Fucking B-I-N-G-O was her name-o. A fist pump and a game of hay bale Frogger later, Rockfish claimed she resembled the cat that had eaten the friggin canary and went back for seconds.

"He's here," Jawnie stammered. "I mean not right now, but he's been here, and odds are he's coming back, if not for the jacket, another round of good times. Raffi and Lynn both mentioned that damn coat."

"And you saw no one else?"

"No one. When I got back to the field, I stopped behind that first bale and looked back to see if I had missed anything, but you saw that."

"I did. Now let's make sure this thing actually works after making the trip." Rockfish pulled out his cell and opened the tracking app. "Good clean signal," he said. "I believe we're in business. I hope someone gets in that Jeep and heads out so we can really test this thing out."

"Based on the Domino's delivery boxes piled up, I think the only destination you'll get off that one is 7/11. Cigarettes and Big Gulps runs."

"Don't forget the rolling papers," Rockfish said. He put his fist out and she bumped it. That was her attaboy, and Jawnie couldn't have been happier.

She sat back on the ground and her heart continued to beat as if it would come through her ribcage. Jawnie tried to relax but had a hard time settling back into the waiting game. The adrenaline rush from that little ten-minute operation was the first on the job, legit high she had experienced. She couldn't wait for the Jeep to head out for Earl or for him to show up. It didn't matter whether the action came at dinner or lunch tomorrow. She'd be ready.

Jawnie's second opportunity came after ten that night before they were ready to call it a day. Rockfish had tracked the headlights as they came down the road and turned into the driveway, sans blinker. An old Chevy pickup pulled in behind the Jeep and backfired before the engine died. The driver quickly climbed the porch steps carrying a twelve pack of beer in his right hand. The small porch light above the door lit Earl Porbeagle in all his glory. Rockfish knew when he saw him. The man could pass for any Kilingess resident, in a tank top and jeans.

An hour passed before the kitchen and living room lights went off, one at a time. A couple of seconds, later Rockfish could see through the telephoto lens a light from a rear window at the back of the trailer had flickered on. It illuminated the far corner of the backyard.

"Hey, I think we're primed—"

Jawnie was three hay bales deep into the field before Rockfish could tell her it was time.

She followed the same path as before and stopped again at the last bale that separated the field from the property. Her breathing was calmer on this second trip, and she looked around the left side of the hay bale at her target. The porch light lit little more than the small landing and the front half of the Jeep. Darkness smothered the old pickup. Jawnie counted to three and stepped out into the open. She slowed this time as she approached the driveway and didn't end up on her ass.

Jawnie crouched down at the right rear wheel and reached up the side of the truck to the bed wall. These old trucks had holes on the top of the bedsides, called stake pockets, or so Rockfish claimed. It would be an undetectable spot; he swore on it. She ran her hand along the top of the bed and easily found the first one. *Clunk.*

Well, I'll be damned. Old man knows his shit. She turned and bent over, stayed low and sprinted back to the confines of the hay bales.

****

Saturday night found Jawnie still scratching at imaginary bugs and knowing two things. She would always be a city girl and second, she preferred to conduct surveillance from a car. Despite how she felt, Jawnie wondered how long it would be for her to feel the rush she experienced yesterday again. *Doing something proactive is a million times more fun than stupid database checks or spreadsheet analyses. No wonder Steve doesn't think twice before throwing caution to the wind. And for the first time in a while, I don't feel the gnawing in the pit of my stomach.*

She looked at her phone. Rockfish was running late. He had knocked on her door, each hour on the hour, since they met for breakfast in the morning. More unsaturated fat for him and only coffee for her. He continued to press the point that she needed to download the GPS tracking data and begin her analysis. While he was content and competent enough to watch the little dot on the map move as either vehicle hit the road, what he wasn't in any position to do was download the data and start making calls based on trend analysis.

Rockfish was itching to get back out there and Jawnie, for the first time, knew what that fever was like. But she stuck to her guns and towed the party line. She would need more data points to accurately assess, or even guess, where the next stakeout should be. She wanted her answer to point to where Earl was spending the early morning hours, not the late evening party ones. Jawnie would need more data to make a call on where she thought Lilith took Roan, either voluntarily or against his will. But her partner—

Knock

Speak of the devil.

She stood up, took the chain off the door, and opened it. Rockfish walked into the room without so much as a hello and sat down on the corner of the bed closest to the door. She caught a whiff of something as he walked past and leaned outside to see if it was the air. It wasn't, and she closed the door, instinctively replacing the chain.

"You went back to the Waffle House for lunch, didn't you? Or does this entire town smell like cooking grease and cigarette smoke?"

"Guilty as charged," Rockfish said. "Yeah, can't get enough of those hash browns. Anyway, all we have back home are IHOPs, so when in Rome."

Jawnie tilted her head. "I thought they were IHObs now?"

"That rebrand crashed and burned," Rockfish said.

"Kind of like your toilet in a few. Got it."

They shared a friendly laugh and Jawnie pulled up her chair. She knew the reason for the visit, but let him make his sales pitch uninterrupted.

"I know I've been bugging the shit out of you today, but this waiting around is driving me nuts. We've got some map points. We need to be out scouting these places, getting a feel for the area. Shit, we might luck across something."

"Like Roan, hanging out on the front porch, whittling or whatever?"

"Now who's stereotyping? You haven't been watching these dots. I have," Rockfish said.

Jawnie looked over at her partner. If his facial expressions could talk, they'd be begging for her to pull out the laptop and do her thing.

"Okay, I'll play," Jawnie said. "We've got roughly twenty-four hours of location data for the Jeep and about fifteen for the pickup. You can tell me Earl left the trailer and went to such-and-such address. What if that's another one of his whores? We stake that place out and get nowhere. Trust me on this one, Rockfish, the more data we can capture, the better our plan moving forward will be."

A blind man could read the disappointment on that face. "I can see you don't like the same answer I've told you half a dozen times today. Well, you've got a kind face. One only a mother could love. But tell you what I'm going to do. Go back to your room and watch the *Impractical Jokers* marathon. I'll give it until six and then download the waypoints. After that, I'll knock when I've got something worth reporting. Positive or negative."

"Deal."

"Oh, this deal is void if you don't bring me a big salad around five," Jawnie said. "I don't care how far you have to drive."

Rockfish stood up, and they fist bumped. Jawnie closed the door and flopped back on the bed. *That man is exhausting.*

By 5:55pm, Jawnie had finished the salad Rockfish had dropped off. She didn't ask how far he had to drive and he didn't offer. She tossed the empty plastic container atop the trashcan. It was too large to fit in, and she made a mental note to walk it out to the dumpster before bed. By seven, she locked the laptop's screen and closed it. She picked up her room key and writing pad. Rockfish would appreciate the old school notes.

Knock

Jawnie walked in and the first thing she noticed was the overflowing trashcan full of takeout boxes.

"I can walk that out to the dumpster when I take mine out later."

"Nah, I'm good. What did you find out?"

Jawnie pulled the chair closer to where Rockfish sat and went into her findings.

"... and based on that, the Jeep goes to 7/11, but it's not taking the most direct route in either direction. It drives out of its way, three times so far today, and traverses a section of State Route 803, which coincidently, or not, is where Earl ended up after his little sex romp last night. 1811-A, State Route 803 to be specific."

"Sounds like someone's jealous he's not spending the night," Rockfish said.

"My thoughts, too. Here's the overhead satellite view," Jawnie said and handed Rockfish her phone. "It looks like a cabin, set way back in what I'm guessing these folks call the hollow."

"That's some freaking windy-ass long road to get back there. Probably all dirt and gravel."

"People who build back there don't want to be seen."

"Or found."

"Agreed. I bet there are trail cameras all over that property. No way we're sneaking up to it." Jawnie said. She watched as Rockfish walked across the small room towards a black box sitting atop his roller bag. *I have to cut this off at the pass.*

"No drone. With the noise that thing makes, why don't you walk up and knock on the door? Either way, you're announcing yourself."

"Don't shoot my idea down before I say it, unless you've got a better one in mind," Rockfish said.

"I do actually."

* * * * * * * * * *

The van crossed the Kilingess city limits and Rockfish glanced down at the directions on his phone. "You'll want to make a right up here and then your first left."

Kilingess was a small town with little, excluding boarded-up storefronts. Fast food wasn't even an option. *I wonder how much of this is due to oxycodone versus the decline in the coal industry? The Discovery Channel would know.*

The Dollar General store was the town's only shopping option, unless you counted the Family Dollar on the northern end and the Dollar Tree further to the east. Walmart would have been a better option, but another forty-five minutes on the road would not fit into their plans. Rockfish wanted Jawnie to have a bit more of a disguise than she thought she needed on this early Sunday afternoon. He also needed to find a spot to position the van somewhat near the cabin so when Earl hit the road, they could make their play. Get in, get out, he kept reinforcing. He wanted to find the sweet spot. A secluded one not too far from the cabin.

Jawnie had come up with the plan, and based on the cabin's isolated location, it was the safest of their few options. Rockfish listened to his partner that morning back at the motel as he made a cup of in-room coffee.

"Fill up the tank with gas and get close. Hang in the area, waiting to pounce. We've got another day's worth of data, and it tells us the man doesn't like to spend much time in their new home. He's out during the afternoon, comes back to touch down, probably for dinner, before heading back out, usually between seven and nine.

"We're not driving up there at night," Rockfish had said. *One nighttime operation on this trip was already one too many.* It also didn't play well with Jawnie's ruse.

"Okay, if he heads out this afternoon, let me drive up and knock on the door. See who answers. He's out in the truck somewhere. The violence meter is going to be way down. They don't know me." Jawnie had machine gunned supporting points at him, and Rockfish countered with playing devil's advocate.

"Or at least we think they don't."

"I dress the part a little. I knock on the door, play a little scenario. See what I can see."

"What about me?"

"The second-row seating folds down into the floor on that van. You can lounge back there. Make yourself a little den. If you hear me scream, come running. Earl won't be there, so no danger I can't handle. Maybe I spot Roan. If that's the case, mission accomplished. Drive away and call in the cavalry." Jawnie wiped her hands for emphasis, but Rockfish was still unsure.

The plan sounded fine. They all do, until the shit hits the fan, and you have to rely on plans B, C and D to get you out of harm's way.

He continued to have his doubts after leaving Scrumsville an hour ago and they remained steadfast as he sat in an idling van outside the Dollar General.

In Jawnie's plan, his primary job was to keep track of Earl and alert Jawnie if Earl bucked the trend and appeared to head back in the general direction of the cabin. *The cell phone in her back pocket on vibrate should do the trick again. And if shit really goes sideways, I can jump out and wave this Glock in the air and hopefully make enough of a distraction so we can get out.* His hand reached down to the small bag under the seat and felt the gun's outline. Jawnie wasn't aware of it being along for the ride and that was how he wanted to keep it.

Jawnie opened the passenger door, and Rockfish jerked back to reality.

"I got these big old sunglasses, a scarf and a hat. I look like an idiot—"

"Or like a good government employee out in the field. Especially if you keep the N95 mask on. You'll be totally inconspicuous. Now let's head out in that direction and hope old Earl feels the need to stretch his legs. Soon."

1811-A State Route 803 was southeast of the small town, roughly a twenty-minute drive, but to Rockfish, the van had time-traveled back to the Great Depression. The road was desolate, hilly, and boarded-up or overgrown houses dotted the landscape. Gravel roads jutted out from the main road every so often, accompanied by large signs stating the shooting of trespassers. 1811-A was no different as they did a drive by, but two faded Trump/Pence 2020 signs were mounted above and below the no trespassing sign.

"You'll want to play up that angle," Rockfish said, and Jawnie nodded in agreement.

Half a mile further down the road, they came across a pond and some shade trees. Rockfish decided nestling the van between a cluster of the trees would be the best spot to wait. He backed the van down towards the waterline and once the engine died, Rockfish and Jawnie traded seats.

"Now remember, flash that badge as quick as you did with that landlord. Then have that card ready to hand to them. Put it right in their hand. One right after the other, so Lilith doesn't have time to think, but her eyes will focus on what the card says."

Cheryl Heinzinger, Field Manager, United States Census Bureau, (800) 555-2020, CHeinzinger@USCB.gov

They passed the time in silence as the minutes ticked by. Ninety in total had come and gone when the alert came across Rockfish's phone.

"He's on the move." He stared at the small screen until the dot turned onto the main road. "Headed northwest up 803 towards town. Let's go."

Jawnie started the van and Rockfish could hear her swallow hard as he squeezed between the seats into the back.

"Stay calm. You've got this. You are quick on your feet, so stick to your story and answer anything she throws at you with confidence. And keep looking. Take it all in."

Rockfish could feel the van turn off the pavement and he sat up to get a good view out the window. The dirt road was half a mile long, winding through the woods, up a hill and then down into a valley, where the cabin sat with a small pond. He had stared at the overhead satellite picture so much, he felt as if he had been here before. As the van crested the hill, Rockfish ducked back down and said a silent prayer for his partner's safety and mental agility.

****

Jawnie brought the van to a stop in front of the cabin's front steps and slid the shifter into park. If the cabin was at noon, the front of the van pointed closer to eight. She positioned it in case they needed to make a quick exit.

Might not have time for a good old three-point turn.

Jawnie got out of the van and heard a faint get 'em kid emanate from the van's backseat before shutting the door and walking over to the porch steps.

The narrow front porch ran the length of the cabin and was bare, excluding a couple of folding lawn chairs to her left which overlooked the pond. *Yeah, let's get 'em.* Jawnie knocked.

Earl Porbeagle opened the door, and Jawnie took the swallow of a lifetime. It stuck in her throat. *Lord, how the mighty have fallen.*

"Can I help you, little lady, since you can't read the goddamn sign at the end of my driveway?" Earl's face was dark red and Jawnie saw a prominent vein on his forehead.

Fuck, who's in the truck? Earl's beard had come in since he applied for his Maryland driver's license. That picture, until this point, had been Jawnie's only visual of the man. *Very Jesus-like, now. Almost as long as his hair.* But Earl had answered the door in a pair of faded blue boxers, a wife-beater and a long tan cotton bathrobe.

"Ah, Good morning, Sir. My name is ah, Cheryl Heinzinger," Jawnie said and pulled out the badge and card as she had practiced. Earl took the card as if on cue. *I pray he didn't notice my hand shaking.*

"Census Bureau, huh?"

"Yes, Sir. I'm a field manager assigned to resolve those residences in the area that were unresponsive to the mailings last year."

Jawnie listened to her own voice as the words left her mouth. It didn't sound remotely familiar, and her anxiety ratcheted up three notches. *Remain calm, stand straight, and don't move off the damn porch into the house. I don't care what he says or offers.*

"And..."

"In that regard, I'm looking for Mr. or Mrs. Highchurch. According to our records from 2010, they lived here with their daughter Lilith. The Bureau had many problems last year with the United States Postal Service and our questionnaires. If I could talk to you or someone regarding the occupants of the house, I could provide that information back to our headquarters. You understand, your or my failure to do so only hurts the state of West Virginia and its representation in Congress."

Jawnie stopped and took a breath. She noticed Earl had stepped back into the house and instinctively, she shuffled her feet a few inches backwards. *Had he noticed?*

"Lady, you got questions about who the fuck lives here. I've got one for you. It's frickin' Sunday afternoon. What government employee works on the Sabbath?"

"Well, Mr... Highchurch?"

"He don't live here anymore."

"Well, Mr..."

"You don't need my name." Earl frowned and a second vein popped out to join the first. He stepped towards the door with an outstretched arm. Jawnie assumed he was about to slam it in her face. She shuffled those few inches forward again.

"As for it being Sunday," Jawnie said. "There's a lot of overtime available for this effort. A matter of fact, the West Virginia Governor has promised funds from the General Assembly to help support the initiative. Getting a correct count is that important to him."

"You've got Maryland tags. This whole thing is fucking squirrelly."

"Sir, please understand. The under-reporting is not unique to this area. It's a state-wide problem and Census Bureau executives have declared this an all hands on deck situation. I work out of our Baltimore office but have been temporarily reassigned to this region in order to assist."

"Listen, I don't give a shit about..."

Earl continued to demean Jawnie, her fake employment and the United States Government as a whole, but her attention abruptly moved to the blur over his left shoulder. *Did I see that?* A man had pushed an elderly woman in a wheelchair past an open doorway. *Roan? Mother Elizabeth?* Jawnie caught a quick glimpse and knew the man was Roan. The same man she had surveilled multiple nights while attempting to catch him stepping out on Claudia. *No doubt in my mind.*

Earl followed Jawnie's eyes, turned and walked back to the door she was obliviously staring at and shut it. As he looked back at Jawnie, she noticed the lock was on the outward facing doorknob. *Were Roan and Elizabeth locked in that room at various points of the day? Was the door open this afternoon because of Earl being home? Was he that much of a deterrent, or are they still fully onboard with what this church had dissolved into? Get your head straight, McGee! He's still standing in front of you.*

By the time the last of these thoughts left her head, Earl had returned to his previous spot and took an additional step towards her.

"Ma'am, are you deaf? I said you need to get the fuck off of my property and don't come back." This time, Earl raised both arms. The left formed a fist and he shook it at Jawnie. The right hand reached for the door.

Jawnie muttered an apology before she turned and headed down the steps. She heard the front door slam behind her. That sound lifted the weight of the world off her shoulders and Jawnie wasn't sure if her feet were actually touching the ground.

He's not coming down after you. Deep breath. Let it out. If he wanted to fuck with you, he could have pulled you inside and then shut the door. Get to the van. Walk slow. Confident. But breathing was hard, especially when she saw spots in front of her eyes that kept time with her heartbeat. She instinctively placed her right hand over it to thwart the escape and didn't let go until she was back in the driver's seat and moved it in order to start the van.

****

Five minutes earlier, while Jawnie carried on her conversation in the cabin's doorway, Rockfish stared at his phone. The pickup had come to a stop in downtown Kilingess. And while this should have brought calmness, his curiosity about what was transpiring on the porch kept his heart beating in the stratosphere.

It ain't gonna hurt anything if I keep one eye on the phone and take a peek with the other.

Rockfish squirmed closer to the open window and lifted his head. Jawnie's back was to him, and she stood close to the open door. But he couldn't see who she was speaking with. Whoever opened the door stood back in the entranceway. From this partial one eye view, he couldn't make out who had answered the knock. The cabin had a front set of windows to Jawnie's left, but the curtains were drawn.

He turned and looked out the windshield, moving his head between the two front seats. He could see what seemed like a garden shed next to the driveway. A wooden door faced the front of the van and a heavy lock hung from a hinge. He could also make out a window on the left side that looked out down the driveway.

What could be in that shed? Most likely yard tools, but why lock 'em up all the way out here in the boonies? Was the drug problem that severe in the backwoods that you need to lock up a shovel and rake? I mean, how much could someone get for a used hoe at the pawnshop?

With little thought other than his concern that Jawnie was taking all the risk, Rockfish spun himself around so that he faced the driver's side and released the sliding door latch. He held the door as it slid open to keep it as quiet as possible. When the door was open, he rolled out, and looked back through the van to Jawnie on the front porch. Her conversation was ongoing. *I need her to keep it going for another minute or two for me to get a decent look through that window.* Rockfish hunched over to make his profile as small as possible and shuffled toward the van's front left fender. It provided his last line of cover before he dashed to the safety of the shed.

Rockfish thought of a countdown but instantly launched himself towards the side of the shed with the window. Three strides later, he was under the window, back against the shed wall, and he listened for a shout from someone who might have spotted him. But his own heavy breathing drowned out any other sounds. Rockfish turned and stood up to peek through the window. The contents surprised him, despite having an idea the moment he spotted the shed.

The boxes that Raffi had found and photographed in the locked office littered the floor, and their contents spilled out across a workbench. Rockfish didn't know one chemical compound from another, but there was no mistaking the stack of colorful candy wrappers, happy kids' faces, and bunches of grapes printed on each side.

Rockfish grabbed his phone, pointed it towards the window and fired off a handful of pictures. *One of these needs to turn out.* He retraced his steps back into the van and slowly slid the door closed but held it short of latching. *Can't blow it now with that noise. Let's fucking go, Jawnie. We need to get out of here.*

Rockfish laid on the floor of the van, holding the door closed, and gave himself a virtual pat on the back for a job well done. *Cautious. In and out in a heartbeat. You still got it, old man.* While he still had it, he was too clumsy to review the pictures with one hand.

But did he really still have it? Because if he had, Rockfish would have noticed the glowing red ember floating in the air off the back corner of the cabin as it watched him sprint to the shed and return to the van. The ember glowed red and dropped to the ground where a foot snuffed it out at the same time Jawnie pressed down on the gas.

CHAPTER ELEVEN

"Jesus Fucking Christ, Rockfish! It was Earl!"

"Calm and cool, Jawnie, until you get us off this property," Rockfish said as he continued to hold the van's side door shut until they had gotten to where he hoped any type of trail or security camera wouldn't pick them up. "Stay in character."

When Jawnie made the left turn onto State Route 803, headed back towards Kilingess, Rockfish let the door roll open a foot to get some momentum and yanked it shut. He sat up and tried to squeeze between the front seats. He leaned forward, his hands on the center console, and he got his first good look at his partner since they had left the cabin. Her hands shook as they held a death grip on the wheel, and her face was flushed. *I need to get us back to The GearJammer. Safe and sound.*

"When you get a chance, pull over. I'll drive us back."

Based on how she appeared, Rockfish worried rehashing what happened could only put her in a worse mental place, but it needed to be gone over while every detail was still fresh. Once Rockfish secured his seatbelt, he pulled the van back out onto the asphalt and turned to Jawnie. "Okay, Earl answered the door. Tell me everything. Leave nothing out, no matter how trivial or minute you think."

Jawnie recounted her ungodly surprise when Earl answered the door, looking as if he had lived in that cabin his entire life.

"... I really think I pulled it off. There may have been a few stumbles in the beginning. Once I got my footing, I don't think he suspected a thing."

Rockfish took his eyes off the road for a minute and glanced over at the life-size giant mold of Jell-O in the passenger seat. The quivering had slowed to an occasional jiggle. Based on how she still looked ten minutes out, Rockfish wondered if she could actually retell the experience with hindsight. He would need to question, at least to himself, her narrative of the performance.

"... and a flash of white caught my attention, over his shoulder," Jawnie continued. "I didn't even think about it; my eyes went from his face to that open doorway over his shoulder."

"You're sure the man was Roan?"

"Yes. I mean, I hadn't seen him in some sort of all white cotton muumuu before, but yeah, I'm sure Roan was pushing Mother Elizabeth in that wheelchair. Bet my next paycheck."

"If you spotted him, technically, we're halfway there. Still, Claudia's paid for us to bring him home. On to the next step. We need to get him away safely. That may or may not involve help by the authorities. But we might have bigger problems."

"What are you talking—"

"Get your head down!" Rockfish said. He had spotted the old pickup truck barreling down the road in their direction, later than he would have liked. *Damn. Pay better attention, idiot. How the hell could you forget about the damn truck having driven to Kilingess?* He dropped his chin to his chest, held the wheel straight, but strained his eyes, looking up and to the left, to see exactly who was behind the wheel. Lilith passed by. He had no doubts. She had her hair pulled back in a ponytail with giant sunglasses, but he recognized her.

"Holy crap. Lilith. Damn, that was closer than I'd like. Shit never ends around here."

"Think she saw us?" Jawnie said.

"Not a chance. Well, maybe. If Earl suspected something and called her, there's a chance. But I'm not buying it." In his head, he definitely bought it, at least partially. Despite their ongoing conversation, he did not have any warm and fuzzy feelings about Jawnie's performance. He noticed long after the pickup had passed, Jawnie remained slouched down in the passenger seat. Again, Rockfish contemplated finishing their conversation back at the motel. *Not a chance.*

"Well, based on what I ran across while you played Census worker, we're not moving forward alone. We're going to have to call in the big guns."

"Wait. You got out of the van? Or did you sit up and spot something?" Jawnie said.

"Yeah, I don't listen to direction really well. Shouldn't be a surprise at this point. All that stuff Raffi saw in the office? It's in a small garden shed next to the driveway. Boxes are open and shit is spread out across a wooden workbench that runs along the back wall. It's not in there for storage. My opinion? Someone's getting ready to, or already has played mad scientist."

Jawnie let out a loud *hmm* and crossed her arms. "You saw the poison. I saw Roan. Now we call Decker. I don't think this is up for discussion."

"I agree. That's kind of what I said."

"Pull over and do it now. It's not like he can be here in ten minutes," Jawnie said. "The earlier he gets to calling the Feds, the cops out here and drives out himself, it could take his army a day or two to rally, at the very minimum."

Rockfish continued to drive for a short distance, looking for a safe spot to pull over. The current stretch of road had a small culvert on the right where the shoulder should have been. His mind traveled back for a second to an earlier time in another state where the partners ended up in a ditch, very much like this one.

"There," Jawnie said and pointed up ahead to an abandoned, boarded-up, overgrown house and Rockfish turned onto the gravel road, which they assumed would eventually wind around to it. He pulled alongside the old house. *This is a good spot.* The van was practically invisible from the road, and he turned off the engine. He pulled out his phone and dialed.

You've reached Lieutenant—

Rockfish hung up and turned to Jawnie. "So much for his desk. The cell's next." That, too, resulted in an automated message and Rockfish dropped his phone into the cupholder.

"You need to call back. Leave a message."

"I've left more than a handful of messages over the past week. Has he called back? Even once? I'll save you the time of guessing. Not one damn time. I would bet you once he pushes play, hears my voice, then deletes it, without listening to the rest. Here's what we're going to do..."

Rockfish laid out his plan. The details were off the top of his head. There wasn't any better option available to him where he could convince anyone in law enforcement to reign hell down on that cabin. Jawnie would grab a few items from her room and immediately hit the road for the seven-hour drive back to Baltimore.

"I want you sitting at his desk waiting for him when he clocks in tomorrow morning."

"And what are you going to do? Hang out at the Waffle House and wait for reinforcements?"

"I'm going to monitor that traveling dot on my phone. In case it takes a left turn and head for the hills. If that's the case, I'll make sure I find a way to get to that property and secure the scene. If Earl left anything behind, I don't want the scavengers laying claim to it. Let Earl run. We know where he's at. We'll catch up."

"Fine. Find me a gas station. I'll need to top off the tank and pick up a handful of those 5-hour ENERGY drinks."

* * * * * * * * * *

Jawnie had unlocked the door to her condo close to midnight and collapsed into bed. She had run the last half of the drive from West Virginia on fumes and way under the speed limit. Despite being back in her protective bubble, she spent another couple of hours staring at the ceiling before finally drifting off. When she did, she soon fell to the floor of a forest. The man behind the curtain directing her dream then took a slice of reality and tossed in a bearded man with a large knife, chasing her through the woods.

When the alarm went off at 6am, Jawnie clung to the ceiling for a few minutes before realizing where she was. She relaxed her muscles and peeled the soaked sheet off her body. Drenched in sweat, Jawnie laid there for a minute, feeling as if she had gotten ten minutes of sleep, instead of the four hours she had rocked. She would need to chase breakfast with yet another 5-hour ENERGY and then a handful of antacids to counter all the caffeine eating away at her stomach's lining. She showered, ate and walked past the rental van for the comfort and calm of her Subaru before heading towards the Southern District Building.

Jawnie didn't have an appointment but assumed that when she told the police officer behind the bulletproof glass that she had vital information regarding the Highchurch/Porbeagle investigation, they would carry her high on someone's shoulders straight to Decker's office.

The man behind the glass seemed uninterested and dead in the eyes. He wrote nothing down, nor did he pick up the phone.

"Have a seat, ma'am. Someone will be with you shortly." He pointed towards a long wooden bench against the far wall.

Jawnie waited for thirty minutes, re-approached the glass and was told the same thing. Instead of returning to her seat, she followed the signs on the wall to the woman's restroom. She opened the door and walked over to the row of sinks. The face in the mirror was unrecognizable. Sunken eyes, large bags and natural hair that didn't want to be tamed that morning was not the look she needed. Add a rainbow hoodie and green leggings and Jawnie realized she didn't scream legitimacy or credibility to old dead eyes.

Jawnie pulled out her phone, unlocked the screen and put it back in the hoodie's kangaroo pocket before immediately yanking it right back out. She opened her options, turned off WiFi, Bluetooth and cellular before walking out of the ladies' room. Jawnie glanced across the room at the individuals on the bench until she spotted one with a cellphone in hand. The young woman looked the worse for wear and appeared to have recently been on the receiving end of a pimp's hand. The swelling had yet subsided. Jawnie walked over and sat down right next to her, probably too close for comfort.

"Hey girl, can I use your phone really quick to make a call? Look at this shit, I ain't got no service in this place. I got a get out of jail free card and I'm desperate to use it." Jawnie held her own phone up at eye level for added emphasis. The woman said nothing and handed her phone over. Jawnie thanked the woman and stood back up. A couple of long privacy strides later, she dialed Decker, and he picked up on the second ring, confirming Rockfish's theory of being blacklisted. Jawnie knew she only had a second to hook him.

"Dan, it's Jawnie. We found them. Scoped out Highchurch and Porbeagle. Please don't hang up!"

"Where are you?"

"I've been in your building for almost an hour, soaking in the bureaucracy and asking to see you..."

Jawnie hung up and returned the borrowed phone with a hearty thank you. She hadn't sat back down when the door next to dead eyes buzzed and out walked Decker. The sight of him shocked Jawnie. The man appeared as if someone had rolled herself, dead eyes, and the pimp slap lady into one entity and then ran it over with a garbage truck. They walked in silence as he escorted her back to his office.

Jawnie sat down across from Decker and couldn't hold it in any longer.

"If you don't mind, you look like absolute shit."

"You've seen a mirror lately?" Decker said.

"Yeah, matter of fact, a couple of minutes ago downstairs. I wasn't thrilled with me either, but I've been awake for way too long and West Virginia tends to wear on you. Mentally and physically."

"West Virginia? You found them there?"

"Yeah. Let me give you the backstory and then touch on my face-to-face with Earl."

Jawnie walked Decker through their investigative process, from the identification of Diane Caruso, straight through to the previous day's encounter. It surprised her when his pen kept pace with her words. Decker had five pages of notes by the time she finished. When he finally looked up from his pad of paper, Jawnie sat back and folded her arms across her chest. "If you had the common courtesy to take a phone call from Rockfish or listen to a voicemail, we wouldn't have lost eighteen hours towards putting these fuckwits behind bars. Probably could measure that in days, but we'll focus on time wasted from not moving forward yesterday."

Decker pursed his lips and gave a slight nod. He rested his chin on his hands and Jawnie wondered what she had said that put him into such a deep trance.

"Jawnie, you've got to understand, after the abortion at the adult bookstore, the FBI took the lead on this case after a lot of pressure from the Mayor's Office. But if what you say is true—"

"Why wouldn't it be?" Jawnie shot back. "Why the fuck would I make myself look like death warmed over, claim to have driven through the night to only come in here and try to play some shitty practical joke on you?"

"Jawnie, relax, it's only a phrase. I should have said it differently. I'm on the task force, but I'm no longer driving this train. I'll reach out now to my FBI points-of-contact. They'll probably call the West Virginia State Police and have them go talk to Rockfish. Based on what you said, we should have boots on the ground no later than this time tomorrow, maybe even tonight if the State Police can get a warrant signed. It will be much easier for them, rather than the Feds. Rockfish still monitoring the pickup?"

"Yes. He'd call if it left the local area, so all quiet."

"Go back home, Jawnie," Decker said. "Get some rest. Someone will call you once they type all this up." He pointed to the notepad on the corner of his desk. "Stay local. Please don't think about driving back to West Virginia. Let us handle it, which is exactly what I'd tell Rockfish in this same instance. You've gotten great intel on these clowns. Now let us do our jobs."

Jawnie threw back her head and laughed. Long and hard. She didn't care who heard. "My partner and I out-worked, out-hustled your so-called Task Force and now you tell me to step aside? Are you working for the FBI now? Because that sounds like something a piece of shit bureaucrat would say, based on my experience."

"Now you know better than that." Decker pursed his lips and shook his head.

"I thought I did until you stopped taking our calls. Now if you'll excuse me, I have a long drive ahead of me. One I'd prefer not to fall asleep on." Jawnie stood up and walked over to the door before turning around. "I'll see you in wild and wonderful West Virginia."

Decker didn't respond, and Jawnie shut the door. She would see her own way out and be on the phone to Rockfish before the Southern District Building's glass front door closed behind her.

"Hey, I finished with Decker. He claims he and the FBI will be there, maybe tonight, maybe tomorrow morning. He's also reaching out to the State Troopers out there. Look for them to come knocking here shortly and get a statement from you. Decker said he'd swing by The GearJammer as soon as he arrives."

"Alright. I'll hang tight and wait for the Troopers. Also, no movement on the truck yet."

"I'm grabbing Lynn for her to drive the van out. I'm going to grab a five-gallon bucket of melatonin to counteract all the 5-hour ENERGYs and try to catch up on some sleep. Be there by supper."

"Copy that. I'm not going anywhere."

****

Rockfish walked out of the front desk area of The GearJammer and headed towards the middle of the parking lot, where Decker, Jawnie, and Lynn were loitering. On this Tuesday afternoon, Rockfish had extended the reservations on their rooms for an additional three days. He wasn't much for administrative tasks, but he wanted to take care of this in case shit hit the fan later in the day.

"All good?" Jawnie said.

"We are until Saturday. By which time I hope to be already home on my deck slowly succumbing to alcohol poisoning."

"Alright, then let's get moving," Decker said. "You ladies in the van, follow me and I'll leave you off at the Fire Hall." The multi-agency task force had used the Kilingess Fire Hall as the command post for this operation. Here, pre-planning for the search warrant would take place and executives from all the agencies involved would get updates and make any tactical decisions if necessary. "Jawnie, I'll introduce you to my FBI Pittsburgh contact. Stick close to him because if the entry team has questions before, during or after, they'll come to you as you've been on scene. Don't be afraid to say you don't know."

"Pittsburgh? What are they doing here?" Rockfish said. "Isn't this a Baltimore and West Virginia party?"

"Their Pittsburgh office's area of responsibility covers the entire state of West Virginia. Their SWAT team will make entry and their

Evidence Response Team has dibs on conducting the actual search. FBI Baltimore and a few of my folks will be there, but more in an observational support role."

"Bureaucracy. Say no more," Rockfish said. *Too many damn cooks. I'm not getting a warm and fuzzy feeling here.*

Decker simply shrugged his shoulders and opened his car door. The rest took the hint and followed suit.

The two-car convoy left Scrumsville and twenty minutes later, thanks to no worries about being pulled over, arrived at the Kilingess Fire Hall. Decker jumped out, leaving Rockfish inside, and escorted Jawnie and Lynn through the door. He introduced them to Supervisory Special Agent Brent Lawlor. After the handshakes and intros, Decker was back in the car and Rockfish directed him to their individual staging area, which was alongside the same pond where Jawnie and Rockfish had waited two days prior.

"Do you have a gun?" Decker said. He had broken the silence with the question Rockfish had expected back at the motel.

"Ankle holster, but with the firepower you're bringing to the show, I doubt I'll need it. Not to mention that we're not driving up on-site until someone gives the all-clear."

"Good. Keep it in your pants," Decker said. "The last thing I need is more paperwork because you pulled it out for some cockamamy reason." Decker turned his head and looked out the driver's side window.

Not interested in my reply? Rockfish tried to ignore the implication of how he could screw this operation up.

"It's not a bad spot, half a mile from the cabin and shaded thanks to these trees."

"I'd have liked to be a little closer," Decker said. "You know, response time if needed."

"You said FBI Pittsburgh is running the show. I doubt that a Baltimore City Lieutenant that had trouble passing his last physical fitness test would be their first call. The SWAT team will have it handled in spades."

"For your sake, you better hope this doesn't turn into a replay of Allison's Adult Superstore."

Rockfish felt the sting of that one and conceded the game of one-upmanship. The men sat in silence and stared out the front windshield until Decker's radio squawked.

"Command post to Lieutenant Decker. Come in Decker."

"Decker. Go ahead."

"Operational spotters request GPS check on the pickup."

Decker looked at Rockfish and Rockfish glanced down at his phone app. The small white circle pulsed almost on top of the house. Rockfish held the screen up so Decker could see.

"GPS shows the pickup is still parked out front."

"Negative. No one's put eyes on it."

"Command Post, repeat that."

"Our spotters can't locate it on property."

Rockfish stared at his phone. The dot hadn't moved. He closed the app and restarted it. The same outcome. Finally, he powered down the phone and, upon restarting, the dot continued to pulse on the same location. *Something's fucked.* Rockfish stared at Decker. "I don't have a good feeling about this."

A second transmission came across the radio. "The team has made entry." A couple of minutes later, "site secured" followed.

"Isn't that our cue?" Rockfish said.

Decker turned his head and looked at Rockfish. *The man's perturbed.* "Maybe the truck was in a garage or something. You know how GPS bounces all over the—"

A third message came over the radio, directed at Decker, "Lieutenant, the scene commander is in route, you need to come up here, stat."

Rockfish glanced back at Decker, who didn't return the favor. Instead, he started the car and stared straight ahead. *He knows it, too. Something's fucked up.* The car rocketed back onto the paved road.

Rockfish made out a line of SUVs and cars as they approached the cabin. Decker parked at the end of the long line, and the two exited the car without saying a word. A woman in a pristine Baltimore PD uniform met them halfway up the driveway to the cabin. *Seems out of place, not in SWAT gear.*

"Hey Lieutenant. I'm warning you now, it's a bust. Porbeagle's in the wind."

Decker shot a dagger at Rockfish.

"Goddamnit. Sargent Tricia Weeds, this is Steve Rockfish. The P.I. that gave us this lead."

Weeds and Rockfish nodded and shook hands before she continued. "Worse, we've got bodies. It isn't pretty."

"Fuck."

They walked towards the cabin while Sargent Weeds provided a brief situational report on the operation until that point. Rockfish listened, knowing better than to ask questions or give Decker any reason to unload what was quickly building up inside him.

"Entry went off without a hitch. They found no one on the property," Weeds said with a wave of her hand across the horizon. "There's five bodies in a back room, arranged on the floor to give the impression of some religious ceremony. Blood everywhere. The Medical Examiner's on the way and the FBI's evidence team has started their search."

"Any idea on the victims?" Decker said. Rockfish wondered how many he would recognize if allowed in the room. *Probably all.*

"Preliminary review shows Earl Porbeagle isn't one of them, based on sex alone. All the victims are female. Per the other person of interest, Lilith Highchurch, she appears to be one of the deceased. Forensics are fingerprinting the rest while we wait on the ME's arrival." Decker rubbed his mouth and chin with his right hand and kicked at an imaginary rock on the ground. He audibly sighed. "Let's go."

As they approached the cabin, Rockfish noticed, to his immediate left, the front door to the garden shed hung open. To his trained investigative eye, it appeared more people than the small space could hold were milling around inside. He could see a couple in Hazmat suits, the rest putting their trust in something other than science.

The three walked up the front steps and to Rockfish, the outside of the cabin looked no different from two days ago. Weeds led them through the front door, followed by Decker, when a firm hand dug into Rockfish's chest. An FBI SWAT team member wearing a helmet and bulletproof vest played gatekeeper and, for whatever reason, he decided Rockfish wasn't welcome inside.

"Dan…"

"Lieutenant Dan Decker, Baltimore PD. He's with me, Special Agent. Let him through." Dan had spun around and flashed his badge. The officer lowered his hand and Rockfish proceeded in and contemplated the disgust he heard in Decker's voice. *This is going to all come down on him again. And shit rolls downhill. Will he even allow our relationship to be salvable? Probably not. Can't really blame him. But isn't a known threat, even if in the wind, better than the unknown?*

As Rockfish walked into the cabin, he noticed what he assumed was the FBI's Evidence Response Team, sitting around a rickety dining room table, bagging and tagging evidence before sealing each brown paper bag with red evidence tape. What caught his attention on the pile of evidence was his GPS tracker. It sat atop the pyramid of evidence and mocked him.

Well, that explains the bouncing happy white dot today. Each time he was asked to verify the location of the pickup, he was only partially wrong. The tracker was here the entire time, but Earl had tied up loose ends and beat feet. *Decker's building rage and impending eruption towards me is going to be justified. Jawnie and I fucked up royally. Earl is in the wind and some innocent people, and one not so innocent person, are dead. Fuck.* Stomach acid raced up his throat into the back of his mouth and Rockfish swallowed hard to keep it down. Jawnie. How the hell am I going to tell her? Let alone do it sober? *She'd take it hard. Damn hard. That I know.* The firm didn't have any kind of Employee Assistance Program, no shrink on call. *Does she have one of her own she could talk to? Who had the hospital assigned to Mack? Maybe that clown has some availability.*

Rockfish reached out to tap Decker's shoulder and point out the GPS tracker, but he had already moved a few steps forward and jockeyed amongst others to stand in the doorway to the small back room. Someone had removed the door, that Earl had closed to keep Jawnie from being nosey, from its hinges. It now leaned against the dining room wall. Rockfish took a step forward and peered in over Decker's shoulder.

Small was an understatement, and Rockfish estimated the room was no bigger than eight by ten. The walls were wood paneling, the same as the dining room and bare. Nylon rope tied the window curtains off to the side. The afternoon sun shone through, illuminating Mother Elizabeth and her chair in the center of the room. Four other bodies lay on a large, blood-soaked blanket at her feet. Rockfish recognized them all. From left to right, they appeared to lie in ascending order of importance. Diane Caruso, Sunshine West, Allison the shop owner, and finally Lilith. His mind went straight to who wasn't there. Roan. Weeds had said earlier the victims were all female, but it had slipped his mind. Dried blood soaked the dead's clothes and portions of the wood floor. Jawnie's research was spot on. Blood out of every orifice. Her words hung in head.

Not a total shit sandwich today. If I can get out of this cabin, with my head and ass intact, Jawnie and I could throw ourselves back into the job at hand and deal with this emotional baggage later. I got a client still to please, and Roan isn't one of these poor souls.

Attaboy son, kick the can. The voice of his father came from deep in the back of his mind. Mack never failed to quickly put things into perspective.

"I can help with the identification, Dan," Rockfish said, and he rattled off the names before stepping back into the dining room. He forced the rising bile back down his throat and pawed at the sweat forming on his forehead. The scene weighed heavily on Rockfish. Decker followed suit and a minute later, Weeds appeared from what Rockfish guessed was the kitchen area. She waved Rockfish and Decker towards the front door. They followed her out onto the porch and then down towards the far end, which overlooked the pond.

"The ME is headed up the driveway, so they want all non-essentials out of the cabin," Weeds said. "Based on the empties in the kitchen, the Vypadium gas that did them in. The All Natural Super Colossal Happy Dunking Snack wrappers littered the floor. The leading theory is that someone, most likely Porbeagle, mixed the chemicals. Mother Elizabeth, the old woman in the wheelchair, and three of the women on the floor appear to have died first. They appear to have gone voluntarily in some sort of religious ceremony. It fits the case's M.O."

"Yeah, moving to the other side, prior to the rapture knocking on their front door," Rockfish said.

Weeds nodded her head in agreement. Decker said nothing and showed no emotion.

"The one on the right end appears to have ligature marks on her arms and feet. She might not have gone along with this willingly and was later positioned on the floor. Of course, this is all from preliminary observation. Oh, also the shed was empty. Whatever wasn't mixed and used on the group inside went the way of Porbeagle."

"Great, so he's taken off with more of this shit to use," Decker said to no one in particular. He ran a hand through his hair and he kicked at the ground again.

"The consensus inside is Canada. Lilith had an address on a slip of paper folded in her pocket."

"Oh, come on, Dan!" Rockfish exclaimed. "That's the oldest trick in the book. No way Earl's headed there."

"That's enough out of you," Decker said, his index finger planted firmly in Rockfish's chest. Steve instantly knew the floodgates were now open. "Newsflash, Magnum P.I. They were all here, alive, but not anymore. Probably would have still been here hiding out, praying, contemplating their next grift, but you had to roll up and knock on the fucking front door."

"Please, what do you mean when I got here?" Rockfish said and held up his hands, palms facing Decker. "Don't shoot the messenger. Your minions were two states over, and if it wasn't for me, you'd still be interviewing every Latino kid you can find in Baltimore, spinning your wheels. Hoping for some Mexican Cartel connection to appease your bosses. They still touching themselves over the thoughts of that press conference? I can tell you—"

The opening notes of Thunder Kiss '65 wafted from Rockfish's pocket. He reached for the phone.

"It's Jawnie," Rockfish said, and took a few steps away from the other two before answering.

"Hey what's up? Absolute shit show here," Rockfish said.

"Steve. Lynn's missing. She walked out down the block to the convenience store and hasn't returned. Her Life Alert charm triggered. Could be nothing, could be something, but I'm scared to death its bad news."

"Me too. On my way." *Christ almighty, can this day get any fucking worse?*

CHAPTER TWELVE

Rockfish spotted Jawnie with her hand up, standing in the parking lot alongside the rental van.

"Sargent Weeds, over there," Rockfish said and pointed towards his partner.

Weeds slowed up and pulled the patrol car alongside Jawnie. Rockfish jumped out of the passenger side and ran around the front of the car.

"Hope your dad's going to be okay," Weeds shouted out of the driver's side window. Rockfish nodded, gave a wave, and jumped into the van.

"Decker didn't drive you back? And what's that about Mack? Is he okay?"

"Decker. We're dead to him. He called me *Steve-O for Two* as I left. Neither one of us should expect a Christmas card from him this year. And Mack's fine. When you called, I said it was someone from back home and Mack was in trouble. Your call was perfect timing. I had to get out of there or he was going to keep chewing my ass. I even apologized. Said, I was sorry this didn't work out the way we planned, but I got full faith in you guys tracking Porbeagle down, but I have to go be with my father."

"Gotcha," Jawnie said. "Here, hold this. Tell me if it changes direction and I'll fill you in as we go." She handed Rockfish her cellphone and dropped the van into drive. A minute later, they were pulling out of the parking lot and onto the road.

"Now what's this about Lynn? This isn't our tracking thingamajig," Rockfish said.

"Yeah, it's Apple's Find My iPhone app. That's Lynn's phone you're watching in real time. Whoever has her has a nice head start on us."

"I mean, by process of elimination, she's got to be with Earl and Roan," Rockfish said.

"Either that or whoever picked her up is taking her to Earl. Either is a winner."

"It's up to us to get them back safe," Rockfish said. "Everyone else will man the northern border waiting for him to cross. And no matter what we find out, no one is coming to help. Up to us and us alone to figure out what the fuck happened here." Rockfish slammed his hand down on the dashboard.

Jawnie didn't respond right away, and Rockfish could see the whites of her knuckles as she held a death grip on the wheel. Something about the sound of those next few words didn't sit right with him. He knew Jawnie was fast approaching the ledge with all she could take.

"Lynn kept saying she was hungry. By the time the SWAT teams were ready to go, we had our fill of coffee, donuts and various other carbs."

Her voice isn't the same, upbeat, everything is going to be alright. He could hear in her tone that she blamed herself for whatever happened. Rockfish thought of interrupting her, letting her know it's all going to work out in the end. They were the good guys, and the good guys always came out on top. But he also knew most of what he wanted to say was pure bullshit and that she'd see right through him. *Did it matter? It needed to be said and I need to convince her, have her believe, even in the short term, that everything will come out in our favor.*

"She said she was going to walk down a few blocks to the convenience store, JJ's Pump and Chomp, to see what they had and then call or text me to take my order. She never called, and I didn't think much of it. Hell, I thought little at all. I was caught in the drama coming over the radio when the SWAT team hit the cabin and found the bodies. I stood there, partially in awe and a good part disgusted, watching the streaming video from the body cameras and how those in the Command Post processed the information coming in from the operators. It was fascinating, repulsive. I took it all in, forgetting about my hunger and my partner. Both of you, actually. Caught up in the moment. It's a stupid thing to say, but I was."

Rockfish noticed as she spoke the whiteness had not receded from her knuckles and the sniffles followed. If she cried, he'd have to ask her to pull over and switch seats with him. She was clearly emotional about the situation and the more Rockfish listened, the more he was, too. Lynn was only in this predicament because Jawnie needed someone to drive her back to West Virginia and felt too exhausted to safely make the trip back herself. *Why was she exhausted? It was simple, stupid. You had ridden her too hard the two days prior and then made her drive the seven hours back herself to speak with Decker. It always comes 'round to you, doesn't it?* Rockfish sighed and ran a hand through his hair. He continued listening while trying to come up with the right thing to say.

"There I was, listening to the live reports, when my phone buzzed. I figured it was her, you know, asking for my order. It wasn't Lynn, but it was. The Life Alert app I had installed when she started working for us was the source of the notification. I had given her the little dongle because it looked like a nice little tchotchke accessory that no one would think twice about. It doesn't track location; it only serves as a something's wrong notification."

"I remember those. The old woman falls and can't get up," Rockfish said. "I remember the commercial."

"Exactly. I thought if she was attending those See You Next Tuesday meetings in the basement and something went wrong, she could push the button and I could run down the stairs and pull her out of there. When I realized what today's alert was, I still thought she might have hit it by accident, but I walked out of the fire hall and looked around the parking lot."

"You had a room full of cops and didn't think to take one with you?" Rockfish said. He could see Jawnie's eyes welling and remembered he's in listening mode here. There would be time to Monday morning quarterback later.

"They had their own job to do, so I started walking down the street to the store. I don't see her anywhere on the walk down, so I ask around, the people loitering outside the store and the clerk inside. But no one's seen her. I panicked, but then I remembered I could track her phone using the app. Again, for safety, we follow each other. I had promised her long ago I wouldn't use it to snoop on her whereabouts unless we were working."

"Is that when you called me?"

"No. I still wanted to handle this without bugging you. I sprinted back to the fire hall and grabbed the first man in uniform I saw. He listened but was of no help. That's when I called you."

"Let me guess, he gave you the standard, not missing for 24-hours, she's an adult, she can wander off if she likes, speech?"

"In so many words, yes."

"Local yokels. As bad as Ringle's men back in Jersey. I'll tell you what, press down on that accelerator a bit, you ain't going to get a ticket today. Every local in the county is back at the command post or out at the cabin. We need to make up some of this distance, or else we'll be chasing them into next week."

Rockfish knew as soon as those last words came out of his mouth, they were the wrong ones to say. Jawnie's eyes sprung several leaks and the tears flowed.

"I'm sorry, Jawnie, I didn't mean it like that." Rockfish searched his pockets for tissues, despite knowing he never carried them on his person. *It's the thought that counts. I'll have to have a friendly talk with her once this whole thing is over. In this business, not everyone involved comes out without a scratch. Sometimes people get involved and things don't end well. But I'll be goddamned if I let something bad happen to someone who's working on my behalf. Can't do shit from the passenger seat.*

"Look, you've been through a lot. Please pull over before you can't see where you're going."

Less than a minute later, the partners had switched seats and Rockfish floored it. Gravel and dirt flew up before the tires gripped the asphalt and the van lurched forward.

"Does that thing tell you how far behind we are?" Rockfish said.

"Yeah, it's right here on the main screen. Lynn's phone is twenty-three miles away, as the crow flies. Speaking of, they made a right on to State Route 606. That leads into the middle of nowhere, according to the map. Maybe we're better off not playing hero?"

"Excuse me," Rockfish said.

"I mean, call the authorities. Call someone. We kinda know—"

"I'm going to stop you right now. All we know is Lynn's phone is somewhere out there. Is Earl driving? What is he driving? We can make a shitload of assumptions but would need something better than those to pull Decker, the State Police or the Feds off of their current search. Plus, no one is picking up our calls again. We are the heroes."

Rockfish shook his head and pressed harder on the gas. He was close to testing the van's suspension and handling ability on this windy road. *Earl isn't thinking he's being followed, but he isn't exactly taking it easy either. He's trying to put as much distance between him and that search warrant as possible. I'm fucking coming for you.*

"Our only advantage is that he doesn't know we're following. I'm going to make up as much time and distance as this van will physically let us. You hold tight."

"Will do, boss. Thanks," Jawnie said, and reached over and gave his forearm a long squeeze.

****

Lynn tried opening her eyes, but the bright light caused them to instinctively slam shut. Shooting stars filled the darkness, and her attention turned to the throbbing in her jaw. Lynn winced and thought to touch the side of her face, to examine the source of the pain, when she realized both hands lifted off her lap. She cracked open her eyes slowly until they adjusted to the light and saw that someone had bound her hands at the wrist.

"Morning, sunshine," a voice to her left said.

"Do what he says," a whisper said from the right.

Lynn shut her eyes again and prayed it was a dream. From what little she heard and could see, she sat in a pickup, between Earl driving and someone else on her right. The rope on her wrists let her know she didn't voluntarily place herself in this situation. She opened her eyes and squinted to her right.

Roan. How the hell did I end up here? The last thing I remember was walking to the convenience store and then a tap on the shoulder. She kept her eyes open and the pain in her jaw filled in the rest of the backstory.

"Now don't you try anything," Earl said. "Roan's got explicit instructions to keep you under control, so don't you try anything."

"Where are you taking me?"

"Well, now, that's really none of your business. I mean, imagine my surprise when I spotted you walking down the street. I know what you're thinking. Why the hell would old Earl risk driving downtown with the cops at the ready to bring the pain? People talk and I've still got my contacts, or should I say, Lilith had. I had to drop off some shit, stuff that was too hot to handle before hitting the road. I knew the cops would be busy with the cabin and I could walk naked down Main Street and no one of any concern would notice. You might say, Earl, you've got some balls on you. I do. Then out of the blue, bam!" Earl slammed his fist down on the steering wheel and Lynn jumped a few inches off the truck's bench seat. "I see you walking down Main Street. Not a care in the world, it seemed. Talk about balls."

Well, that jives with my last memory. Pieces and small flecks of it came back. She remembered reacting to the tap on her shoulder and turning around to see Earl. *Had I screamed? Had anyone leaped to my defense or did they pull out their phones hoping to get TikTok famous?* Lynn recalled going for Jawnie's warning thing but couldn't be positive she had activated it before her head bounced off the concrete. *Do they know? Does anyone care? Why couldn't I have chosen a different alley?*

"That can't be, I thought, but sure as shit, there you were," Earl said. "Too strange, too much of a coincidence. First, I always knew something was up with you. You, Rockfish, and that dope that ripped me off, all started showing up at the same time. Lilith was too stupid to put the pieces together, but I had a hunch..." Earl tapped his index finger to the side of his head. When he moved his arm, Lynn noticed the men on each side wore matching flannel shirts, albeit different colors.

"... fuck, I'm pretty sure you're the blur on the edge of the video when Pérez broke in. Lilith didn't believe it. Maybe I didn't back then either, but when I saw you walking down Main Street, a couple of days after Rockfish shows up at my cabin, well, that sealed the deal. I was right all along, and it was time to claim my prize. Honey, you got a glass jaw, and I learned old Roan here, he has trouble carrying a sack of potatoes."

Screw you, dirt bag. Lynn quickly lifted her bound wrists towards the gearshift on the column. Her goal was to throw the vehicle into park and damn what happened to any of them, but the shifter only moved up into neutral before Earl's right elbow connected with the already throbbing side of her face.

"Shit, Roan!" Earl said. "I fuckin' told you to keep an eye on her. Hold her goddamn arms down now until I can figure something else out."

Lynn was woozy from the elbow, but it didn't knock her out as Earl had hoped. She could feel Roan twist on the small bench seat and grasp her forearms with his hands. Now, for the time being, Lynn was content to be the victim. She had shot her shot and promised herself it wouldn't be her last. She closed her eyes to think about anything other than the pain on the left side of her face. *Happy thoughts. Think happy thoughts. I've got to have some somewhere in this memory.* She leaned away from Earl, only to have Roan back in her ear.

Roan squeezed harder. "I told you to do what he says. You don't want to end up like the others."

"What's that Roan?" Earl said. "You giving the little lady some advice? How'd that work for the rest of your flock? I wouldn't listen to anything he says. He's still pissed that he missed the Rapture Express with the rest of the crew. Cut the shit, man. You're not as important as you once were."

Rapture Express? Had Lilith and the others that fled Baltimore died? Murdered? Those thoughts only made the pain worse. She could feel Roan's torso retreat away from her and move towards the truck's door with each word Earl shouted across the cab. Roan shuffled his feet and Lynn noticed her pocketbook on the floor between his legs. *My phone's in the bag, but no fucking way I'd be able to finagle a call stuck between these two. It also contains some pain relief. Maybe they'd take pity and allow me to dry swallow a couple. Can't hurt to ask. I have to put the pain behind me before trying to think straight.*

"I have some Advil in my bag. Can I please have a few?"

Lynn looked at Earl first, as he was clearly running the show and tried to give the saddest puppy dog eyes ever. She followed his eyes as they went from her down to the bag and then to her hands. He glanced back out over the hood of the truck before answering.

"Roan, dig through that fucking purse and see if you can find the damn aspirin. And as for you, Miss, don't move those hands of yours again. He'll drop them in your mouth or I'll drop you. Your choice."

Lynn watched as Roan bent over and pulled her pocketbook up onto his lap. He unzipped the top and dug down inside. He pulled her phone halfway out and instinctively tapped the screen. A dozen notifications filled it.

"They know—"

Lynn grabbed the purse strap before Roan could finish speaking and pulled with both hands. Roan automatically pulled back harder. Lynn lurched to her right and found her upper half lying across Roan's waist.

"Handle her!" Earl said, slamming his fist on the steering wheel. Lynn winced. She waited for the blow to her back that didn't come. Earl was too busy driving. She reached across, still holding on to the strap, and released the door latch. The passenger door flew open and then the pain came. Earl's fist landed square on her back and Lynn screamed. His hand moved from her spine, up to her collar, and jerked her back into a seated position.

"Shut the fucking door!" Earl said. Roan leaned over and reached out with his right hand, while his left remained firmly entrenched in the game of purse tug of war. Lynn could feel the truck slowing down as Earl became more concerned with his passengers than traffic.

"I can't reach it," Roan said.

"Close the damn door now." Earl repeated the order.

Roan leaned out to his right again. Lynn felt like everything slowed down. Not only the speed of the truck, but all of their actions. Roan leaned hard, causing him to pull more on the purse's strap, which pulled Lynn further towards the open door. She released her grip on the strap and watched as Roan tumbled ass over elbows out of the pickup and onto the side of the road. Lynn tried to sit back up and avoid the same fate, but Earl locked up the brakes and she was thrown hard against the dashboard. She found herself in the fetal position on the floor, previously occupied by her purse and Roan's feet.

Lynn looked up and watched as Earl stared at the rearview mirror. He shifted the truck into reverse and then immediately into park. He reached down and pulled her back up onto the bench seat by her shirt and pulled her close. His hand moved inside her collar and gripped her neck. Lynn winced, and a small yelp of pain escaped from her lungs. Inches from his face, his rancid breath filled her nostrils and bile rose up her throat. *Hold your breath. Concentrate on that scar along his chin. Don't give him anything.*

"You ain't going nowhere," Earl said. "Don't you fucking move, do you hear me?" He didn't wait for an answer. "Don't even think about making a run for it, because you ain't." He gave her neck a hard squeeze for good measure. "Now I'm going to let go. Don't you move a goddamn inch." Earl moved his hand from her neck, down the back of her shirt, and stopped at the top of her jeans. He tugged up on the denim and adjusted his grip.

Lynn tried to keep her head still and look at the rearview mirror. She could make out what she thought was Roan, lying motionless on the side of the road. *Is he dead? Does it matter?*

"No. You won't get far. Do as I say and lean over and shut that door. Try to run for it and you'll do it with no britches on. And I will catch you. Yeah, you'll have a couple of minutes before the blood fills your mouth and lose consciousness, but know, I'll beat you to death."

With the grip he had on her, Lynn knew she couldn't pull away. She leaned across the seat and reached for the door. She fell a few inches short and scooted her ass across the bench seat. Earl didn't loosen his grip but leaned with her. Lynn pulled the door shut.

"Lock it."

She leaned over again, and this time pushed the door lock down. Earl's hand remained on the back of her pants until he was back on the road and rapidly gaining speed.

They sat in silence for the next few minutes. Lynn never saw the backhand coming, but she welcomed the darkness as it flooded over her.

* * * * * * * * * *

"They're still on Route 606, but we've made up some distance thanks to your driving," Jawnie said.

"She's no Lana, but this old van is holding her own."

Rockfish was still behind the wheel as late afternoon turned to early evening. He continued to push the van to its limits as Jawnie gave periodic updates, as the app refreshed the data every couple of minutes.

"Down to twelve miles," Jawnie said. "Do you think we'll catch them this evening or lie back until they stop for the night?"

"Neither of us plan on stopping today, as far as I can tell. But we're going to have to soon, though." Rockfish pointed at the gas gauge on the dashboard. It had recently dropped below a quarter tank. "We're going to have to stop for gas, but it's not like they're traveling on an unlimited fuel source either." Rockfish looked over and winked at Jawnie. He was still trying to lighten the mood and keep her attentive and not languishing within her own head.

"According to Google Maps, there's a Valero station up on the left, roughly four miles. Hell, the only thing around for miles."

"Good, we'll resupply there."

Rockfish spotted the gas station as they approached and put on his blinker. He pulled the van alongside an open slot and paid at the pump. He secured the nozzle's latch so the gas would continue to flow as he walked inside to take a leak and pick up some snacks.

The inside of the store was riddled with half-stocked shelves and brand names Rockfish had never heard of. He found Jawnie already talking to the attendant. The kid couldn't have been over seventeen and his grease-stained clothes showed he might have been working on a vehicle outback before having to come up and man the register. Jawnie stood there holding up her phone and Rockfish assumed it was a picture of Lynn. He didn't stick around for the conversation, as she could fill him in when they were back on the road. He followed the wall signs to the restrooms. Jawnie was still at the counter when he came out. Rockfish trolled the two aisles of the small gas and go, filling his arms with bottled water, sunflower seeds for her and small bags of Fritos for him. He dropped the supplies down at the register and looked at his partner.

"He said he hasn't seen Lynn or an old white Chevy pickup recently."

"Yeah, man, like I told the lady, this here is Ford Country," the attendant said. "Ain't no man driving a Chevy round these parts. Those rusted out pieces of shit ain't worth a damn unless you're some underage turd learning to drive. Beaters, that's all they're good for."

"Well, thanks for all that," Rockfish said. "This will be it for us. I paid for the gas at the pump."

Jawnie took the plastic bag from the man behind the register and followed Rockfish out the door.

Rockfish looked at the total price on the pump and returned the nozzle. He closed the gas cap and made a mental note to call Marvin at Baltimore Pike Motors. They had agreed to an open-ended rental, but it had already been five days and Rockfish couldn't see the end of this mess no matter how hard he tried. *Marvin won't bug me as long as he's holding Lana as collateral in this deal. Hell, I may need to call him to make sure he doesn't sell her out from under me. I hate this van. I don't want to keep it a day longer than I need to.* Rockfish hopped back in the driver's seat and pulled the van back onto Route 606.

"Can you toss one of those water bottles in the cup holder for me and gimme one of those bags of Fritos?"

"Look down, dummy. Already put one out for you," Jawnie said. "And here's your snack bag."

She tossed the small bag onto his lap and Rockfish picked it up while keeping one hand on the wheel. He tore into the bag with his teeth and poured the single serving into his mouth.

"That's a good look. No wonder you're single," Jawnie said with a laugh.

Rockfish held up a finger. He couldn't talk until he emptied his mouth and then downed half his water bottle. He smiled to himself at her remark. *She's coming around. Let's keep the guilt express on the other set of tracks. I need her on her toes and that her mind firing on all cylinders when we get within striking distance.*

"How are we doing?" Rockfish said.

"Uh-oh."

"That doesn't sound good. What's up?" Rockfish said. He took a quick glance at his partner before turning back to the road. She stared down at her phone with a puzzled expression on her face.

"According to this, the pickup hasn't moved since we pulled over to get gas. Ten minutes, to be exact. The signal is stuck at eight miles away. Probably a tad less now with the speed you're driving."

"Meh, things happened," Rockfish said. "Maybe they pulled over like we did, or there's a GPS glitch at the moment. It's happened with these elevations. Give it a minute or two."

Three minutes later, as the app refreshed, Jawnie confirmed the diagnoses. "It has not moved a hair and we're only five miles out now. I pulled up the satellite view, and there wasn't any gas station or anything around that spot. For all we know, Earl may have tossed the phone out the window."

"Agreed. No way he's lying in wait for us. Can't know he's being followed," Rockfish said. He continued to think aloud. "Might be a tire problem, or that old piece of shit Chevy broke down. IF that's what Earl's driving. Out here, he'll wait all day for someone to drive by and offer help. The only other option is that he arrived at some pre-arranged rendezvous spot. In that case, we need to be careful."

"We're at about four miles now. Do you think he'll recognize the van from the other day?"

"No clue, but with this guy, I wouldn't put it past him. Keep giving me the mileage as we draw closer."

Rockfish retreated into his mind to come up with an on-the-fly plan.

I could stop a mile or so short and hike around and come at him from the side. Full on surprise mode. Yeah, you do that, and he'll end up pulling away the moment you get close and then you're stuck risking a heart attack in a mad rush back to the van. Fuck.

"Three miles."

I could drive past and circle back, hoping to get some worthy intelligence on that pass-by. Pray that Earl doesn't recognize the damn van and take off in the opposite direction. If his truck didn't break down, that is. What if he is lying in wait and I walk our dumb asses headfirst into it? Come on brain, work with me.

"Two miles."

Too many damn ifs. I need to slow down before I arrive with my hand on my dick. Rockfish let up on the gas pedal and leaned out over the wheel. He tapped his right ankle with his left foot. *Of course, the gun is still there. Where the fuck did you think it went? How would Jawnie fare if this turned into a shootout? Christ, stop with the sidebar thoughts. Think. What do you plan on doing two goddamn minutes from now?*

"One mile."

Okay, drive up alongside the truck, hit the brakes and put this thing sideways in front. Block it from the front. I could use the van as a shield in case things turn hot and heavy right off the bat, and it would also force Earl to reverse out and around if he made a run for it.

"Should be coming up on them any minute now."

Rockfish went with the last option and leaned further out over the steering wheel to see what waited ahead. He pushed back down on the accelerator and went with the last option.

"When I stop, get down. I'll go for Earl and when I've got him occupied, grab Lynn from the pickup and get her into the van if you can. If not, stay with her until I get there. With some luck, Earl will run for the hills and this thing will go off without a hitch." *I hope.* He reached down for his gun. "Either way, say a prayer."

"I don't see a truck," Jawnie said.

"I don't see shit either, only clear open spaces. I bet he tossed it," Rockfish said.

"Ah, I see something, something lying ahead, on the dirt shoulder. Slow down," Jawnie said.

Rockfish ignored the instruction and stuck with his plan. Pickup or no pickup. He hit the brakes and brought the van to a stop past what they both quickly recognized as a body. A person. Neither said a word as they jumped out and sprinted towards the back of the van.

Rockfish reached the middle-aged man first. He was on his side and Rockfish gently pulled on his shoulder, and with a loud moan, the man rolled over onto his back.

"You can't do that. You don't know what injuries he's suffered."

"I don't see any broken bones sticking out, so he'll be fine. Lynn didn't have this much facial hair, so do you think..."

"It's Roan," Jawnie said. "That bruise on his face means he's probably concussed. Hopefully, that is the extent of his injuries. Appears he was thrown from the truck. Or saw his chance and jumped."

"You think? Look at him. Not at a high speed, but I'm betting he was thrown out. It pays to be fat sometimes, and this might be one of those," Rockfish said. He was already contemplating how to get the man up and into the van. *I don't see any bleeding. No need to call the authorities. We need to get him back to The GearJammer and see what he can tell us. Before driving him back to Claudia, of course.*

"Stay with him for a second," Rockfish said. "See if he can tell you what hurts. I want to take a quick walk around and see if I can find that phone."

Rockfish found Lynn's purse with the phone still inside, a few paces off the road. It seemed to fair better than Roan. He walked back towards where Jawnie remained hunched over.

"I've poked and prodded and he only moans when his head moves."

"Good. Think we need to call the EMTs?"

"He's definitely concussed," Jawnie said. "Nothing appears to be broke or bleeding, other than these scrapes on his arms and forehead."

"If he's not better in the morning, we'll get him help," Rockfish said and tossed Jawnie the pocketbook. "Put this in the van, fold down those second-row seats and back that thing up right alongside him. The less we have to carry him, the better."

"Are we going to continue after Earl?" Jawnie said.

"How? Are we going to Rock Paper Scissors at the next intersection on which way to go? We don't know where he's headed. But you know what? This one might." Rockfish glanced down at Roan and smiled.

****

Rockfish kept one eye on the road and the other on their currently incapacitated passenger.

The van ride back to the GearJammer was long and anything but smooth. Roan moaned after each bump or sharp turn in the road. Jawnie apologized after each, but after the first couple of miles, Rockfish kindly told her to knock it off. If she wanted to play nursemaid, she could climb in the back and rest his damaged melon on her lap. And that's exactly what she did.

The partners agreed on a plan, or at least Rockfish hoped they did. He did most of the talking and hoped Jawnie's silence didn't show her anxiety's return to where it was prior to picking up Roan. The shit sandwiches were coming fast now, stacking one on top of the other, before Jawnie could fully resolve, digest, or deal with the one prior. Rockfish had faith. She was excellent when it came to learning on the job.

"We'll get him to The GearJammer and go from there. Baby steps right now," Rockfish said. "Technically, we've closed our missing person case. Mission accomplished, excluding the delivery of this guy, but we're still down one potential receptionist candidate. She's headed who knows where, in what direction. This guy is our only clue, our only hope for a point in the right direction."

Jawnie agreed, but Rockfish couldn't look past that thousand-yard stare coming from her. He continued anyway.

"We get this guy some rest, make sure he's got no internal injuries, and see what he can tell us. Then we call Claudia and tell her the good news. If need be, you can take him back in the van and collect our money. I'll figure out transportation on this end and go in whatever direction he gives us."

Roan eventually had fallen asleep or passed out. Rockfish couldn't tell the difference. It seemed the slightest bump or nudge would cause him to cry out in pain, despite not being conscious. *What the heck did Earl put this guy through? Was he reliving it in his head?* Each time Roan cried out or moaned, Rockfish thought back to his grandfather's last days. The old man, lights out to the world around him, laid in a hospital bed and groaned in pain every time the blanket shifted, or a nurse gently touched him.

Rockfish pulled the van up to the parking spot directly in front of his room. The GearJammer's parking lot was mostly empty, and he hoped the number of lookie-loos would be at a minimum as they carried Roan to his room. It took some doing, but they finally had him sitting up in the van with his legs dangling outside. Each partner laid an arm across their shoulders and lifted on the count of three. They half-dragged, half-carried Roan into the room and let him flop, face down, onto the extra twin bed. *Probably not the right medical thing to do. But hey, what can you do?*

Rockfish removed the red flannel shirt and black track pants from Roan, leaving him on the bed in a pair of tighty-whities. They examined the man up and down to further check for injuries or bleeding they may have missed with their roadside overview. At the conclusion of the examination, Doctor Rockfish inferred Roan would be sore for many days to come, but he suffered from no real serious injuries other than the concussion.

"With that bump on the noggin, he's going to be pretty sensitive to light," Rockfish said. "Let's keep the shades drawn tight and only use the overhead light outside the bathroom door." *Hey buddy, how scrambled are those brains? Did Earl slow down prior to pushing you out? If that's what happened. What would have happened in that small cab for Earl to slow down and leave you behind? And how the hell did you end up with Lynn's purse?* These questions needed answers, but Rockfish was content to let Roan rest thru the evening but come the morning, the fifth degree would happen, minus the glaring spotlight. It would be useless to question him now.

Jawnie brought food in that evening, and Roan surprised them by eating, but not doing much of anything else. He remained quiet and withdrawn as Rockfish watched an old John Wayne, black and white movie. Jawnie had propped herself up in the chair by the door after dinner. Even in the dark room, Rockfish could see the exhaustion that covered every inch of her face.

"Go to bed, kid," Rockfish said. "I got it from here. Grab a key to let yourself in, in the morning." Those words were the last thing Rockfish remembered and not even the mortar fire and machine guns on the beaches of Iwo Jima coming through the TV could keep his eyes open.

The following morning, Jawnie used the key she had picked up last night and let herself back into Rockfish's room.

"Morning, sunshine," Rockfish said. "Ten o'clock, someone needed their shut eye."

"Yeah, I'm feeling better, but I could sleep for another six or seven hours," Jawnie said as she came in and shut the door behind her. "I brought breakfast. How's Roan holding up?" She put the plastic takeout bags atop the table in the corner. "I mixed it up this time for you. I went to casa del Waffle."

Rockfish laughed and realized the night's sleep did his partner well. He didn't answer her question, but tilted his head towards the small bathroom alcove where they could talk somewhat privately.

"He's a little more with it this morning," Rockfish said. "Able to move around, albeit slowly. The bruises are beginning to show."

"When we drive him back to Baltimore, we can take a couple of these comforters and wrap him up good before we strap him into one of the back seats," Jawnie said. "The front desk has our corporate card. They can bill us."

"Yeah, about taking him back. I called Claudia this morning and filled her in. She expects us to be on the road with him yesterday."

"We can get on the road within the hour, if needed," Jawnie said. "I'm sure that might brighten him up, if he knew he could be in his own bed by nightfall."

"Oh, he knows. I put him on the phone with her after she got done barking orders at me. I handed him the phone, and they talked. Well, she talked. I'm pretty sure he didn't mumble more than a dozen words. You should have seen his eyes light up. There might have been tears, but I didn't get that close to see."

"Did he say anything to you after?"

"Not a word. His eyes said thank you, but he's been staring at the television since. Do you want to take a crack at him? Maybe kid gloves will work?"

Jawnie cracked a smile and gave Rockfish a fist bump before spinning around. She took the one chair in the room and put it right next to Roan's bed. He was sitting up, his back against the headboard, but there wasn't any room for Jawnie on either side. She sat on the edge of the chair and leaned forward while Rockfish hung in the alcove. *Out of sight, out of mind.*

"Hi, Roan. My name is Jawnie. I'm not sure you remember me, but you gave me this," she said and pulled out Roan's *Wilhelm, Gicobe and Stottlemyer* business card.

"McDonalds," Roan whispered. His eyes lingered on the card for only a second before returning to his lap.

"I'm glad you remember. You were doing a lot of good back then, loading up with food to feed the less fortunate. That was an uplifting thing you did for those people. I bet they're all wondering what happened to you. Since you remembered that, I'm going to ask you some questions about what's happened since you left Baltimore."

Roan didn't respond or lift his head. Jawnie reached out with her hand and held his. Roan initially jerked his hand back, but he didn't pull it completely away.

The kid's got skills I don't have the patience for. Rockfish shuffled to his right to get a better view.

"Do you know where Earl is going to now? He's got a good friend of mine with him, and I'd like to get her back to us, safely." When Roan didn't respond as quickly as he did to the first question, Jawnie reached out with her free hand and stroked the top of his hand she held. It took a minute of coaxing, but Roan spoke. The man's voice still didn't register above a whisper, and Rockfish could barely hear. He took a step closer and then a second. Roan and Jawnie hadn't noticed his presence.

"There's a guy... stole money... caused all this. Earl wants it, needs it back."

Raffi! They're headed back to Baltimore. Why risk going back to settle a debt with someone, when every cop in that state, not to mention the Feds, is on the lookout for you. Maybe he thinks they're as stupid as I do, setting up roadblocks on all major roads and bridges leading into Canada.

"Roan, how did you get injured?" Jawnie continued her line of questioning. "Did Earl do it?"

There was a longer gap of silence here before he answered.

"Asked me to get something... from her purse. She grabbed it... opened the door... pushed me out."

"That's my receptionist!" Rockfish said under his breath.

"Why didn't Earl come back for you?" Jawnie said.

"I don't know. I think... I'm of no use... the cards... don't work anymore."

Rockfish nodded in agreement. Claudia had mentioned on the call earlier that she and her lawyer had successfully frozen all accounts Roan had access to. *If she had forced that issue sooner, instead of piecemeal, a lot of this shit wouldn't have happened. Nothing like paying for a service and not listening to reason.*

"Roan, can you tell me what happened back at the cabin before you and Earl rode away in the truck?"

This time, there was no delay in Roan's reaction. He shook his head slowly, side-to-side and then faster. He pulled his hand from Jawnie and cradled his head with both hands. Roan moaned in pain.

"That's gonna leave a mark," Rockfish said, and took the last step from the alcove and into the room proper. He walked over behind Jawnie and bent over. "Excellent job, partner," he whispered in her ear with a light pat on the back.

Rockfish stood there like a dope waiting for the thank you that didn't come. Instead, Jawnie shuffled out of the chair, squeezed half her ass on the side of the bed, leaned in, and wrapped her arms around Roan.

"We're going to get you home now," she said. Her comforting words were muffled, but Rockfish could make a few out. He watched as Roan's arms slowly moved from his head and returned the favor.

Rockfish let them have their moment and walked past them and out the door. He wanted to let the front desk know they'd be checking out early. *It's 11:30. Too close to noon and I don't want to get charged for another day here in Wild and Wonderful West Virginia.* He looked forward to sleeping in his own bed tonight for the first time in almost a week.

On the walk back to the room, Rockfish loitered outside for a few. He ran through Roan's answers again and tried to fill in the blanks on his own.

Earl needs cash. Allison's riding the Hale-Bopp comet to heaven, and Roan's cards were declined. Ergo, Earl needs the cash Raffi stole. Lying low doesn't cost much, but the minute he decides it's time to flee, there are palms that will need to be greased. His goal is probably the same as it was when Lilith thought she was running the show: cross the border, eventually get to the Seychelles Islands, and access the money. Then on to French Polynesia or some other faraway place, where he feels the Government can't get at him.

Rockfish kicked a stone across the parking lot when it hit him. He cursed and smacked the palm of his hand to his forehead. He cursed a second time, this time in pain.

We need to find Lynn. The sooner the better. She knows the money is in the office safe. How much can she take from Earl before spilling her guts to literally save her guts? We need to be on the road like three hours ago. Fuck bringing Roan directly home. I gotta get to the office and move that money.

Then it's a waiting game because he's gonna come looking for it. Fuck, Lynn's not collateral damage, you dumb fuck. She works for you. You lie in wait for Earl, you're signing Lynn's hospital admission forms, or worse. A memory of the scene in the cabin's back room flashed before his eyes. *Have to get to her before Earl breaks her.*

Rockfish fumbled for his room key, threw open the door and took in Jawnie and Roan, still sitting on the bed.

"Let's go get our receptionist."

CHAPTER THIRTEEN

Lynn awoke in a fog, her head leaning against the pickup's passenger door window. A line of drool stretched from the window to her mouth as she tried to sit upright. Fog enveloped the truck also, as she squinted to see outside but couldn't see past the front bumper. *Things were better when they were shut.* Lynn closed her eyes.

Pain. The throbbing across her head, and particularly her jaw, never dissipated. It hurt so much she couldn't even move it. *Worse than when Jimmy Buffalo kicked the shit out of me while I was on the floor withdrawing. But that was another lifetime, a long time ago.* The current pain was all she could deal with at the moment, no time for old memories. Her attention returned to the line of drool and she remembered she couldn't close her mouth. The bone no longer wanted to cooperate. Mouth-breather was the first word that came to mind, but the pain wouldn't even allow a forced smile.

Did the old truck have a passenger side visor mirror? How bad is it? Was it worth looking at? It's not like I can do anything other than get more upset. These thoughts alone exhausted Lynn and, with her defenses down, uncontrolled memories of the previous day came flooding back. Her brain winced at the visuals and the physical pain that stuck around long after the blows stopped. *What if I hold my jaw? Cradle it and try to stop any sudden movements. The pain should lessen. PLEASE.*

Lynn's brain signaled her left hand, but both hands moved. Confused, Lynn tried again and both hands lifted. She cracked her eyelids to see what the problem was and remembered the rope. It still bound her hands as it had when she'd tussled with Roan over the pocketbook. *Roan. Had he gotten up? Could he? Did he limp down that back road? Had a Good Samaritan stopped and helped him?* A small voice in the back of her head countered. *Stop worrying about the fat man and instead come up with a plan to get yourself out of this dilemma. You will not take much more pain before you succumb to whatever he wants.*

Lynn eased her head against the window and prayed for sleep to take her away. The truck hit a bump and her head lifted an inch off the glass before bouncing back. She wanted to scream and tried to, but what came out was more like the cry of a wounded bird after flying into an unforgiving patio door. Lynn slowly eased her head back onto the window and noted a large green sign as it passed.

I-68 Cumberland

Back in Maryland. Was Baltimore Earl's end goal? The pain was too much, and Lynn succumbed to the welcomed darkness again.

The next thing Lynn knew, her door opened, and her body leaned further to the right. Panic filled her mind. She pictured herself falling and then rolling down the shoulder as 18-wheelers sped by. Her body moved less than a couple of inches before Earl's hand grabbed her shoulder and pushed her upright.

"Here, got you this milkshake. I didn't think you'd be too good with solids. Plus, I need you somewhat alive," Earl said, and he pushed her back upright and closed the door.

Lynn slid the end of the straw between her lips and siphoned with all the strength she had. It wasn't much, but the coolness felt good sliding down her throat. The shake rivaled those she used to get with her sister, in better times, when they rode their bikes down to the General Store. Tension in the back of her neck followed the coolness and as it tightened Lynn knew what was coming. *Brain freeze.* She welcomed it, or any other pain, to take the attention away from the constant throbbing on the side of her face. The cold from the cup against her hand gave her an idea. Lynn put the milkshake against the side of her face. *It isn't an ice pack, but should work as well.* She held the cup against the left side of her jaw and felt nothing. Lynn panicked and moved the cup around, but the result was always the same. The pain never receded, and she couldn't feel the cold, other than against her hands.

Later, she finished the shake and wondered what her sister was up to. *Maybe she was right about a lot of things and I shouldn't have stormed out. Someone's help doesn't mean you owe them. Maybe it means they care.* Sister thoughts quickly turned to Jawnie. *Was she out there? Did that piece of shit alert button work? Was she out there looking, searching, trying to find her? Was it possible for Rockfish to be rocketing up the highway behind*—

The empty McDonald's cup slipped from her hands and fell towards the dirty floor mat. Lynn was unconscious again before it settled between her feet.

"Hey! Wake the fuck up!" Earl shouted, and Lynn jerked awake. She did not know how long she had been out this time. Her vocal cords wanted to yell, but what came out of her mouth was nothing close. "Damn, you sound like a shot coyote. We're almost home, sunshine. You got a place you're staying? Alone? I'm going to need a place to crash. Rest up, recharge those batteries for a couple of hours and then you're going to help me with something very important. And then, maybe then, I'll let you go." Earl held his fist up towards Lynn. She winced and felt it, even though he faked the punch and dropped his hand.

"Ha! You're learning," he said. "Now where were you staying?"

Lynn tried to explain the best she could that her voice didn't work. She used a combination of moans and wrist-bound, two-handed sign language. It took Earl a bit, but he finally understood. He nodded back at Lynn and pulled the truck over on the side of the Interstate. A second later, he walked around to the passenger side and threw open her door.

"Right or left-handed?" He said.

Lynn wiggled the fingers on her right hand and Earl untied her wrists. Lynn flexed them, but the relief was short-lived.

"Left hand behind your back," Earl said, and he didn't wait for Lynn to process the request. He grabbed her arm and put it behind her back and pulled. She could feel the shoulder joint being stretched to its limit. He re-tied the rope around that wrist and then to the door handle. Earl stepped back to admire his work before opening the glove box. Lynn's eyes locked on the handgun piled atop a stack of papers.

A gun? There's been a goddamn gun sitting inches away from me this entire time. Goddamnit. Her chin sunk to her chest with the realization her one chance had only been inches away. She didn't care to even try to stop the tears this time.

Earl picked up the handgun, stuck it in his waist, and gave a wink before continuing to rifle through the glove box. He pulled out a square pad of Post-it Notes and a fat rectangular carpenter pencil.

"I ask, you write," Earl said. He dropped the items on Lynn's lap and asked his first question. "Do you have a place of your own? I got keys to the Superstore but damn if that ain't the first place someone would look."

Lynn had trouble gripping the large pencil in her hand and fumbled with it.

"I don't have time for your bullshit," Earl said. He raised and cocked his fist back. "No fake-out this time."

Lynn scratched out a shaky *yes* on the pad, and Earl dropped his arm back to his side.

"Where?"

Super 8 Brooklyn Pk Rm 107

Lynn looked from her answer to Earl's face, but his head was down. *Glaring at his phone, searching the address.* When he finally glanced up, he smiled, slammed the door shut, and returned to the driver's seat. Lynn eased her forehead back onto the window, but the pain-free sleep eluded her grasp and instead it was a painful last hour and a half of the drive.

Earl didn't speak until the Super 8 was within eyesight and simply pointed out the window as they approached. Lynn pointed with the tip of the pencil to the note she had previously scribbled *yes* on and had stuck to the dashboard.

Earl pulled the truck into the parking lot and parked directly in front of Lynn's room. As he got out of the truck and walked around, Lynn looked at the old analog clock next to the oil pressure gauge.

2:15pm, if it was even correct. Tuesday, Wednesday, Thursday? She had lost track a while ago.

"Gimme your key."

Does he not remember my purse flying out the door with Roan? Lynn scribbled down her one-word answer.

Purse

"Fuck!" Earl said and spat on the ground. "No. I don't fucking believe you." Earl lifted her right arm out of the way and dug into her jean's front pockets. When they came up empty, he checked the back pockets. The same result awaited him there.

Earl took a step back and scanned the row of rooms. Lynn followed his eyes and spotted a cleaning woman pushing a cart, walking in their general direction. Earl leaned in.

"Don't you move, don't you moan a goddamn word. If you try either, I'll not only beat you to death, I'll make sure Consuela there gets a taste of these fists *first*." Earl gave her jaw a squeeze and winked. Another level of pain washed over Lynn.

Earl left his door open and strolled in the direction of the cleaning woman. He stepped in front of the cart to the left of Lynn's room as the woman approached. Lynn could hear every word and wanted to shout out to the woman, but couldn't. *If there was some sort of fucking signal I could give.* But mentally, she'd never forgive herself if the woman took a punch to the head and was unceremoniously dumped into her own cart and pushed behind the dumpster. Only to be found by junkies later that evening.

"Hey ma'am. My girlfriend over there lost her key," Earl said and pointed back towards the truck. "She was in a nasty car accident and the keys were in her purse, which is still in the car, on the back of a wrecker."

Lynn could see the woman's mouth move, but she couldn't make out her response.

"I know, the front desk," Earl said. "I'm going to hit them up, but I'd like to get her off her feet and some ice to help with the swelling. The EMT at the scene said she needed to elevate her feet and put ice on her head. If I can lay her on the bed and get her all settled, I swear I'll run right up to the front desk and get a new key."

The woman looked over at Lynn in the truck and slowly shook her head from side to side. Lynn wondered what Earl's next play would be. But, the woman pulled out her skeleton key card and walked over to the door. Her head never stopped shaking until the door was open and Earl thanked her with a hug.

"Never a doubt," Earl said. A second later, he untied the rope, scooped up his bride and carried her across the threshold.

* * * * * * * * *

Six hours after the happy couple crossed into their honeymoon suite, Rockfish put on his blinker and guided the van towards the I-70 exit and the Baltimore Beltway. He had driven the entire way, with Jawnie keeping Roan company in the second-row seating. Rockfish kept the music loud and his eyes on the road, but he occasionally checked on his passengers through the rearview mirror. Jawnie's lips were always moving, and while Roan didn't reciprocate at the same speed, he seemed to hold his own.

Good for them. If he clams up when the police come to interview him, maybe Jawnie could fill in the gaps and even get him talking. Instances like this made him thankful, yet again, for the completely unique set of skills she brought to the team.

The van merged onto the Baltimore Beltway and Rockfish felt a tap on his shoulder. He reached down and lowered the volume on the radio.

"If you can find a place, I need to stop."

"We're literally a half-an-hour out. Nothing I can do to get you to hold it?"

"Not unless you want to pay for the cleaning fee when you return this mom-mobile."

"Next exit it is," Rockfish said. Four minutes later, he flicked on the turn signal and exited off the highway. A blue sign pointed the way to a bevy of fast-food restaurants, half-a-mile down Pole Green Road. He pulled the van into the first one, a combination Long John Silver's and A&W.

Jawnie jumped out the side door and Rockfish shouted after her, "I'll stay here with the big guy." He got out of the driver's seat and took over Jawnie's spot in the second-row. "Hey Roan, almost home. We'll have you there soon buddy, but I gotta make one small stop on the way. It will be a quick detour, I promise."

Rockfish looked to his left for a reply or any kind of emotional recognition, but Roan's face was unresponsive. He tried again.

"I know Jawnie's been talking your ear off, but after all of this, I really wanted to ask about how you got involved with this group. Did you fumble across them, or did they come after you with some sort of full court press?"

"Embarrassing," Roan replied and lowered his head.

Rockfish waited to see if there was more, but that was it.

"I get it. Totally embarrassing. Same for my dad and a friend, who fell for their schtick. I understand why you don't want to talk about it. But you're going to have to at some point. The police will want a statement from you. A lot of shit has happened."

This time Roan closed his eyes and only nodded. Rockfish called it a day with his questions and not long after, Jawnie exited the restaurant and walked towards the van.

"Does this mean I'm driving the rest of the way?"

"No. I'm going to finish the rally," Rockfish said and jumped down out of the back seat. "Why don't you sit up front with me the rest of the way, so we can talk. I think he'll be okay for a little while. But first, let me try Raffi again."

Rockfish picked up his phone and pushed send for the fifth time since they'd cross the Maryland state line.

You've reached Pérez, Longmire and Associates, recently profiled in Financial Markets Quarterly. We are—

Rockfish dumped the phone down into the cup holder without leaving another message. There were three already cued and waiting. With an outgoing message like that, Rockfish could only imagine the type of scam that Raffi was currently running.

Boy, there's a ton of shit headed your way. You better pick up soon, or fucking buckle up.

"Do you think Earl's already got to him?" Jawnie said, interrupting Rockfish's thought.

"I think if he did, we'd have already heard from old Earl. You've seen this movie as many times as I have. Earl applies the pain. Raffi rolls over on us, and then we set up a meeting to exchange the cash for the hostages."

"Yeah, but in those movies, the shit hits the fan, and everything goes wrong."

"Don't worry. I follow directions very well," Rockfish said with a wink.

Rockfish pulled out of the parking spot. He headed back towards the Beltway with the next stop being their office. He turned up the music and shifted the sound towards the back set of speakers to give them some privacy.

"We're stopping by the office first," Rockfish said. "I know with him our case is closed. But I don't have to tell you that until we have Lynn back in the fold, safe and sound, it's really not. I want to grab that cash box since it's our one element of surprise."

"Huh?"

"If I have it with me, and no matter if we run into Earl or if Raffi calls and says Earl wants the cash, I'm ready to wheel and deal that instant. Not to mention Earl doesn't know we're already back here and we know that he's here. I'll go out on a limb and assume Earl wants to trade Lynn for the cash box. Once Raffi says he doesn't have it, he'll sell us out in a heartbeat to save himself. No anger towards him, it's who he is. That is why it's imperative that he answer his goddamn phone!" Rockfish slammed his fist on the center console.

"Nice guy to have on our team," Jawnie added.

"Most times, the good outshines the bad. But when Earl's call comes in, I'm ready to go that instant. I can do the deal right then. If I needed to get the money first, then there's time for shit to go south. I want to do it immediately after he calls. Put that fucker back on his heels and keep driving."

Jawnie nodded.

I wonder if she's buying it. Or does she hate the idea but have nothing to throw against it?

After a minute, she spoke. "I get it. But we have to think about what if he broke Lynn? What if she's already told him the money is in the safe? I mean, it's not beyond belief."

"Now you're talking nonsense. You know how I know? If Lynn told him where the money was, he would have already driven through the door with that damn truck and the alarm company would have reached out. Come on, kid."

Jawnie sighed, nodded. "Yeah, I'm tired and not thinking straight."

"But I got faith in your girl. Like I said, I'm going to get it out of the safe. And newsflash, while I'm opening the safe, you're going to return our package back there to its rightful owner. Don't gimme that look, I'll help you get him into the Subaru. You left it in the parking lot before we left, right?"

"I did, but how the heck am I going to get him out of the car?"

"Claudia? Plus, she's got that guy, James. I guarantee you he's live-in help. Make sure you get the check from her, then head home and get some rest. I'll be in touch."

"Yeah, I'm going to use my trump card here," Jawnie said. "With him running around out there, we're not splitting up. He could be watching Roan's house or even the office for all we know. I'd feel safer if you were by my side."

Rockfish took in what she said and couldn't find fault with her reasoning. Two against one sounded better after she said it.

"I agree. You're totally right on this one. Let's stop by the office, drop him off, get Lana and then try to track down Raffi. After I grab the cash, I want to put a note on the door in case Earl shows up. Save our insurance deductible at least."

"Say what?" Jawnie said.

"You know, in case Lynn lets anything slip. Something short to say I've got the cash on me with my phone number. Call me, we'll trade. Something like that."

"You think it'll work?"

"We each have something the other person wants. Couldn't be easier. If we don't hear back and it's relatively early, I know a few places Raffi likes to hang. We'll find him, don't worry. "

They debated the merits of Rockfish's plan for the rest of the drive. When they pulled into the parking lot, both let out an audible sigh of relief when their door was in one piece and the parking lot, empty. Rockfish pulled up front and left the van running.

"Keep the doors locked until I'm back," Rockfish said. He unlocked the front door and went inside.

As he walked into the office, Rockfish thought back to the original call he received from Claudia. A simple cheating husband case turned into a search and rescue, cult exfiltration, and wild ride that somehow tied all back to Mack and Iggy getting ripped off by some online boobs. *What a long, strange trip, indeed.* He turned off the alarm and fluorescent light filled the space.

Rockfish took nothing for granted and he walked across the office floor to make sure there were no surprises hiding behind a door, waiting for the perfect time to strike. When the coast was clear, he opened the safe and pulled out the cash box. From the outside, nothing had changed and when he popped the lid, the inside remained full.

Now, if I can swap Lynn for this damn cash. Wash my hands of this total mess. Fuck Earl. Gimme Lynn and he can go wherever the fuck he wants at this point. I'm done. Let Decker track him down and put him behind bars and play asset forfeiture monkey. Somewhere on the other side of the world was a bank account waiting to be emptied. Earl or the authorities. Does it really matter who got to it in the long run?

Rob Zombie interrupted Rockfish in mid-thought, and he looked down at the Caller ID.

Raffi!

"Raffi, where are you?"

"Me first. Stevie, why you blowing up my phone?"

"I don't have the time to fill you in right now. Listen to what I say. Stop whatever you're doing and get to my house as soon as you can. I'll meet you there in a bit, and I'll call Mack to let him know you're on your way."

"Stevie—"

"Please. Do what I ask for once in your fucking life. Keep your head down and get moving!" Rockfish said and hung up without waiting for an answer.

I got the money. I got Raffi. Lana's the only one left before the home stretch. And Lynn. Can't forget her. He walked around behind the bar and poured himself a much-needed celebratory drink.

"I got to him first, Earl." Rockfish said aloud and downed his shot. "Now where the fuck does Jawnie keep the Sharpies?"

****

Jawnie watched as Rockfish taped his ripped sheet of loose-leaf paper to the inside of the door, facing out.

Yeah, that won't raise any eyebrows of anyone traversing the sidewalk over the next day or two. For the ride to Claudia's, never mind how short it was compared to how far they came, Jawnie jumped back next to Roan for the ride. "We're taking you home now," she told him and reached out for his hand. "It's all going to be over shortly. We'll all be happy to sleep in our own beds tonight." Roan said not a word, but squeezed her hand back. Jawnie needed nothing more.

"Next stop, the Coyne estate," Rockfish said as he jumped back behind the wheel. "It's almost eight. I hope Claudia's waiting up for us. Heck, I know she will be."

"Yeah, didn't you already call her and make sure she had our check waiting?" Jawnie said. She hoped he could hear the sarcasm in her voice.

Rockfish saw the spotlights at the far end of the long driveway as soon as he cleared the front gate. The closer he got, he made out three people waiting on the van's arrival. Claudia, a short, stout man, and James. *I guess he really lives on premises.* James seemed to stand next to what appeared to be a hospital gurney. *It very well could be. I wouldn't put it past Claudia to put on such a show that she would need to be wheeled back inside as the van pulled away.*

Rockfish brought the van to a stop next to where the three stood, and Jawnie reached over and slid open the door on Roan's side. Claudia ran to her husband.

The partners exited the van on the driver's side and walked around to take in the reunion. Rockfish gave a nod in James' direction and the butler returned the gesture.

Claudia stepped back out of the van and shuffled in Rockfish's direction, and he helped her out by meeting halfway.

"Thank you, Steve," was all she said before burying her face in his chest, sobbing.

"Hey, no need to thank us, all in a day's work for *Rockfish & McGee*," Rockfish said, waving Jawnie over to get in the hug so he could step away. It took a couple of minutes longer for Claudia to compose herself and Jawnie to join the escape club.

"Steve, Jawnie, this is Doctor Winchester, the Coyne family private physician," Claudia said and stepped aside so that Doctor Winchester could step forward and shake Rockfish's outstretched hand.

"Nice to meet you two, but if you'll excuse me, I want to get started on Roan's examinations to see if we need to transport him off the grounds."

Rockfish and Jawnie watched as James and the Doctor worked like a well-oiled machine and got Roan up on the gurney. James moved around to the back end to assume the pushing position when Roan lifted his hand and everyone stopped. He held his hand out to Jawnie and she stepped over to take it in hers and gave it a squeeze.

"Thank you," Roan said. There were words that followed, but Doctor Winchester wasn't having any of the sappiness, and placed an oxygen mask over Roan's face. Jawnie smiled, waved, and mouthed a silent *You're Welcome*, as the gurney sped through the open garage door.

"Well, I don't want to keep you from your husband, Claudia," Rockfish said.

"He's not going anywhere he won't be in five minutes, Steve," Claudia said. "Now if I can talk to you and your associate about hiring you for another job."

"Ah, Mrs. Coyne, we brought your husband home after a harrowing time," Jawnie said. She was clearly interrupting but could not care less. "No matter what you hear or read about this in the future, your husband's experience was ten times worse. What could be so pressing you'd proposition us in the middle of your driveway while your private doctor checks Roan's vitals?"

"I'd like you to get my money back. All of it. My accountant says the final amount will be slightly over three hundred thousand." She held her palms together and rocked her forearms. Pleading.

Jawnie pictured her eyes as big as saucers, but hoped she was a little more professional than that. Her brain was fried and couldn't calculate the finder's fee for a sum that large. She assumed her partner was all over it. She looked over at Rockfish and he was still recoiling from the figure Claudia threw out, all nonchalant.

"That's above my pay grade," Rockfish said, surprising Jawnie. "I'm going to pass you along to Lieutenant Dan Decker, of the Baltimore Police Department. I don't have his card with me at the moment, but I can get you the number. If you speak to him, whatever you do, don't mention my name. He'll point you in the right direction. But when this thing ends, the way I hope it does, it will be the US Attorney's office doing the asset forfeiture on the bank account, or accounts that these clowns have overseas. It will be a long and tedious process, but you'll get it all back. But for the time being, I'd recommend reaching out to Lieutenant Decker."

Jawnie laughed inside. Rockfish was trying to help the woman out, but he was antsy as hell to get the hell out of here. She watched as he shifted his weight from foot to foot.

"Well then, that wraps up our association, for the time being," Claudia said and reached out to shake Rockfish's hand. "I almost forgot. Here, I had this prepared for you," Claudia said as she reached down into the pocket of her robe and pulled out a check. "I had my accountant round the total up. I believe that thirty-thousand should make us close to even. Please put it towards your itemized bill and let me know if there remains an outstanding balance. Mr. Rockfish. Ms. McGee, I can never repay you for what you've done for us." Claudia dabbed her eyes with a tissue.

With the transaction complete, Claudia spun around and entered the house through a side door.

Rockfish and Jawnie got back into the van, only to be met by the sound of Rockfish's phone vibrating in the cup holder.

"Hot date?" Jawnie said with a laugh.

Rockfish glanced down at the screen and sighed. "Raffi's safe at the house. Only one more thing on tonight's to-do list. Let's go swap this piece of shit out for Lana."

****

Earl surprised Lynn with how gently he had laid her on the bed. Her eyes followed him as he walked around between the two twin beds, picked the phone off the nightstand, and ripped the cord out of the wall.

"Can't have that now, can we?" Earl said with an evil grin. "No noise. No squawking or loud shrills. Got me?" He walked over to the door and disappeared outside. Lynn promptly sat up and weighed her options. She didn't have a chance to review the first one before Earl walked back in with a roll of duct tape in his hand.

"Forgot this bad boy was in the bed of the truck. Just a bit to make doubly sure," he ripped off a healthy strip and covered her mouth, "I won't take the chance that this whole can't talk thing isn't a scam. Never underestimate someone, mom used to say." The grin returned to his face.

Lynn tried to bite her lip, but found her injuries prevented even that, as Earl tossed the small room. She assumed he was looking for anything a man on the run with very little in the way of planning could use. He dumped bag after bag on the floor and sifted through the contents until he laughed and stood up.

Fucking handcuffs. She hadn't seen what he found, but the metal clang and the location he stood were dead giveaways.

"Kinky, but don't think I'm going to go that way with them. Nice of you to leave the key in the lock, too. Saves me some time searching through all this mess."

Earl raised her hands above her head, ran the handcuffs through a section of headboard, and secured them. He ran the rope that previously held her wrist tight around her ankles and secured them.

"I apologize if I'm awakening any BDSM memories in that pretty little head of yours." Earl blew Lynn a kiss from across the room and the evil grin returned. "I'm about at my wits' end, and these old eyes of mine don't want to stay open. It used to be easy staying up for a couple of days when I was younger. Much easier if I had some crank. You wouldn't have anything hidden in this shit hole, would you? I didn't think so. Recovery's a wonderful thing, isn't it? Tell you what. I'm going to get myself a couple of hours of shuteye. Don't you go anywhere." Earl laughed at his joke, and Lynn rolled her eyes. He walked over to her and sat on the side of the bed. He grabbed her chin and gave it a hard squeeze. Lynn winced in pain.

"Also, what you need to do while I cat-nap is have that come to Jesus moment, the one Lilith always preached to you losers about. If you know where the money is, you best remember and tell me. If you know where that fucking kinky haired mother fucker is, you better tell me. What happens to you is totally up to you. I'll see you in a few." He moved back to the other bed and laid down. Lynn watched as Earl closed his eyes and folded his hands across his chest.

Come to Jesus, my ass. I know where it's at. Have all along, fucking bonehead. Would Rockfish and Jawnie understand if I reached my breaking point and rolled over on what I know? They don't know what I've been through. Could they? What if I point him toward Raffi? Would he let me go? Would the old alley take me back with open arms? Say goodbye to all these people in order to save myself? What if I could somehow get back into the office, maybe find his number? Hell, if I'm in the office, I might as well look for the combo, give Earl the money and call it a day. Dumb ass.

Lynn laid there, and it wasn't long before the pins and needles started in her arms. That pain was a welcome distraction from her jaw. She cursed the day that Mack talked Raffi into giving her a ride home.

Why couldn't I wait? Simply hung in Rockfish's backyard for Jawnie to finish whatever she needed to do. And then I wouldn't be in this situation. Well, I'd probably still be. But Earl wouldn't have anything concrete to tie her to Raffi, only that they started showing up around the same time. Fuck.

She glanced over at Earl. He had started snoring.

Come on, sleep apnea, stop his fucking heart! It won't, but I can dream. Another reason to hate this—Mack—of course! Why didn't I think of it earlier? What if I tell Earl I know of someone who might give me a lead on Raffi's location? Would he take me there? Would he let me walk up to the door? Alone? With him a step behind, while he listened as I got the information he so desperately needs? What if he stood alongside of me? Would I be able to get close enough to dive through the door and slam it shut before he could react? I wouldn't put Mack in any danger that way. Get him to dial 9-1-1 as I twist the deadbolt and watch old Earl run with his tail between his legs. I have to. I need to try something. Her belief that someone, anyone, would come for her, grew more faint with each stoppage in Earl's breathing. But then, as if right on cue, it started up again. She needed to act.

Lynn ran through each of the various scenarios in her head, trying to hit on all options. How each could play out and where she could take advantage to escape. She meticulously considered Murphy's law and what monkey wrench could be tossed her way; at what point and how to successfully play it off in order to get away from this lunatic. By the time Earl's alarm went off and he sat up, Lynn was confident she was actually in control of her destiny. One of her plans would work, she was sure of it.

Once she had his attention, he took the handcuffs off, ripped the tape from her mouth. Lynn winced long and hard before pointing towards the small pad of Super 8 stationery. *i know old man might know Raffi*

"What's his phone number? I'll call him." *in my phone - long gone*

"Can you direct me to his house?" *yes what time is it?*

"A little after nine." *should be okay*

Ten minutes later, Lynn was back in the truck. This time, Earl handcuffed her right hand to the door handle.

"Pull any funny shit and I'll dump that old man in the back of the truck and not stop until both of you are floating in the bay. Hell, that might be our outcome, anyway." Earl leaned over and gave her chin another squeeze to emphasize his point. She ground her teeth and tasted blood.

Lynn pointed the way, and upon arrival, Earl backed down the driveway. Lynn could only fathom it was in case he needed to make a quick getaway. She watched as he turned off the truck and shoved the keys in his pocket. He stopped, looked at her, and raised his fingers to his lips. "I don't want to hear a peep out of you." He opened his door and Lynn stared back with wide eyes. She managed a small gargle sound from her throat as ALL of her plans revolved around her not being handcuffed to the goddamn door.

"You hang tight. I ain't gonna let you walk up to the door and pull some shit. Honey, I've been doing this a lot longer than you. I'll talk to the old man, persuade him if needed." Earl reached down and pulled the handgun from underneath his seat and slid it into the small of his back. "For your sake, this guy better give me a line on Pérez. Back in a minute." With that, Earl stepped out of the truck, shut the door, and headed for the cement walkway. At the same time, Lynn's hope for escape or rescue—she was open to either—didn't really have a preference, shrunk to near impossibility. A tear started its journey down the injured side of her face as she contorted her body enough to watch Earl approach the front door.

I'm so sorry, Mack. Lynn shut one eye but squinted through the other as the front door slowly opened.

Raffi!

From her vantage point, it looked as if it took each man a second to comprehend what they saw. Earl's right arm swung behind him, fingers grasping for the cold steel before the hand even cleared his side. The whites of Raffi's eyes were huge. As Earl's arm swung, Raffi lowered his shoulder and charged forward. The perfect form tackle sent the men tumbling over the azaleas and into the front yard. Lynn now had a front-row seat.

Earl lay on the bottom, his right arm twisted, sandwiched between the grass and his back. Raffi was atop the pig pile and hoping for a submission. Lynn watched Raffi's body rock right and then left as Earl attempted to buck him off. Raffi hung on for dear life until Earl threw his head forward, catching Raffi's nose. Cartilage broke and blood splattered the pair. It dazed Raffi and Earl easily tossed him off to the side.

Earl rolled over and pulled his right arm out from under. He reached a second time for the gun and sat up. Both of Raffi's hands met Earl's right as he tried leveling the gun to fire. Raffi held on and pushed the gun away with all his might as Earl used the opportunity to punch Raffi in the head with his free left hand. The men were on their knees, struggling for control of the gun. Raffi dove to his left to escape the continuous roundhouse lefts and brought Earl's gun-hand down so it was parallel to the ground.

A shot pierced the night and slammed into the side of the pickup truck. Lynn tried to scream, wanted to scream, but nothing emerged. She leaned against the window to see better, and a second later, the entire front yard was lit by oncoming headlights. As quickly as the light arrived, it disappeared, plunging the front yard back into darkness.

* * * * * * * * * *

"Hear that?" Rockfish said as he pumped Lana's gas pedal. The guttural moan of the engine's roar filled the used car lot. "Good to have the power back. Let's go figure out what we're going to do with Raffi until Earl's behind bars."

"Marvin always leaves the keys to his cars hidden on the front tire? Seems a dangerous way to do business," Jawnie said.

"He knew I was coming. Speaking of it, I really have a feeling this is all coming to head now," Rockfish said as he steered Lana out of the lot and onto the street. "Like, whether I lose all this cash, as long as Lynn's out of harm's way, we can chalk this one up in the win column."

"I'd like that. I'd also like some work that involved a little less fieldwork, at least for the time being. To be honest with you, it's been harder than I thought. Hard to hold it all together right now. Highs and lows, one after another. Goddamn."

Rockfish looked over and gave his partner a squeeze on the arm. "I'll tie you to that computer, if it means you won't pack up and head back to Jersey."

"Deal. For the time being. I need to get over this case before I venture out from my desk any time soon."

The partners shared a small laugh, and Rockfish gunned the engine. He, too, wanted to get home and a return to some sort of normalcy.

Lana crested the small hill leading home, and her headlights illuminated a strange vehicle in her driveway. Jawnie put one and one together first.

"Earl!"

"Mother Cocksucker," Rockfish blurted out and pressed down on the accelerator. He brought Lana to a skidding stop, perpendicular to the pickup, blocking the driveway so there was no escape.

This ends now.

"Stay here," he ordered Jawnie. Rockfish reached down and pulled the gun from his ankle holster. He killed the engine and threw open the door. Crouching, he moved between the two vehicles, and a pounding to his right drew his attention.

"Lynn!"

She punched the windshield with her free hand. Rockfish doubled back to his door.

"Jawnie, get Lynn out of that truck. I'm going inside."

Rockfish moved back to the rear of his car and assessed the situation the best he could in under half a second. The front porch light was on, and he could see straight through the glass storm door to the kitchen and the far end of the house. He could hear Zippy barking up a shit storm. The thought of his dad in the house with Earl moved him forward, across the front lawn. *Was Zippy all bark, or did the old boy have some bite to him?* Rockfish took the straightest line between the two points.

The barking stopped for a second and grunts, this time to his left, drew his attention. He stopped in his tracks. Two men wrestled in the yard, closer to the house.

"Dad!" Rockfish shouted.

The sound of a gunshot filled the darkness, followed immediately by air leaking from a tire. Rockfish sprawled out on the ground, his body hugging the grass. He turned to see where the bullet had struck. What he caught out of the corner of his eye was Jawnie standing at the pickup's passenger door.

"Jawnie, get down!"

"Stevie, help me," came the reply. It had clearly come from the men fighting for control of a handgun.

Raffi! And for a split second, he felt better about the entire mess. Mack was safe. Somewhere.

A second shot soon rang out, and this time, Rockfish caught the flash from the muzzle. Jawnie screamed and Rockfish jumped up and moved towards the men without giving it any real thought. He pointed his gun, but couldn't tell the men apart in the dark. He took two steps closer when the house's front spotlights illuminated the entire yard. A second later, a third shot.

Raffi screamed and scampered away like a wounded crab. It drew Rockfish's attention away from where he thought the shot had come.

Earl's lifeless body, minus half a head, lay on the ground. Rockfish's eyes traveled from Earl to Raffi and further up to the front porch. There Mack stood, long rifle hanging at his side.

"Because I was in the Navy, doesn't mean they don't teach you how to shoot."

All Rockfish could manage was a thumbs up to his dad and ran over to where Jawnie sat on the driveway, her back against the pickup's passenger door.

"Where are you hit?"

Jawnie looked up at Rockfish, eyes wide, and then dropped her chin back down to her chest. She did not speak.

"You gotta snap out of it, kid. There's going to be a ton of people here in the next couple of minutes and they're all going to want to speak to you. Hear your version."

Jawnie raised her head. She pulled her hoodie away from her body and wiggled a finger in the bullet hole. "I'm good, but I'm going to need a new pair of pants. I don't know how it missed me."

"Don't worry, it's all over," Rockfish said. "Mack got 'em." He wrapped his arms around Jawnie and helped her to her feet. She was so unsteady he was afraid to let her go.

"Steve, if it's okay with you, I'd like to take the next couple of days off."

"Couple? Take five. I'll see you next Tuesday."

EPILOGUE - POSITION FILLED

Six weeks after the Baltimore Police Department contracted with Wolf's Crime Scene Cleaners, new grass finally started growing back on that portion of the front yard where Earl's brain matter had scattered. The small group hadn't gathered on Rockfish's back deck to celebrate the new grass taking root, but Lynn's jaw being unwired and her liquid diet finally being put to rest.

Zippy let loose with a series of loud barks and Rockfish spotted Lynn and her sister, Kim, coming through the side yard. He stood up and walked down the stairs to meet them, but Zippy outraced him. Lynn bent down to say hi and when she stood up, Zippy turned his attention to Kim. She folder her arms across her chest and step away from the dog. *She treats him with the same love and affection she has for us. Don't worry, boy. You'll get used to the cold.*

The sisters had reconciled after her ordeal with Earl, and Lynn had moved back into Kim's house. Despite their differences, the sisters were getting along well.

"I mean, for Christ's sake, it's not like we twisted her arm. She was free to say no to anything we asked her to do and go back to the confines of her alley," Rockfish had said when Jawnie passed along what she had heard about Kim's animosity with the firm.

As Rockfish approached the sisters, he felt the telltale slight dip in the temperature. *It's all in my mind, right?* Kim led Lynn by the arm towards Rockfish and for a Friday afternoon in early June, Kim seemed better dressed for a colder season. She wore long sleeves, jeans and a Yankees cap. *Shots fired. She's clearly in Orioles country.*

"Ms. Hurricane-Tesla, welcome to your party," Rockfish said with a wide grin. He stepped forward and gave Lynn a long-lasting hug. "And you must be Kim."

"Nice to meet you, Mr. Rockfish," Kim said and held out her hand.

"Call me Steve please," Rockfish said and shook. The hand was limp and the skin clammy. *Gotta force the fist bump next time.*

"Mr. Rockfish will do fine, thank you." Kim said and retracted her hand.

He escorted them around to the back steps leading up to the deck, where the rest of the party people waited. Jawnie, Mack, and Raffi lined up and welcomed Lynn back.

Rockfish noticed that when Kim stepped away from her sister to make a drink, Lynn walked straight over to him.

"Are you going to catch me up, or what?"

"Let's grab up a couple of chairs, stare out over the water and I'd be more than happy to talk your ear off."

Rockfish pulled two chairs to the far end of the deck and they sat down.

"Well, you had to walk right by the crime scene grass I'm growing on your trek back here," Rockfish said. "Looks pretty good for Kentucky Bluegrass, don't you think? Zippy likes to try his best and kill it. It's the only spot he'll piss on in the front yard. Fuck Earl."

"Not that," Lynn said, and she playfully punched him in the shoulder.

Rockfish laughed and gave his shoulder a playful rub. In doing so, he glanced behind him and saw the glare emanating from Kim. *Ah, screw her.* Rockfish caught Lynn up with a condensed version of the events since Earl's death. The FBI had located all the overseas accounts associated with Lilith and Earl, but as with anything involving the Federal Government, the wheels to repatriate that money to its rightful owners had slowed to a crawl.

"Decker told me the total is upwards of $740,000," Rockfish said.

"He's finally talking to you again?"

"Bits and pieces. More of when he needs something type of deal. He still makes himself scarce when I need something. But this was all official business. I might have to invite him over for crabs to build that foundation all over again. Maybe half a dozen times after that. Although he'll never forgive me for giving his name to Claudia Coyne. Until the Feds make final restitution, that woman has him on speed dial all day, every day."

"Better him than us."

"Amen," Rockfish said, and they laughed.

"Hey, Sonny, sorry to butt in," Mack said as he stepped between their chairs. "Lynn, I wanted to let you know I made plenty of soft type food for you to enjoy and here's a glass of ice water. I know you're probably on pain killers and want to stay away from liquor for a while."

"That's thoughtful of you, Mack. Thank you. I mean it," Lynn said and stood up. "I don't think I ever got a chance when everything was all said and done to properly thank you." Lynn wrapped her arms around Mack and Rockfish could see the red in his dad's neck slowly move up, throughout his entire face.

Lynn took a long sip from her ice water when she sat back down before turning to Rockfish.

"Okay, last question. What about the cash? Did Decker and the Feds confiscate that along with everything else?"

"I do not know what you're talking about," Rockfish said with a wink. "Off the record: once we paid back Mack and Iggy, although I don't think we can ever really pay back Mack, there was a little over eleven thousand left. We donated that to the Anne Arundel County's Women's Shelter. Decker came sniffing around when the pictures of Jawnie and I made the local paper. Asked a lot of questions, but we all played dumb. Really easy on my part."

Jawnie walked over and tapped Rockfish on the shoulder. "Our guest of honor is requested."

Lynn had not gotten completely out of her chair when Mack walked through the sliding glass doors carrying a monstrous sheet cake. Once everyone gathered around, Jawnie tapped the side of her glass with a fork.

"I wanted to thank everyone for coming this afternoon, especially Kim for taking the time out of her work schedule to bring Lynn by straight from her doctor's office. Speaking of Lynn, Steve and I wanted to thank you for all the work you've done for us over these past couple of months. Granted, some of it was like playing solitaire and the rest like being the last girl alive in any slasher horror movie. We are grateful for all you endured on behalf of our firm."

"Here, here," Raffi said, and Rockfish quickly gave him the cut sign by swiping his hand under his chin.

"And we're especially thrilled that you're almost back to one hundred percent health. In such, we'd like to officially offer you that receptionist position we've talked so much about. It'll keep you safe and in the confines of the office. Now I can't promise that I won't throw some research projects your way, but the job pays more than you and I had discussed on that long ride out to Kilingess. If you accept, here's a little signing bonus we threw together as an incentive." Jawnie held out an envelope and waited for Lynn's answer.

"Of course, I'll take the job!" Lynn said, bypassing the envelope and practically leaping into Jawnie's arms.

"That should make for an awkward drive home," Rockfish said, leaning over into Jawnie's ear after the women separated. "And here's to our next big case." He didn't wait for her to reply. Instead, he reached out and clinked her glass with his.

"I'd settle for a few very uneventful, but well-paying ones between now and then."

"Deal."

ACKNOWLEDGEMENTS

Much like last time, I have to start by thanking my awesome and extremely patient wife, Nicolita. From reading printed out scenes and chapters to being handed multiple three hundred-page, three-ring binders, she was there to tell me what worked, what didn't, and when my inside jokes or witty dialogue fell flat. Lastly, her vision and hand-drawn sketches led directly to the awesome cover art of this sequel.

My editor Ben Eads, who for the second straight time showed me how to better my craft in a short time and had me realize how good a story this actually was.

Thanks also to my beta readers, Val Conrad, Tim Paul, Jason Little, and Susan Niner. Your input and catches of all my screw-ups are greatly appreciated.

Lasty, I am grateful to Reagan Rothe and Black Rose Writing for their support in allowing me to continue this wild ride. The opportunity to give life to these characters in a sequel is something I'll always cherish.

ABOUT THE AUTHOR

Ken Harris retired from the FBI, after thirty-two years, as a cybersecurity executive. With over three decades writing intelligence products for senior Government officials, Ken provides unique perspectives on the conventional fast-paced crime thriller.

He spends days with his wife Nicolita, and two Labradors, Shady and Chalupa Batman. Evenings are spent cheering on Philadelphia sports. Ken firmly believes Pink Floyd, Irish whiskey and a Montecristo cigar are the only muses necessary. He is a native of New Jersey and currently resides in Northern Virginia.

The Pine Barrens Stratagem - From the Case Files of Steve Rockfish published January 27, 2022.

NOTE FROM THE AUTHOR

Word-of-mouth is crucial for any author to succeed. If you enjoyed *See You Next Tuesday*, please leave a review online—anywhere you are able. Even if it's just a sentence or two. It would make all the difference and would be very much appreciated.

Thanks!
Ken Harris

We hope you enjoyed reading this title from:

www.blackrosewriting.com

Subscribe to our mailing list – *The Rosevine* – and receive **FREE** books, daily deals, and stay current with news about upcoming releases and our hottest authors.
Scan the QR code below to sign up.

Already a subscriber? Please accept a sincere thank you for being a fan of Black Rose Writing authors.

View other Black Rose Writing titles at
www.blackrosewriting.com/books and use promo code
PRINT to receive a **20% discount** when purchasing.

CPSIA information can be obtained
at www.ICGtesting.com
Printed in the USA
BVHW071622050722
641299BV00012B/1534

9 781684 339891